RISING

BY STEPHANIE JUDICE

This is a work of fiction. All of the characters, organizations, and events portrayed in this novel are either products of the author's imagination or are used fictitiously.

RISING

Copyright © 2011 by Stephanie Judice

All rights reserved. No part of this book may be used or reproduced in any manner whatsoever without written permission except in the case of brief quotations embodied in critical articles or reviews. For information address StudioKae Publishing: VOICE at studiokae@gmail.com.

ISBN-10: 0615500099
ISBN-13: 978-0615500096

For my beloved, Kevin

Acknowledgements

This book, the first in the *Saga of the Setti* series, has found its way to publication on a long and winding road. My gratitude is great to many. First, I must thank that group of students who urged me on while I was writing the book and kept me working with their persistent pleas for new chapters. Cheers to you—Alex, Taylor, Kayci, Kali, Laura, Zach, Drake, and Seth. Thank you to Logan for your contribution of the name 'Vanquisher' during that very special fire drill one afternoon in the school parking lot. Your name stuck. To Sarah Trosclair (then Metz) and Matthew Smith, I appreciate both of your diligent early edits and encouragement. To my niece and literary kindred spirit, Jessen Judice, thank you for the many wonderful book talks and inspiration over Frappuccinos and chocolate cake. A special thank you to my dear friend, Cheryl Freyou, who has ever been my number one cheerleader, in writing and in life. I must also recognize Devon Poole whose amazing skills continue to transform my words into art. I still marvel at how you bring my characters to life with your pencil. And, to my managing editor Karen Theriot-Eileraas, for rekindling our friendship and starting us on this thrilling journey—may it be long and fruitful. I must also thank my parents simply for their unconditional love and constant belief in me. And, finally, I thank my husband Kevin and children—Justin, Jacob, Noelle and Jackson—for sacrificing family time so that I might pursue this little dream of mine. May God continue to bless me and all those in my world—both the real one and the imagined.

Part 1:

The Awakening

"Deep into that darkness peering, long I stood there wondering, fearing, Doubting, dreaming dreams no mortal ever dared to dream before."

--Edgar Allan Poe

Rising

✸ ✸ ✸

Powdery dust floated into the air, revealing the carven images etched into the surface of the ancient piece of pottery. Dr. David Malcolm brushed the artifact gently then blew once more to reveal the full picture that had been hidden for centuries. He could not believe his eyes.

"This is astounding," he reflected quietly.

Click. His assistant and translator, Theresa Miguez, snapped a photograph of the bizarre artifact. She had asked very few questions since the moment they had crossed into this mountainous jungle in the heart of Cuba, but she was instantly curious at the sight of this pottery.

"What is it, Dr. Malcolm?" she asked.

"These figures are like nothing I have ever seen before. Look at this one here."

He pointed to the central figure, which appeared to be a giant human. It was double in size next to the others, but abnormally thin. It had no facial features at all except for a gaping, rounded mouth. The smaller human figures to each side lay prostrate on the ground.

"This appears to be their god," said Dr. Malcolm, pointing to the unnatural figure at the center, "but the surrounding people do not necessarily appear to be worshipping the god. They seem—"

"Dead," said Theresa bluntly.

"Dr. Malcolm! Over here," yelled a disheveled man jogging toward them who was besmeared with black dirt. His glasses continued to slip off the bridge of his nose. "I'm so glad you've finally arrived. How was the flight?"

"Well, from Miami on out, it was terrible if you must know. We were held in customs for hours until they could finally verify with your university in Brazil that I was actually who I said I was."

"Sorry to hear that," the young man said. "I'm Abraham."

"It's nice to meet you face to face," said Dr. Malcolm, shaking his hand, then wiping the dirt that passed between them on his khaki pants. "I must say that your description and photographs of the artifacts far exceeded my expectations."

"Yes," agreed Abraham, almost smirking at the strange piece of pottery Dr. Malcolm was still holding in his hand. "But, I must take you to Dr. Hernandez right away. He is down in the pit."

"Aren't most of your discoveries right here?"

Dr. Malcolm gestured to the array of lined artifacts he had not yet had the pleasure to investigate closely enough—tables of rudimentary spearheads and utensils, fragments of pottery, pieces of ornate cobalt and copper jewelry.

"No, sir. This isn't what we called you for. There's much more, but you have to see it for yourself."

Theresa clicked a few more pictures before following Dr. Malcolm and Abraham along a well-worn trail into the dense jungle. The foliage thickened, blocking out the sun high above them. Theresa tripped, grabbing her Nikon camera before it touched the ground. Dr. Malcolm knelt down and helped her up quickly, trying to keep up with their speedy leader. Suddenly, they stepped into an opening in the jungle, revealing a vast circular space 200 meters across. However, the canopy of green overhead blocked all sunlight from finding this hidden archaeological treasure. Theresa paused behind Dr. Malcolm. The entire formation appeared to be charred earth; blackened soil that had been scarred long ago, where no vegetation was able to take root.

Assistants to Dr. Hernandez spread wide, digging in patchwork formation along the edges of the site. They had not taken notice of the two newcomers. Click. Click. Theresa snapped a few shots of them diligently at work. A shadow appeared at the corner of her lens. She glanced sideways, but no one, nothing was there. It was sweltering here even in the shade, but something made the hair on her arms stand up. She stared into the cover of trees, thinking an animal might have fled across the clearing into the brush. There was no sign of anything at all.

"This way. Please, follow me," urged Abraham.

Theresa followed them toward the center of the site where she first saw make-shift *stairs descending downward.*

"You have excavated straight down?" Dr. Malcolm asked, perplexed.

"Not exactly. When we started digging, one of our men fell through a hollow space. He found, well, come and see for yourself."

Theresa stared down into the pit after them, wiped her brow with the back of her sleeve then stepped cautiously into the abyss. She felt a strange sense of dread, but shrugged it off as her own fear of tight spaces. She crossed herself quickly then descended step after step, seeing only a hazy hint of light below. At long last, she reached a rocky, earthen floor covered over by wooden planks for easy passage. It had the look of an old mine, with gas lanterns hung at regular intervals along the dark corridor.

"Dr. Hernandez is this way, at the wall."

"The wall?" asked Dr. Malcolm ahead of her, but received no reply.

They walked down the corridor, passing other workers digging with trowels and whisking dirt away in niches every few feet. The cold dampness seeped into her skin. Theresa felt as if she had entered a tomb. She peered into a rather well-lit recess where several workers were digging even further down into the pit that had a seemingly endless amount of charred soil. A sturdy man with a grim expression carried out a misshapen, blackened boulder the size of a small child.

"Have you tested the soil? Why is it so black?" she asked Abraham a few steps ahead.

"Our preliminary samples of the topsoil showed nothing more than what it appears to be—black dirt. As we've dug deeper, we've found an overabundance of one element appearing in the samples."

"What's that?" she asked.

"Sulfur," he replied, pushing his glasses back into place.

"That's bizarre," said Dr. Malcolm as they resumed their walk deeper down the corridor.

"That's what we thought, but we keep finding more and more concentrations of it. We're sending some of the rocks from down here as well. Shipping them out today, actually."

Theresa tripped again. Dr. Malcolm was too absorbed to notice this time. She looked down at her feet and found a small malformed rock. It appeared to be a chip off of a larger black one. Thinking someone was standing just behind her, she glanced around. Again, no one. Her mind was playing games with her. She quickly pocketed the find. Her background in geology compelled her to do a few studies of her own once back in her laboratory in Albuquerque.

"Hurry, Theresa," called Dr. Malcolm, winded by the shallow air in the tunnel.

Finally, Abraham led them through a narrow niche into a chamber, well-lit by dozens of lanterns. Theresa stared in awe at the far wall of the cavity, completely covered with large pictographs. The left side of the wall had been carefully brushed, revealing a perfectly preserved history of a primitive people. Two workers continued to brush away the layers of time along the right.

"Amazing, isn't it?"

Theresa jumped, not seeing the rather short bespectacled man standing next to them.

"I'm Dr. Hernandez. I am pleased that you've come." His words rolled with a thick Hispanic accent.

"I—I had no idea you would show me this," stammered the awestruck Dr. Malcolm. "When Abraham e-mailed me pictures of your artifacts, he had not included this."

"No, Dr. Malcolm. I wanted you to see it for yourself. While my expertise is in geology, I still know enough about anthropology to realize that this is a spectacular find. When we started this project, we had not planned on finding an underground city at all. I wanted your professional input before I prepared a report for my sponsor in Brazil."

Theresa had stumbled into the room, speechless. Without any command from Dr. Malcolm, she programmed her digital camera for low light and began to work. She methodically zoomed in on each individual pictograph and snapped rapidly, panning from left to right. However, she quickly realized that the glyphic stories were not in chronological order from left to right. Seeing a kind of pattern, she mentioned her finding.

"Dr. Malcolm," she interrupted, "I believe these are in order from bottom to top."

"Your assistant is correct," said Dr. Hernandez, "the stories seem to be in order from the bottom going up. There is a certain fluidity in the connection of each pictograph as you scale up the wall."

Theresa edged closer to the wall for a better look. In one pictograph, a bald man had dropped his staff and was crouching in a fetal position. A looming figure with a darkened face had a skeletal, cylindrical arm that jutted out several feet, like a long, sharpened blade. He pointed his appendage at the crouching figure.

"How amazingly detailed they are, but what could they mean?" asked Theresa.

"Well, the Egyptians lived and recorded their lives for thousands of years through hieroglyphics," said Dr. Malcolm, "but there is nothing the likes of this. How old does your carbon dating tell you this place is, Dr. Hernandez?"

"That is the most remarkable thing of all. My dating puts this wall before 7,000 B.C."

Theresa recalled her undergraduate anthropology classes, knowing full well that any discovery older than 1,000 B.C. was an historic event. She had successfully begun from the bottom left corner, snapping detailed shots of each pictograph. She found herself at the very edge where assistants continued to whisk away dirt from the crevices in the wall. In an effort to capture every detail, she zoomed in on one of the pictographs toward the right side. A sudden horror struck her. The many crouched and stricken figures reminded her of her visit to Pompeii, where ancient Romans had been frozen in time by the lava and ash of Mount Vesuvius. These cowering humans had the same look of fear and horror upon their paralyzed faces. Theresa roved the scene, staring in awe at the delicate drawings of the dark figures with sword-like arms. She zoomed in on one of these dark creatures, standing in a dominant posture above a kneeling woman and snapped a picture. Bleep. Her camera gave the warning signal that her memory card was full.

"Of course," she mumbled under her breath. She had no one to blame but herself after having photographed every city and small village they passed through into this vast jungle. "Abraham, will you hold this for a minute?"

She ejected the memory card then buttoned it into her shirt pocket. She looped the strap off of her neck and passed the camera to Abraham. It had been cumbersome enough climbing down with the swinging, bulky camera; she did not want to haul it back up unnecessarily.

"I left the camera case in the Jeep. I need to get another memory card," she explained.

"No problem," said Abraham, listening in on Dr. Hernandez and Dr. Malcolm interpret an unusual scene at the bottom, depicting several of the dark figures with thin, slanting eyes.

Theresa traced her way back down the long corridor toward the exit. She passed the many workers in the niches. As she passed one darkened corridor, where men had been carrying out large volcanic-looking rocks, she heard vehement whispers bouncing from one digger to the next. She peered down the hall, seeing workers arguing near two tall pillars of stone about ten feet apart. It looked like they had uncovered an entryway of some kind. Something made her shiver. She thought she heard a slight humming sound. Dismissing it as being too long in this unbearable heat, she moved on quickly.

Climbing the ladder, she stepped onto the shaded formation where workers excavated remnants of a bygone people. As she walked briskly along the well-worn path toward the vehicles in the clearing, a ghastly sound quaked from deep within the pit. Theresa stopped short and turned. The deep sound of a throaty growl bellowed forth with a deafening din. The sound reverberated louder and louder until Theresa was forced to cover her ears. She could see workers on top of the pit in anguish from the bestial sound, then suddenly she saw no one. They vanished as the earthen floor gave way and collapsed. A sudden blast of wind blew Theresa backward. She flew off the path into the underbrush, knocking her head on a gnarled root twisting out of the ground. Then darkness. Silence.

Awakening dreamily, a faint breeze brushed her cheek. With closed eyes, Theresa sensed a strong wind rising. The trees shook their branches in defiance against an oncoming storm. For a moment, she had forgotten the noise, the explosion, the fall. Her eyes fluttered open, unable to comprehend what flashed and floated nearby. At first, she thought her mind still lingered in a dream. No, a nightmare. The etched figures in stone had somehow come to life in horrifying forms—streaks of shadowy men; giant, menacing figures with long, sharpened limbs; and dozens upon dozens of ghastly, willowy figures lurching behind the others with gaping, hungry mouths.

✳ 1 ✳

GABE

The road was open and empty. The wind whipped around me in the Jeep, waking my senses after a fitful night's sleep. Morning mist rolled over the blacktop from drowsy fields of sugarcane. I glanced at my watch, aggravated that I was running late for 1st period. Again. It was these nightmares that had been haunting me. I could never remember any details, only fleeting images—lightning splintering the sky, a field of sugar cane, a burning black stone in my hand, and an eerie creature in the distance. It irritated me more than anything, breaking my night into chunks of unsatisfying sleep.

Swerving into my parking spot, I jumped out of the Jeep and hooked my backpack swiftly over one shoulder. Instantly, my other sense threatened to overwhelm me with someone else's heartache. I honed in on the source to my right. A whimpering sophomore with puffy eyes was leaning against a car with a posse of clones surrounding her, all wearing the exact same clothes with the exact same make-up and the exact same hair. They corralled around the weepy one, commiserating the loss of this week's boyfriend. I was in no mood to deal with someone else's issues on

Monday morning. I tried to give them a wide berth, still catching clips of their absurd conversation.

"It's his loss, girl. Don't you worry," said Clone 1.

"Yeah, you're too good for him. I always told you that," said Clone 2.

"We'll do a girl's night out this Friday and make him regret he even thought about leaving you," said Clone 3.

Their insanely melodramatic feelings were draining me dry, giving me a headache from trying to block them out. I couldn't get away from them fast enough. Close proximity with anyone in distress amplified my other sense so much that I couldn't even think straight. Teenage girls were the worst at setting it off. I couldn't wait to graduate this year and get the hell out of high school to escape all of this adolescent angst. I tried to imagine what life would've been like if I hadn't been born with this ability to sense the emotions of others, this curse that made me want to bang my head against a wall around foolish, infantile girls. It would even be comforting if I could just tell people to stay away from me when they were feeling emotionally volatile, because their erratic feelings made me want to commit myself into an institution. Of course, that's exactly what people would do to me if they knew I had this so-called gift.

When I first discovered that I could sense the emotions of others at age six, I also realized that it was an ability I had to keep hidden. It was at the Sugarcane Festival Parade on Main Street. I had held my grandfather's hand as row after row of baton twirlers flashed by in a blur of red and gold. The booming drums and blaring trumpets of Beau Chêne's High School band followed them. What I remember most of all was a sudden overwhelming feeling of anger. A jolt of fear shot through me, and I couldn't help but find the man in the crowd that was giving me this feeling. He was just on the other side of my grandfather, wearing a bright red shirt. There was no emotion at all written on his face. All the same, I felt a tingle of fury vibrate from him toward me. I had squeezed my grandfather's hand, partly afraid of the man and partly afraid of what I had sensed.

"He's very angry, Pop."

Pop had peered down at me, furrowing his bushy eyebrows. He followed my gaze.

"Who, Gabriel? Who's angry?" he asked, picking me up to eye-level.

"That man there," I said, pointing with a crooked finger then quickly tucking it into a fold of my grandfather's jacket. "He's very, very mad."

That was when the angry man had lost all control, suddenly hauling back and punching the man behind him. Pop pushed backward out of the crowd as people moved toward the brawl. Three policemen were breaking their way through the mass. Pop carried me quickly toward Rue de Rouge and away from the scene. At the center of the bridge that crossed Bayou Rouge, Pop stopped and knelt before me. He peered into my eyes which I knew reflected my guilt and confusion, feeling like I'd caused the scuffle.

"How did you know that man was so angry?"

"I don't know," I had shrugged, looking down at my shoes. "I just felt it."

Pop had stared intently down at me, causing me to shiver.

"Why did he hit that man?" I asked.

"I don't know, son. Sometimes people act without thinking, especially when they've got bad feelings all built up inside them."

As Pop had walked on, pulling me by the hand, he gave me a bit of grandfatherly advice.

"It may be best if you don't always share your feelings with everyone in the future."

"Yes, Pop."

I took his advice. Knowing that my senses were abnormally heightened, I chose to wall the world outside of me, disguising this strange intuition with a mask of indifference. It was so weird for me to feel emotions so intensely from those around me and to always camouflage my own. It was better than them knowing the truth and thinking me a freak. I spent a lot of free time wondering at this irony, way too much free time, which might've been where my brooding nature was born. I learned over the years that hiding my ability kept me safe from ridicule, though I did share my secret with one other person.

"Dude, did you see that fight last night? Clovis tried one of his jiu jitsu moves, then BLAM! Spencer knocked him to the ground with one blow under his jaw. Rocked his world, man!"

"No, Ben, I missed that," I said casually.

Benjamin LeBlanc was my best friend. To see us together was probably like seeing two polar opposites, in looks and personality. Ben had sandy blonde hair and was insanely upbeat, often whistling or humming some ridiculous tune wherever he went. He smiled easily and always seemed to be laughing about something. You know those people. The ones who make you wonder what happy pill they took or what they drank to be in such a good mood all the time. That's Ben. Only he never drank any mood-altering substances, unless you count Red Bull. Of course, no one would describe me as depressed or anything, but I'm definitely his opposite—more serious, more studious, and undeniably more sarcastic.

"Hey, did you read that poem by Robert what's-his-name for Mrs. Jaden's class? I totally forgot," said Ben.

"Robert *Frost*. Yeah, I read it. I'll catch you up at lunch."

"Hey. What's wrong?" asked Ben, noting my irritability.

"Oh, nothing really. I just couldn't sleep last night—bad dream."

"What was it about?"

I tried to remember, but again only snatches came to me—streak of lightning, the burning stone, sugar cane, and a hissing creature coming toward me. It was what I felt more than remembered that troubled me; that ominous feeling that comes before something terrible happens.

"That's the weird thing. I can't really remember."

"Who wants to remember? I just forget about bad dreams. Wake up and brush 'em off. No worries, man."

I laughed. Life seemed so easy for Ben. He always lightened the mood. I guess that's why he was my best friend.

"We better hurry. Bell's gonna ring. See ya at lunch," he called back to me as he headed toward the B Wing to his Chemistry class.

Beau Chêne High School had a central commons area with benches and tables where students gathered for lunch. At the center of the commons area was the statue of our mascot—a fierce bobcat, one claw up and ready to strike. The rest of the school spread out around the commons area. The A Wing housed the business and principals' offices as well as the library and teachers' lounge. The B Wing housed all of the Science and Math classrooms; the C Wing held the English and Fine Arts classrooms; the D Wing housed Social Studies and Languages; and the E Wing jutted out into large classrooms for Woodshop and Home Economics then fattened farther out into a connecting gym. If viewed from above, I always thought the campus would look like a giant left hand spreading its fingers wide.

I walked briskly to Mr. Hampton's World History class. I always looked forward to 1st period because Mr. Hampton's monotonous drone about the ancient pyramids or Roman battles or whatever the subject was of the day nearly put everyone to sleep. Personally, I'd always been interested in history. It was just poor Mr. Hampton's pathetic delivery of the facts that made it so boring. The advantage for me was that I felt content from everyone's lulled senses in the room. It gave me a sort of break from my emotional intuition.

Sidling into the third row, my friend Mark was already there. His usual Cheshire-cat grin spread across his face.

"Hey, dude. Check out Deanna's new tat," he whispered.

Mark pointed to the girl in the second row, leaning forward so that her shirt lifted and revealed her lower back. There was a golden guppie swimming up her spine. Mark made a fish-mouth face as if he were gasping for air. I shook my head.

"Hey, maybe I ought to give her another shot at going out with me," he said, smirking.

"I thought you said she was too childish for you."

"Looks like she's growing up. I'm thinking about going fishin'."

He pantomimed casting an invisible fishing pole and reeling her in.

"Maybe you ought to try to go one week without a new girlfriend," I suggested, although I knew I was wasting my breath.

"Hey, that's an exaggeration. It's about every two weeks."

The bell rang for the morning announcements. I disregarded Mark's comments. He was always excited about some girl, whether it was an incoming freshman he had never laid eyes on or a girl he had known since middle school that suddenly developed curves. Summers could do wonders for late-blooming girls.

World History was predictably dull, although I wondered how anyone could make Roman gladiators sound boring. Calculus was no better. On the other hand, physics was very different. For the past few weeks, my classmates and I had been tortured by a number of feeble-minded substitutes for the former physics teacher, Ms. Perry, who abruptly moved away with her new husband to some small mountain town in Kentucky. I'd been cursing her ever since for abandoning us to this torture by boredom. Today was the first day of the new teacher, an *actual* teacher with an actual degree.

"Mr. Phillip Dunaway," said the tall, intelligent-looking man in the front of the room after the tardy bell rang. "I have been teaching for 13 years. I am excited about this opportunity to run the Science Department here at Beau Chêne High School. I've mostly taught biology in the past, but physics is my second love of the sciences. So, this will be great fun for me. Well, enough small talk. I'm a man of action, so why don't you all gather around over here."

I was wondering, 'what small talk?' I was so used to at least a twenty minute speech about nothing important from new teachers, blabbering away about their goals and dreams yet to be accomplished in the classroom.

Mr. Dunaway stepped away from the front of the room to the lab tables in the back. At first, no one moved. Since early September, the entire class had been wasting day after day completing worksheets, texting friends, sleeping, studying for other classes—anything but actually learning Physics.

"Well, come on. Don't be shy. I don't bite, not very hard anyway," urged Mr. Dunaway with a forced chuckle.

No one laughed, but it encouraged us all the same. I followed him along with the rest of the class. On the table was a glass filled to the very rim with water. He then demonstrated an experiment on surface tension, dropping quarters in one by one. The water became concave, bending and swelling with each fallen quarter, able to withstand much more weight from each quarter than expected before finally spilling over the edge. He then went on with a cool explanation about liquid particles being drawn together when in contact with a gas, such as air. I know, most kids wouldn't find that cool at all. Actually, most of the class seemed to drift away the longer he talked, but it was my kind of thing. He kept most of us captivated with another experiment where a needle floated on the water's surface until the bell rang for lunch.

As I wandered out to our lunch table, I was still pondering the malleability of water and other elements when hit with powerful forces when I felt a stirring tension in my chest. Ben and Melanie were already seated at our usual table nearest the bobcat statue. They were obviously debating something rather excitedly. This was nothing new for those two. I felt their heated exchange before I even heard their voices.

"You are absolutely insane, Benjamin LeBlanc," said Melanie in her dry tone, "Slaves did not *want* to remain enslaved by their masters. They simply had few options to go elsewhere."

"Exactly! They knew they had it better with their old slave-owners rather than trying to go out and make it on their own."

"How ludicrous. The reason they had no options is because no one would give them a chance because they had been slaves. Even after the treaty ended the war, people didn't suddenly start seeing them as equals."

"It just seems they would've been happier where they were born and raised with the people who took care of them. What makes you the expert anyway?"

"Um, I think I have a better idea than you do, my fair friend," she said, pointing to the darker complexion of her arm.

"That doesn't make you an expert. You weren't a slave."

"Chances are that my ancestors were."

"Whatever," said Ben matter-of-factly, taking an overly large bite of his hot dog, completely unflustered.

Poor Ben. He was entirely outmatched. He didn't have a chance of outwitting Melanie. Somehow, I think he knew it. He just liked pushing her buttons.

"Should I sit somewhere else while you debate?" I asked casually, sitting anyway.

"It wasn't a debate," said Mel. "It was a silly boy's view on the luxurious lifestyle of a share cropper."

"Silly *boy*? I see no boy," said Ben in his light-hearted manner, his mouth full.

"Here, let me help you," said Mel, stuffing her compact mirror in front of his face.

"Mr. Hampton would be proud that he actually stirred someone up in your class. No one stays awake in mine," I added, trying to lighten the mood.

"It wasn't Mr. Hampton. It was that idiot Trey Hawkes in 2nd period, who is only in our class because he failed last year," said Mel. "He said that sharecropping was the best thing the ex-slaves had, and they probably preferred it since it was the closest thing to slavery and they couldn't think for themselves anyway."

Mel spit the entire sentence out in one breath, obviously perturbed. My other sense started to pinch in my chest.

"Trey is an idiot," I said, feeling the anger rising in her, "just ignore him. Why were you talking about sharecropping in World History? He was lecturing about gladiators in my class."

Ben suddenly pretended not to hear the question, staring off in the other direction.

"This one here," said Mel, pointing to Ben, "thought that since gladiators were slaves, but were getting money for their fights that they were just like sharecroppers. How's that for a dumb analogy?"

I laughed, despite Mel's scowl. She looked like she wanted to set Ben on fire.

"What's so funny?" asked Jessie, sitting next to me.

None of us acknowledged Jessie at first. We were all looking at the girl standing next to her.

"Hey, guys. I think most of you know my cousin Clara," said Jessie. "She's taking English IV this year, and I was hoping one of you might have it next period, so she'll know somebody in the class."

Jessie introduced each of us to her. Clara nodded politely around the table, letting her eyes rest a second longer on mine. My other sense awakened with a blow, nearly knocking my head back. As always, I kept my face blank and stayed in control. I'd trained myself not to show any outer signs of my feelings. And now, I couldn't even put it into words if I tried. This girl gave off an unearthly wave of calm that somehow felt overwhelming to me. It made me lightheaded.

I'd seen her with the girls' soccer team before. They usually practice the same time we do. I remembered Jessie talking about her every now and then, but I'd never met her face to face. She's a pretty girl, very pretty. But, hell, there are lots of pretty girls here. That wasn't enough to interest me. Most teenage girls were so moody and emotionally hysterical that it was exhausting just being around them; for example, the pity party in the parking lot this morning. Blocking all of those feelings would drive me crazy. Jessie and Mel were fairly level-headed, emotionally speaking, which made it easy to be around them.

They were all talking about something to Clara, but I was just trying to get a grip on whatever it was I was feeling. It was aggravating, annoying, and completely mesmerizing all at the same time. I'd never been put off-balance like this by anyone.

"Gabe and I have Mrs. Jaden next. You can come with us," offered Ben.

"That would be great. Thanks," she said, seemingly unaware of my gaze.

Yeah, that would be just great, Ben. Now I can stumble like a drunken idiot back to class with this girl.

"Why are you taking English IV?" asked Mel.

"Oh, well, when we moved here from New Orleans last year, I was ahead in a few classes. Guidance forgot when they set the schedule and just now got it straight."

"Yeah. They move a little slowly around here. I'm sure you can catch up quickly. We've only been in class two weeks," said Mel.

"Are you a genius or something?" asked Ben, stuffing several Pringles in his mouth at one time.

"Uh, no."

"Uh, yeah," interrupted Jessie. "She took physics last summer. Homeschooled by her dad."

I could tell Jessie harbored a little jealousy over her cousin.

"You can do that?" asked Ben.

"I had to take an exit exam," explained Clara, trying to sound modest. "It was really hard."

"Wow, she could give you a run for your money, Gabe. He's the big brains in our group."

"You're forgetting about the National Merit Scholar next to you," I added, pointing to Mel.

"He always forgets about me, and *my people*."

"Come on, Mel. Stop being that way. You're not still mad at me?" asked Ben, giving her his sweetest smile.

"I'm still thinking about it," she said, already softening a bit.

"What happened?" asked Jessie.

"Don't ask," I said, relieved that Mel's vibe had calmed.

While the entire conversation rattled off in a matter of seconds, I was completely transfixed by Clara. It was nice the way her auburn hair waved past her shoulders, making her fair face that much more striking. She tucked one side behind her ear nervously. She had bright amber eyes that seemed to notice everything. No one seemed affected by her presence at all, but I was almost numbed by it. I hid my emotions well—as always. How had I never noticed her before?

"Yeah, well, in Clara's defense, she kinda couldn't help doing the Physics thing, her dad being a teacher and all," said Jessie.

"Wait. Your father is Mr. Dunaway?"

I was a little distracted before to make the connection.

"Yes," she replied shyly. "I'm Clara Dunaway."

"Your dad is so cool," I said, trying to sound as normal as possible. "I just had him for physics."

"Cool? Wow. That's the first time I've heard my dad described that way."

"Well, compared to the last few science teachers I've had, he ranks at the top."

"Speaking of classes, you were supposed to explain that Robert Frosty poem to me," said Ben before gulping down his orange Gatorade.

"Well, hello friends! How are we doing today?" asked Mark, shoving Ben over so he could maneuver himself next to Clara. "Hi, I'm Mark Mouton. I know I've seen you around campus before. Were you in my Fine Arts class?"

Mark shook her hand a little too eagerly. Clara smiled politely, but I detected a change in that ethereal air of hers. It dimmed to a more defensive mode. I couldn't help but chuckle under my breath. She glanced at me curiously, while Mark continued with his not-so-subtle introduction.

"No, Mark, I don't think I've had the pleasure of having a class with you," she replied sarcastically.

Evidently, Mark didn't detect the sarcasm. He just barreled ahead.

"Really? Well, we must fix that," he said, flashing his most charming smile.

"Don't you have some freshman to harass or something?" I asked lightly.

Before he had time to respond, the end of lunch bell rang.

"Saved by the bell," mumbled Mel before leaving.

"What class do you have next?" Mark persisted.

"Don't worry, Romeo" Jessie said annoyingly, "Ben and Gabe are showing her where it is."

Jessie had always been the oddity in our group of friends. She had little to nothing in common with any of us. She wasn't very brainy or athletic or artistic, but she was eccentric. We had just accepted her when other cliques refused to. Jessie was a bit too odd for any of them. She was into graphic novels and underground punk bands no one had ever heard of. Even though the other cliques had all rejected her, she seemed to reject them as well. Mel felt sorry for her one day when she saw her eating alone by the vending machine, completely absorbed in her comic book, *Dr. Strange*. She had been hanging out with us ever since. Even now, she mostly spent lunch time flipping through her latest issue of *Punk Magazine*. Somewhere along the line, she picked up Mel's dry sense of humor, but it sounded crueler coming from her.

"No problem. I'll catch up to you later," said Mark, giving Clara a wink before he headed off to B Wing.

"Mark's a sweet guy," Jessie said to Clara. "But, he's in love with a new girl every minute of the day. Don't get too excited."

"Oh, um, I wasn't actually," mumbled Clara.

Ben walked alongside Clara and Jessie, chatting lightly. I followed behind, taking in that serene sensation once more. It wafted over me like a sweet balm, drawing me nearer. Clara glanced over her shoulder once or twice. She must've noticed me staring. I wanted to move closer to feel its full effect, but restrained myself from doing so.

Ben offered her the seat next to him on the last row near the windows. I sat in my usual desk in front of Ben.

"Hey. You better bail me out if she calls on me about that poem," Ben whispered.

I nodded. Mrs. Jaden was writing a quote on the board as students trailed in late from lunch. The quote read, 'Most powerful is he who has himself in his own power,' with the title Seneca, Roman philosopher, beneath it. Just after the bell, Mrs. Jaden turned dramatically to the class and asked a question.

"What does this mean?"

No one said anything. Mrs. Jaden was accustomed to our pensive silence, always a little sluggish after lunch. So she read the quote aloud then asked her question again. It was Mary Sullivan, a know-it-all on the front row, who spoke first.

"It means that you control your own destiny and your own future."

"Very close, Mary, but not quite," said Mrs. Jaden.

Hah.

"I think it means that if you can control yourself, then you can do anything. You have real power," said Derek Touchet, a skinny, disheveled kid in the second row.

"Yes, Derek, but what does it mean to control yourself?"

"It could be anything," he replied, "your actions, your dreams, your feelings."

I flinched. I didn't think that anyone noticed.

"Yes, Derek, very good. Now, this is going to be our philosophy for this month. We will periodically have assignments related to this quote, so you might as well jot it down in your notebook and become familiar with its meaning. Okay, class," she said, putting the dry erase marker on the lip beneath the board. "You were supposed to read and interpret Robert Frost's poem 'Fire and Ice' last night. Let's get those out and hear what you think."

There was a minute of shuffling papers, binder rings popping open and shut, and zippers sliding on backpacks. Mrs. Jaden walked down the fourth row and placed a copy of the poem on Clara's desk.

"Here you go. I'll speak to you after school on what we've covered so far. Don't worry about being behind."

Clara nodded politely.

I stared down at the poem:

> Some say the world will end in fire;
> Some say in ice.
> From what I've tasted of desire
> I hold with those who favor fire.
> But if it had to perish twice,
> I think I know enough of hate
> To know that for destruction ice
> Is also great
> And would suffice.

"So, what is Frost trying to tell us?"

Lots of hands went up, including Derek and Mary. *Suck-ups.* Ben lowered his head, avoiding any eye contact with Mrs. Jaden.

"Steven, why don't you share your thoughts?" she asked that dopey guy on the basketball team in the middle of the room.

"He's saying that there are two ways to die—through fire or ice. And, he prefers fire because it's through his desires that he would die. But, he also thinks that if he had to die a second time, he wouldn't mind the ice."

Although Steven only gave a literal interpretation of the poem, Mrs. Jaden always offered a little encouragement to her students before she corrected them.

"Okay, I could agree with that. However, there's more here. He is proposing his opinion on whether fire or ice would be the better way for the earth to end. You could say that he might be simply making a preference on which way he would prefer to go. Which end would any of you prefer—fire or ice?"

"Fire, definitely. I would want to burn up from desire," answered Steven, with a smirk. "'It's better to burn out than to fade away.' Am I right?"

His friends laughed a bit overenthusiastically. A few girls giggled in the back row. He was such an idiot.

"I don't think fire only represents desire," came Clara's clear voice right next to me.

Mrs. Jaden was excited that Clara joined in the discussion. She moved to the front of her row.

"How do you mean, Clara? Please explain."

"Well, desire can encompass more than the physical. It might be other desires—longings of the mind or passions of the heart."

"Interesting," said Mrs. Jaden, smiling. There was no response from the rest of the class, but silence only encouraged our flamboyant teacher. "Which would you prefer, Clara?"

Clara glanced warily around the room at the many pairs of eyes bearing down on her, except for me. I'd remained very still with my eyes fixed forward, pretending I wasn't that interested. I waited anxiously for her reply.

"Fire."

"Yeah, baby," howled Steven, high-fiving his dorky friend Alex next to him.

"Settle, boys," warned Mrs. Jaden. "Would you explain, please?"

"It seems," began Clara hesitantly, "it seems that Frost compares ice with hatred, which can kill just as easily as passions. I wouldn't want to die from hatred."

I felt my own emotions mounting, and I didn't even know why. I had taught myself how to manage and control the feelings I felt coming from others, but I constantly struggled with managing my own. Mrs. Jaden made it a point to persuade her students to express their inner feelings on a regular basis. Somehow, this very topic made my blood rise.

"I would prefer ice," I said abruptly before I even knew that I would. Now, all eyes swiveled to me.

"Excellent. Please go on," said Mrs. Jaden, excited by the debate.

"I just don't see how being smothered and burned by one's emotions would be preferable to sleep. I mean, I know that when people die from freezing temperatures, they simply go to sleep and peacefully drift into death. Wouldn't that be better than actually burning to death?"

"Well, I think Frost is using these terms metaphorically, not that you would actually die from burning or freezing," said Mrs. Jaden.

I looked at Clara, who had her bright eyes fixed on me. I could feel a redness flush my neck. She seemed not to hear or notice Mrs. Jaden.

"I would prefer to live and die by my passions than to turn cold with hatred," she told me, holding my gaze.

"At least you would be in control of yourself in the end, just as Seneca suggests," I snapped back, gesturing to the board but never taking my eyes from her.

"But, what kind of life would that be, without passion?" she asked pointedly.

The last question lingered in the air. I had no response. I was trying to cool my thoughts and emotions. They had flared into a fury whenever Clara spoke to me, and I was still trying to figure out how she could make my blood boil so easily. The entire class seemed transfixed by our heated exchange.

"Well," said Mrs. Jaden, "that is the perfect place for us to jump off to our first Anglo-Saxon poem. Now, I know many of you were probably wondering why I would assign the reading of an American poem for homework when we are beginning British Literature."

"Actually, Mrs. Jaden," said Steven, "I was wondering why we have to read a poem at all."

His entourage of brainless followers laughed again. Mrs. Jaden ignored him, but shot an icy glare down the aisle.

"The *reason* I wanted you to read Frost's poem was so that we might have an intellectual compare and contrast discussion with the Anglo-Saxon poem 'The Seafarer.' Does anyone know who the Anglo-Saxons were?"

Although I knew exactly who they were, having paid close attention to Mr. Hampton's ramblings about the fierce Norsemen the first week of school, I was still regaining control of my overheated temper and couldn't answer. Derek's hand shot up.

"Um, they were the pagans who conquered Britain, establishing their new country as Angle-land, later becoming England," pronounced Derek in his overly arrogant way.

"Very good, Derek. Close enough. The Angles and Saxons were both a warlike people from lands now known as Denmark and Germany, who conquered the British Isle. We know them mostly by the name of Vikings."

"Awesome! Is this poem about killing and pillaging?" asked Steven, proclaiming himself an idiot—again.

"Actually, this poem is an *elegy*, which is a sorrowful poem about the good old days of this seafarer. And, it is set after Christianity has taken root in England."

Steven slumped back in his seat, completely distraught that there would be no blood and guts. Poor guy.

" 'The Seafarer,' which is anonymous, tells us the sad tale of a wandering Viking sailor. So, let's read."

Mrs. Jaden pointed to the page number posted on the board and began to read in a melodious rhythm. I became entranced by the words and the grief in the sailor's heart as he wandered alone on the sea. Steven and his crew began to nod off since the poem was more than a page long and their attention span was about the same as a five-year-old's. There was something inexplicably stirring about this poem, and I couldn't figure out why. It felt so familiar, like a distant memory. I became aware of the sudden increasing of Clara's dizzying sensation passing over me again. I glanced sideways. She was engrossed in the poem. I couldn't take my eyes off of her. I could hear Mrs. Jaden's muffled voice as my thoughts grew more distant. What had compelled me to speak so violently toward this girl? Was it that I couldn't control whatever wicked vibe this was she had about her? I wasn't an irrational person, so why take it out on her? I'm sure she had no idea what effect she was having on me just sitting there so properly, answering all of Mrs. Jaden's questions. That's when I finally tuned in and listened to what she was saying.

"The Viking sailor knows that no matter how much he longs for the warmth of home, it is the icy call of the sea that is his true home."

"Absolutely right, Clara," beamed Mrs. Jaden. "It appears that the icy realm that he longs for is actually where he finds the fiery stirrings of his heart."

And then it came to me, why I'd furiously debated with Clara earlier. It was because I longed to cloak my emotions from the world forever. I knew that I was actually arguing that it was best to live my life without ever opening myself up. I didn't know what would happen if I ever allowed my wall to crumble and my supernatural sense to take over entirely. Now, this strange girl comes along and basically announces to the class that I'm a fool for thinking you should bottle your emotions forever.

I faced forward, unable to hear Mrs. Jaden or anyone else for the rest of class. I refused to even glance in Clara's direction. When the bell rang, I left in a hurry without a word to anyone. I robotically moved through my last few periods—French II, Astronomy, and Art. Everything felt like a blur, because I couldn't get her out of my head. My emotions bounced from curiosity to anger to admiration, dramatically jumping up then down until I was exhausted. What was so strange was that wave of tranquility coming from her. I couldn't grasp how someone with such a depth of calm could goad my own feelings into a violent storm. I made it to my Jeep before Ben could catch up with me, then tore out of the parking lot. Thankfully, I had the canvas top down. The gusting wind blew away my anxiety, ridding me of this heaviness. By the time I drove down Sugar Mill

Road toward home, I felt lighter. Clara was out of my thoughts, and I was at ease again. The tall green stalks of sugarcane whipped wildly as I passed. I was so distracted that I'd forgotten all about my haunting dream.

✶2✶

GABE

A sheet of white mist covered and smothered the morning. I sped through the empty streets toward the practice fields at BCHS. Most of the town was at Sunday mass or happily sleeping late. I wish I could sleep at all. I didn't mind early morning soccer drills since I'd been having these nightmares. Every time I fell into a deep sleep I found myself surrounded by cane stalks scraping against my bare chest, a dark burning stone in my hand, and something whispering in the shadows ahead of me. This dream was persistent, but what did it mean? Troubled by night, I found comfort in the day, even after my bizarre first encounter with Clara Dunaway.

This past week, I'd successfully avoided any more outbursts in Mrs. Jaden's class. Once or twice, Ben tried to get me to join in a conversation with Clara, but I pretended to be doing something for another subject. When Mrs. Jaden launched into *Beowulf*, outlining the traits of a true hero and of the monstrous villain Grendel, I never said anything that might start some new argument with Clara. The truth was that my supernatural sense was strangely off-center when she was around. The numbing sensation I felt whenever she was near me had not dimmed at all. Actually, it had grown stronger. So much so that when she accidentally bumped into me as we left class one day, I nearly passed out. It made me feel weak. I hated it. I always left class quickly to try and get away from her. No one seemed to notice any change in my behavior. I guess everyone was used to my withdrawn personality by now. That shouldn't surprise me. Every now and then, I'd let down that wall I'd built around me, letting down my defenses. Then someone devastated by a family tragedy—divorce, abuse, or death—would pass by me in the hall and send my emotional sense off the charts. It was at these times that I'd spend time in silence, trying to recover as if from a physical injury. Ben always knew what was up. He would make excuses for me and everyone would just leave me alone. So, no one noticed that I'd become suddenly abrupt and rude. Or, they pretended not to. This girl Clara troubled me, because I couldn't figure out why she was affecting me. I was almost glad that today I wouldn't have to find some reason to avoid her. *Almost.*

I slowed my Jeep to let a tractor hauling sugar cane turn into the mill. Harvest time was at its peak. Tractors bumbled along the back roads, dropping mounds of mud as they went. Clouds of puffy white smoke churned into the morning sky from the stacks of the mill. The bittersweet stench of burning cane filled the air. As the musty odor blew around me, I was reminded that Fall was coming. There was something else coming, but I didn't know what.

I made it to school a few minutes late and wheeled into a parking spot behind the gym. I jerked my duffle bag from the backseat and jumped out of the Jeep when a shadow flitted in the corner of my eye. I glanced to the right, thinking another player might be running up late, too. There was no one there, just a few empty cars in the lot. A wave of negative energy flowed through me then was gone. An eerie chill crept up my spine. I glanced behind me. No one. Nothing. My dark dreams must be playing with my head.

There were already a number of different athletes using the practice fields. The football team had right field. They were still standing around waiting for their coach. I saw Mark among the players. The girls' soccer team had center field and had already begun dribbling and passing drills up the field.

"You've got to be kidding me," I mumbled to myself, seeing the streak of auburn hair flying downfield.

Ben and my other teammates were stretching on the left field. I dropped my gear on the sidelines and jogged to meet them.

"Goddard!" yelled Coach Louviere.

I looked up to see the coach tapping his watch.

"I know. Sorry," I said, then began stretching my hamstrings in a hurry.

"What's up, man? Sleepin' late?" asked Ben.

"Not really. I've just been having trouble sleeping at all. When I finally do sleep, I can't get up."

"Yeah, I know what you mean."

"Gabe, can you give me a ride to the game this week? My truck's completely died on me," asked Zack, who was bouncing a soccer ball on his knee.

"Sure. What happened?"

"Transmission," he replied shortly.

"Ouch."

"Yeah. My dad completely lost it. I can't use his car right now."

"No problem," I said, stealing his ball then sprinting downfield while maneuvering the ball toward the goal.

"Hey!" yelled Zack, chasing after me.

Zack was our star blocker and I was one of the team's three strikers. We had a constant duel going between us to see who was best. Today, Zack was winning.

"Not already!" yelled Ben.

The sophomore Sean jogged down center toward the goal, calling out to Zack.

"I'm open, man! Over here!"

Sean, a new sophomore on the team, tried to join in the game. He didn't realize that this was a one-on-one competition that had been playing between us since middle school. I managed to steal the ball twice before Zack shot past me. I dribbled twice then knocked the ball right over Sean's head into the goal. I laughed, circling back behind the goal.

"Nice," said Zack, giving me a little credit.

We walked back toward the other players, still stretching on center field. The coach was making his way toward us. Loud laughter suddenly carried across the practice field behind us. I glanced across to the football players, catching sight of Trey Hawkes making a vulgar gesture in a huddle of players. He happened to be glancing toward the girls on the other field. No, he was gesturing toward one in particular leaning over to tie her shoe. I felt a sinking in my stomach to see who he was glaring at—Clara. What an ass.

"Yo, Gabe, let's go!" shouted Ben.

I turned away and focused on the practice. Coach Louviere called a series of drills. My body reacted instinctually each time. I dribbled, passed, then aggressively tunneled into the strike zone and scored nearly every time. It was easy. I just imagined the ball was Trey Hawkes' head and I slammed it home without fail. Though my body was fully in sync with the calls, my mind was far away. I thought I could be rid of her for at least one day. Why did she bother me so much? And, why should I care if Trey and those other losers got a few laughs at her expense? She had no idea what they had been thinking. But, I felt it surely enough, even half a mile across the field. Anger boiled in my gut just thinking about it. The ball zoomed toward me through the air. I blocked it with my chest, let it drop at my feet, and then kicked it toward the goal. Zack dove for the ball, but it swished by him, missing his head by an inch.

"Dude!" shouted Ben, catching up to me. "You are *on* today."

The whistle blew three times.

"Five laps then you're done, boys," shouted Coach Louviere.

Ben fell into stride next to me as we started laps around all three practice fields. Coach Louviere demanded that we keep our cardio up. The girls had broken into offensive and defensive teams and were planning strategy for next week's game. I caught sight of Clara with the defense, intently listening to the coach. She hadn't seemed to notice she was being watched.

"What's up with you?" asked Ben. "You're silent. You're moody all the time. I mean, more than usual."

"Sorry, man. I'm just distracted lately."

"With what? The dream thing again? I told you, don't let that kind of stuff bother you. I never do."

I hadn't even thought about that, but Ben was partly right. As we jogged along the other side of the practice field, we drew closer to Clara's group of players. I was hoping she wouldn't even look in our direction.

"Hey, Clara!" shouted Ben.

I wanted to disappear. Leave it to Ben to draw attention toward us when I was doing my best to be invisible.

"Shut up, man," I mumbled under my breath.

It was too late. Clara glanced up. She looked intently at us for just a moment then lightly waved with a smile. Ben waved enthusiastically back at her.

"What's wrong now?" asked Ben when we made the corner. "Whoa. Wait a minute. Don't tell me that all of your insane grumpiness is because you have a thing for Clara?"

"No, man, no way. Not her."

"Oh, yeah. Now it all makes sense. But, dude, if you like a girl, the point is not to avoid her. You have to actually talk to her for her to notice you, and be *nice*."

"I don't like her, Ben. It's not that. I mean, I don't dislike her. It's just--"

"What? It's just what?"

"Well, it has to do with, you know, my sensory thing."

"Ohhhh," said Ben casually, "does she give you a bad vibe or something?"

"No. Actually, she gives off a really calm vibe," I said, speeding up the pace without realizing it.

"Oh, yeah. Those calm vibes can be so annoying. I see why you avoid her like the plague."

"It's hard to explain," I said, feeling kind of stupid about the whole thing.

"Well, we've got four more laps, so let's hear it."

"It's like she's void of any emotion at all. I mean, it's almost numbing when she comes around."

"Dude, sounds like a crush to me."

"No," I argued, not willing to even consider it. I tried to explain another way. "I mean, when you come around, you give off a certain happy, easy-going vibe."

"Thanks," he said with a goofy smile.

"When Melanie's around, I feel her kind nature pouring out. Although Jessie gives off a certain anxiety, it's always just on the surface, never too strong. And, Mark's eagerness and self-confidence gives off a good vibe, even when he's being a jerk. What I'm trying to say is y'all are all easy to be around. Your emotions are steady, not overpowering or negative."

"So? I don't get it," said Ben, pausing to catch his breath. "How can Clara's calmness be a bad thing?"

"It's not just that. It's like my other sense gets whacked out and fuzzy when she's around. I mean, yeah, I feel a super-strong sort of, I don't know, quietness come over me, but it makes me almost dizzy. It's just weird, Ben."

"Weird? *You're* talking about weird?" he asked, giving me a shove.

I tried to laugh, but I was nearly out of breath, too.

"Come on," I said, "one more lap."

※ ※ ※

I toweled off and downed a Gatorade while walking back to my Jeep. I felt her before I saw her. On a bench near the parking lot, Clara was sitting cross-legged with a book in her lap. I had to pass her to get to my car. I walked slowly, trying not to make any noise. She looked up anyway. When she saw that it was me, a playful smile lit up her face. It made me even more uneasy.

"Hi," she said pleasantly.

"Hello," I said, feeling that numbness come over me the closer I walked toward her. "Uh, you waiting for a ride?"

"Yeah. My dad. He's always late, *when* he actually remembers to pick me up."

"Uh, huh. Well, see ya later."

I walked past her, giving a little nod. She gave me a quick puzzled look then went back to her book, which I noticed was Mrs. Jaden's latest assignment—*Lord of the Flies*. I jumped in my Jeep and started it up. Clara glanced at her sports watch then pulled out her iPhone and made a call. I rolled out of the parking space and glanced in my rearview mirror when I passed her. She slipped her phone back in her bag without speaking to anyone, frowning out at the main road.

"Damn," I whispered to myself.

I sighed then stopped my Jeep and reversed.

"You want a ride?"

I was hoping she would just say no politely, then I'd be on my way without any guilt.

"Definitely," she said with a wide smile. "I'm sure Dad forgot again."

Without hesitating, she closed the book still open on her lap and jumped up. I chunked a pile of books and a pair of sneakers into the backseat while she threw her gym bag on the floorboard and hopped in.

"Sorry about the junk," I said.

"It's okay."

As soon as Clara slid into the seat and fastened her seatbelt, I felt that wave of dizzy tranquility. I had a sudden flashback to my ankle surgery two years ago. I felt like I did right before they put me under, like I was slipping into sedation. Glancing sideways, Clara was staring strangely at me.

"Thanks for saving me there," she said quietly.

"No problem."

"Dad is a great guy, but he gets sidetracked sometimes."

I shook my head clear for a minute, trying to push her feelings from me. I turned on the radio and pulled out of the parking lot. Clara checked her phone, but still no message from her dad. I noticed her background was a picture of Einstein sticking his tongue out at the viewer. Odd girl. Most girls used pictures of themselves with their "BFFs."

"Which way?" I asked stiffly.

I was making a serious effort to focus, but it was hard when it felt like I just drank a whole bottle of nighttime Nyquil.

"Oh, uh, left."

We were both quiet while we drove down Main Street. No shops were open, except for Mirabelle's Café. A few coffee-drinkers sipped and talked under the awning. I flipped on the radio to hear the tail end of Paramore's latest hit. The disc jockey then rattled off the mid-morning news.

"Traffic is next to nothing in Lafayette today, so enjoy the open free roads, people. One caller let us know about a wreck on Congress Avenue, so avoid that area if you can. Weather looks great today; cloud-free with a high of 75°, so get off your PlayStations and laptops and get outside. But, look out, Hurricane Lucy is brewing off the coast of Cuba. This one's got meteorologists scratching their heads. She just popped up out of nowhere and is spinning her wheels, growing larger by the minute. More about that later. In international news, the Summit meeting has been postponed in Tel Aviv due to the bombing on Saturday. Protestors have inundated the streets—"

"Take a right at the next light," interrupted Clara.

I turned then crossed over Bayou Rouge. The morning fog had lifted, revealing the glassy surface of the slow-moving bayou. I had used all of my energy to push back the cloudiness that came with Clara, and I almost felt normal now.

"I was wondering," she said finally. "I was wondering why at school you're basically rude to me, then all of a sudden today you offer me a ride home."

I was caught off guard. Most girls I knew would never be so straightforward about what they were thinking. I glanced at her again. Her eyes were fixed on me. Actually, she was looking all around me in this bizarre way. Was there something wrong with my hair or something? I combed my hand over my head. She had a sort of surprised look on her face then focused forward.

"I'm not rude to you," I said defensively.

"That's a lie," she said, chuckling to herself.

"I, well, I don't mean to be."

"It's okay, you don't have to admit it," she said with a little sigh. "At least tell me why you suddenly decided to be nice for once. I mean, I'm grateful, but it was kind of strange since we never speak at school. Like, ever."

Was she for real? I'd never heard a girl just say whatever she was thinking. They were usually more calculating and secretive, trying to hide their thoughts and feelings. This was always pretty funny to me, since I knew exactly what they were feeling and could usually figure out what they were thinking from there. Somehow, whatever came out of their mouths usually contradicted what I sensed on the inside. I figured this was probably why I rarely dated.

"It just looked like you needed a ride," I finally said, trying not to sound irritated.

"Fair enough. I suppose I'm being rude pointing out your rudeness, huh?"

She was infuriating to say the least. I laughed under my breath.

"What?" she asked with a straight face.

"Are you always like this?"

"Like what?"

"Do you just say whatever you're thinking whenever you want?"

"Oh, yeah, pretty much. My mom says I'm too much like my dad, always blurting whatever pops into my head. Sorry."

"Don't be," I said. "It's nice."

I meant it.

"Oh, a compliment. I'm going to remember that the next time you shun me in Mrs. Jaden's class."

I glanced at her again, wondering how she could say such blunt things in such a carefree way. She tossed her ponytail lightly and looked out the window. I found myself staring a little too long at the back of her neck. A horn honked. I jerked my head straight again. Clara seemed not to notice.

"Turn right onto Gardenia Drive," she said.

I made the turn then pulled into the last driveway on the left.

"You want to come in and see my dad's project? He's bragged about you so much from class that I know he'd love to show it off to you."

I felt tired. After a long practice and using the rest of my energy to block her hazy air, I thought it would be best to just leave. I looked at Clara. Her amber eyes shimmered up at me—steady and unwavering. I found myself nodding before I'd completely decided. She smiled widely.

"His lab is in the back."

I followed her across the wooden porch and into the house. There was a television on somewhere, but there seemed to be no one around.

"You have any brothers or sisters?" I asked.

"Nope, just me," she said.

I passed a wall of photographs—a toddling Clara in a red dress by a Christmas tree; six-year-old Clara on a bicycle next to Dad; ten-year-old

Clara with both her parents at the beach; and, a photo of her with her last soccer team in New Orleans. There was also a wedding photo of Clara's father and beautiful mother—simply dressed under an outdoor canopy. Clara looked like her mother.

"Is your mom home?"

"No. She's gone shopping in Lafayette, her favorite pastime."

I caught a sudden ripple against my sensory wall to block her emotions. There was a definite change in that serene air of hers when she mentioned her mom.

"This way, through here," she called, leading me through the kitchen and past a breakfast nook to a door leading to what looked like a greenhouse. I was accustomed to the many plants, herbs, and vegetables my mother nurtured in her own greenhouse and garden. I was expecting that same strong herbal aroma when I stepped through the door, but was nearly knocked backward by what hit me. A cool, earthy smell poured from the greenhouse.

"Hey, Dad! Did you forget something?"

"What's that, hon?" he called from the back where he leaned over a microscope not looking up.

"Uh, me!"

Mr. Dunaway looked up with a puzzled expression, his glasses still firmly in place.

"Soccer practice, Dad. Ring a bell?"

"Oh, no, Clara. I'm so sorry. Was it my day to pick up? Oh, hello there, Gabriel."

"Hi, Mr. Dunaway."

"He gave me a ride, Dad."

"Oh, thanks ever so much," he said absentmindedly then moved back to his project. "Well, come look at this, Gabriel. You're a man of science."

"What is all this?" I asked, gesturing to the many pools of algae in all shades of green.

"Ah, this is my wetland project. Well, these are my test samples. My real work is out in the swamp."

"Algae?" I asked.

"Oh, yes. Did you know there are 30,000 species of algae?"

"Uh, no sir, I didn't know that," I said, smirking at Clara who arched one eyebrow at me.

"Yes," continued Mr. Dunaway enthusiastically. "It's an amazing organism. It can be used as a fertilizer, to reduce toxic waste, and look at this species here I am studying now. This green alga can spontaneously switch from producing oxygen to producing hydrogen. Do you know why?"

"No, sir."

"When there is a lack of sulfur in its environment, it just switches gears to producing hydrogen!"

Mr. Dunaway clapped his hands together as if he had just made the discovery himself.

"Amazing, isn't it?"

"Yes, sir," I replied politely, only half interested.

Although I'd always liked science, I had more of a flair for physical science as opposed to biology. Immediately caught off guard, I felt a wave of numbness filter through me. I knew she was near me.

"Told you," said Clara right by my shoulder. "Okay, Dad. Well, I'm going to let Gabriel make his escape now."

"Oh, alright then. I suppose you have better things to do. But, Gabriel, I'm expecting you to sign up for the Science Fair. Have you decided what you're going to do?"

"Not yet, Mr. Dunaway. I'm still thinking."

"Okay, but you better make a decision quickly. Deadline is next Friday."

"Yes, sir."

"Enough Dad."

Clara led the way back through the house, stopping at the refrigerator.

She pulled out two bottled waters from inside.

"One for the road?" she asked.

"Sure. Thanks."

As she handed me the bottle, my fingers overlapped hers. My other sense reeled as a full wave of her vibe shivered through me. I tried not to look surprised when I stepped back suddenly.

"Are you okay?" she asked, stepping quickly toward me.

"I'm fine," I said, trying not to frown. "Thanks."

I left the house hastily, knowing she was close behind me. I stopped and turned abruptly at the Jeep.

"So, are we on speaking terms now?" she asked. "Even though you won't tell me exactly why we never were in the first place?"

"Yeah," I said, breaking into a smile.

"Wow, that's nice. I'm not sure that I've ever seen one of those on you before."

I found myself laughing, despite concentrating very hard on blocking her wave of fuzzy feelings.

"He laughs, too," she said with mock amazement, widening those tawny eyes.

"You're kind of different, you know that?"

"Yeah, well, with the nutty professor as your dad, it's kind of hard not to be," she said with a wide smile that lit up her whole face.

She gave me that bizarre look like she had done before. It was like she was examining me for some reason. I jumped in the Jeep and backed out of the driveway.

"Thanks again for the ride," Clara called, bounding back up her porch steps with her auburn ponytail swinging behind her. I sped back down the street, smiling.

✶3✶

GABE

    I stepped steadily through an endless field of sugar cane in a haze of night fog. I'd been here before in this eternal nightmare. Knowing I wouldn't wake up until I saw them, I walked on. I gripped the cold, black stone in my palm, disturbed by its familiar presence. The stone was always there in this nightmare, freezing my palm till it burned. I never knew what it was or why I held it, but there was deep power in it. Something compelled me to move on. The thin blades of cane sliced my exposed skin. The row of green stalks lashed at my arms and bare chest as I pushed my way farther into the field ahead. Abruptly, the cane field ended. I found myself standing alone at the edge of a brackish swamp. Pain seared through every vein in my body, pulsating from the burning stone in my hand. I stood still, staring into the darkness. A storm was brewing. Lightning flashed, revealing cypress trees bending in the wind and waves of rippling black water. I held the stone tightly in my fist. A sudden gust of wind swept across the water. I stood firm although the gale threatened to topple me. A whispering, rustling sound began to build. A streak of purple lightening split the sky. To my horror, hundreds of ghastly shapes flew toward me. The whispering was not the wind, but the movement of these creatures drawing closer. I was frozen to the spot, doomed to watch them advance. Another flash of lightening. One of the creatures hovered right in front of me. At first, I thought it wore a sleek, gray cloak, then realized instantly that it was not cloth, but wings that fluttered with every breath of wind. A sheet of ashen skin hung in tatters over its skeletal body. Its cloak-like wings were dry, cracked and frayed at the edges. What horrified me most about the monster was the lack of any facial features at all, except for a black, gaping hole for a mouth. It hissed once then inhaled deeply. I felt excruciating pain, like needles pricking along every surface of my skin. I looked down at my chest, which began to break like glass. My skin literally shattered into tiny shards and pulled away from my body. The creature inhaled again, sucking the pieces toward its mouth. Instinctually, I pressed the black stone to its head. Piercingly, the creature screamed as smoke rose from seared ghastly flesh, then—

"Gabriel! Wake up!"

I shot up in bed.

"You'll be late for school," my mom was yelling. "And I don't have time to check you in. I've got to get Pop to his doctor's appointment."

I jumped up, still dizzy from the dream. The digital clock next to my bed read 7:26. After a two-minute shower; pulling on jeans and a t-shirt; and grabbing a bottle of Sunny-D, I was out the door. I backed out of the drive and tossed my backpack onto the passenger seat, where I saw a paper bag with the top neatly folded.

"Lunch," I mumbled, thankful for a thoughtful mother.

The take-in bell rang just as I squealed into a parking spot. I made it to my locker and into Mr. Hampton's class as the tardy bell rang overhead. After morning announcements, the classroom television popped on for Now News, a nationwide news channel anchored by teens. Bleary-eyed from another night of restless sleep, I was barely listening until I saw a hurricane tracking chart with red routes bee-lining for Louisiana.

"Let's ask expert Stan Wallace at the National Hurricane Center here in

Miami, Florida, what he thinks," said an overly serious-looking brunette of about 18. "Can you give us your expert opinion on where and when Hurricane Lucy will make landfall?"

"Well, it's too soon to tell either of those things. This is an extremely unusual hurricane."

"How so?" interrupted the stern teen anchor, trying desperately to look older than she was.

"For one, it did not organize and form in the Atlantic as most hurricanes do. It formed off the coast of Cuba, which is unprecedented. There have been reports that there was a very large and intense electrical storm over Cuba just prior to the formation of this hurricane. We have had only limited information from Cuba about the storm as most of the populated areas are still out of power and communications have been down. Some meteorologists believe this anomaly had something to do with the formation of Lucy. At this point, we are using prior knowledge of hurricane routes. As Lucy is heading northwest at a sluggish half mile an hour, there's no telling exactly when and where, which brings up another strange thing."

"What's that?" asked the teen anchor.

"The winds are already exceeding 125 miles per hour, which makes her a strong category 3 hurricane, *and* she's already 90 miles wide."

"Why is that unusual?"

The meteorologist blinked stupidly at the anchor.

"It is highly irregular for a storm to be so large in size with such intensely, strong winds and to barely be moving at all. But, the good news for us is that radar shows a bank of cooler air sweeping down into the Gulf of Mexico next week, which we expect to disband Hurricane Lucy altogether, downgrading her to a tropical storm. We're certainly going to keep our eye on her and see what happens."

"And, you'll let us know as soon as you have more information, won't you, Mr. Wallace?" asked the brunette.

"Absolutely."

My mind wandered as the newscast began its collage of video clips from past devastating hurricanes along the Gulf coast—Betsy, Andrew, Katrina. It was always the same. The news would feed on people's fears of the next storm that would sweep in, crushing and destroying homes and lives in the Deep South. I knew it was their job to warn those in harm's way, but I wondered why they must always make it sound apocalyptic in scale. They spread more fear to these people rather than actually helping them prepare for the disaster.

"Yeah, right. Like any of you know what's gonna happen or when it's gonna happen."

I turned to the boy who had mumbled at the television. It was Jeremy Kaufman, an awkward skinny kid who kept mainly to himself. He had a few friends, but I couldn't name one of them. I only knew Jeremy because we'd been in art classes together since freshman year. He was really good, too. Most of the time, Jeremy had his ears plugged with his iPod, hiding it under his tattered Hot Topic hoodie. He only got caught by teachers when he forgot where he was and broke out singing lyrics from whatever metal band he happened to be listening to. I smirked when Jeremy started playing an air guitar, wishing I could blow the world off like him.

World History was dull as always because of Mr. Hampton's complete inability to interest anyone. It gave me more time to wonder why that newscast bothered me so badly. I zoned out all the way through Pre-Calculus, unable to focus. Even in Mr. Dunaway's class, I found myself staring out the window for most of the period. As the bell rang for lunch, Mr. Dunaway caught me.

"Hey, Gabriel? Are you okay? You seem a little distracted?"

"Oh, yeah, I'm fine. Just a little tired."

"Have you given any more thought to the Science Fair?"

I hesitated, but I already knew what had my interest now.

"I'd like to research this hurricane out in the Caribbean, its unusual formation and the course it runs."

"That sounds like a terrific idea. Science that is current and evolving—love it!"

I headed toward my table of friends—and Clara. As I got closer to them, I noticed her watching me. I noticed something else, too. Although that same dizzying vibe of hers was there, it was laced with something new. A steady warmth filtered out from her. I knew this feeling. I'd felt it before. There was Tammy in fifth grade; the Weber twins in seventh; my first girlfriend, Chelsea, in ninth; and a slew of underclass girls, none of whom I was interested in, since I hit seventeen. Once upon a time, I'd even felt it from Jessie, but it faded long before I had to tell her I saw her only as a friend. I stifled a smile when I sat across from Clara.

"Hello, stranger," said Ben, biting into a Twinkie. "I thought you were sick or something when I didn't see you this morning. Sleep late again?"

"Uh, yeah."

"Look who decided to join us today. Clara's going to actually help me with Mrs. Jaden's homework, unlike certain people who claim to be my friend and never do."

Clara had the book *Lord of the Flies* open to the homework chapter for last night.

"Hi," she said.

"Hi," I replied.

Clara shifted back to the book, showing Ben where the tragic death of Piggy happened.

"But, why did they kill him?" whined Ben.

"Because he was weak," explained Clara as she ate her chips.

"So what. We don't just kill people because they're weak."

"No, *we* don't. But, there are plenty of wicked people out there who do. Look at the terrorist attack in Paris this summer. I mean, who would've thought people would bomb the Eiffel Tower on Bastille Day. That's just awful."

"Yeah, well, if they weren't so laissez-faire about everything," chimed in Mel, as she usually did when the conversation reverted to politics, "they might've gotten a hint they would be next when Buckingham Palace was hit at the last Summer Olympics."

"That's not the same thing," Ben said to Clara. "You can't compare Piggy's death to terrorist attacks."

"Why not?"

Clara looked as if there were no way to argue against her.

"Well, because," stammered Ben. "Because, because—"

"We might be here a while," interjected Mel. "On a different note, I hear that all of Dunaway's students have to do the Science Fair."

"Yeah," I complained loudly, "I can't believe he's making it mandatory. Some teachers."

Clara chunked a chip at me from across the table without looking up from her book. I caught Mel and Ben exchanging a look.

"Well, what are you doing?" asked Mel.

"Actually, it's funny you ask. I just told Mr. Dunaway that I'm going to research that hurricane off the coast of Cuba."

Clara clapped her book shut.

"Really?" she asked. "That's interesting, because I was going to do the same."

"Well, you two better duke it out and quick, too, before someone else beats you to it. Have you filled out the official form?" asked Mel.

"No," I said.

Clara shook her head.

"Then I guess it's the first one of you to Mr. Dunaway that wins."

Clara and I stared at each other for a minute. I felt that warmth again coming from her.

"Why don't we do it as a team?" asked Clara matter-of-factly.

"Sure," I agreed.

The warmth multiplied. I smiled as I bit into a sandwich. Ben and Mel exchanged another look. I just ignored them.

"So," Ben asked Mel, "what are you going to do?"

"I'm doing a study on *traiteurs*. Since my grandmother is one, I'll have first-hand access to a primary source."

"Sounds more like Social Studies than Science," I said.

"Yeah, you're right. I had to do a lot of convincing with Mr. Dunaway to get him to let me do a comparison of modern medicine to old medicine. He said I could do it as long as there was, as he said, 'an equal share of real medicine versus faith healing.' "

"Sounds like my dad. Don't be offended," said Clara.

"I'm not. Very few people actually believe in the healing arts of traiteurs, but it doesn't matter to me. I know she's for real. She even thinks I could be the one to pass her secrets onto."

Clara looked like she wanted to ask another question, but then Mark and Zack took a seat.

"Our game is tomorrow afternoon," Zack was saying, "so I know ours won't be canceled."

"By Saturday, it may be here," said Mark, "and I'm supposed to be starting receiver. I'll be pissed if I don't get my chance because of a stupid storm."

"What's up?" I asked.

"Coach Jackson just told us we may have to postpone the game if we have to evacuate because of that hurricane," said Mark bitterly.

"What are you talking about? As of this morning, it hadn't even moved out of the Caribbean."

"It's on the move now," said Zack. "It's not going fast, but Coach said it's definitely headed for the Gulf."

Ben shivered visibly.

"What's up with you?" asked Mark.

"I hate storms," said Ben, his brow pursing.

"What? You afraid of a little thunder and lightning?"

"I don't care about thunder. It's the lightning that freaks me out."

"Why?"

"Because," I answered for him, "he was struck by lightning when he was a kid."

"What! How come I never knew that? You didn't die?"

"No, Mark, he didn't die," said Mel dryly. "Can you tell?"

Mark ignored her, urging Ben to tell him more.

"There's nothing to tell, really. My dad took me to the golf course with him, and out of nowhere a freak storm rolled up and struck me while I was holding his putter."

"No way! Did they have to do CPR?"

"I was six. I don't know. I just woke up in the hospital. But, I'll tell ya, I hate storms. Every time we have a bad one, I get all jittery."

Ben shook again. The bell rang to end the conversation.

"You still picking me up tomorrow for the game, Gabe?" asked Zack.

"Oh, yeah. Sure."

Ben rambled on about what a pain it was the last time they had to board up his house and leave for a hurricane, while Clara and I listened silently. As we walked into C Wing, Mrs. Jaden stood at her door, handing out half-sheets of paper to students as they entered.

"Hello, lady and gentlemen," she said playfully. "You may form your own literary discussion groups, but if you can't do it cooperatively then I'll make your group for you."

"Not a problem," said Ben lightly. "I've got my group right here."

Ben hooked one arm around both of us.

"Groups of four, Benjamin," said Mrs. Jaden.

Most of the desks had already been filled. I pointed to the group of desks where Derek Touchet sat alone.

"Oh, man," whined Ben. "Do we have to?"

"He's not that bad," I said.

"Are you kidding me?"

"Come on, Ben."

"Whatever."

The three of us sat down as Mrs. Jaden closed the door.

"Alright. You have your discussion questions in hand. Now, as we've done before. This is for an open discussion of your assigned reading over the weekend. You must all participate and answer the questions. You may have one recorder in each group, although I advise everyone to take notes. Decide amongst yourselves. Now get started. You have fifteen minutes."

"Okay," said Ben, pushing the pen and paper toward Clara. "You can be our recorder."

"Why me?" she asked defensively.

"Well, because you're—"

"Because I'm a *girl*?" she drawled.

Her eyebrow arched in a threatening manner, and her fiery eyes flashed at all three of us. Derek stared at his desk, Ben's mouth dropped open, and I smirked at Ben.

"No," protested Ben, "I was going to say because you're new, you know, to our group. And, my handwriting's just terrible, and—"

"Right."

"I'll do it," I offered, saving Ben before he shoved his foot in his mouth any further. "Okay, first question is 'Having nearly completed the novel, what do you think the overall theme is? Explain your answer.'"

"Well, that's obvious," said Derek haughtily. "The theme is about survival at all costs."

"Yeah, that sounds pretty good," agreed Ben.

"How do you mean?" asked Clara.

"Yeah," said Ben, "How do you mean?"

"Did you even read all of the chapters?" I asked Ben.

He shrugged. Derek ignored us both and puffed up a little with the attention from Clara.

"It's simple really. It's about survival of the fittest, which includes intelligence as well as brawn. Ralph survives because he uses his intelligence and inner strength to make it."

"So, you're saying that those who are good and moral like Simon and Piggy shouldn't survive?" asked Clara accusingly.

"I'm not saying they should or shouldn't," said Derek, "but obviously being good or moral has nothing to do with survival. They're weak characteristics."

"So, what exactly made them weak?" continued Clara.

"Mostly their fear. At first they felt strong with Ralph as their leader, but as more boys left their group, they lost confidence and gave in to their own fears. That's when Golding decided to do them in."

"Who's Golding?" asked Ben, but nobody answered him.

It looked like Derek's arrogance made Clara want to scream. I could feel her anger rising since I was so close to her. She couldn't argue with this logic that the more fearful, weaker characters were doomed to die in the savage wilderness. I think she knew he was right.

"I don't think it's about survival at all," I said, trying to relieve the tension.

"What do you think, Gabe?" asked Ben, pretending to be interested while stifling a yawn.

I ignored Ben who obviously didn't know what the hell was going on.

"I believe the theme is more about the breakdown of humanity when removed from civilization. I mean, whether they were good or bad back home made no difference in whether they survived or not on the island. I think Golding was showing how the primal instincts of people, even in our good guy Ralph, start to take over when civilization is no longer there to keep those instincts at bay."

"Yeah," said Ben, "I'm going with what he said. Who is Golding again?"

Derek looked around the room as if he were no longer interested, while I jotted down a few notes.

"I put what everyone said. Okay, next question is, 'How would this story be different, if at all, if it were a group of girls instead of boys stranded on the island?'"

"You've got to be kidding me," said Ben, looking at Clara in angst.

Clara giggled then said, "Let *me* answer that question."

I listened attentively to Clara as she explained the wickedness of adolescent girls and how the island would have gone up in smoke had girls been in charge—all to Ben's absolute amusement. I was just watching her, enjoying that warmth coming from her. It only barely dulled that dizzying sensation of hers, but it made it much more bearable. At least I understood this emotion, probably because I was feeling it quite strongly, too. When class ended, I felt an unwillingness to leave. I found myself following Clara toward the exit when I still had a class in this hall. When we reached the double doors, Clara stopped and leaned back against a locker.

"I'll talk to my dad about us doing that science project as a team."

"Mm-hmm," I said, taking in the way her auburn hair fell across her brow, partially covering one eye.

"I mean, is that okay with you?"

"Mm-hmm."

I couldn't stop admiring her—the way she stood with her head slightly tilted to the left, the way she bit on her bottom lip, the way her eyes sparkled like gold in the bright sunlight.

"It's hard to believe we may have a storm coming soon with nice weather like this, huh?" she asked nervously.

"Mm-hmm."

I leaned one shoulder against the locker, completely unashamed of being overly friendly. Clara laughed. I finally pulled myself out of my little dream-world and noticed she was giving me that strange examining look again.

"What?" I asked, half smiling.

"What do you mean what? You're the one who's acting all—"

"All what?" I asked, knowing I had that tilted smile still plastered on my face.

"Never mind. I'll catch up to you after 7th period."

I found it strange how last week all I could do was find ways to get her out of my head. Now, all I wanted to do was think of her. I was making myself crazy with my lack of focus in school lately. It wasn't until Art class that I was finally distracted from thoughts of Clara. We were supposed to be working on our abstract art project, but I still hadn't started. Jeremy Kaufman sat across from me, streaking his painting with deep blues and purples. He was completely in the zone, painting away and bobbing his head to *Ratt* or something along those lines. Mrs. Fowler never minded Jeremy listening to his music, espousing the philosophy that music inspired art. I just sat there staring at a blank canvas when Mrs. Fowler leaned over my shoulder.

"You know, Gabriel. You don't have to use paint and canvas. Why don't you try another medium? That charcoal sketch of yours was so wonderful last semester. Why don't you try that?"

I pulled up a stool to one of the long design tables with a large white sheet and a piece of charcoal. I started to streak the edge with bold lines then shaded with my finger, not knowing where I was going with this. At first, I had no inspiration at all, but then my fingers began to move fluidly on their own. Tall contour lines formed the trunk of a cypress tree. I smudged in moss on its limbs with my thumb. A few shaky lines streaked down from the sky in the background. Then the figure in the forefront took shape—the slouching, skeletal body covered in a crackled-skin cloak—no—wings. Finally, I anxiously darkened the wide, gaping mouth in a screaming 'O.' A distant aching swelled inside me as my heart raced. I heard the far-away hiss and—

"Gabriel," Mrs. Fowler set her hand on my shoulder and I jumped suddenly. "Oh, sorry, dear, I didn't mean to startle you. Well, that's quite interesting—*very* surreal."

I noticed Jeremy Kaufman across the table, staring at my drawing with his mouth hung open. I'm sure he was thinking I was some pathetic psycho obsessed with death and darkness when I really just wanted to get away from it all.

"I've got to go, Mrs. Fowler," I said, quickly rolling up the parchment. "I forgot I'm supposed to meet with Mr. Dunaway about the Science

Fair."

"Alright. See you tomorrow."

I hated to lie, but I had to get out of there. I felt overwhelmed by the sudden memory of the nightmare. A nightmare that crept under my skin like a distant memory coming back to haunt me. I could hardly ever remember it during the day, but it was so clear now. I was struggling with thoughts of why this was all happening to me when I rounded the corner and stumbled right into Clara. An overpowering surge of her numbing vibe made me stagger backwards and fall.

"Oh, Gabriel, I'm so sorry."

Luckily, it looked like the physical contact had knocked me over. She didn't seem to notice that I was reeling from some invisible force. I wondered what she would think of me if she knew. I wondered how long it would take for that warm sensation of hers to disappear.

"It's okay. I was going to see your dad."

"About the Science Fair? Already taken care of," she said, helping me to my feet and picking up my rolled parchment.

"I'll take that," I said, "you don't want to get your hands dirty. It's charcoal."

"I want to see your work."

Clara pulled away teasingly.

"No, Clara," I said, knowing I sounded defensive.

She opened it anyway and stared dumbstruck at the charcoal figure. I felt a sharp pang of fear burn through me. But, it wasn't my own fear. Clara's fingers began to tremble while still holding the paper.

"Clara? Are you okay?"

"You drew this?" she whispered, almost inaudibly.

"Yes," I said, taking the paper and rolling it back up.

The look of sheer terror pained me, but more than that was the fear that I could still feel radiating from her.

"How did . . . how did you draw this?" she stammered, looking up at me with a confused expression.

I was worried by the tearful look in her eyes. I also began to fear why she reacted so personally to an imaginary creature from my nightmares.

"What do you mean, Clara? Tell me why you're so afraid of this."

She seemed to calm herself just for a minute.

"It's the monster from my dream."

✳4✳

GABE

Dumbfounded, I just stared down at Clara. Classes had ended and students began shuffling past us. I realized we had to get out of here, so we could talk. Now.

"Come with me," I said gruffly, taking her by the hand and leading her to my Jeep.

All I could feel from her was that painful fear brought on by seeing that skeletal figure in my charcoal drawing. How could we be dreaming of the same creature? It wasn't possible.

I stuffed the drawing underneath my backpack on the floorboard so it wouldn't fly around. I had put the top down this morning to wake myself up on the way to school. I refused to take the time to put it back on and get stuck in this parking lot.

"Buckle up," I said sharply.

Reversing quickly, I sped out of the lot. A few students had been quicker than us and were blocking the exit by talking between vehicles. I wheeled hard left, jumping the curb and spinning through the grass to the street. One of the drivers was Jessie who gave us both a puzzled look.

"Where's the fire?" she called out the window.

I turned away from town, shifting into fifth gear and zooming past the sugar mill. Clara had said nothing at all. Skillet pulsed out of the radio, singing about secrets beneath the skin and monsters within. I sped down the open country road where no more tractors bumbled along hauling loads of sugar cane and blocking our way. I downshifted into second and turned onto a dirt road, almost hidden in a nest of trees. If you didn't know it was there, you'd pass it right up. Glancing sideways, I couldn't help but think how wildly striking she looked with her reddish hair whipping around her face and her gaze set steadily ahead. All her fear had disappeared somehow, and that hypnotic numbing sensation was back again. What was it about her that made me feel this way?

Tall maples, oaks, and elms hovered closer as we wound our way deeper into the woods. This place always made me feel calm. After a bumpy ride about a mile in, the trees opened up and we rolled into a small clearing. I came to a sudden halt at the bank of Bayou Rouge. There was utter silence when the engine died. Clara glanced at me, obviously wondering where we were.

"Come on," I urged, heading toward an oak tree fallen halfway into the water.

Clara followed me. I stepped out onto the thick trunk first, offering my hand to her. I was prepared, pulling up that emotional wall to block out her vibe as much as I could. When she touched me this time, all I felt was a stream of warmth shooting through my body. I couldn't help but smile, guiding her along to a flat spot where we could look out over the bayou. She was not as comfortable as I was balancing over the murky water. Our bouncing movements caused the trunk to send waves of ripples out toward the opposite bank. Once we were settled, she finally broke the silence.

"Okay. I give up. Where are we?" she asked.

"It's my grandfather's land. He has a cabin a little ways in that direction."

I pointed toward a trail behind us and to the left that had once been used regularly. Now, weeds and brush had taken over the well-worn path.

"Don't you go to the cabin anymore?" she asked.

"No, not really. We used to come when I was little. And, my grandfather came here a lot with my grandmother. But, since she passed away, he just doesn't want to anymore."

"Oh, I'm sorry," she said.

"It's okay. That was two years ago. Pop's been living with us pretty much since then and he's fine now. Well, I guess as fine as a crazy, old man can be."

Clara laughed. It was a nice laugh. I didn't tell her that I come here sometimes when I'm completely exhausted from feeling the emotions of other people or when I'm just too tired of holding up that wall to block everyone out. There was nobody out here. It was the perfect place to find some peace.

For several minutes, we both refused to talk about the dream and what it could mean. We just sat there looking at the water. We both had our hands bracing our bodies on the tree trunk. Clara shifted her weight and her hand, pressing it right against mine. I felt a sudden jarring shock. It was a hypnotic feeling being so close to her, skin on skin. It was Clara to finally break the silence.

"Gabriel. How could you draw something from my dreams?"

I thought a minute, staring out at a white heron dipping its beak along the shallows. A fat turtle that was sunning itself on a cypress stump plopped into the water.

"Because I've been dreaming about them, too."

"What? But, how?"

"I don't know," I said, shrugging. "Tell me, do you dream about a storm and a swamp and several of these creatures flying around?"

"Well, yes and no. I don't dream of a storm or a swamp, but I do dream about several different monsters. They're like the one in your drawing, but different, too. There are also the shadow men and the giant black ones."

"Tell me about it, Clara."

She paused for a moment and inched even closer. I pretended it had no effect on me, while inside I felt amazingly serene.

"My dream starts at a football game," she said.

"What?"

"Yes, I know, but it's a dream after all. It doesn't have to make sense. I'm at a football game and everyone is cheering. Then the shadow men come, but no one sees them but me. They're so horrible because all you can see are their yellow eyes glaring at you. They have dark bodies, like shadows. It's so weird, and creepy. Then the black giants come with their sharpened swords. I can't remember how, but they freeze everyone. The whole time I'm screaming for everyone to run away, but it's too late. No one can hear me. Then the gray ones come, the one in your drawing. All I see is one coming toward me and sucking the life out of me."

I felt her steady emotion falter, overwhelming me with a deep sadness. I couldn't help but try to comfort her. I reached out and took her hand in both of mine. It was natural, and she didn't seem to mind.

"Don't be afraid. It's only a dream."

"If it's only a dream, then why are we dreaming about the same thing?"

I thought for a second.

"Maybe it's some kind of warning. I don't know. I can't help but think it has something to do with Hurricane Lucy. I mean, I've heard of people having dreams that are like premonitions of danger. Ever since this morning, I've been obsessed with that storm and with—"

I stopped. I'd almost just blurted out 'and with you.' That was too much honesty for one day.

"But, I've never heard of people dreaming of the same thing. And, Gabriel, they're just," she broke off for a minute, "they're horrible."

"I know, Clara, but they're not *real*. They're just symbols of danger that our minds have created. Why we both see them in our dreams, I'm not sure."

"That's just so strange."

"There are lots of strange things in the world. They're not always bad," I said.

I was of course thinking of myself and my bizarre ability to feel other people's emotions. The sympathy in Clara's eyes as she looked at me made me feel like she completely understood what I meant. A chill tingled up my spine; this time, a good one.

"Come on. I think we need to do some research," she said.

Clara wobbled when she stood up. I jumped up and caught her around the waist before she tipped over. She immediately grabbed my shoulders for balance and froze, looking up at me.

"Sorry," she whispered weakly.

"It's okay," I said with a half-smile.

There was a sudden rush of heat flowing through me, but I knew it was my own emotions this time. There was no denying my deep attraction for this outspoken, copper-haired girl. I didn't know what brought on such a strong feeling. At this point, I didn't care. All I wanted to do was be with her. I was very aware of her light fingers on my shoulders. She was biting her bottom lip again and struggling to get her composure. She finally did and gently pulled away. After clearing her throat, she finally spoke.

"So, where should we go to research?"

"We can go to my house if you want."

"Okay," she said meekly.

"If you don't mind meeting my crazy, old grandfather," I added.

"Crazy? Um, have you met my dad?"

"Yeah, that's right. You're pretty familiar with crazy."

Clara giggled, giving me a playful shove.

"You and your dad don't come here together?" she asked.

I was shocked by the question, but I shouldn't have been. I guess it was normal for her to think both my parents were still together.

"No. My dad lives in D.C."

Clara didn't say anything and I could tell she was feeling bad about asking.

"Don't worry about it," I assured her. "My parents divorced when I was really young. I see him once or twice a year, and that's enough for me. My home's here. My family's here."

I winked at her. Clara nodded and took my hand.

As we pulled away back through the woods, the sun dipped low behind the treetops. The light was fading. A cool wind rustled through the thicket even when the air was still hot. It felt like the hint of autumn, but that just wasn't possible. The seasons changed late in the Deep South. A twinge of dread trickled through me. There had never been a storm of this size to hit the United States when the cool winds of fall had already begun to blow. Yet, somehow I felt something ominous was coming all the same.

✵ ✵ ✵

"Try 'dreams + omens,' " said Clara.

I typed that into the Google search box which brought up over 416,000 hits.

"Wow."

"It all says the same thing anyway, Clara. That dreams and premonitions are mythical, fictitious. And, there's nothing on two people having the same dream."

"Here you are, you two, some iced tea," said my mom, setting down two glasses by the computer.

"Thank you, Ms. Goddard."

"You're welcome, sweetheart," she said, seeming to examine the two of us closely. "You can call me Ms. Nancy."

"Thanks, Mom," I said, giving her the go-away look.

She shuffled away with raised eyebrows and a silly smile. So embarrassing.

"Don't you ever bring girls home, Gabriel?" asked Clara.

"Uh, no," I said.

"What is Einstein's Theory of Relativity?" shouted Pop from the den behind us. "Oh, come on! Everybody knows that!"

The voice of Alex Trebek mumbled out of the television that the contestant was incorrect.

"Do you see why?" I asked, thumbing at my grandfather in the other room. Clara giggled.

"Your grandfather sure likes his Jeopardy," she teased.

"Yeah," I said, rolling my eyes. "Let's try something else."

I emptied the search box then entered 'Hurricane Lucy.' I clicked on the National Hurricane website which popped up on the first page. The tracking chart displayed several possible routes for the hurricane, one of which plowed directly through Beau Chêne, Louisiana. The current speed was up to 2 miles an hour, which was still five times less than the average speed of a hurricane.

"Why is it moving so slowly?" asked Clara as if she read my thoughts.

Scrolling back to the list of hits, I clicked on one titled 'Hurricane Lucy's Movements' by a meteorologist in Georgia. The website summarized the odd formation of this large hurricane off the coast of Cuba, stating that the super-charged electrical storm stirred the warm waters into a massive thunderstorm then to a hurricane.

"This is all just the same thing," I said. "It doesn't say anything about, no, wait a minute. Look here. 'The slow-moving mass may be due to the fact that it is currently over warm waters in the Caribbean. The hurricane should dissipate once in the Gulf of Mexico where a cold front is expected to sweep across the span of water later this week.'"

"So, the storm may die soon before it even crosses the Gulf. That's good," said Clara, sipping her tea.

"Let me try something else."

I typed in 'Hurricane Lucy + Cuba + storm.' Thousands of hits popped up again. I scrolled down until my eye caught something in the blurb following the title, "Hurricane Lucy: More Than Meets the Eye."

The words in the partial blurb underneath that caught my eye were, "creatures of unparalleled force."

As soon as I clicked on the website, Clara gasped. Neither of us read a word. It was the photographs of wall carvings that stunned us both. Three pictures of primitive carvings depicting the monsters from our dreams stared back at us.

"My God, Gabriel. What does it mean?" whispered Clara.

"Is this a magazine article?"

"No, there's no organization's name attached. Look here at the bottom—Theresa Miguez is the author. Well, what does it say?"

I scanned really fast through what others had already theorized about Hurricane Lucy, clicking the down arrow speedily through the summary of what we already knew.

"Here, listen to this. 'Although my colleagues believe I suffered a concussion with hallucinations from my fall in that Cuban jungle, I am one hundred percent positive that what I witnessed was real. Somehow, I survived. But when I awoke, every human on that archaeological site had vanished. Not only that, but I followed through the path of these creatures' destruction. All that I found in the next town was one survivor—an invalid—and a town misted in ashes.'"

Clara sucked in her breath quickly. I sat back, staring at that last word on the monitor.

"Do you realize what this means?" she whispered.

"Yes. It means we need to talk to this Theresa Miguez."

I scrolled down the page where an e-mail address was posted. I copied the address then pulled up my Gmail account and pasted in the address. After clicking the cursor into the text box, I paused for a second, just watching it blink.

"Clara, what should we say exactly?"

"How about—"

"Would you like to stay for dinner, Clara?" shouted my mom from the den. "We're having shrimp and okra gumbo."

"Uh, yes, ma'am. That would be nice."

I heard Mom hurry back to the kitchen. We didn't have company often, so I knew she was going to pull out her good dishes.

"Scoot over," said Clara, inching her chair over.

I read along silently while she typed:

> Dear Ms. Miguez,
>
> We are both high school students in a small town called Beau Chêne, Louisiana. We have been searching for information about Hurricane Lucy, because we believe that it could be very dangerous.

"Add, 'more dangerous than locals think,' " I said. "It will make her want to talk to us, since no one will believe in her."

"Good call, Gabe."

"Gabe? When did I become Gabe?"

"Just now," she said with an impish smile, while continuing to type.

> More dangerous than locals think. We really would like to speak with you about the pictures posted on your website. We have reason to believe every word you're saying. Please contact us ASAP at this Gmail account.
>
> Clara Dunaway and Gabriel Goddard

She clicked the send button and turned to me.

"Okay. Now, we wait."

"Dinner's ready," said Mom.

The table had been set more formally than when it was just the three of us. She had set the white rice in a large, orange ceramic bowl on the table along with a basket of sliced French bread. Four large bowls of gumbo had been placed on the table.

"Just sit anywhere, Clara," Mom said, carrying in the potato salad.

Clara tucked her iPhone back into her pocket after calling home then took the seat across from me.

"So, Carla, your dad's a science guy Gabe tells us," said Pop, completely embarrassing me by letting Clara know I've been talking about her at home.

"It's *Clara*, Pop," I corrected him.

"Um, yes, sir," she said, staring at how Pop was dipping every bite of potato salad into his gumbo.

"What's wrong?" I asked. "You look like you've never seen anyone put potato salad in their gumbo?"

"I haven't," she said. "We didn't eat it like that in New Orleans."

"You never saw that before?" asked Pop, raising his bushy eyebrows. "Shoot, when I was a boy, my mama used to put boiled eggs in our gumbo. Mmmm, now dat was good. Can't seem to get Nancy to cook it that way though."

Pop grunted toward his daughter.

"You get pretty much whatever you want anyway," Mom said. "So, Gabriel told me that you and Jessie are cousins, right?"

Damn it, Mom. Didn't she understand that it was totally uncool to let a girl know you'd been talking about her at home?

"Yes, ma'am. My mom and her mom are sisters," said Clara, taking a bite of French bread.

"That's nice to have family close by."

"Mm-hmm," nodded Clara, still chewing.

"I bet you and Jessie are close cousins," said Mom.

"Well, not too close. Jessie's got really unique interests," said Clara. "I mean, we get along, but I'm more the athletic type, and Jessie's more the, well, die-your-hair-a-new-color-every-week type."

I laughed, trying not to spit out my food.

"You sure do speak your mind, like Gabriel said."

"Oh, really? What else did Gabriel say?" asked Clara with a gleam in her eye.

God, this was embarrassing.

"Mom, don't you have any dessert or something in the kitchen?" I asked quickly.

"I only have that leftover brownie cake from Sunday," she said, hopping up to go fetch it.

Clara grinned across the table at me. She seemed so pleased to find out how much I'd been talking about her at home, and I was growing more humiliated by the minute.

"So, you talked about me to your mom, huh?"

"Yep, he's been gibber-gabberin' about the new girl in his English class quite a bit around the house," said Pop, wiping his chin with his napkin and patting his belly. "You're not quite what I pictured though."

"Oh? What description did he give?"

I couldn't stop the slight groan that escaped me. There was no telling what might come out of my Pop's mouth.

"He never gave one directly. Sounded to me like you were kind of a pest, the way he was carryin' on. You're quite a bit prettier than I pictured."

"On that note, I'll be taking you home, Clara."

I grabbed Clara's brown hoodie on the sofa and my red BCHS sweatshirt, then headed for the door.

"Well, it was very nice to meet you," said Clara, shaking Pop's hand. "I hope to see you again."

"I'm sure you will, darlin'. My grandson's not stupid, you know? You're a keeper."

"Thanks," she laughed.

"But, I have the brownie cake," said Mom, carrying in a plateful. "You can't leave yet."

"Thank you so much, but I'm so full. It was wonderful, Ms. Goddard."

"Alright then. You have a good night," she said, putting the plate down.

"I'll take one of them brownies," said Pop, shuffling over.

"Be back in a few minutes, Mom," I called, heading out the door before my family could humiliate me anymore.

The air was warm and balmy, very typical for August here. I left the top down on the Jeep.

"Gabe, it doesn't feel like a cool front is coming. Do you think the weathermen are right? Do you think the hurricane will break up before it gets here?"

"I don't think so. I'm convinced now that the hurricane has something to do with our dreams. I hope that Theresa Miguez e-mails us back soon."

"So, I'm a pest, huh?" she asked, changing the subject.

I knew this was coming.

"No, it's just that when I first met you," I said, stumbling over my words. There was no way to explain how I felt without telling her about my other sense. This was a confession I wasn't prepared to make. "I guess I just had a wrong first impression."

"I see."

"But, I changed my mind fairly quickly, as you can tell."

I settled back onto my headrest at a red-light. I felt Clara's numbing vibe trembling through me. I thought it funny how I was so used to it that I only noticed it now when there was a quiet moment between us. I still didn't understand why she affected me this way. As I pulled into her driveway and parked, I found her examining me again. There was a look of complete wonder in her eyes as she stared at me.

"What? What is that look you give me all the time?"

"Huh? Oh, nothing," she said hastily.

"Clara Dunaway doesn't have some quick and smart reply? Come on, tell me."

"It's just your good looks. You're so mesmerizing, you know," she said with a wry smile.

"I asked for it, I guess."

I stepped out of the Jeep. Clara jogged around to meet me as I walked her to the front door. The living room light was on.

"Your mom's probably worried I kidnapped you or something."

"No. Mom's in her bath right about now, soaking the world away."

I felt that ripple of anxiety again that I'd felt before. I decided it wasn't the right time to ask about her mom. There was obviously tension there.

"Now, if my dad is not discovering some new way to cure cancer with phosphorescent algae or something, and he actually realizes I'm missing? Then you'd be in trouble."

She poked me in the chest. My hand went up naturally to take it. I knew I had that half-smile plastered to my face again. A shot of adrenaline ran through me when I tugged on her to come closer. She leaned into me easily, then the porch light went on and the front door opened.

"Clara? Is that you?" asked a gorgeous, red-haired woman in a floor-length white bathrobe.

"Yes, Mom. Um, this is Gabriel," said Clara, stepping up to the porch.

I waved politely, deciding it would feel a little awkward to go up and shake her mother's hand who stood there in her nightclothes. Weird.

"Sorry, we were so late," I said.

"Oh, that's okay," she said in a crooning voice. "You can come have dinner over here next time."

I suddenly felt like I was being examined again, but not by Clara. I nodded to them both then returned to my Jeep and cranked it up.

"Hey, wait," called Clara.

She had come partly down the walk and pulled out her phone.

"Smile."

She took a picture, glanced at her phone then gave me a funny expression and waved.

"I'll see you tomorrow at school," she said as I backed out of the drive.

Clara had a sort of sorry look on her face when she disappeared through the doorway. I wondered if she was thinking what I was thinking. I was wishing that her mother hadn't come out onto the porch so soon.

✴5✴

CLARA

    I sprinted downfield, dribbling the ball in front of me. As soon as Penny was open, I kicked it diagonally for the set-up. Running parallel to her, I waited. Penny shot the ball at an angle toward me. I made one long stride then smack—the ball flew over the goalie's head into the upper left pocket of the net. Yes!

    I screamed, elated with the first goal. Penny ran over to me.

    "Awesome moves, Clara."

    "You too."

    We high-fived then jogged back up field. A whistle blew. The coach was waving in two substitutes for us since we hadn't had a break the whole game.

    "Nice job, Dunaway and Blanchard!" called the coach when we sat on the bench.

    The air was cool, but my blood was pumping feverishly. I couldn't bear to sit idly on the bench. Needing to pace, I went to the cooler for water. I tried to catch my breath while gazing out across the field at the bleachers. I loved a gathering of people—the colors of their energy auras made an ethereal light. The energy I gained from a crowd made me almost giddy. Although I'd never seen the beauty of the Northern Lights, I knew that it must look just like this. Glancing over the crowd, I saw an array of colored light—yellow and gold haloed several children; blues and violets speckled over relaxed adults and one distracted grandmother; vibrant orange and red spread over the passionate, shouting parents; and, many shades of green sprinkled the rest. But, there was one in particular I was searching for. And there he was. Gabriel, who radiated a rainbow of color, always drew my eye.

Lately, it was more than my eye that was lured in by him. Every waking moment, I felt my heart tying itself to his. Unwilling as I was to part with it, there was no denying whatever hold he had over me. I'd noticed him several times before from across campus because of his bizarre aura, not to mention that he was positively gorgeous. Most girls couldn't help but notice him. He had that whole tall, dark, and handsome thing going on. Except his eyes looked at you less like Prince Charming and more like Count Dracula. I had to admit, I couldn't help but stare like the other girls. But, it wasn't until Mrs. Jaden's first class that I felt seriously attracted to him, like metal to a magnet. From the second I glanced in his direction and saw his multi-colored aura radiating over his head, shoulders, and along the length of his body, I felt an inner tug, uncontrollable and fierce. Never before had I felt such a connection with anyone. Perhaps, I sensed that if I told him about my gift of seeing energy auras around people, I knew he wouldn't laugh. Or, perhaps, I was just fooling myself. I only ever told one person—my mother.

When I was five years old, my mother had taken me to see Santa Claus in the shopping mall. It was the first memory I had of seeing auras. From the moment I entered the long corridor of bustling people, I began to feel a tingly elation from the energy and all of the beautiful hues of color.

"Look, Mommy! Look at all the lights!"

"Yes, Clara. The Christmas lights are pretty," Mom said to me, tugging me along, not getting my meaning at all. If I was old enough to understand it, I would've known that this event would mark the beginning of my rocky relationship with her.

There was already a group of anxious parents stacked in a winding line toward Santa's throne at the center of the mall. Many mothers were fretting over the curls and lace of their little darlings, wanting the picture to look just right. I smiled at the little blonde boy in front of me with a mass of freckles dappling his nose and cheeks. The blonde boy had been crying. He forced a little smile back. By the time we wound our way toward the front where I could finally see Santa, I instantly clutched at my mother's hand, completely terrified of what I saw.

"Who's that?" I whispered.

"That's Santa, of course. We've come to take your picture with him, remember?"

I remember staring at the red-faced man with a grizzled beard in a red suit. I shrank from him, because of the smoky bluish-gray aura hovering over his head. He looked like a red ghost, clouded in mist. It scared the heck out of me.

"No," I whispered to my mom.

By now, the little blonde boy was being placed on Santa's lap. He was telling Santa that he wanted a Spider Man action figure for Christmas. I watched as that smoky aura swirled frighteningly around the little boy as if to smother him. I pulled back on my mother's hand.

"What is it, Clara? It's nothing to be afraid of. I'm right here with you."

"No," I said defiantly. "He's got darkness over him. No!"

"What are you talking about, Clara?" she asked, looking around her embarrassingly.

"His halo is dark, Mommy," I said, my little voice shaking. "I don't want to go."

I looked up at Santa, who was now waiting for me to approach the throne. He had a look of total sadness in his eyes, which only increased my fear of him.

"What do you mean?" demanded my mother. "We've come all this way in your pretty new dress."

"His light over him, Mommy, it's dark," I repeated frantically.

"Hush, Clara! There are no lights over him."

"Yes. Yes, there are. I see them over everyone, but his is bad."

I remember watching as my mother's aura transformed from violet to orange to red, while I tugged away from her.

"What on earth are you talking about? No, you don't."

"Yes, I do! I see lights over you now. I see them everywhere!" I screamed, completely panicked.

At this point, some of the parents and their children had staggered out of the line to witness my meltdown at the head of the row. My mother suddenly jerked a bit too hard on my arm. I felt her nails digging into the underside of my flesh. Her tone became stony, which was scary, but still not as scary as the ghostly Santa.

"No, you don't, Clara! And, I don't ever want to hear another word about this again! Do you understand me?"

I nodded my head tearfully as she spun me around, leaving the sad-faced Santa gawking after us.

I kept my word and never mentioned the halos of light to my mother again. I did try once to tell Dad. He took me to the planetarium when I was ten. I loved our little adventures to science and art museums. Dad was adamant about education, and I liked the time with him. We watched an awesome show about the cosmos—all that mankind understands about the universe and all that is still a mystery to us. I became particularly interested when the mellow voice of the broadcast speaker mentioned that the electromagnetic energy produced by stars reflects off the planets and the moon, making them glow with light in the darkness of space. As we left the auditorium, I turned to my father.

"Dad, do you think it's possible for some people to see human energy shining off of them like we can see energy in space?"

"Well, now, Clara. That's more science fiction than it is science.

Some people have claimed to see such things, but I don't believe it. Where did you read about that?"

"Oh, just in some magazine."

I closed the door on that conversation quickly. As soon as I knew his views on the subject, I decided not to even try. I already knew that my dad was a man of scientific fact, steeped in the mindset of what can be proven and disproven. There was no way to prove what I saw was actually real. Knowing that he would only look at me with disbelief and confusion if I confessed my gift to him, I decided to keep it to myself. It was easier to pretend to be normal. But, how I longed to share it with someone.

Gabe waved at me when the coach put me back into the game. I felt a fluttering in my stomach. I could hear him cheering enthusiastically above the others.

"Stay focused, stay focused," I whispered to myself.

I put all my energy into dribbling and striking. The opposing team had adjusted their strategy now with a stronger defense against us. I don't remember where they were hiding this Amazon girl, but their new blocker knocked the ball back every time it crossed the center field line. She was a monster. After what felt like an eternity of trying to score with no success, the referee finally blew three times, ending the game. Both teams lined up and we passed the opposing team's line, high-fiving as we went.

Sweaty and breathless, I grabbed my gear and headed toward Gabe who was standing with Ben and Zack. His colorful aura blazoned brightly from head to toe. I couldn't help but smile as I walked up to him.

"Hi," I said with what I knew was a silly grin on my face.

I couldn't wipe it off.

"Hi," he said.

"Y'all are all finished?" I asked.

"No, we're still playing, Clara," said Ben. "I'm actually a hologram of Ben. Gabe didn't want you to feel unloved or anything, so he had a virtual copy of us put here to cheer you on."

I rolled my eyes. Gabe just took my hand and headed for the car, ignoring his best friend's jabs at me.

"You look so real," I said, teasingly to Ben.

I reached out and poked him in the arm.

"Amazing, isn't it?" said Ben with that goofy smile of his.

"Well, virtual Ben, did you win your game?" I asked.

"Yes, as a matter of fact we did, thanks to Zack, who completely shut down the Hornets with his awesome goalie skills."

Zack smiled modestly as we walked along. I liked Zack. He was a nice guy.

"Seems like you needed our help out there, Dunaway. You might want to try a new strategy when the other team figures your game out," Ben advised.

"Is there any way to shut virtual Ben off?" I asked Gabe.

"I wish."

Gabe took my bag and chunked it in the very back with the rest of our gear. I unthinkingly hopped in the front seat.

"Oh, I see. Girlfriend's got the front seat now, huh?"

I felt my cheeks flush pink at hearing Ben call me that, but I recovered quickly.

"It doesn't seem to me that holograms need preferential seating. That's for the humans."

"She got ya," said Zack, jumping into the back seat.

"Let's stop at Mirabelle's," said Gabe. "I'm starving. Is that okay, Zack?"

"Sure, man. I'm in no hurry."

"What about me? You didn't ask me? Am I invisible or something?" whined Ben.

"Ben, I've known you since 1st grade, and you've never passed up an opportunity to eat."

He shrugged in agreement and hopped in next to Zack.

There were few customers at Mirabelle's Café on a Wednesday

afternoon. It was crammed with customers during the week for lunch, being conveniently located near the businesses on Main Street. We ordered a round of burgers and fries, which flew out of the kitchen speedily. There was a radio droning on behind the counter somewhere.

"Hurricane Lucy may certainly be headed to Louisiana. The latest tracking update has her eye travelling over New Orleans, which is bad news for New Orleans, but good news for us here in Acadiana. We still expect to have strong winds, but the experts are saying there is little moisture in this vast storm to cause flooding. We're not in the clear, but we may have dodged a direct hit. . . ."

Gabe and I shared a knowing look. I glanced at Ben whose unwavering golden aura beamed brightly as he shoveled five fries in at a time. He didn't have a care in the world.

"Ben, how do you eat like that and stay in shape?" I asked.

He grinned widely.

"Jealous, huh?" he said through a mouthful, then gulped his Coke.

"He's got the metabolism of a racehorse," said Zack.

"Yeah, and I can run like one, too. Hey, Clara, you've got to come to our game next week, so you can catch a look at my super, awesome speed."

"He is pretty fast," agreed Gabe.

"Absolutely," I assured him, dipping a fry in ketchup.

"Hey, did you hear they might move the football game up to Thursday night?" asked Zack. "Some people are planning on evacuating if that hurricane comes this way, and it will probably be pretty windy even if we don't get a direct hit."

"Oh, yeah, we've got to go and see Mark. It's his first game as starting receiver, and he'd be pissed if we didn't make it," added Ben, shoveling his last bite of burger into his mouth.

"You wanna go?" Gabe asked me.

"Sure."

"Don't tell me you wouldn't go if she didn't go," accused Ben. "We're not already at that stage of the game, are we?"

"No comment," said Gabe teasingly.

I grinned as Gabe took my hand and pulled me out of the booth. Ben harassed us both for the duration of the ride to Zack's house behind the sugar mill. He finally shut up when we pulled up the drive where a somber man poked his head out of the hood of Zack's truck. It was his father.

When I first saw him, I instantly flinched, unintentionally squeezing Gabe's hand. A swirl of smoky black mist hovered over the brawny man.

"See you guys," said Zack, hastily grabbing his bag and heading into the house.

His father followed in after him. We could hear the shouting before we had backed out of the driveway.

"Poor Zack," said Ben.

"What's wrong with his dad?" I asked distractedly.

"He's an alcoholic," explained Gabe, who seemed suddenly gloomy.

We rode the rest of the way in silence to drop off Ben. He waved over his head as he loped up the driveway. I was looking down at my lap, thinking about Zack, when a long, slender piece of ash settled on my knee.

"Ah!" I yelped, slapping it off of my bare leg as if it were a poisonous insect ready to bite.

It left a black smudge mark that I began rubbing frantically.

"It's okay, it's okay," assured Gabe. "It's just sugar cane," he said, pointing at other wispy black flakes floating through the air.

"What?" I asked, sounding a little panicky.

"They burn the dried husks to make it easier for harvesting. They do it every year at this time," he explained, gesturing to the charred leafy ash floating through the air.

"Oh," I said apologetically, feeling embarrassed at my overreaction.

I'd been living here for over a year, but had only been through one sugar cane season.

"You've never noticed?"

"Um, I guess not. Our house is nowhere near the sugar mill."

I didn't need to explain to Gabe that my first thought was of the creatures from my dream when the flake of ash landed on me. Gabe lightly brushed the sooty smudge on my knee, before shifting into third on the main road. I felt a different kind of shiver that time.

There was another silent ride back to my house. The day waned into dusk as hues of orange and pink settled in. Shadows elongated and deepened to the east. My thoughts lingered in the darkness.

Gabe pulled up my drive and walked around to my side. He braced both his hands on either side of the door. I gave him a puzzled look, wondering what that determined expression on his face meant and why he seemed to be blocking my exit.

"Okay. So, tell me exactly why you reacted the way you did when you saw Zack's father."

My heart lurched. He must've noticed me flinch when I saw that dark aura. I just stared at him like an idiot, watching his rainbow halo glowing, and trying to figure out a way to lie to him.

"I just saw that he looked angry, and—"

"No. That's not true," he accused. "Please, Clara. Tell me the truth."

His brown eyes were intense and steady, holding me still. His dark, wavy hair fell forward. I didn't think I could lie to him, but I was scared to death to tell him the truth. My pulse raced wildly, knowing I was about to confess something no one else knew. Also, because I was very aware of how close he was standing to me.

"I know what people are feeling or thinking, Gabe."

"What?"

His tone didn't sound skeptical, but it had a scary edge of disbelief.

"Gabe, there's something I need to tell you about me. It's going to sound really weird."

"Go ahead," he urged.

"I see energy auras around people, which generally correlate to what kind of mood they're in or what kind of person they are. And, Zack's dad's aura was very dark. I knew that something was wrong."

Gabe was shaking his head, but at the same time smiling broadly.

"What? You don't believe me, do you? I knew you wouldn't. Why did I even bother?"

I was ticked off. Why did I tell him? I'm such an idiot.

"Yes. Without a doubt, Clara, I do believe you."

Huh?

"How can you?" I asked aloud, trying to understand the bizarre smile on his face.

"Because, Clara, there is something really weird I need to tell you about me."

"What is it?"

He sort of chuckled first.

"I can feel what other people are feeling, Clara. I've been able to do it since I was very young."

No. Way. I was speechless for several seconds.

"Really?" I finally asked, feeling a smile come to my lips.

"Yes, really. At the very same moment that you squeezed my hand in Zack's driveway, I felt a wave of anger come over me from his dad. I knew that somehow you felt what I felt. I didn't realize that you actually saw his feelings."

Gabe exhaled deeply, as if a monumental boulder had cracked and fallen away from his shoulders. I finally hopped out of the Jeep, leaning against the side.

"So, you know when people are happy or angry. You just feel it?"

"Yes."

"You know what I'm feeling when I'm around you?" I asked. Very nervously, I might add.

"Yes," he said.

That tilted smile came to his lips, and that crazy butterfly in my stomach was flapping like its wings just caught on fire. I blushed even though I tried to act casual.

"What do auras look like?" he asked.

"Well, they're like transparent colors of all shades. They sometimes hover only over the head. Sometimes, they flow down further over a person. I'm not sure why."

"What color is my aura?" he asked.

I grinned. This was something I'd been wanting to tell him since I met him.

"That's the funny thing about you, Gabe. You don't have one color. You have every color. Maybe it's because you have so many feelings of others bouncing off of you. Yeah, now that I think about it, that explains it," I said.

"Well, I think I finally know why you numb my other sense," he said, edging toward me.

"Numb you?" I asked, feeling my heart pick up speed erratically.

"Yeah, when we first met, the reason I didn't seem to like you is because I couldn't figure out why my other sense got all fuzzy around you. It must have something to do with your ability to see these auras, the energy or something. It messes with my ability somehow."

"That's crazy," I whispered, realizing he was leaning ever closer to me.

I've had little experience with kissing. Sadly, very little. There was Shane Bradford in eighth grade behind the gym. Yes, a cliché, I know, but it really was my first experience. All I remember is that Shane was a sloppy kisser. He was all over the place with his mouth to the point that I started giggling and quickly ended our blooming middle school romance. There was David Weber at my freshman homecoming dance in New Orleans. David was sweet. Our first and last kiss, while we swayed to Jewel's 90's hit "Pieces of You" on the dance floor, was nice. Just nice. Then, there was Jordan Blanchard, a friend of Trey Hawkes on the BCHS football team who took me to a party in the back of a cane field my first year here. I'd just moved here and didn't know any better at the time. I don't remember his kissing abilities, because I spent too much time fending off his roaming hands.

Now, Gabe, whose hands were perfectly still on my hips, were sending me an insanely intense vibe. He moved slowly, tenderly. A shot of heat flowed through me as his lips gently met mine. My heart beat frantically when he pulled me to him, continuing his slow, soft kiss. After what felt like the longest, most pleasant minute of my life, he pulled away and looked down at me. I realized to my embarrassment that I was a little breathless. His dark eyes never moved from mine. Piercing, motionless, they held me still. He was so close, I could feel his heart beating against me.

"What color am I now?" he whispered.

I watched his aura flicker and flame like a maddened blaze.

"You look like you're on fire."

"Funny," he whispered, smiling, "I feel like I'm on fire."

His hands were still on my hips as he pulled me closer. Our second embrace was stronger, deeper, longer. I wound my hand into the back of his hair, marveling at how soft it was. He slipped a hand behind my neck. Through my closed eyelids, I could see his aura glowing brightly. A current of electricity coursed through both of us, and I wondered if this was normal, or if our powers amplified our attraction. Whatever force drew us to each other; it bonded us permanently with that deep, lingering kiss. The sun disappeared beneath the horizon, but we hadn't noticed. We were lost in each other. I felt dizzy when Gabe finally pulled away. I steadied myself with one hand on his chest, not wanting this to end. We didn't speak, but simply basked in this hypnotic feeling that had woven itself around us, tying us together like an invisible string. Gabe traced the line of my chin with his thumb and down my neck to my collar bone, which made me hitch my breath in sharply. Looking into his eyes, I knew he was feeling everything I was. That half-smile lingered on his lips, driving me absolutely crazy.

The coolness of night settled in around us, reminding us eventually that we had to go in. I had forgotten my earlier angst about the smoky aura around Zack's dad as Gabe walked me up the drive, his hand intertwined with mine. Somehow, everything else felt far, far away. He gave me one last swift kiss on the porch.

"See you tomorrow."

I smiled and nodded. As I turned, something flashed darkly in the corner of my eye. I glanced toward the old oak tree to the right of the house, but there were only shadows cast by the setting sun moving slightly in the breeze.

"You okay?" he asked, standing at the foot of the porch steps.

"Yeah. Of course."

I wasn't. This had happened too many times lately. My fears had manifested into fleeting shadows that haunted me daily. I wouldn't burden Gabe with this now. I couldn't ruin what was possibly the most perfect ending to any day I ever had. We could deal with shadows and nightmares tomorrow.

✶6✶

GABE

    Pale moonlight slipped in through the window, tinting the white walls blue. I lay on my back, staring at the ceiling. I'd never thought there might be someone out there like me who also had a strange supernatural sense; especially not someone like Clara, who apparently had similar feelings for me. It was like fate or destiny or something.

    There was no way I could go to sleep, knowing some hellish creature waited to haunt me there. I only wanted to think of Clara—the way her auburn hair brushed my neck and cheek when I held her, the way she leaned into me when I kissed her, the way she couldn't wipe the smile off of her face afterward.

    I rolled over on my side and glanced at my cell phone on the table. Should I call her? I picked it up and saw a text message waiting.

> Hey. Are you asleep?

It only took me a few seconds to reply.

No. Call me.

I punched the volume down, knowing my mom was a light sleeper. She never was too restrictive with me or anything, but I still didn't want her wandering in, asking me why I was on the phone at midnight. A few seconds ticked by then the phone vibrated in my hand.

"Hey."

I was glad to hear her voice.

"Hey."

"Can't sleep?" I asked.

"No."

"Me neither."

The conversation came to a dead halt after that. I was thinking about this afternoon, but didn't know what to say. Clara broke the silence with a new subject.

"Hey, did you hear from Theresa Miguez?"

"Oh, I almost forgot about her."

"Why? Was something else distracting you?" she asked.

I could feel a sly smile spread across her face.

"No comment."

There was a thud as I rolled off the bed and knocked my Physics textbook to the floor.

"What was that?"

"Nothing," I replied. "Just give me a sec. I'm gonna pull up my e-mail."

I pulled up to my computer desk and moved the mouse around to wake up my desktop. I double-clicked the Internet Explorer icon and waited. Again, Clara broke into the silence. I don't think she liked the quiet.

"So, do you think the hurricane is going to miss us? The newscasters seem to think so."

There was an edge to her voice. I knew she didn't believe it any more than I did. There was something about this hurricane that made me feel tense and guarded. I didn't know for sure that it would hit us or not, but I knew something was coming our way.

"I don't know. I can't tell you why or how, but I think it's still coming here."

"I know. Me too."

"Hey! I have a reply from her. Wait, I've got four replies from her."

"Wow, didn't you check your e-mail this week?"

"Well, I checked the day after we sent it, then I just kind of got distracted and forgot."

"Really? By me?"

Again, I could feel the smile coming through the phone.

"You sure are pretty blunt, you know that?"

"Yes, I know. So, what does she say?"

I clicked on the oldest e-mail first. It went on and on.

"Okay. I'm gonna forward this to you and sum it up while you're pulling up your e-mail."

"Alright. Read away."

"The first part talks about her experience in Cuba. She says, 'After a horrible explosion where the entire site sank into the ground and buried everyone alive, I stayed under cover in the jungle for fear of the beings I saw pass nearby. I stayed the whole night, hiding in the hollow trunk of a tree. The next day, I wandered into the next village where the only person left was a mute boy of about twelve. He could not speak and tell me what had happened. He seemed confused and lost. The strange thing about the village was the thin coating of ash spread over the place, and I had found no evidence of fire.'"

I paused. There was no response from Clara on the other end, and there was no need. Neither of us wanted to talk about the creatures from our dreams that seem to be made of ash. I had a prickly sensation thinking about the one that inhaled the breaking pieces of my chest.

"Keep going," said Clara, "I've almost got my e-mail pulled up."

"Okay. She says, 'I went on to the next village and the same thing apparently happened there. When I finally found a town that seemed untouched by these beings, they all were oblivious to any sort of catastrophe. The locals thought I was crazy. I got out on the first plane and just in time, because a severe electrical storm hit right after I left. It apparently knocked all of Cuba out of power. When I arrived home to Albuquerque, I could not convince anyone of what I saw. They all think I suffered a severe concussion. But, I know what I saw. I know something is terribly wrong.'"

"Wait, Gabe, scroll down to her last paragraph."

"Man, you're quick."

"Look, she says that her pictures are of the archaeological site before the disaster. She thinks the creatures depicted on the wall were the very same things that destroyed those towns."

"So, what she's telling us is, these things are for real."

There was a long pause on the other end.

"Gabe, what do the other e-mails say?"

I clicked open the second one.

"Wow. She wants to come visit us in person. She wants to know how to reach us."

"Gabe, what if she's some psycho? I don't think we should give her our numbers."

I thought about all I'd just read. Although I couldn't sense Theresa Miguez's emotions through cyberspace, I knew she was being sincere.

"Clara, do you really think she is making all of this up? I mean, why would she create some crazy story like this? She already says she's lost her reputation at work. She apparently needs to speak to someone who believes in what she's saying."

"What do the other e-mails say?"

I clicked them open. They were brief.

"Well, yesterday's was another request to come and see us. She says that she thinks the hurricane has something to do with the creatures."

There was another pause. Both of us knew now that Theresa was more than a deluded head-case.

"Send her your cell number," said Clara finally.

"The e-mail she sent this morning says she'll be arriving on a plane in Lafayette tomorrow, and she lists her cell number to contact her."

"Seriously?"

"Yeah."

The excitement I felt from our afternoon together had faded with the sinking feeling that our dreams were not just dreams. They were premonitions of some dark evil coming closer and closer. This woman Theresa Miguez was solid proof, having seen with her own eyes what we feared from our nightmares.

"Well, Clara," I finally said. "Let's not talk anymore about what this could or couldn't mean. Not tonight anyway."

I was more than aware that we would both be asleep soon and with the possibility of dreaming about man-eating monsters, I didn't want to worry Clara anymore tonight.

"Tomorrow should be an interesting day," I added, trying for lighthearted.

I almost pulled it off.

"Yeah, you're right," was all she said.

"You want me to pick you up for school?"

I knew it made no sense to pick her up, since her dad was a teacher at BCHS, but I didn't care. I just wanted to see her as soon as possible. Lunch time seemed too far away. I actually wished I could crawl through the phone receiver and hold her and tell her it would all be alright. Since I certainly didn't have the power of teleportation, which actually would've been a useful paranormal power, I asked for the second best thing, to see her as soon as I could.

"That would be great," she said.

I wanted to hear that smile spreading across her face through the phone, but I didn't. I hated to go to sleep, knowing she was upset, but I didn't know how to erase this waking nightmare from her thoughts.

"Goodnight," I said.

"Goodnight."

* * *

CLARA

I lay awake for some time after hanging up with Gabe. I couldn't help poring over the entire day in my head. It went from good to great to *amazing* to downright depressing. Somehow, I was able to slow my racing thoughts. I began to drift into that place between dreams and awake. As my mind pushed Theresa Miguez away and pulled Gabe's face to mind, which was a very pleasant sight, I heard a slight noise at the foot of my bed. Thinking my silver tabby cat, Misty, must have jumped up, I murmured to her in a fuzzy haze.

"Misty, go to sleep."

There was no mewing response or tiny, soft footfalls leading to my pillow as usual.

"Misty?"

I rolled over and looked at the foot of my bed. A panicky flood of spine-tingling fear jolted through my body. A black figure stood there, watching me. Though the room was dark, this shadow was darker. I froze, utterly petrified. My heart threatened to beat right out of my skin. It didn't move, but continued to watch me. A faint smell of something like burnt hair passed over me. I realized it wasn't a transparent shadow at all, but as solid as I was. It lifted an arm to point at me, and I noticed the dim light from the curtained window glimmering on its scaly, black skin. I could not make out the features of its face, but the eyes, those glaring, menacing yellow eyes bore through me. It hated me. I could see its aura. It flowed out over its entire body like a black sheet of powdery soot. There was no transparent light at all like I see around other people, but the substance of ash hovering all around this shadow man. Then, it spoke in a throaty whisper.

"Setti."

What did this mean? It continued to point at me as if accusing me, damning me. Of what, I didn't know. A faint hiss slid from its invisible mouth, making every hair on my body prickle. Then, it took three quick strides toward the wall and vanished through it.

I still couldn't move. A cold sweat dampened my skin. What in the world had I just seen? What did it say to me? What did it want? When my senses calmed and I realized it wasn't coming back, I fumbled on the bedside table for my iPhone. It had been over an hour since I spoke to Gabe, but maybe he was still up. I let the phone ring until I got his voicemail. Remembering that he had probably put his phone on vibrate or silent when I called him earlier, I put the phone down, leaving no message. What was I going to say? *Good morning. I know you just got up, but I wanted to let you know that an evil entity stared at me from the end of my bed tonight and I'm in fear for my life. See you soon.* No, I'd tell him as soon as I saw him tomorrow.

I trembled at the dread of that thing I'd just seen coming back through my wall. It seemed like forever, but was probably only a half an hour, then I finally crept from under the covers and down the hallway. There on the living room sofa, I found what I needed—Misty. She was curled into a tight ball, sleeping soundly. If only I could do the same. She purred softly in response, which I found more comforting than usual.

I tip-toed back down the hall and stopped at my parents' door, which was cracked open. I had a sudden fear that the shadow man might have gone into their room. Very quietly, I poked my head in the door. There was no shadow, no black aura anywhere. Dad slept on his side, wheezing slightly. Mom slept on her back with one of those ridiculous satin, eye shields like rich women wear on those stupid soap operas. I still couldn't get how the science geek and the beauty queen ended up together. Dad always said he had dazzled her with his knowledge and intellect, but somehow that didn't make any sense to me, even as a joke.

I crept back down the hall and slipped into bed, cuddling Misty to my chest. Her purring increased. I listened to the rhythmic sound which lulled me into a safe place. I didn't remember falling asleep, but I was relieved the next morning when pink sunlight shone throughout my room and I didn't remember having any dreams. There was only the stinging memory of that shadow man.

✳ ✳ ✳

GABE

As soon as Clara stepped off of her porch, I felt a wave of anxiety pour over me. The expression on her face matched the emotion. I instantly tensed.

"What's wrong?" I asked her when she belted in.

"Just drive. I'll tell you."

Her appearance matched the angst-ridden emotions she was sending out. Her face was paler than usual. She left her hair down, which kept sliding forward to hide her face as she stared into her lap. At the first red light, she inhaled deeply and looked up. I still had the top down. It was a cloudless, blue sky, which for any other teenager would've brightened their day. Clara wasn't any other teenager, with nothing more than a Chemistry test to worry about. There was something more on her mind. I grew impatient.

"Well?"

She paused for only a heartbeat.

"I saw one of those creatures last night."

"What? In your dreams?"

"No. It was standing at the end of my bed."

"What!"

I punched the brakes. The car behind me nearly slammed into the bumper. It veered around me, and I barely registered the driver cursing me and making a vulgar gesture as he passed. I pulled along the side of Main Street. I couldn't focus on the road and digest what she was saying at the same time.

"Say that again," I said gruffly.

"One of those shadow men, the ones that come to me in the dream and no one sees them but me. It was there, in my room."

"Okay, do you mean you saw a shadow flicker at the foot of your bed and when you looked, it was gone?"

I was thinking how this had happened to me several times in the past few weeks. I'd figured it was stress, causing me to see things when nothing was there. Maybe Clara was having the same problem.

"No. I heard something near my bed. At first, I thought it was my cat, Misty, but when I looked, it was that creature. Oh, God, Gabe it was horrifying. It had black, shiny skin. And, it stared at me as if it wanted to kill me. Then, the freakiest part was that it said some word to me that I've never heard before."

"What word?"

I felt her fear spreading through me, mounting my own. My heart sped up quickly. It was her emotions causing this, not mine.

"It said, 'Setti.' Do you know what that means?"

"No, I've never heard it before either. But, you really actually heard it speak?"

"Do you think I'm making this up?" she asked defensively.

I heard her voice crack. There were bags under her eyes and her cheeks were even paler. I felt kind of insensitive, but it was just so hard to wrap my head around this.

"I'm sorry. Of course, I don't. I just, I just can't get over the fact that this is happening. I mean, what are they? What do they want?"

"I don't know," she murmured, staring into her lap and twisting a loose strap from her backpack around her finger. "But, it's not good."

There was a sickening feeling stewing in my chest. I realized it was Clara's quickly increasing anxiety. That gentle, fuzzy tranquil sensation that I'd come to long for was nowhere to be found. I took her hand and closed it in both of mine.

"Don't worry. We're going to figure this out," I assured her.

As I said the words, I truly meant it. I pushed her anxiety away from me, thinking only of how to soothe her. Lifting her chin with one hand, I leaned in and gently kissed her. The growing adoration I had for her filled me with hope. I couldn't help but wish that she could feel this, too. For the first time in what seemed like forever, I pulled down that wall I always held tall and strong; the barrier to prevent other emotions from coming in. As I kissed her again, she inhaled sharply as if she'd been shocked. I pulled back quickly.

"What happened?" I asked.

"What did you just do?"

"Uh, I thought it was kind of obvious. I was kissing you."

"No, Gabe," she said seriously, "I felt a kind of shock, like a vibration when you kissed me."

"Wow, I didn't know I had that kind of effect on you, but what can I say."

I know. It was a bad joke, but I thought a little humor might help if my affection didn't have any effect on her. I hadn't realized that it had had more effect than I imagined.

"Gabe. I'm being totally serious. It wasn't like when you brush your feet on the carpet and shock someone. It was, it was really, *really* strong. That wasn't normal."

I pulled back slowly. I wasn't sure what she was telling me, but I knew the look on my face showed my shock. I was at a loss for words.

"And your aura, it's changed. It looks like ropes, mostly purple and blue, all tied together around you."

I thought about what she'd said. This was the first time I had pushed my emotions out instead of walling my own in as I'd done my whole life.

I couldn't imagine what that would mean if I was able to force my energy onto Clara, or onto anyone else for that matter. What kind of power was I releasing? This was beyond weird.

"Your gift is changing, Gabe."

When she said it, I knew it was true. I felt it somewhere deep inside. A slight vibration burned in my chest. While the warmth of Clara's kiss still hung on my lips, I knew it was more than that. It was like my power was willing me to draw it out again. I smiled confidently, not knowing exactly what this meant, but knowing it was good.

As I maneuvered back onto Main Street and shifted into high gear toward school, I grabbed her hand and held it tightly. She was still staring at me with what seemed like awe.

"Don't worry, Clara. This is a good thing."

She didn't ask me how I knew or what this meant. She accepted what I said as true, and I felt a heaviness lift. I'd apparently kept her from spiraling into a depression with a distracting kiss, or actually with my other sense. Now, she was light again. The longer I held her hand and pushed my newfound confidence out to her, the sweeter her feelings became. That fuzzy tranquility spread over me, giving me what I needed to work my head through this.

During 1st period, I listened to that ditzy anchor on *News Now* interview more experts on how the hurricane seemed stalled in the middle of the Gulf of Mexico. It was odd. Even the meteorologists couldn't understand what was going on. The front they'd expected had rolled through, but it hadn't diminished the hurricane at all. Actually, the hurricane continued to grow bigger, although it was at a complete standstill.

"What d'ya think of that?"

I turned to Jeremy Kaufman who'd asked me the question. His usual black hoodie was pulled up over his head.

"Me?"

"No, my invisible friend here, Harvey."

He was straight-faced, and his sarcasm was borderline rude, but I knew it was just his way.

"There's not much to think about," I said.

"Really? You don't think that's a little strange?"

It was weird. Jeremy Kaufman had barely said three words to me since ninth grade. All of a sudden, he was interested in my opinion on a hurricane. I knew it was no ordinary hurricane, but what was up with him?

"Yeah. It's strange," I finally added. "There's lots of strange things in the world."

"You got that right, man."

With that, he plugged his earphones back in and sank down in his desk into silence. I just shook my head. He was a hard one to figure out.

The first few periods crawled by at an outrageously slow pace. I saw Mr. Hampton's mouth moving, but I heard nothing. Even Mr. Dunaway, who was a great teacher, couldn't pull me from my thoughts. I felt like I was in a Charlie Brown episode listening to adults ramble nonsense. At lunch, Clara and I sat, picking at our lunch quietly while the others babbled away. I perked up when the conversation turned to the hurricane.

"Yeah, we're not going anywhere. Chances are, it'll turn toward Florida. That's what my dad says," said Ben.

"Awesome. That means the game is still on for Friday," said Mark. "Y'all are comin', right?"

"Of course we are," said Zack. "You just better make it worthwhile and actually catch the ball, make a touchdown or something. We've gotta beat the Trojans."

"I'm just glad this thing looks like it's turnin'. That girl on *News Now* this morning said the hurricane's got little rain, but is highly electrical. That means lots of lightning," said Ben with a shiver.

"You really are scared of lightning, aren't you?" asked Mel.

She seemed to be amused by finding out this phobia of Ben's, but she wasn't to the point of teasing him. Not yet.

"Yeah. You would be, too, if you were struck by lightning as a kid," he said defensively.

"Not this again," said Zack. "We know. We know. It was a traumatic event. We get it."

While they were distracted, Mark turned to me and whispered.

"You're awfully quiet," he said with a nudge. "Is there trouble in paradise?"

He winked and nodded to Clara who seemed to be analyzing exactly what was on her sandwich rather than eating it.

"Oh, no. Everything's fine. Just tired. You ready for that game?"

I knew if I turned the conversation to him, he would easily get distracted. It worked, of course. He launched into a detailed explanation of all the plays he planned on using to score points against the Trojans on Friday. Finally, the bell rang. Just as we found our seats in Mrs. Jaden's class, there was an interruption over the intercom.

"Excuse me, Mrs. Jaden?"

It was Mrs. Brewer, the front office secretary. She had a thick southern accent. She had moved here from Mississippi after marrying a local from Beau Chêne years ago, but she'd never lost that twang.

"Yes," Mrs. Jaden called up to the loudspeaker.

"Could you please send Gabriel Goddard to the front office for a few minutes?"

"Yes. Gabriel, go ahead."

I turned to Clara who mouthed the word 'what' to me. I shrugged then shuffled out of the classroom. I wondered what I could've possibly done to get called to the office. Maybe it was about a scholarship or something. No, Guidance would've called me to their office. Maybe my mom needed to get me a message. No, she would've texted me. Unless, of course, it was something about Pop. Maybe the doctor had some kind of bad news. I was suddenly afraid as I opened the door to the front office. Mrs. Brewer was on the phone. There was a freshman in the waiting area. From his freakishly negative vibe, I knew he was in some kind of trouble. He was seated closest to the principal's office. Mrs. Brewer looked up and cupped the phone.

"Your cousin's here to give you that paper," she whispered.

What cousin? I know the confusion showed on my face. She pointed back to the waiting area, then resumed her phone call. I hadn't noticed the other person sitting in the waiting area. She was a petite woman in her early thirties with shoulder-length dark hair and bright brown eyes. She was eyeing me cautiously.

"Hi, Gabriel," she said, walking up to me very casually. "I brought that English paper you typed at my house and forgot in the printer."

I knew right away this must be Theresa Miguez. Obviously, she was hiding her identity to give me something. In general, high schools don't allow personal visits from paranoid scientists who think the world is on the brink of an invasion by supernatural monsters. She handed me a manila envelope and gave me a loaded look. By this time, the secretary had finished her phone call.

"Okay, Mr. Goddard. I did you this favor and let you get that paper. I don't do that for everyone. Now, get on back to class."

I nodded my appreciation to Mrs. Brewer and glanced at Theresa.

"I'll see you after school," said Theresa.

"Yeah," was all I could reply.

On my way back to class, I opened the envelope. There was Theresa's business card and a note attached to a thick stack of papers with four photos on each page. I glanced at the photos then stopped mid-stride. I nearly dropped the stack of photos as my brain tried to register what I was looking at. My mouth went dry. My hands began to shake.

"Are you alright, Gabriel?"

I glanced up to see Mr. Dunaway slowing down in front of me with a concerned expression on his face.

"Yes, sir. Fine," I managed. "No problem."

I quickly moved on my way, studying the pictures as I went. Although the carvings were primitive, they were definitely visions of these people at some kind of stand-off with the ash-eaters that haunted my dreams and tall, dark creatures with arms that extended into killing rods that stabbed some of the human figures. I had only dreamed about those creatures once. All I could remember from the dream was these unbelievably huge beings with black bone-like appendages they used to kill my family. There were also some other dark human-like figures watching these scenes from nearby. These primitive carvings proved that some people thousands of years ago had faced them before. What had been their fate? I was almost back to Mrs. Jaden's class, so I flipped back to the note on the front.

Gabriel and Clara,

I know why they're coming. I'm staying at the Holiday Inn near the Interstate. Meet me in the lobby after school.

--Theresa

Clara was obviously waiting for me to return. Ben apparently hadn't even noticed. He had nodded off on his desk and was beginning to drool, while Mrs. Jaden continued to spout the morals of the epic hero *Beowulf*.

"What was it?" Clara whispered.

"Theresa Miguez," I answered.

"Gabriel and Clara, unless you are enlightening one another on the difference between the Saxons and the Geats, then I ask that you keep quiet. Unless of course you would like to enlighten the whole class?"

I shook my head. Mrs. Jaden always had an interesting way of saying 'shut up.' My mind raced wildly, wondering what news Theresa had to *enlighten* us on the fate of mankind. Normally, I enjoyed the lengthy speeches Mrs. Jaden gave on literary heroes and heroines, but right now it all seemed ridiculously trivial. Learning about *Beowulf* wasn't going to help us figure out what to do with these supernatural creatures. Could they truly be real? Or, were we letting fantastical dreams and odd coincidences make us believe the impossible?

I watched the clock. So did Clara. As soon as the bell rang, she headed toward the door, grabbing my hand then dragged me toward the end of the hall. We stood right at the back exit.

"Tell me," she demanded.

"It was Theresa. She gave me pictures of the carvings we saw on her website."

I pulled them out and let Clara shuffle through them. I immediately felt that familiar fear coming from her.

"These are the shadow men," she said pointing a shaky finger at one carving in particular. Many of the dark human-like figures crowded around one woman who held her arms out to stop them from coming closer.

"She says she knows what they want. She wants us to meet her after school," I said, drawing her attention away from the pictures.

A group of cheerleaders whizzed by us, gossiping about who knows what. Clara pulled me out the back door that led to the track field. No one was out here at this time of day. I could sense Clara was on the verge of a breakdown.

"I know why they're here, too. They're coming for us."

"Which ones?"

"All of them," she nearly shouted, her voice was cracking. "The shadow men, those giant things, those ashy creatures, all of them!"

I grabbed Clara by the shoulders, trying to calm her. Tears pooled in her eyes and were spilling down her pale cheeks. I swept one away with my thumb, cupping her face. She was giving me a pitiful look, but slowly, her eyes lost that wildness. I was about to pull her to me when I heard a movement from behind us. We both turned quickly. Jeremy Kaufman was watching us with a strange smile spread across his face. His iPod earphones were dangling loosely out of his hoodie and his arms were crossed. He looked as if he were casually watching a sporting event, although I doubted he ever attended sporting events. Clara and I glanced at each other, wondering if he'd heard everything and if he thought we were completely insane. What he said surprised us more than anything else we could've imagined.

"So, you're seein' 'em, too, huh?"

7

GABE

"Excuse me?" asked Clara.

Jeremy stuffed his hands in his jeans pockets and walked toward us.

"The shadow people? The others? You're seein' 'em in your dreams, aren't you?"

Clara and I glanced at each other. This was unbelievable. I was getting a strange vibe from him, not angry or upset or intense in any kind of way. It was just steady and even like this was a normal conversation.

"How long have you been dreaming about them?" I asked.

"A couple of weeks now," he replied casually. "I figured out that I wasn't the only one when I saw that masterpiece in charcoal of yours."

"Why didn't you say anything to me?"

"I don't know. Would you?"

Good question. I doubt that I would.

"Jeremy," said Clara, "have you ever seen a shadow person in real life? I mean, up close."

I could sense that her fear had turned into something more like excited curiosity.

"Well, no. But, maybe."

He had a sheepish smile, like he enjoyed his little mysteries.

"Are you going to tell us or what?"

I knew there was an edge to my voice that told him to cut the crap.

"I've only seen them in my dreams. But, lately, I keep seeing shadows in broad daylight. Everywhere, man. It's always in my peripheral vision, you know, but when I look, there's nothing there."

I couldn't believe this.

"Me too," I said.

"What?" asked Clara. "You never told me this."

"I didn't want to scare you."

"You've got to be kidding, Gabe. I'm having visits in my bedroom from one of these creepy things, and you didn't want to scare me? At least I would know that I'm not just going crazy."

"You saw one in your room?" interrupted Jeremy. "Wicked."

"Well," continued Clara, "I think we should all go see Theresa. I mean, if Jeremy's having these dreams, too, then maybe he can help figure this out."

"Who's Theresa?" asked Jeremy.

"We found her on this website," I tried to explain. "She says that she's actually seen these things in real life. She wants us to meet her after school at the Holiday Inn."

"Whoa. Are y'all into some kind of kinky on-line dating thing?"

"No!" Clara and I snapped at the same time.

"Just kidding," he said with that annoying grin again. "So, let's ditch school and go meet her. I'm game."

"Absolutely not," said Clara. "It would look a little suspicious, Gabe, if we just disappeared since everyone knows we were in our first four periods."

"And, no one would notice if I was gone, right? Because I'm already invisible?" asked Jeremy.

I could tell that he hurt Clara's feelings, which pissed me off, but then he saved himself from my interference.

"Just kidding. You really need to get a sense of humor. Besides, nobody would notice if I took off. That's my whole plan, man, to be *in cognito*."

"Oh," said Clara.

I could tell she didn't know how to respond to his weirdness.

"Well, let's just go after school like we planned. Okay?" she added.

"Whatever," said Jeremy, "catch you on the flip side."

He plugged his earphones back in, pulled his hoodie up tight and went back into the hall. Clara was fidgeting with a loose thread on her shirt.

"Are you okay now?"

"Sure," she said, but not very convincingly.

I brushed a long strand of her hair away that had fallen in front of her eyes. Those light hazel eyes seemed so sad, too sad. I bent down close to her.

"Goddard, better get back to class and kiss your girl later."

It was Coach Louviere coming up the walk from the track field. His warning sounded casual but meant business. I gave him a quick wave then Clara and I hurried to our fifth period classes.

Surprisingly, the rest of the day sped by, especially when I got to last period. Jeremy and I spent the whole hour pretending to share art techniques, but actually recapping our dreams. I also caught him up on Theresa Miguez and what we knew about her. Mrs. Fowler was so impressed with our intense "art" discussion that she never once told us to be quiet and get back to work. When the bell rang, we were still talking about it while walking to my Jeep.

"The weird thing is, we've all dreamed about the same creatures, but at different places. It's always a swamp for me in a storm," I told him.

"Really? And, mine have been on streets with shops, like in town at the plaza."

We made it to the parking lot when I heard someone behind me.

"Hey, Gabe. Where's your prettier half?"

It was Mark who usually parked his pick-up a few spots down from me.

"She's coming."

"You missed it, man. Ben was snoring so loud in French that Ms. Toussant knocked him awake with her yard stick right on the back of his head. Whack!" he said, giving me the full effect with an invisible slap in the air.

"What's up with him?"

"I don't know, but pretty boy better get his beauty sleep or he's gonna have a row of knots on the back of his head."

Mark was laughing, but at the same time he kept glancing at Jeremy who was now sitting in the backseat of my Jeep. He gestured me over.

"What gives, dude? You hangin' out with that headbangin' geek now?"

He clearly spoke loud enough for Jeremy to hear. To his credit, he slipped on his earphones and ignored Mark.

"He's cool," I said. "We're working on a science thing for Dunaway."

"Oh," he said, easily accepting that lame explanation. "Alright. Catch ya later."

Clara practically ran across the parking lot a minute later. She threw her backpack in and swung herself into the front seat in one quick movement. I was still highly impressed with her athletic ability.

"Let's go."

I was glad to feel that her stressful vibe was gone. There was a new sense to her now. Not that warm and fuzzy feeling that I so often got, but one I could only describe as eager anticipation of something.

None of us talked. The radio station was doing their Afternoon Oldies Hour. An 80s band called The Police was wailing that Roxanne didn't have to wear that dress tonight when Jeremy poked his head in the front seat.

"Do you really listen to this crap?"

I shrugged. I liked my music, but I wasn't as obsessed as Jeremy.

"No, no, no. We need some *real* music."

I watched him in the rearview mirror pull out an iPod car adaptor from his backpack.

"You carry that with you?" I asked.

"Always be prepared. Boy Scout motto," he replied, shoving it into my battery plug.

"You were a Boy Scout?" asked Clara.

He just grinned.

"Here we go, ladies and gents. I give you one of the best albums ever made, *Destroyer*, by the almighty Kiss."

"Wasn't that the weird band who wore all the make-up and high heels?" asked Clara.

"You've gotta be kidding me. Just relax, listen, and learn what real music is all about," said Jeremy snidely.

I caught a glimpse of Clara smiling to herself. I mean, who hadn't heard of Kiss? It was good to see her playful side coming out again. Jeremy air-guitared with Gene Simmons and sang along with Paul Stanley for the rest of the ride to the hotel, which was a short one.

Beau Chêne was a small town, but it was settled along a busy Interstate that connected New Orleans to I-10. There were a couple of hotels located right on Beau Chêne's outskirts to lodge any businessmen in the oil industry who happened to be passing through. It probably looked a little strange for three teenagers to be wandering into the lobby after school. We didn't know any of the people drinking coffee or surfing the Internet, but I wasn't thrilled with the way the curly-haired receptionist was watching us when we walked through the door. Theresa stood up and joined us as soon as we came in. She offered her hand to me first.

"Hi, Gabriel. It's nice to officially meet you. I'm Theresa Miguez. And, you're Clara, right?"

She turned and shook Clara's hand then finally turned to Jeremy.

"I'm sorry. I wasn't prepared for a third person."

"It's okay," I said. "It might sound crazy, but we just found out that he's dreaming about the same thing we are."

Theresa eyed him skeptically, which seemed kind of ironic to me since she was having so much trouble convincing people in her profession that she actually saw what she saw. I guess anybody would be suspicious of a third wheel jumping on the oh-I'm-dreaming-of-monsters-too bandwagon.

"It's for real. He really is," Clara assured her.

"That's very interesting," she said. "Do you know if there are others?"

"No. I hadn't thought about it," I answered.

"But, why would just you three in this little town be dreaming of them?"

She seemed to be asking the air around her rather than any of us. It was a question I had been wondering myself. I was hoping Theresa might have the answers.

"What is it that you have to tell us?" Clara asked anxiously.

Theresa's face turned dark.

"I think it's best if I show you," she said. "Come with me."

We followed her outside and up to the second floor on the outside staircase. Her room was just at the top with a 'do not disturb' sign hanging on the doorknob. She glanced around nervously as she unlocked the door. She seemed a little paranoid, even though there wasn't a soul in sight. Expecting the typical white-walled, cheaply furnished hotel room, I was shocked to see an entire wall covered from top to bottom in photographs. The television was set to the weather channel, which was continually looping weather reports and routes for Hurricane Lucy.

"Come in, come in, hurry," she said, ushering us through the door and closing it behind Jeremy.

"Cloak and dagger," he whispered hoarsely as he slid through the doorway, "way cool."

Theresa ushered us to the wall of photographs.

"This is an actual representation of the underground wall at the archaeological site in Cuba. I posted each picture as it appeared on the wall. As you can see, it stops here because that's where my memory card on my camera filled up. I was unable to get the complete wall of pictographs."

"That sucks," said Jeremy.

"Actually," she added, "that was the only thing that saved my life."

"Oh, then I guess it doesn't suck."

"So, how do we read them?" asked Clara, ignoring Jeremy. "Just start at the top? Did you figure out what any of these meant?"

Theresa's brown eyes brightened. She apparently had done more than just a little thinking on the subject and was happy to finally share it with someone who took her seriously.

"Begin here, from the bottom up and go across to the right. It was actually the last thing that I discovered about the wall of pictographs before I left Dr. Malcolm and--"

Theresa fell silent, looking dazedly at the pictures. We all remained silent. The weather forecaster rambled on, listing possible landfalls in Georgia or Florida if Hurricane Lucy continued to head northeast.

"Are you okay?" asked Clara, touching Theresa's arm gently.

I felt a pang of grief come from Theresa. I could only imagine what somber color her aura must be. The look in Clara's sympathetic eyes told me enough.

"Yes, yes, fine. It's just that it still is very jarring when I think about it. It almost feels like a dream, since no one witnessed it but me and no one believes it but me."

We didn't know what to say though I think all of us wanted to comfort her in some way. She obviously went through something terrible and has felt very alone for a long time.

"Well, now. Let me show you what I think I've discovered. Come closer."

As we stepped up to the wall of photos, we noticed that she had marked several pictures with different colored stars. The first few she had marked had orange ones in the left corners.

"If you look at this set of pictographs, you'll notice that the people, the humans, are doing normal chores—cooking around the fire, tanning hides, harvesting a garden. Everything seems normal except for one thing. What do you see?"

It was Clara that stepped closer first, staring at each pictograph. Though the engravings were primitive, they had been shaved and shaped to show definition. There were several human-like figures that had been completely dug out rather than just an outline of a human. These other figures appeared darker and were simply standing in each pictograph, watching the humans do their work.

"They're shadow people," said Clara unflinchingly. "All of these."

She pointed to each one in each picture.

"Shadow people? That's what you call them?" asked Theresa.

"Yes," she replied.

"Well, they keep popping up throughout this history on the wall. I know now that this primitive people who died out long ago wanted to tell what happened to them."

"So, these things have obviously been here before?" I asked. "How long ago?"

"Thousands of years ago."

"What are they doing? The shadow people?" asked Clara, now examining other pictures with the orange stars.

"Nothing, actually," said Theresa. "Or, at least that's what it seemed like at first to me. I've been studying these very closely since I returned home from Cuba, but things suddenly change for this primitive people when a disaster occurs—a flood. Look here," she pointed to several pictures along the second column marked with blue stars.

The pictographs showed how this devastating flood killed livestock, ruined crops, and put these people into a famine. While these cryptic pictographs could not show great detail like in a painting, there was a definite look of sadness and fear upon them. This is where other figures appeared.

"After the flood," narrated Theresa, while pointing to each picture, "more shadow people as you call them appeared. Then came the dark giants. It seems that some sort of catastrophe precedes their coming."

"Like a hurricane," added Jeremy.

We all considered that quietly. Theresa's eyes flicked to the television. I looked at the wall of photos where Theresa had marked each one with a red star that had the dark giants as she called them. In the pictographs, it looked as if these huge, black creatures had swords for arms that they stabbed right into the chest of their victims.

"So, why do these demon monsters or whatever they are want to come and kill people? Just for fun? I don't get it," said Jeremy. "I mean, what do they gain from it?"

"I don't think they're killing for the fun of it," said Theresa. "Do you see these sword-like hands they have? They seem to be killing each person in exactly the same spot."

My limited knowledge of anatomy from Biology and just watching enough blood-and-guts movies told me that these monsters thrust their "swords" directly into their hearts.

"Perhaps, it's some kind of ritual," said Clara.

"That's what I was thinking," said Theresa excitedly, "like the ancient Mayans who sacrificed humans to the gods. Hell, maybe they even got the idea from these things. It seems that they could be performing this ritual to gain power amongst their own kind when they conquer another people."

I looked closely at the dark giants in each pictograph. After each killing, from frame to frame, there was a subtle difference. They seemed to grow larger and stronger each time they killed a human in this way. There were subtle wavy lines around them, as if they were glowing or shining with some new power. A flash from that nightmare slammed into my head where I met one of these huge demons on a swampy shore. Its black, sword-like arm struck me directly through flesh and ribs, straight into my heart. It wasn't a sudden death, but a seeping out of all my strength. It was as if this thing was literally sucking the life out of me. The demon's electric eyes glistened brighter with each ounce of life it took from me.

"No, it's not a ritual," I finally said, shrugging off the memory of the nightmare.

"What is it?" asked Clara. "Why do you have that look on your face?"

There was no way to sugarcoat this. I had to just tell them straight up.

"They're feeding," I said. "They feed on our energy. They're coming here to eat."

I knew how gruesome it sounded. No one could say anything for a minute.

"How do you know?" asked Theresa quietly.

"Because of how they kill me in my dreams. I can feel them draining me dry, while at the same time they grow stronger from it."

"He's right," said Jeremy.

He didn't elaborate on why I was right, but I knew Jeremy must've had the same experience in his dreams.

"So, what about the third ones?" asked Jeremy somberly, pointing to a pictograph with a yellow star. "The ash-eaters."

"Interesting name," said Theresa, "because that's exactly what they are. The pictographs aren't very clear, but if you look closely the people who built that wall tried to show it as best they could. Look here, this is what the humans look like after the giants are done with them. I remember when I first saw this pictograph there in that hole in the ground in Cuba, I thought this looked like the remains of people I once saw in Pompeii. The Pompeiians had been killed by the eruption of Mount Vesuvius and then buried in lava and ash. Hundreds of years later, archaeologists found the perfectly preserved city and were able to show us just what the victims looked like when they died. They looked like these people, who are frozen in statues of fossilized humans. When I was in Cuba, I took something with me, thinking it no more than a souvenir from the site at the time."

Theresa pulled out a small, brown velvet pouch from her suitcase. She untied a knot then poured something into the palm of her hand. It was a small black rock. As I got closer, I recognized it from the stone in my dreams, the burning stone.

"I know this," I said.

"You do?" asked Theresa.

"But how?" asked Clara.

"I don't know. It's always in my dreams. I'm holding it as I walk through a cane field, just before I enter the swamp then see the creatures. What is it?"

Theresa looked at me curiously. I couldn't read her emotions, because I was caught up in my own.

"It was a piece of rock, so I thought, from deep underground. They were hauling and packing pieces of it the day . . . the day the site was destroyed. I had picked this up and put it in my pocket, thinking it would be fun to do my own study of it. You see, my degree is in geology."

She paused and looked out the window, getting that glazed look again.

"Well," said Clara, "what did you find?"

She turned back to us, still holding it in her hand for us to see.

"It's the petrified remains of human bone."

I instantly felt a jolt of shock and fear from both Clara and Jeremy.

"There are traces of sulfur on the surface. There were much larger pieces of the same thing, but they're all buried now. I'm sure whoever funded the dig will eventually get back to it again. At some point, they will listen to me when they realize an entire group of workers has disappeared."

All three of us were staring at it.

"How come they didn't look into Dr. Malcolm's disappearance?" Jeremy asked distractedly. "I mean, they knew that the two of you traveled together then you came back alone."

"Yes, well, actually they finally were the day I flew here. They were trying to communicate with the officials in Cuba about it, but that entire

God-forsaken island is still without power. For some reason, I knew I had to come here."

I wasn't really listening, because I was so mesmerized by this object from my dreams being very real, very tangible. I reached out my hand, palm up.

"May I see it?"

Theresa nodded then placed the black stone in my hand. I was expecting the pain of the cold burn just like in my dreams, but not the intensity of it. I sucked in my breath at the stun. Then, there was something I didn't expect. A distant woman's scream was ringing in my ears and all went black. A spinning vision jerked into my head. An amazingly fierce and beautiful woman stood before me. She was fair-skinned with reddish-blonde hair spilling wildly around her shoulders. She had the look of a warrior with some sort of tribal tattoos swirling up her forearms though she had no weapon. There were four of the giant creatures towering above her as she crouched, ready to pounce while she guarded some kind of gateway. Two huge monoliths, perhaps twelve feet tall, easily as tall as the creatures stood behind her. There was a weird humming sound coming from the tall stones. In between them was a black hole, outlined by threads of electricity. The scream I'd heard had apparently come from the woman after seeing her fellow warriors killed at her feet. There were five others—all of them with similar tattoos on their arms. They were men and women with the same fair looks as her, except for one large dark-haired man near her feet. I knew this was only a memory from someone else. I still didn't even know how I was even seeing it, but the overwhelming sensation of vengeful anger flowed from her like a primal instinct. She drew herself to her full height, which was only half as tall as the dark beasts but taller than most men. She seemed to be waiting for them to do something. Lifting her arms outward in a cross, she waited. I couldn't help but think how triumphant she looked, even with death breathing down on her. The beasts let loose an eerie growl, impaling her all at once through the chest, two from the side and two from the front. Her eyes never dulled with defeat. She purposefully grabbed the two black arms extending to the tallest creatures in front of her. I felt a trembling vibration, growing and growing. It was coming from her. It was the same vibration I felt when I sensed the change in my supernatural sense, except this was much, much stronger. She looked first at the ground, at her fallen friends then pausing at the man near her feet, speaking quietly to them in a language I didn't understand.

"Setti, valr, svá váru þeir allir hraustir at engi talaði æðruorð."

She then stared menacingly at the beasts, with a terrifying fierceness in her voice.

"Myrkr jötnar, tekinn minn lífdagar. Vér nálægr þessi dyrr. Vér vili neinn andask. Minn kyn vili nálgask endr. Vér ávalt hafa."

Her head bowed just an instant, and I thought she whispered something else then she glowered at the menacing creatures in front of her. A glimmer of what I can only call pure hatred came from her eyes, then a shuddering, violent vibration rose out of her body. She yelled, but not because she was in pain. It shot out of her throat at the same time her full power blasted from her body, shattering all four of the creatures into splinters and dust. She continued to wail, unleashing her killing power on ash-eaters that were circling the kill. There was a feral squeal from every creature she destroyed with her force. The black abyss and electric circle between the two stones behind her blurred, crackled, then vanished. She continued to cry out until I saw her own skin begin to shudder, shake, then split and explode into tiny fragments of shimmering light.

"Gabriel!"

It was Clara, leaning over me. I had fallen back onto the bed with the stone in my hand. Theresa had pried it loose from me. A piercing pain throbbed in my head, and I felt sick to my stomach.

"Are you okay?"

I could barely open my eyes without pain. I couldn't even feel the fear coming from Clara that was obviously written all over her face as she peered down at me.

"I'm okay," I said, trying to sit up.

Clara helped me to a sitting position. Slowly, the world came back into focus. The throbbing was fading.

"Dude, you look like hell," said Jeremy.

"It's getting better. Just give me a minute."

"What happened?" asked Clara anxiously.

"I saw something."

I looked up at Theresa, who was now holding the black stone in her hands. The more minutes that passed without me holding it, the better I felt.

"What, dude? Don't keep us in suspense. You looked like your head was gonna pop off or something."

"I saw that person's death," I said, pointing at the stone. "She was like me."

I realized after I said it that I'd have to confess to two other people about my supernatural sense, that weird secret that I'd kept hidden for so long.

"What do you mean like you?" asked Theresa.

I glanced at Clara who simply smiled and nodded.

"I have this other sense," I said, unable to find the words.

Jeremy was looking at me way too seriously, and Theresa looked confused. But, neither of them was staring at me like I was crazy. Not yet anyway.

"Go on," said Clara. "Tell them."

I sighed heavily.

"Ever since I was really young, I've been able to sense people's emotions, especially strong emotions. When someone's really angry or sad or happy, I can sense it the moment they walk in the room or come close to me."

"And so, you could sense that the woman you saw was like you?" asked Theresa.

"Yes. Well, no, not at first. It wasn't like that. It's so complicated," I said, feeling my own frustration growing. I looked at Clara.

"She could use her emotions as a weapon," I told her.

"What do you mean? Like what happened this morning?" she asked.

"What happened this morning?" asked Jeremy.

"Clara and I were on our way to school when she got really upset about seeing that shadow man in her bedroom."

"What!" said Theresa in a completely horrified voice. "One was in her room?"

"Hey, hey, one thing at a damn time. I'm tryin' to keep up here," said Jeremy.

"Okay, let me explain," said Clara. "Yes, Theresa, one of the shadow men was in my room last night. He didn't do anything but stare at me hatefully then say some weird word '*setti*' then he vanished. Then on the way to school, I got really upset thinking about it. Gabe was trying to comfort me, so he kissed me and—"

Clara stopped short, obviously embarrassed at confessing a little too much.

"Kissin' and drivin'? You're a multi-tasker, huh, Gabriel," said Jeremy.

I punched him in the shoulder, but not too hard.

"Ow."

"Well, when he did," continued Clara, "it was like being shocked, and I felt a sort of vibration. I knew that it was this gift he had."

"Vibration, huh?"

Jeremy was grinning sheepishly again. I leaned over to punch him. He flinched back.

"Just kidding, just kidding. Geez, dude."

"I don't understand," said Theresa, ignoring all of the stupidity. "How can that be a weapon?"

"In the vision, the woman I saw used her anger to kill the giants. She projected it out somehow."

"She survived?" asked Theresa. "Then how—"

She was looking down at the stone in her hand, which we all knew now was a fossilized piece of the woman.

"They had already stabbed her before she killed them."

For some reason, I couldn't explain everything I saw. I didn't know what the warrior woman said before she died, but I knew it was some kind of sacrifice. I wanted to keep this to myself for now, but I had to tell them about the monoliths and what I thought it was.

"I couldn't understand what she said, but I know that she was blocking a gate so the creatures couldn't get back through."

"What kind of gate?"

"It was between two tall stones, monoliths, like what we learned in Mr. Weber's World History class last year," I said, turning to Jeremy.

"Do you think I really paid attention in that class?"

"Anyway, that's what they looked like. There was an electric field between them, but she used her power to close it."

"Why wouldn't she want them to leave?" asked Clara doubtfully.

"Honestly," I said, "I think she wanted to kill them for what they'd done to her friends. Maybe she closed the gate so no more could come through."

"Wait a minute," said Theresa, "what did these monoliths look like? You said there were two of them?"

"Yeah. They were about twelve or thirteen feet high, rounded at the top, and made of dark stone."

"I don't believe it," murmured Theresa.

"What don't you believe?" asked Clara.

"I saw these stones," she said, her brown eyes widening. "Right before I left the excavation pit for my camera's memory card, I heard a weird humming noise and saw some workers sort of bickering around two tall stones they had nearly dug out."

"Wow," said Clara, "then you actually saw the portal right before they came through."

"You said, Gabriel, that she closed the portal between the gate, right?" she asked.

"Yes," I agreed.

"But, somehow they found a way to reopen the gate, didn't they?" she asked thoughtfully.

"Where do you think they come from?" asked Jeremy.

Theresa looked at all of us somberly.

"I don't know."

She turned the pouch holding the fossil of the ancient warrior in her hands over and over.

"You must have a connection to the stone, because of the power you shared," she said to me, then turning to the wall of photographs. "You said she had friends, this warrior woman?"

"Yes. There were others around her. They were all dead. I knew they were warriors like her because of the similar tattoos on all of their forearms."

"And, you said she spoke to the creatures?"

"Yes, but I didn't understand it. It was a strange language."

"Interesting. I only wish we were able to see the entire wall before, well, before it was all buried again."

"Dude, I'm gonna need to get home soon," interrupted Jeremy. "My dad will think I'm stealin' cars or somethin' if I'm gone too long."

"Really?" asked Clara, sounding rather shocked.

"No, not that bad, but not far off. He doesn't get me. But, what parents do?"

I sensed a sudden shift in Clara to bitterness. My supernatural sense was clear now, reading everyone in the room. Jeremy was anxious, apparently about his dad, or maybe something else. Clara had that sort of uneasy vibe I felt whenever I knew she was thinking about her mother. Theresa was completely detached, absorbed in the photos on the wall. There was still more to talk about, but it was getting late. It was enough for one day.

We left in silence. While I knew the others were unsettled by what they saw and learned, I felt something entirely different. I felt empowered. For the first time in my strange life, I felt a purpose for this curse of mine, this gift. More than that, I could feel it inside, pushing its way upward from the depths of my gut. Strange that I knew some hellish monsters from another world were coming to kill me and everyone I knew, but all I could feel was a heightened sense of confidence and control. I was connected to an ancient warrior who had learned to use her power to destroy the invaders. I would learn, too. I would be ready for them.

✶8✶

CLARA

Dad was devouring the fried pork chops, rice, and gravy I had cooked for dinner. I was just picking at mine. I watched him, sunk down in his comfy chair, chuckling at another rerun of *The Andy Griffith Show*. His earthy green aura waved out around him.
"Dad?"
"Yeah, hon," he said forking in another piece of pork chop.
He snorted a laugh. Barney Fife was parading around ridiculously the jail of Mayberry, playing king of the castle. I definitely didn't get my dad's sense of humor, but I loved his simplicity. Right now, I wondered if I should even bring up what I was about to.
"It's a little weird what's going on with this hurricane, isn't it?" I asked, trying to sound casual.
"Yes. It's quite an anomaly," he said, glancing toward me. "How's that science fair project coming along with Gabriel?"
"Fine."

I wasn't exactly lying. Gabe and I were definitely doing lots of research on the hurricane. Only, we were trying to discover how it was linked to the murdering monsters from another dimension that planned on eating humankind rather than its bizarre scientific origins.

"Don't you think it's more than a little strange how it started off the coast of Cuba instead of out in the Atlantic like other hurricanes? I mean, it seems sort of supernatural, doesn't it?"

I tried to sound casual, but I heard my voice squeak a little. Dad gulped some of his iced tea and turned to me.

"Yes, it does. Do you and Gabe have some theories?"

I knew he thought I was nervous because I had some radical scientific theory that I wanted to get his expert opinion on. What I wanted was for him to open his mind to something totally non-scientific.

"No, but do you ever think there might be some things that we can't explain? I mean, scientifically speaking?"

"Like what?" he asked, sounding curious.

"Oh, I don't know, like the Bermuda Triangle? You know, some people believe that the disappearances have something to do with other dimensions. They think that's where those boats and planes disappear into."

I spit out the first example I could think of, but after I said it I wondered if it was true. I mean, now that I actually believed in other dimensions and gates opening up from other worlds where scary monsters popped out. Was it so crazy to think there were dimensions randomly opening up and swallowing things in our world?

"Oh, Clara, you know that's not true. We've talked about that. It has to do with the earth's gases and plate tectonics under the ocean-bed. None of that crazy stuff is true. I'm sure this hurricane formation seems odd, but it has more to do with a shift in our planet's weather system than anything else. Everything can be scientifically explained."

"Well, what if something couldn't?"

He gave me a concerned look. I kept rambling, trying to get that crease in his brow to disappear.

"Hypothetically speaking, if something happened that you couldn't scientifically explain, would you take advice from others who had some knowledge of it?"

"What's this about, Clara?"

I was grasping for a better explanation, wondering why the heck I even brought this up when Mom stepped through the front door. She was carrying several new hanging outfits and dresses, rustling in their plastic coverings, and one bag dangling on her arm with her Coach purse.

"Hello there. Oh, Philip, don't spill on my carpet. And, Clara. Didn't you make something fried on Monday? You'll get fat and ruin that pretty figure eating all that greasy food."

"Clara will not ruin her figure," said Dad, turning back to the TV.

"Come see what I got you," Mom said, beaming down at me. "Oh, but wash your hands first."

She clip-clopped down the hall to her bedroom. Resigned that I wasn't going to eat anything anyway and I might as well play like I had something in common with my mom, I followed her to the bedroom. She spread her day's worth of shopping all over the bed. Ordinarily, she didn't bother showing me her new things. She knew I never shared her ridiculous obsession with new clothes and shoes. I mean, I like shopping as much as the next girl. I just wasn't plagued with the need to constantly decorate myself with something new every other day, like my mom.

"Look at these," she said, opening up a long box to reveal black stiletto boots.

"Oh. They're cool," I said flatly.

"They'll be great with this black velvet skirt for my next Ladies of Beau Chêne meeting. Don't you think?"

She whisked her new skirt around, flaring it out next to the boots. I wondered if all the Ladies of Beau Chêne put this much effort into their wardrobes to impress each other. Probably so. The entire purpose of the group seemed to be just to show off. Mom said that it was a club to discuss current events and social issues. I thought it was an excuse for all the socialites of Beau Chêne to hang out and admire themselves and feel important.

"Uh-huh."

"Well, then," she said, eyeing me closely, "maybe this will get your attention."

She pulled out three dresses, obviously in my size, and displayed them on the bed. There was a red halter-top style dress that flared at the bottom near the knee. The second was a black strapless that draped to the floor. The third was an emerald green sweetheart-cut with spaghetti straps and black beading along the bodice that disappeared at the waist.

"What's this?"

It was a stupid question. Obviously, they were dresses, but what for?

"Clara. Homecoming is next month. I'm sure you'll be going with your new boyfriend. I thought I'd get a head start shopping for you."

"Oh, Homecoming," I said, sounding kind of dense.

"Come on, Clara. Everyone dresses up for Homecoming. So, go try them on and come show me."

She was actually giggling. I couldn't believe it. I knew Mom loved to see me primped and pretty. My childhood pictures in Christmas and Easter dresses made me look like a pageant girl, complete with bouncing curls. As soon as I was old enough to choose my own style, I shed all of the prissy skirts and dresses for t-shirts and beat-up blue jeans. I was way too casual for my mom's taste. Maybe that's why she got excited about high school dances. That was when she knew she could get me in a dress, and I really couldn't protest. I mean, I liked dressing up and looking good. I just didn't want to look like my mom's version of pretty. Maybe it was my only way to scream at her—*I'm not like you.* My mom was gorgeous—tall, slim, great skin and reddish-brown hair thicker than the average forty-year-old should have. I knew it was a compliment when people said I looked like her, but I winced all the same. It's just that as long as I could remember, she's been more interested in appearances than anything else. At my first dance recital when I was nine, I was so excited because my parents were there beaming and clapping excitedly at my performance. My mom's only comment afterwards was, "You looked so pretty up there. I swear you look just like me at your age." The next year, I turned to soccer and baseball, which really ticked her off. I think that's when the gulf between us grew wider and wider. Every now and then, I would try my best to connect with her in some way. But it was always through something like this—homecoming dresses.

I took the three dresses into her bathroom and tried them on one at a time. I hated the red dress. It made me look a little skanky. The neck line plunged way more than I was comfortable with. I had to admit that the black dress made me feel very grown up—tall, thin, and elegant. But, the best was definitely the emerald-green dress. My pale skin, auburn hair, and hazel eyes stood out strikingly with this dress draped on my body. I couldn't help but smile at my reflection. I wondered how Gabe's expression would look when he saw me in this dress. My smile faded.

What was I thinking? Would there even be a Homecoming dance? It was like I was caught up in a mirage for a few minutes, dreaming of high school dances and a normal teen's life, when I knew very well that what was coming would change everything forever. My reflection looked a little ridiculous and sad now. I couldn't explain to my mom that there was no point to keep the dress since I'd probably never go to the dance because I was seeing shadow men and dreaming of monsters that I was pretty sure were coming to kill us all. Instead, I flounced out of the bathroom, spinning around in my best act of teen giddiness.

"Oh, Clara. It's beautiful! I just knew that would be the one."

"You're right, Mom. It's perfect."

I smiled as genuinely as I could while a sick feeling swelled up in my stomach.

"Just wonderful. Now, see how easy it is to dress up?"

She still talked to me like I was five. Hadn't she noticed I'd grown a little? She was pleased with herself and all of her accomplishments for the day and some part of me wanted her to have that feeling. Who knew how quickly all of this would change? Handing her the other dresses, I wore the green one back to my room. After I changed into my white tank and blue cotton pajama pants, I hung the dress up regretfully in my closet. I stared at it for a minute, sighed, then went back out to the living room and stretched out on the sofa. I was in no mood for sleeping right now, especially not after my encounter last night. Surely, it wouldn't happen again, but I still needed an hour or two of mindless television to wind down.

Dad had already gone to his "lab," in other words the greenhouse, which he usually did for an hour before bedtime. Misty jumped up to the couch and cradled herself in the curve by my stomach. That queasy feeling had gone away. I flipped through the channels, finally resting on *Extreme Home Makeover*. Ty Pennington was once again making the ultimate dream come true for a sweet family who had been struck with an illness and poverty. I couldn't help it. I knew this would probably make me cry like a sap then feel ridiculously happy when the family got their dream house in the end. Every episode was the same, but I liked the feeling it gave me. It was hopeful and happy. I needed that like I needed air and food and water.

Just like I thought, I teared up at the end, all gushy for that unfortunate family. I flipped through the channels again and stopped abruptly on the National Weather Channel. Hurricane Lucy was just sitting there right in the middle of the Gulf, not moving. The red trajectory lines for the different routes it could take looked like a giant spider web attached to the entire southeastern coastline of the United States. Why was it just sitting there? It was so weird. I sighed heavily then kept flipping.

"Goodnight, Hon," said Dad, pecking me on the top of my head. "See you in the morning."

" 'Night, Dad."

I heard him shuffle down the hall and close the door. I turned down the volume, so I wouldn't keep them up then settled on a rerun of *The Office*. If that couldn't lift my spirits, nothing could. The show was nearly over when it happened.

Misty let out a slow growl from deep in her belly. I could feel the hairs prickling on my neck and arms, but there was no one in the room but the two of us. Static fuzzed up the TV screen, which just doesn't happen with digital television. I glanced toward the kitchen, thinking something might creep up behind me then turned back. I jumped in my skin and sat up in a heartbeat. There they were. Three shadow men standing in front of the coffee table, staring at me. They were motionless. You would think they were statues if not for those glowing yellow eyes boring down on me with sinister hatred. Their dark, powdery auras lingered around their black, scaly bodies, like living cloaks of dust. An overpowering burnt smell passed over me; not a woodsy smell like a campfire, but a nauseating, rotten stench. The middle one took a step toward me. Misty hissed and spat, arching her back to puff herself up. I couldn't move. I was paralyzed by my own fear. The middle one pointed a long, bony finger at me.

"Setti. You cannot stop us. You will not."

It's voice was deep and gravelly like someone being choked by water. My heart pounded feverishly in my chest. I was fighting the fear that threatened to spin me out of control. The menacing shadow man took another step closer as if it was being cautious for some reason. I flinched backward, pressing myself into the sofa. Misty spat again then leapt down to hide in some corner. Thanks for the back-up, Misty. Then, the leader of this hideous crew did something entirely unexpected. It smiled, and then laughed at me. I felt my back stiffen as that guttural cackling sound filled the room. Its teeth were a coarse gray or metallic color, if what lined its mouth could be called teeth. The two behind him shared wicked smiles. That's when my fear turned into anger. I mean, what was going on? What were they doing here? Why me? As soon as my emotions shifted, I felt something flare like fire deep within. I noticed a change in the leader's stance. It leaned away from me, just barely. That flame burned inside, intensifying my anger. All three of them stepped back in unison, their eyes widening almost invisibly. But, I caught it. Whatever stirred inside of me wrapped my body in a shell of heat. I could even see my own aura waving out from my arms and torso in golden ripples, fueling my courage. I no longer felt fear. I felt strong, stronger than them. I jumped off the sofa to face them and whatever attack they had planned. I was about to say something, although I didn't know what, when they turned, and vanished through the wall. In a blink, they were gone.

I stood there for what seemed like an eternity, unable to move. Something grazed my ankles. I shrieked and jumped. It was Misty, staring up at me with her big green eyes, like nothing at all had just happened.

"Oh, now you come to my rescue," I said, picking her up, "you scaredy-cat." She purred softly against my chest. That was as close to an apology that I was going to get. "They're gone. Don't worry."

The air felt light again. No creepiness. I took Misty to my room and curled up in my bed with the side lamp on. I didn't have the feeling they would be coming back tonight, but I still wasn't ready to sit in the dark. Not yet. I had to calm down before I could ever fall asleep. Picking up my phone, I texted Gabe.

HEY. DON'T FREAK OUT. 3 SHADOW MEN WERE HERE.

There was a chance he'd already gone to bed. I figured he might not even respond, but as I set my phone down, it bleeped.

WHAT!!! ARE YOU OK?

I quickly texted back. He was freaking out like I said not to.

YES. I'M FINE. DON'T WORRY.

There was about a 10-second delay.

I'M COMING OVER.

Oh, crap. I texted back again.

NO! I'M REALLY OK. WE'LL TALK TOMORROW. SEE U THEN.

There was no response after that. He might be ticked off at me for not letting him come over, but my dad would freak out if he woke up. He was a light sleeper. I was, too. Sometimes I would wake up in the middle of the night and go to the living room to fall back asleep to the TV, only to find that Dad had beat me to it.

I lay back in bed, bundled under the covers. Misty rested on my other pillow, purring softly. It was nice to see at least one of us wasn't completely shaken by what happened tonight. I'd just turned off my bedside lamp when I heard a tapping at the window. I froze. Could the shadow men be back? Of course not. Shadow men didn't tap on your window and announce their arrival. They just zapped right in your house and scared the pee out of you. I knew it was Gabe.

I pushed the window open and leaned out. Our house was a one-story Acadian style house set up on pillars. Gabe had found our recycling bin and turned it upside down so he could reach the window. We were eye level. Even in the darkness, I could see a shimmering wave of all the colors in the rainbow hovering around him. They were dimmed more than usual, but they were there.

"What are you doing?" I whispered.

"I told you I was coming over," he said, bracing his hands on the windowsill to lift himself into the room.

"No, no, no, you can't come in."

"Why not?" he asked, as if it was perfectly fine for him to crawl through my bedroom window.

"My dad will kill us both if he wakes up and finds you in here."

Gabe gave me that flat expression that said he wasn't going to leave until we talked.

"Okay, okay. Meet me on the front porch," I whispered.

I didn't own a robe, but I wasn't going out there in just my pj's. I pulled on my long, black peacoat from my closet then padded quietly down the hall and out the front door, wincing when the screen door creaked. Gabe was leaning back against a corner post on the porch. His ankles were crossed casually and his hands were tucked into the front pocket of his BCHS sweatshirt. He had that tilted half-smile that made me melt. His dark, wavy hair looked more of a mess than usual, but somehow that made him look even better.

"Um, expecting snow?"

I glanced down at my coat, unable to come up with a response. Before I had time to think of one, he was across the porch and had me in his arms. The night was warm, but there was a chill on the wind. It was an eerie paradox. I shivered.

"It's okay," Gabe whispered into my hair. "I'll stay all night if that's what keeps you safe."

"Oh, no you won't," I protested, pulling back a little to look up at him. "I'm not kidding. My dad might act like a goofball, but he's very protective of me. He won't take it very well if he finds some boy sneaking into my room at night, even a boy he likes."

Without warning, he leaned down and pressed his lips to mine. It was a gentle kiss, slow and soothing. It definitely shut me up and made me forget whatever I was just saying a minute ago. Right then, with Gabe, I did feel safe—completely safe.

"He won't wake up," he said.

He brushed his lips lightly, but deliberately against mine, more teasing than kissing.

"He might," I whispered, completely breathless.

"He won't."

Gabe pulled back, grinning at me.

"What?" I asked.

"Nothing."

That grin on his face didn't say 'nothing.' Then I realized it. He was reading my feelings. I knew that what I was feeling had nothing to do with me being worried about my dad catching us. I felt a flush of heat fill my face.

"I wish you wouldn't do that," I said flatly, not meeting his brown eyes.

"What?"

He gave a little laugh.

"You know what," I accused. "You know my feelings."

"Sorry, Clara. It's not anything I can control. At least I know you're feeling, um, better."

I turned and looked out into the night. It was nearly a full moon in a crystal clear sky. A ghostly blue light bathed the trees, grass, and nearby houses. I thought about the shadow men. Gabe must have sensed my immediate change. He took me by the hand and we leaned back against the railing.

"Tell me what happened," he said soberly.

I exhaled deeply.

"I was watching TV by myself. Well, my cat Misty was with me, but she wasn't much help when they showed up."

"They? Last time it was only one. Now it was three?"

"Yeah, and this time one of them spoke to me."

"Really? It was a weird language, wasn't it?"

"No. It spoke English."

"You're kidding. But, I thought when I saw that vision of the warrior woman that she was speaking their language. That's so weird. What did it say?"

Gabe held that look of disbelief on his face.

"It called me 'Setti' again then it said, 'you cannot stop us. You will not.' Then the worst was that it laughed."

"Laughed? Are you sure?"

"Uh, yeah. I'm pretty sure. It wasn't like 'ha, ha what a nice place you have here.' It was dark and gross and completely creepy."

I shuddered again. He wrapped his arm around my shoulder and still held my hand with the other.

"The weirdest thing wasn't even that though," I said. "It seemed like they were a little scared of *me*."

"How do you mean? What made you think that?"

"Well, at first I was totally terrified of them. You haven't really seen them, Gabe. Not like I have. They're really, *really* scary looking. But, when the leader of the three laughed at me, something in me just snapped. I got so upset, I mean angry. I didn't even know where it came from. All of a sudden, I felt a hot sensation in my gut then it came all the way out of me until I could even see my own aura. Gabe, I've never seen my own aura."

"What happened? What did they do?"

"They stepped back away from me then just vanished."

I watched a frown crease his face. His brown eyes were shadowed by that crazy hair.

"What are you thinking?" I asked.

"I think something's happening to us."

"What do you mean?"

"I mean with our other senses. I think we're supposed to use them somehow against the creatures. I can feel it, Clara. I feel it in my gut, too, just like you did."

He looked at me more seriously than I'd ever seen him. His aura had darkened to shades of blue, indigo, and purple all blurred together. It looked like ribbons of light weaving in and out of each other, cocooning his whole body.

"Can you feel it right now?" I asked softly.

"Yes."

"I think I'm looking at your true aura, Gabe. It's different than when you've got everyone's emotions bouncing off of you."

"What does it look like?" he whispered.

Something in his eyes drew me toward him.

"It looks beautiful."

Like a magnet, I was lured into him. His arms slipped under my peacoat and held me tight. Then our lips met again. No teasing this time. Our mouths were persistent, not playful. My hands went up behind his neck in a tangle of hair. That electric current was back, pulsing between us, making me want to get even closer. I felt my heartbeat racing through my veins at a dizzying pace. Then I felt something else—a subtle, humming vibration. Gabe clutched at my back then without warning . . . wham! A heavy blow knocked me unconscious.

✳ ✳ ✳

When I woke up, I was laying on something soft. My coat had been removed and I was tucked in my own bed. The room was dark. Gabe was at my side with a terrible look on his face.

"Are you okay?" he asked in a shaky whisper.

"What happened?"

My voice was raspy. My entire body felt sore, like someone had taken a hammer and beaten every inch of me.

"Are you okay?" he asked again more eagerly.

"I . . . I think so. What hit me?"

"It was me," he murmured.

There was a pained look in his eyes. He combed a hand through his hair nervously.

"I don't understand," I said.

"I didn't mean to," he explained. "I was thinking about my other sense, and I could feel it building. Then, when we were, you know, I lost control of it. It was like what I was feeling built up into a ball of energy, and just came out of me all at once."

He was gesturing wildly with his hands.

"I still don't understand."

I felt stupid, repeating myself, but I couldn't make sense of it.

"Do you mean," I stammered, "that your feelings can hurt someone physically?"

"Only really strong feelings," he said, emphasizing 'strong' and moving closer to me. "I didn't mean to hurt you. I would never—I just lost it, Clara. I completely lost control. I'm so sorry."

He reached for my hand lying outside the covers then pulled it away before he touched me.

"It's okay. I know you wouldn't," I said.

I sat up and made sure I didn't wince to make him feel any worse, then I took his hand. He sighed and seemed to be still beating himself up in his head.

"Wait a minute," I said, "you just carried me down the hall right past my parents' bedroom? Are you crazy?"

I was yelling in a whispery voice.

"Would you rather I'd left you by the front door, so your dad could find you in your pajamas on the front porch?"

I opened my mouth to make a snappy comeback, then closed it shut.

"Still, you better get out of here," I said, pushing him off the bed and standing up. "We can talk about this tomorrow."

"If you're sure you're okay?"

"Yes, really, I'm fine. It's not like I'm made of glass or anything. I'm a pretty strong girl."

"Yeah, I see that," he said, laughing at me as I pushed him toward the door.

"Wait, no, what am I thinking. Don't go down the hall. Use the window."

I unlocked the window and shoved it up. Peeking out, I saw that Gabe had already put the recycling bin back where it belonged.

"You'll just have to jump," I said.

"No problem," he said, swinging one leg out the window and sitting on the sill.

He reached out and took my hand gently. I could tell he was still worrying about me.

"Stop it," I said. "I'm fine, really. What I'm really worried about is what this all means, with your other sense. If yours is changing, then maybe mine is, too."

"Didn't you just say that you saw your own aura tonight for the first time when those things were in your living room?"

I nodded.

"Well, that has to mean something. I also don't think it's a coincidence that we're dreaming of the same creatures, which Theresa said she saw with her own eyes crawl out of that pit in Cuba right before a weird, massive hurricane formed just off the coast."

"The massive hurricane which happens to be headed for us," I added.

"Yeah," said Gabe a little calmer. "I think it also means that Jeremy is hiding something from us."

"Jeremy? What would he be hiding?"

"Clara, if all three of us are dreaming of the same thing and the two of us have a supernatural sense, don't you think it's probable that he has one, too?"

"Yeah, I guess you're right."

I hadn't made the same connection that Gabe had. I had to admit that he was right. I was used to being the one to figure things out quickly. I'd always been in the top of my class. Somehow, I hadn't even thought that our connection to Jeremy had more to it than creepy nightmares. I heard Gabe chuckling at me.

"What?" I asked.

"You always bite your lip when you're worrying about something."

He pulled me down to him. Cupping my cheek, he gave me a brief, but tender kiss. Nothing like the last one on the porch, but still very nice.

"We'll have to be a little careful, you know. I mean, until I can figure out how to control this thing," he said.

What he was really saying was that we couldn't make-out and act like animals until he knew how to control his changing power. Obviously, it was intense feelings that brought it out, and I'd say what happened earlier was pretty dang intense. I felt my face flush pink. I was glad it was dark, and he couldn't see me. Then I heard that mischievous chuckle again. Dang it! He always knew my feelings, whether he could see my face or not. I hated that.

"Get out," I whispered hoarsely, practically pushing him out the window. "Goodnight."

"Goodnight," he said before swinging his leg over and dropping into the night below.

I closed the window and watched Gabe disappear into the cover of oak trees surrounding our house. I could no longer see him, but I could make out the blue and purple silhouette meshing into the shadows. I'd decided not to tell him that whatever force he had released tonight was still with him, clinging to his body and glowing in that rich, dark aura.

✳9✳

CLARA

"Look at this, Gabe. It says that SETI stands for Search for Extra Terrestrial Intelligence. There's an institute here that says their whole purpose is exploring the universe," I said, pointing to the computer monitor.

The library was practically deserted at lunch time. The only other people besides us were Mrs. Fairfax, our school librarian, and some guy snoring in the study cubicle next to us.

"I don't know, Clara," said Gabe, "it just doesn't seem right. They're calling you this like it's your name. Even in my vision, the warrior woman called her dead friends that name. Try spelling it with two t's."

I punched in "Setti" into the Google search box then started to scroll. Nothing that was listed seemed to have anything to do with what we were looking for—some connection to our supernatural senses. I rolled my shoulders back, trying to work the ache out of them then quickly stopped, realizing Gabe was eyeing me carefully. I didn't want him to know how much he'd hurt me last night. It felt like my coach had forced me to run up and down the stadiums twenty times, then run ten miles, then do 100 push-ups, then do weights for two hours. In other words, I felt like crap, but I still didn't want Gabe feeling guilty about it.

"Maybe there isn't anything in our records that would help. I mean, you said the woman spoke another language. Maybe this word comes from their world, not ours," I said.

"Probably so," said Gabe, "type in 'shadow people.'"

"What?" I asked.

"Just humor me here."

I typed it into the Google search box then pressed enter. Wow. Over 10,000,000 results posted at the top of the screen.

"You've got to be kidding," I said.

"Click on that one," said Gabe, pointing to the third site that read "Sightings of Shadow People."

It was some kind of on-going blog, where people posted their experiences seeing shadow people. Some claimed to have seen them disappearing under their refrigerator; some saw them in their shower, glaring at them with red eyes and growling; then others claimed to have only seen them out of the corner of their vision before they vanished through walls.

"Most of these are hoaxes or crazy people," said Gabe, "but some of them seem very similar to what we're seeing."

"Of course there's no contact information for any of them. What would we say anyway? 'Hey. Are you seeing shadow people, too? Let's chat.'"

"Shadow people?" came a voice behind us.

Gabe and I spun around to see Mrs. Fairfax staring at the computer screen over our shoulders. Her glasses had slipped down to the tip of her nose. Mrs. Fairfax had a knack for sneaking up on students.

"Um, it's for a science project," I lied.

Wow. We seemed to be doing lots of "science projects" lately.

"That reminds me of crazy old Homer," said Mrs. Fairfax.

"Who's he?" Gabe asked quickly.

"Oh, he was a classmate of mine many years ago."

"In high school?" I asked.

"Yes, here at BCHS. I remember it because Homer Rivers not only presented a research project to the class on these so-called shadow people, but he insisted they were real."

"How did he know? Did he see them?" Gabe asked.

"No, no, nothing even as conclusive as that. He claimed to see them in visions. Not only that, but he claimed to have visions of ancient warriors fighting black demons from other dimensions," said Mrs. Fairfax, chuckling to herself.

Holy crap. I felt my heart race ahead quickly. Gabe nudged my knee.

"Poor guy," continued Mrs. Fairfax. "We all just thought he'd been doing some special experiments to see these visions, if you know what I mean."

We must've looked completely clueless.

"It was the 70s after all," explained Mrs. Fairfax.

"Ohhhhh," Gabe and I said, sharing a knowing look.

The seventies—the decade of freedom, love, and lots of hallucinatory drugs.

"Well, whatever happened to him?" asked Gabe.

"He went off to college as far as I know. He was always extremely intelligent. I think he was one of those crazy geniuses, you know. I don't know what he did after that. Then he came back here a few years ago. I saw him in Walmart of all places. It took me by surprise. The years haven't been exactly kind to him."

"How do you mean?" I asked.

"Oh, he looked awfully unkempt. I thought he must've finally fallen off the deep end. I was polite and said hello, because he recognized me right away. I suppose I haven't changed too terribly much," she said, smoothing her skirt. "He said he was working for the farmers, living over on Canebrake Island. I knew then he certainly had finally lost his mind, because I'd never heard of a soul living out there all alone."

"Is he still there?" asked Gabe anxiously.

"I don't know, but I wouldn't try to contact him or anything for this project of yours. He really is crazy," she said with glaring eyes before walking away.

Before Gabe and I had a chance to say a word, Jeremy stalked up to us.

"There you two are. I've been looking everywhere."

He pulled up a chair from the table behind us, turned it around backwards and straddled it. We hadn't said a thing yet. Both of us were reeling in our own heads from this new discovery.

"What? What's that look for?" asked Jeremy.

"We've got to go see someone," said Gabe.

"Who?"

"His name is Homer, and he lives out on Canebrake," I said.

"He could just be a crazy hermit, but I have a feeling he's not," added Gabe.

"O-kayyy. Are y'all feeling sick or something?"

Jeremy was leaning back away from us in his chair.

"I know it sounds weird," I explained, "but we were sitting here looking at these websites when Mrs. Fairfax comes up and says that there was this guy in her class who used to have visions of shadow people."

"And demons from other dimensions," added Gabe speedily. "Everybody thought he was insane and didn't believe him. Now, he lives out on Canebrake Island by himself."

"There's no way this is just a coincidence," I said, more to Gabe than to Jeremy.

I could feel the excitement leaking into my voice.

"Geez," said a groggy voice from the cubicle next to us. "I thought I was dreaming about them again. It's just y'all."

All three of us turned to see a sleepy Ben peering out from the cubicle beside us. He yawned and stretched, scooting his chair out of the enclosure to face us. His tousled blonde hair was a mess.

"*Who* were you dreaming about again?" asked Gabe soberly.

I could feel the tension in his voice. His brown eyes darkened. His multi-colored aura shimmered more blue than any other color.

"Oh, you know, shadowy, creepy guys," said Ben casually, stifling another yawn. "I was dreaming about this super cool black giant, ya know, and he was about to stab me with this long sword then all of a sudden I heard Mrs. Fairfax's voice come out of his mouth saying 'he was a classmate of mine.' Weird, huh?"

Ben was chuckling to himself. None of us laughed.

"Have you been having dreams like this for a while?" asked Jeremy.

"Uh, yeah, I guess so," said Ben, "but that stuff doesn't really bother me. Now, this hurricane that might be comin'? *That* bothers me."

"Why haven't you told me about this?" asked Gabe, sounding like a concerned parent.

"Why should I?" asked Ben. "It's just dreams. I told you before I never pay attention to stuff like that. It has cut into sleep time though. Besides, I haven't seen you much lately. You've been too busy with your *girl*friend."

I realized that Ben may not be teasing about being resentful of me. I made a mental note to try and be more sensitive to him.

"This is unbelievable," I said, looking at Gabe.

"Why are y'all lookin' at me like I'm a freak or somethin'?" asked Ben.

Gabe's phone bleeped from his pocket. It was a text. He pulled it out quickly and read the message.

"It's Theresa. She has to go back to Albuquerque. She wants us to meet her after school at the hotel before she goes to the airport," he said, glancing from me to Jeremy. "And, Ben, you're coming with us. We've gotta talk but there's no time now."

As if Gabe had a magic wand, the bell suddenly rang above us. There wasn't much talking as we made our way to Mrs. Jaden's class. Ben didn't appear rattled at all. He had that same goofy, carefree look like he always did. I swear, Gabe and I must've looked like zombies as we sat in our desks, completely lost in our own thoughts. I couldn't get over it. First Gabe, then Jeremy, now Ben. How many of us were there out there dreaming about these things? What could it all mean?

I couldn't even follow what Mrs. Jaden was doing flitting around in the front of the classroom, pulling out speakers or something. I was trying to imagine what this crazy old Homer looked like and what kind of life he led all by himself on Canebrake Island when I heard Gabe make a sort of gasping noise. I glanced over at him and he was staring scarily toward the front of the classroom. Then he turned and looked at me. His face had gone totally white.

"That's it," he whispered, pointing to the front.

I finally tuned in to what Mrs. Jaden was doing. She was playing some audio clip that I couldn't understand at all. Across the board, she had written 'Beowulf in Old Norse.' I turned back to Gabe with a puzzled look.

"What?"

He seemed completely frustrated with me. His foot was twitching like 90 miles a minute. Why was he freaking out? He pulled out his phone and hid it behind his textbook. In a few seconds, I felt my phone vibrate in my pocket. I pulled it out.

Thats the language from woman in my vision.

I listened to the strange, fluid words coming from the speakers. Mrs. Jaden was smiling broadly with closed lips, all proud of herself for impressing the class with these ancient words of the epic poem. The other kids did look impressed. As for Gabe and I, it had a completely different effect—more unanswered questions. Ugh.

Whatever else happened that day in Mrs. Jaden's class, I really don't remember. Nor could I recall any other class for that matter. I wonder if I would've paid more attention and tried to cherish the crazy antics of the teachers, the excitement in the halls for the upcoming football game, or the quiet camaraderie between friends if I had known that it would be my last day of high school. Ever.

✳ ✳ ✳

"Old Norse? Why would a Viking be in Cuba?" Jeremy was asking, leaning forward between our two seats.

"If I knew, I'd definitely tell you," said Gabe.

It was the three of us again, heading back to the Holiday Inn. Gabe had asked Ben to come along so we could talk to him, but he said he'd just catch up to Gabe later. I wondered if Ben was in some sort of denial about the whole thing. There was no telling with Ben.

When we pulled into the parking lot, we saw Theresa rolling her suitcase to her rental car. Gabe pulled up right next to her then we hopped out.

"Hi," she said, "well, they finally want to talk to me and hear my story."

"What made them decide that you might be telling the truth?" I asked.

"Apparently, the university in Brazil where Dr. Hernandez was working contacted our Anthropology department, wanting to know if they'd heard from Dr. Malcolm since apparently there was some sort of disaster throughout the villages in the southern part of Cuba. So, I'm off to try and explain it again."

Theresa let out a little laugh, but there was no happiness in it.

"Well, at least you know they'll listen this time," I offered.

"Yes. At least there's that," she said dryly. "Well, I copied these for you so that you can look at them more closely when you have time. Hopefully, they'll be of some use to you."

She handed me a manila envelope, which I could tell held a copy of each of the pictographs she had shown us before.

"I also tried to find the meaning to that word 'setti.' At first I only found references to this institute that searches for extra terrestrials, but that didn't seem right."

"Yeah, we found that, too," I said.

"I decided to search foreign languages. I nearly gave up, but I did find one translation of the word. The meaning of 'setti' was sixth."

"In what language?" asked Gabe briskly.

"Old Norse," she replied.

Gabe made a sort of choking sound that might have been a laugh, but I doubt it.

"Maybe it's a reference to a sixth sense," said Jeremy, his eyes lighting up.

"That was what I thought, too. But I have no idea how it could connect to these shadow men," said Theresa, now turning toward Gabe. "Gabriel, I'd like you to have this," she said, holding out the velvet pouch with the black stone. "I think it belongs with you."

"Are you sure?" he asked. "I mean, won't the university want to see this?"

"It doesn't matter," she said.

I could tell she wanted to say something else, but she didn't. I wondered what she meant. It didn't matter because they'd recover the old samples? It didn't matter because they'd start a new excavation and find more samples? Or, it didn't matter because all would be lost soon enough.

"Maybe they'll take you back to Cuba and you can dig up more of them," said Jeremy, sounding somewhat apologetic. It was strange hearing a softness to his voice.

"Maybe," she said quietly.

"Thank you," said Gabe, taking the pouch. "This means a lot to me."

"Yes, I thought it would. Well," she said, glancing at her watch, "I don't want to be late. It takes three hours just to get through airport security these days, so I'll wish you all luck. I'll be watching the news and praying that the hurricane doesn't turn in this direction."

She had an awful look in her eyes, like a mother sending her son off to war. Her aura rippled around her like liquid light in hues of baby blue. I smiled genuinely at her, knowing she must feel terrible about what was coming toward us, with no way to help. I stepped forward and hugged her. It was strange, hugging a complete stranger who I knew cared for me so deeply. She squeezed me tightly then finally let go.

"Good luck," she said in a somber tone. "I'll be in touch."

I wondered if she meant it, or if that was just one of those things you said in parting to lighten the mood. We watched her get in her car and leave, zooming onto the Interstate toward the airport. Then finally, we piled back in the Jeep, heading back toward town. I glanced at Gabe. He had that brooding look again with both hands fixed on the steering wheel and his dark hair blowing crazily in the wind. I looked out at the passing trees, hoping that maybe these creatures weren't as bad as we thought they were, that maybe our military would find some way to stop them, when Gabe suddenly swerved off the main road and into an abandoned gas station. I held onto the roll bar above me. Gabe was a crazy driver—fast and unpredictable. It was amazing that he hadn't had an accident yet. He pulled along the side of the building without any explanation.

"Piss break?" asked Jeremy, popping his head up front.

Gross. I rolled my eyes.

"No," said Gabe sternly, pulling out both of Jeremy's earphones with the tug of one hand on the dangling cords. "What's your sixth sense?"

Gabe's voice was demanding and exact. It always made me feel a little nervous when he got this intense. His aura was very dark blue and swirling in a torrent around him.

"What are you talking about?" asked Jeremy, a little aggravated.

"You heard me," said Gabe, "what's your other sense? Your power? What can you do that most people can't do? You know mine, now I want to know yours."

"What about her?" he asked pointing at me. "Does she have one?"

"*She* is sitting right here, Jeremy. You can ask me directly."

What the heck? Was I invisible or something?

"Okay, what can you do?" he asked me.

"I can see auras, which usually correlates to people's personalities or feelings."

"Really?" he asked, a sly smile coming to his lips. "What color is mi—?"

"Red," I answered before he could finish, "sometimes hot pink."

"What! You're lying. Hot pink? No way," he protested.

I didn't bat an eye. I could see the wheels spinning, trying to determine if I was joking or not.

"Really?" he asked more quietly. "Hot pink?"

"Yeah, but most the time it's reddish-orange, like now."

"Whoa, that is sooooo wicked. I bet I look cool."

He was laughing to himself or by himself, I don't know. Jeremy was a weird one.

"So," said Gabe, "spill it. What about you?"

He suddenly got a thoughtful look on his face, eyeing Gabe carefully. Gabe was quite a bit bigger than him and although I don't think Gabe would pin him down and beat it out of him, it didn't look like Jeremy was going to take the chance. He jumped out of the Jeep.

"I can't explain it in words, but I can show you," he said gesturing to the back of the abandoned gas station.

We filed out behind him and followed. The building had been empty for years. The panes of glass had been long shattered and broken. There was a rusted ice machine sitting uselessly under the tin awning and graffiti painted up and down along the wooden siding. The back door was left ajar with its window panes intact except for one diagonal crack. Jeremy stopped about twenty feet away from the building, and grinned at both of us.

"You ready?" he asked.

We nodded, wondering what in the world he was about to do. Then the crazy boy starts fumbling with his iPod until he finally found whatever song he was looking for.

"This'll do," he mumbled to himself.

He plugged his earphones back in and started humming with the music.

"You've got to be kidding me," I said, wondering why we were getting a serenade.

Gabe wasn't bothered at all. He had that expression of concentration that made him look way older than he was. So, away Jeremy went singing along to his iPod. At least this was a song I actually recognized, "Toxicity" by System of a Down.

"I didn't know you listened to anything written in the past two decades," I said, noting the bitter sarcasm in my voice.

Jeremy didn't hear me. He was completely in the zone, having a good old time in his little world, revving up for the chorus.

"What is he doing?" I asked Gabe who put a hand out to quiet me.

"Don't you feel it?" he asked me.

Then, I did feel it. A low rumbling hum was building, coming from Jeremy.

"Somewhere between the sacred silence and sleep," he was singing, and I have to admit sounding pretty good, too.

Like an amplifier turned all the way up, there was a humming sensation coming from Jeremy. His reddish-orange aura vibrated around him then the pitch of his voice grew heavy and loud with the chorus.

"Disorder, disorder, dis-oooorrderrrrr. . . ."

As he sang the last word, I could see a ripple of blurry, transparent sound waves streaking toward the abandoned building. The door shook on its hinges, rattling fiercely, then all at once every pane shattered. Shards of glass blasted outward. I blocked my eyes. Gabe suddenly pulled me protectively behind him. Only a few pieces hit us, but did no harm. Jeremy had stopped singing and was grinning from ear to ear.

"Awesome, huh?"

Gabe had that half-smile and was nodding in agreement. "Pretty cool. How long have you been able to do this?"

"It started not that long ago actually. I've been getting stronger and stronger. It works best when I'm rockin' to Metallica."

"How did it start?" I asked.

"I think the first time I noticed it was one Saturday a few weeks ago," said Jeremy thoughtfully. "My parents were out doing errands and I was sitting at the kitchen table, listening to Motley Crue while I ate Frosted Flakes."

"Are you ever without your iPod?" Gabe asked.

"No," he said emphatically, "anyway, I started doing Tommy Lee's drum solo on the table with my spoon and was singing along with one of Vince Neal's high notes then my bowl of cereal just exploded. I was pissed at first because milk splattered all over me and my iPod, which is very precious to me, ya know."

I suddenly got a vision of Jeremy cowering in a cave like Gollom from *Lord of the Rings*, stroking his iPod and whispering 'My precious.' I had to restrain myself from giggling, because he was so dang serious about that thing.

"Then," he continued, "I realized what I'd done. I thought maybe it was just a freak accident, because I'd seen on TV how some opera singers can break glass, ya know. And I knew I was pretty good. Then, something inside me sort of changed. Sometimes when I'd start really getting into a song that was awesome and intense, I'd feel something in me kind of spark, ya know."

"How do you mean exactly?" asked Gabe.

"I don't know how to explain it. It would just start from the pit of my stomach then come out the more I sang. That's when I noticed I could shatter not only glass but plastic, too. I had this cool plastic model of Darth Vader in my room—"

"Darth Vader?" I asked, raising my eyebrows.

"Yeah," he rambled on, "and it happened again. Plastic is a lot harder than glass, so I realized that it wasn't just an accident. I had some kind of cool super power."

"But," I interrupted, "I don't see how breaking glass or plastic is going to help us against these creatures. No offense, Jeremy, but I just wish we knew what all of this meant."

"That's why we're going to see Homer on Canebrake Island tomorrow," said Gabe. "I don't know why, but I think he'll know more than any of us. Mrs. Fairfax said that he's been having visions since the 70s. That's longer than we've been alive. Hopefully, he's not just some crazy hermit and he can give us some answers."

My iPhone started buzzing in my pocket. I realized I hadn't taken it off vibrate yet. I glanced at the front to see my cousin's purple hair and "shoot me" expression that she gave me when I snapped this pic.

"It's Jessie," I said, answering it.

"Jessie?" asked Jeremy with a funny look on his face.

"Hey," she said, "listen, I was wondering if you were going to the game tonight."

"Yeah, I mean, I'm not really friends with Mark, but Gabe promised him we'd all go."

"Oh, are you riding with Gabe?" she asked. "Because if not I was wondering if you wanted to ride with me. Mom gave me her Durango. I just felt like getting out of the house tonight."

"Sure," I said, "um, how about 6:30?"

"Cool. I'll see you then."

I stuffed my phone back into my jeans.

"That's funny. Jessie wants to go out tonight," I said. "I didn't think she liked football games."

"She's hard to predict," said Gabe, "none of us have been able to figure her out."

"Well, she wants me to ride with her," I said, looking at Gabe.

"That's fine," he said, "it gives me time to talk to Ben. He's a part of all this, I'm sure, but I don't think he knows it."

Somehow, that didn't surprise me. I adored Ben. His fun-loving outlook on life could be infectious, but he was so daffy. He rarely had a clue what was going on around him.

"Excuse me, guys," said Jeremy, clearing his throat and sounding timid which was definitely not Jeremy, "um, I was wondering if I could go along with y'all tonight."

"You go to football games?" I asked, a little too surprisingly.

"No, not really, but I wouldn't mind going if your friend Jessie is going," he said, looking at me pleadingly.

"She's my cousin," I said, grinning because I finally got it. "Sure, you can come."

"We'll pick you up," said Gabe, clapping Jeremy on the back and smiling at him with a shake of the head as if to say 'good luck.'

We both knew Jessie wasn't easily impressed by anyone. I laughed to myself, wondering how she'd react to the attentions of Jeremy—the Darth Vader-lovin', heavy metal bangin', air-guitarin', glass-breakin', wicked-awesome dork.

✸ ✸ ✸

I was waiting on the sofa for Jessie, while Dad was studying a bunch of his papers on the kitchen table. The six o'clock news was droning on about Hurricane Lucy spinning in its place out in the center of the Gulf of Mexico. An interview of a local from New Orleans in the 9th ward popped up on the screen.

"Nobody's tellin' us nothin' about what to do," said the haggard-looking woman standing in the front of her weathered house. "I can't afford to pick up and 'vacuate unless I have to, and nobody knows what to do. I tell ya, they better figga it out or it'll be too late."

The male anchor then turned to the camera with a serious doomsday look on his face.

"You heard it here in the 9th ward, where tragedy has struck before and just may again. The question is: will it be too late or will we have a devastating repeat of history here in New Orleans?"

"God, I hate it when they do that," I said.

"What's that, hon?" asked Dad.

"They make everything sound so end-of-the-world. The newscasters only add to the fear and hysteria," I said, feeling heat flush up my neck.

What I didn't want to admit to myself was that it just might be the end of the world. Who could tell what was going to happen?

"Don't worry about it, Clara. They've been very prepared for these kinds of things in recent years. The newscasters are doing their job, trying to get ratings."

"Yeah, well starting a panic doesn't seem like a very good job."

Dad didn't respond. He was absorbed back in his papers on the table. He had that furrowed frown pressed into his face.

"What's wrong?" I asked, picking up Misty and scratching her head.

"I just can't figure out what's going on here. My green algae samples in the lab and in the field are all producing oxygen now. It's strange that they all are. There shouldn't be large amounts of sulfur in the environment that would cause this, but I've observed and tested them several times this week. It keeps coming out the same."

"Well, don't you look pretty," said Mom, swishing into the room in a brown suede skirt and cream-colored top.

I had decided to dress up a little more tonight; at least, what I considered dressing up. I was wearing dark blue, skinny jeans, a slim-fitting, red American Eagle shirt to show my BCHS spirit and I flat-ironed my hair, which made it fall to the center of my back. I even put on dark eye-liner, black mascara, and a bronzy lipstick, which I rarely bothered to do during the school week.

"Thanks, Mom."

"Do you have a hot date tonight?"

Ugh. Who says that?

"I don't mind you having a date," chimed in Dad, "but I don't want to hear the word 'hot' mentioned in any reference to an outing with a boy."

He was so overly protective. Geez.

"It's not a date, Mom. Well, not really. I'm riding with Jessie to the BCHS football game. We're meeting Gabe and some other friends."

"Oh, Gabe?" Dad said, his voice perking up a bit.

"Yeah, Dad. Remember Gabe, the guy I've been dating for a little while now."

A horn honked in the driveway. I plopped Misty on the sofa and headed out the door.

"Have fun, dear," Mom crooned, primping herself in the mirror.

No telling what social event she was headed out to tonight.

Jessie's hair was mostly black now with several chunks of fuchsia streaking over the right side of her face. When we were little kids, her hair was light brown, but I hadn't seen that Jessie in a long time. It actually looked pretty with her violet aura hovering over her head. Her faded jeans were ripped at the knee and her neon green t-shirt read in all caps "I DARE YOU TO STARE." Jessie wasn't really scary or depressed or anything. She was just incredibly independent. If I could imagine anyone in the world who didn't need another human soul, that would be Jessie. At least, that's the impression I got from her. Even as kids, she preferred to suntan alone rather than play in pool games with our other cousins. That's why it was a little weird for her to want to come along to a football game. I had no idea how she regularly spent her Friday nights.

"We've gotta swing by and pick up Mel, too," she said when I hopped in.

"Cool."

We wound our way out of the neighborhood in silence. Then she started a conversation I definitely did not expect.

"So," she said in that ultra-casual way that wasn't casual at all, "you and Gabe are a thing now."

She didn't say it like a question.

"Yeah, I guess we are."

I couldn't hide the small smile that came to my lips.

"Well, I can't imagine anyone else I'd want him to be with."

Okay. Anyone else, other than you? I really didn't know what to say. Jessie and I had never exactly been best friends, but we always had a decent, comfortable friendship. This was so not comfortable.

"He's a good guy," she continued.

"Yeah, I know."

"No, I mean, he's a really good guy, not like what you'd expect from someone like him."

"What do you mean? Someone like him how?"

"You know, guys who are that good looking are usually such . . ."

She seemed to be at a loss for the right word.

"Jerks?" I suggested.

"Egotistical, vainglorious, narcissistic dweebs."

"Oh, uh, yeah. That about sums it up."

"Gabe's not judgmental about people."

Ohhhhh, and therein lies the attraction. Jessie spent her whole life scaring off people with her super-tough exterior, and Gabe was one of the few she'd consider dating who never judged her. If I know him at all, he probably tried his best to make her feel included. That's just how he was. I wondered if that was because he always felt different on the inside, even though no one could ever see it on the surface. She didn't seem resentful of me for dating Gabe, so she must be over him by now. I debated whether to tell her she had an admirer, decided not to, then decided to go ahead anyway.

"You know, Jessie. I just found out today that there's a very interesting boy who has his eyes on you."

Her eyes flicked in my direction as she made a right turn onto a country road with only a few houses.

"Yeah? Who's that?"

"Jeremy Kaufman," I said casually.

"Jeremy Kaufman?" she asked, wracking her memory. "The metal head?"

"Yeah," I said giggling. "I think you ought to give him a chance. He's very unique."

"Unique, huh. Like me?"

"Well, not exactly like you, but I definitely think you'd have interesting conversations."

"Humph," she said as we pulled up a shell drive-way on the outskirts of town.

I stared at the two rocking chairs on the front porch. One was more used than the other. It only took a few seconds before Melanie came out to meet us. She was dressed conservatively as always—khaki pants and a white cardigan sweater over a blue tank. I thought we were quite the trio. We didn't look like we belonged together, but it definitely felt like we did. Mel's presence was always soothing, even when she was picking a fight with Ben. I thought she downplayed her beauty too much. She had that flawless Creole skin and pretty almond eyes that were usually hidden behind her reading glasses. She had soft, wavy hair that she always smoothed into a ponytail that dropped just below her shoulders. Tonight was no exception.

"Hello, everyone," she said.

I thought it funny how she always sounded so proper, even when she was trying to be casual.

"Hey, Mel," said Jessie, pealing out backwards down the driveway.

"Hey! Slow down, Jessie! You'll give my Gram a heart attack right in her living room."

"Sorry, Mel, but my mom's got a Hemi. I'm not used to it."

"Your *mom's* got a Hemi?" she asked.

After about ten seconds of tension, we all started laughing. It seemed funny, but fitting somehow, that the three of us were piled into a very manly vehicle. My Aunt Vanessa had never been one for conformity. I suppose that's where Jessie got it all.

The boys were conveniently pulling into the back parking lot near the stadium at the same time we were. I saw Gabe's Jeep veer into the last parking spot on the third row. We followed and found a spot close by.

Gabe, Ben, Zack, and Jeremy met us in the drive as we piled out of the Durango. It was mostly dark with just a few streetlights, but it didn't keep me from noticing how good Gabe looked. He was wearing just some plain jeans and a black t-shirt, but it accented all the best parts of him. As I got closer, I saw how his eyes flickered up and down my body with that tilted smile lingering on his lips. How I wished he wouldn't do that. My stomach started flip-flopping around again. We didn't say anything at first, but he intertwined his fingers through my left hand as soon as I was close enough.

"What?" I asked as casually as I could manage.

"You know what," he said, taking a deep breath and brushing a light kiss on my cheek. "Let's go."

The rest of our group had already started walking a little ahead of us. Ben seemed sullen, which was not like him at all.

"Did you talk to Ben?"

"Yeah," said Gabe, pausing a minute. "He's just in sort of a state of shock. He looked at me like I'd gone insane when I asked if he knew what sixth sense he had. If he has one, he apparently doesn't know about it."

I noticed that Jeremy had sidled in next to Jessie. I also noticed something else very peculiar about him tonight.

"Hey, Jeremy! Where's your iPod?" I asked.

"Oh, I decided to leave it at home tonight," he called over his shoulder then resumed his conversation with Jessie.

I gave Gabe my raised-eyebrows look. He chuckled.

"I know," he said.

I had to admit. From where I was, they looked kind of cute together. Jeremy was at least a foot taller than her, but they both had the same gangly walk and lop-sided black hair. Well, at least there was no fuchsia in Jeremy's hair, but his aura certainly was tonight. How weird is that. They matched.

The stadium lights burned brightly and the bands were in full swing, banging their drums and exciting the crowds to cheer. There were still tons of people mingling outside and inside the gates. Like any small town, a Friday night football game was a regular social event. It seemed like everyone in a twenty-mile radius got all dressed up and piled into the bleachers for the occasion. We passed through the gate quickly, showing our school i.d.'s. I was feeling on top of the world. It was a beautiful night out with all my friends and Gabe was holding my hand, standing wonderfully near me. Then, in a heartbeat, the perfection shattered like a devastating mirage. Fear stiffened my body to the spot.

"What is it?" Gabe asked, suddenly very close to me.

I couldn't believe what I was seeing. It was a living nightmare whirling in front of me in and out of the crowds. Black shapes with evil, yellow eyes.

"Shadow people," I whispered as if they might hear me.

"Where?" asked Gabe, his voice low and deep. "Where are they?"

"Everywhere," I gasped, "They're everywhere."

✱10✱

GABE

Clara shrank into me, facing the milling crowd. It was an eerie moment. There was a sea of faces in blithe oblivion—smiling in conversation, laughing at friends' jokes, shouting excitedly at the football field. Along the edge of this façade, I could feel a menacing presence slithering around us like a breath of icy wind.

"I can't see them, but I know they're there," I said, still holding onto Clara's hand which was clinching mine too tightly. "What are they doing?"

I thought for a minute that she didn't hear me, then she whispered back to me.

"It's like they're just watching and listening to people."

"Do they see you?"

"Not yet."

"Man, I feel better. I was starving," said Ben, walking up behind us, stuffing cheesy nachos into his mouth. "Y'all waitin' for me?"

The rest of our group had stopped at the base of the bleachers. Mel and Zack were quietly observing Jeremy while he gestured intensely about something. Jessie was listening with something like a smile on her face. No one could see or sense the company of intruders circling them, except for Clara and me.

"Come on," said Ben, urging us toward the others.

"What should we do?" asked Clara, her breath short and quick.

"Just act normal. Tell me what's going on, and stay close to me."

I could hear the tension in my voice. Ben had bounded ahead of us, joining the others. We moved closer. Mel and Zack were now leaning against the chain-link fence. Zack was pointing out to the field, obviously to Mark. Ben moved up beside Mel, offering her a nacho. She shook her head. He continued to chomp away, bobbing his head to our band's rendition of "Doctor Who." Jeremy was absorbed in a conversation with Jessie as we moved up beside them.

"I can't believe you've never heard of Iggy Pop," Jessie was saying in disbelief.

"And I can't believe you haven't heard of Zebra," said Jeremy just as arrogantly.

It seemed they were having a good time testing each other's knowledge of music history, or lack thereof. Across the field, blue and gold dappled the bleachers of the Trojan fans. It seemed surreal to see their pom-poms waving while something sinister lurked in our midst.

Clara suddenly jerked on my hand. I stopped and turned to face her, leaning down.

"Look at those women right there," she said urgently, "One of the shadow men is standing right behind the blonde lady."

There were three women—a blonde and two brunettes. They were decked out in red shirts and too tight jeans. The blonde had a layer of make-up on that shined under the stadium lights. Clara nudged me a little closer within earshot.

"It doesn't look like it's coming here, anyway," said one brunette.

"I don't know," said the blonde. "It's hard to predict these things. We booked a hotel in Shreveport the minute we saw it in the Gulf, but we keep having to rebook since it's still just sittin' out there."

"Well, John said we're not goin' one way or another," said the other brunette. "Last time, we spent six hours in traffic before we crossed into Mississippi. That was sheer torture with a toddler in the car."

Clara flinched back and pulled me down to her.

"It just touched her, the blonde," she whispered in a panic.

I watched as the blonde woman's face bunched up into a frown, creasing her caked-on make-up job. I could feel a wave of frightened hysteria wash over me from her direction. She started talking in a frenzy.

"What if it does come here?" said the woman, her eyes widening abnormally. "What if it heads straight for us and we can't get out? Remember when that one came straight into the port, flooding the whole town. That could happen again. We could be stuck here."

"It touched the lady next to her," said Clara.

I felt Clara's own fear growing next to me. The brunette chimed in with the blonde.

"You're right. They say we don't have to worry on the news, but what if they're wrong? They've been wrong before. It could be a lot worse than losing power and a few fallen trees. We could be trapped by water like. . . ."

The banter continued. The three women fed off one another's fears. Clara was following something through the crowd, pulling me along. Every person I passed seemed to be in some frantic conversation; either about the hurricane or the latest terrorist attack in Europe or the crappy economy. Where I first saw happy faces, I now saw fear welling up like an incoming tide.

"They're just grazing people with their fingers as they pass them," said Clara. "I don't understand it."

"The crowd is changing, Clara. Listen to what they're all saying."

"Wait," she said in an icy tone, "they're on the sidelines and the field, tapping players, all of them. What are they doing?"

As if to answer her question, a yellow flag flew onto the field. The referee made a holding call against our defense. Coach Jackson stormed toward him, yelling into the ref's face, chest to chest. Players slowly inched onto the green, shouting protests. A huge Trojan lineman pushed one of our fullbacks, Trey Hawkes. A fuming, brawny man stomped out of the bleachers, leapt the chain-link fence, then barreled into the frenzied crowd on the field. I recognized him as Trey's father. Hysteria followed. Players from both sides rushed out, swinging and cursing. Before I could stop him, Zack was over the fence and running headlong to help Mark, who was in the middle of the fight. Ben started to do the same, but I grabbed him by the collar.

"No, Ben! Look around you."

We turned to see frightened, angry faces pushing toward us, pinning Mel and Clara against the fence. Mel's dark eyes widened. She was petite and would be crushed if the crowd continued to press us forward.

"We've got to get them out of here," I said.

Ben pulled Mel behind him and started pushing through the mass of people. I followed with Clara's hand in mine. There was no need to warn her to stay close. Her other hand had a fistful of the back of my t-shirt.

"So much for a fun Friday night football game, eh," said Jeremy at my shoulder.

Jessie was close behind him. I lowered my voice so only he could hear me.

"They're here, the shadow people."

"I thought something was weird," he said, glancing warily around us. "Clara sees them?"

I nodded, shoving a middle-aged man aside who tried to break my hold on Clara to get through to the field. I wasn't about to let any of these deranged idiots pull her away from me. As soon as we were out of the gates, we could hear police sirens in the distance.

"What about Zack?" asked Ben.

"He's a big boy. I'm sure he'll find a ride with Mark," I said, leading the group in long strides to the parking lot.

"If he doesn't get arrested," said Jeremy, loping up beside me.

"What in the world was that all about?" asked Ben.

Clara was at my side, panting a little, and not from our brisk exit.

"Do you see them?" I asked her.

"No," she replied quickly, glancing back over her shoulder.

"I don't get it," said Ben. "One minute, everyone was fine then all of a sudden people went nuts."

"Remember what we talked about earlier?" I asked him.

"Yeah."

"Well, those 'shadowy, creepy guys' as you call them are here."

"What? You mean from my dreams? That's crazy. I didn't see anything."

"I did," said Clara.

"Can someone please tell me what you're talking about?"

Mel had been listening closely, as she always did, and had overheard a little too much. We passed underneath the last streetlight, throwing our shadows long in front of us, stopping at my Jeep. All eyes and somber faces had turned on me. I realized that there was no sense hiding what I knew to be true anymore. If I continued to keep this façade up, then others would be hurt because of it. I had to tell them the truth.

"Okay, I'm going to be completely honest, because it's obvious that it's only going to get worse from here."

"What's going to get worse?" asked Jessie.

"Clara, Jeremy, and I know that the hurricane is going to come here."

As if to offer me encouragement, Clara and Jeremy nodded on either side of me before I continued.

"Also, it's not a regular hurricane."

"What do you mean?" asked Mel.

A whirring blast of sirens made us all jump and turn. Three police cars, blue lights flashing, squealed through the parking lot straight to the stadium. The din of screaming voices and mayhem from that direction echoed around us. We still seemed to be the only ones with the bright idea of getting the hell out of there.

"Look, let's go somewhere safer and then talk. How about Mirabelle's?" I asked. They all nodded in agreement. "You want to ride with me, Clara?"

"Yeah, let me get my bag."

"I'll ride with the girls then," said Jeremy quickly, following Jessie. Yeah, of course he would.

Ben had already jumped in the Jeep. I was standing near the streetlight with my hands tucked in my jeans pockets. There was an edge in the air. I glanced up to the night sky where wispy gray clouds spun swiftly in front of the half-moon. Then it happened.

I felt a crackling sensation filter around me before a slap of mortal terror flooded my veins like ice. My muscles became rigid. I couldn't move. I saw Jeremy, Jessie, and Mel turn and face me with looks of confusion a few yards away. It felt as if I was being held to the spot, not by hands, but by sinking despair. I knew these weren't my own feelings, but someone, or something else's. Then I heard it, so close to my ear that an electrical current passed between the thing and me.

"Setti," it whispered in a gravelly voice, "our masters are coming. There is no hope in fighting. They will kill you all. There is only slavery, or death."

In a flash of fury, my power awakened, rising up against the tide of fear that threatened to freeze me forever. I stopped it, suppressed it. Standing before me were my friends, and I had no idea how to control whatever it is that I could do. Then, Clara stepped from behind them; her face pale and mouth open in shock and horror. I couldn't imagine what she could see. A surge of true fear, my own, passed over my heart. My terror had found a focal point. I couldn't hurt her, not again. That invisible wall I had built to block out my other sense all my life came up to hold my own power in. I wouldn't let it destroy those I cared about, those I loved, to save myself. That thing snickered in my ear, like the serpent in the garden, gloating over its victim. I restrained my anger still.

Clara. It was like slow motion in a movie. I saw her running toward me, screaming as she came.

"Get away from him!"

Her auburn hair streaked like fire under the lamplight then she outstretched her arms as she drew closer, moving as if slowed by water. My own will was faltering. That internal wall of mine threatened to crumble and free my power uncontrollably on whoever was near. I held that burning power inside myself, knowing that I would certainly suffer for what I was doing. It was against nature, but I wouldn't unleash it on these creatures, not knowing whether I would hurt my friends in the process.

Like a flaming angel, I saw light burst from Clara. Out of her fingertips, the ends of her hair, and blasting from her body, waves of undulating gold reached out to me. The invisible creature hissed in my ear, then another. There was more than one. My power surged up; I resisted again, only to feel a crippling pain shatter through my body then all was dark.

✷ ✷ ✷

CLARA

I felt something change as soon as I slammed Jessie's car door shut. I broke through Jeremy, Jessie, and Mel to see utter horror. Two huge shadow men had their fingers clamped down on Gabe's shoulders, holding him to the spot. There was such a painful conflicted look on Gabe's face that I felt my heart sink into my stomach. He seemed unable to move at all. The tallest of the two was whispering something in Gabe's ear.

I didn't know what I was doing; I only knew that I had to help him. I ran in a fury, wanting only for those hideous things to get their hands off of him. I didn't even know what I yelled. They leered at me as I went charging ahead. A look of torment and rage played on Gabe's face, altering between the two. I was only a few feet away when I felt the surge of fire and light shoot from my insides, flaring out around me, in front of me, like a warm blanket. The shadow men hissed, glaring with slits of yellow eyes at me. I didn't care. I was furious. They had somehow paralyzed Gabe, my Gabe, and I wouldn't let it happen. The halo of gold light flared out from my body, pouring over him. The creatures leapt back in surprise then vanished into shadowy smoke and air. Just as I reached Gabe, a look of pain swept over his face before he collapsed to the concrete. Ben was there and caught him before his head hit the ground. The others were at my side within seconds.

"What happened?" yelled Ben, putting Gabe down gently.

I lifted Gabe's head into my lap, calling his name. Mel leaned over him, reaching up to his neck. Her fingers found his pulse then his eyes shot open. He sat up quickly, too quickly.

"Ow," he said, "is this what it felt like when I—"

He turned to me. I wasn't sure what he was talking about.

"What did you do?" asked Jessie, glaring at me.

"I was helping him," I stammered.

"That was awesome," said Jeremy with his crazy grin.

Jessie ignored him. Her violet aura was tipped with orange.

"It looked like you hurt him, Clara. You knocked him out with, well, with whatever that was you just did."

"You could see that?" I asked, finally realizing that everyone was staring at me, because *they* could see my aura, too. Wow. This was new.

Jessie looked at me angrily; Ben looked shifty-eyed and worried; Mel had a look of sympathy for me; and Jeremy, well, it could only be called a look of admiration. Gabe wasn't looking at me at all. He was flexing and unflexing his hands as if to see that they still worked.

"It wasn't her," said Gabe. "I knocked myself out."

"What do you mean?" I asked.

"I couldn't do the same thing again like last time," he said.

His dark eyes finally found mine. Then I realized what he had done.

"You held it back?" I whispered.

He nodded his head once.

"Can someone please, *please* explain what is going on?" begged Mel.

I took a deep breath and plunged ahead, barely thinking as the words spilled out of my mouth.

"Okay, here it goes. Ever since I was little, I've been able to see auras. Yes, lights around people that tell me what kind of person they are or what they're feeling. When I started hanging out with you guys a couple weeks ago, I realized that Gabe has a kind of sixth sense, too. He's always been able to tell what other people are feeling when they're close to him. Then, we discovered that we've been having similar dreams, about these shadow people, and big, black giants, and ash-eaters. Just this week, we realized that Jeremy is having the same dreams, too. Not only that, but he's got this cool sixth sense where he can break glass when he sings."

"It's really cool," assured Jeremy.

"Can I continue?" I asked, more haughtily than usual.

Jeremy nodded and looked down.

"Gabe and I found this woman on-line who had pictures of these ancient pictographs that were these exact same creatures we've been dreaming about. Weird, right? So we shoot her an e-mail then next thing you know she's here in Beau Chêne all the way from Albuquerque. We met her and she told us how she saw these creatures come right out of a pit in the ground in Cuba, right before a severe electrical storm hit and this hurricane formed."

Jeremy started to say something, but I jerked up my hand, palm out, to stop him from saying a word, then continued.

"She told us that our dreams aren't just dreams. They're some kind of warning of what really is heading this way. Then, I see one of these shadow men from my dreams standing at the foot of my bed."

Mel gasped, clapping her hand to her mouth.

"Yeah, I nearly peed on myself. But, it just said this weird word then left. The next night, three of them show up in my living room while I was watching TV. This time, they seemed scared of me when, well, it was like I was starting to do what you saw me do tonight. I realize now that my sixth sense is more like a power against the shadow people. Not only that, but Gabe has a power, too, which seems to have less to do with sensing emotions and more to do with using it as some kind of weapon against these things. Tonight, I think he refused to use it in order to save all of us from getting hurt."

That's when all eyes shifted toward Gabe, much softer than they looked at me earlier.

"And, today in the library, we found out that there's a guy who lives out on Canebrake Island who's been having visions of these creatures for about thirty years. Then, tonight, as soon as we walked through the gates, I must've counted about forty or fifty shadow people wandering through the crowds," I said as confidently as I could. "Oh, and Ben's having these dreams, too."

All eyes swiveled to Ben.

"Hey, don't look at me. I might be having these dreams, but I don't know anything about sixth senses or freaky powers or anything like that."

"So," said Jessie quietly, "you must've seen some of these, uh, shadow people standing by Gabe?"

I nodded, thankful Jessie was no longer looking at me like I was a hateful witch.

"Sorry I fussed earlier. I just didn't—"

"Don't worry about it," I said quickly. "So, you all believe me?"

"Of course they do," said Jeremy. "Damn, Clara, that was wicked what you did with the burning aura and bright light and everything. That was sa-weet."

His voice went up an octave on his last drawn-out word.

"These shadow people," interrupted Mel, "You think they have something to do with what happened here tonight?"

"I know they do. When they started to touch people as they passed them, that's when the arguments started between everyone."

"What happened when they touched you?" Mel asked Gabe.

He combed a hand through his wavy hair, trying to push it out of the way, but it fell right back in place. A couple with a young boy in tow scurried to their car one row over, not bothering to wonder why a group of teenagers was crouched on the pavement.

"I felt fear," he finally said, "intense, raw fear. I couldn't even move."

"Why did they seem so angry back in the stadium?" asked Jessie knitting her brow together into a frown.

"They only touched those people," I said, remembering how the black, scaly creatures slipped through the crowd brushing their bony fingers along shoulders as they passed. "But, those two I saw right here, they were clutching at Gabe's shoulders. I could see their fingers pressing into his t-shirt."

"It's like a mob mentality," added Gabe. "One person reacted to that touch of fear, then the next, then the next. It was bound to end in violence."

A small group of Trojan fans was headed down the aisle. One woman clung to her husband who held a Ziploc of ice to his head that seemed to be dripping blood.

"Let's go," I said.

"Yep. That's our cue," said Jeremy.

"We'll see you tomorrow," I told Jeremy, not as a question.

He gave me a two-finger salute, then walked with Jessie to the Durango.

"What's tomorrow?" asked Mel.

"We're going to see that man on Canebrake Island," said Gabe, standing up and heading toward the Jeep. "You want to come?"

"Uh, no thanks. You just let me know how that works out," said

Mel, then she stopped Gabe by the shoulder, her tone very serious. "Thank you, Gabe, for whatever you did tonight. I don't pretend to understand it, but I know that you were thinking of us. And, you too, Clara. I know how it must've felt to keep all of this in."

I remembered how Mel had only briefly talked about her grandmother, the *traiteur*, as if hiding a family secret. *Traiteurs* were faith-healers, a mystical thing that not everyone believed in, especially in this modern world of science and technology. I gave her a quick hug. She seemed surprised, but smiled sweetly in return. Gabe just waved then we jumped in the Jeep and headed home.

I had become used to silent rides in Gabe's Jeep, but this one had to be the worst. Usually, there was no awkwardness or tension. Tonight, I could tell there was more brewing in his head than the incident with the shadow people. He walked with me up my drive-way then stopped me before we reached the porch.

"You lied to me."

What? I didn't lie to him.

"What are you talking about?"

I heard the tightness in my voice.

"You told me that it didn't hurt you when I made you pass out that night."

His voice was stern, but it wasn't cold.

"Oh," I said dumbly.

Um, oops.

"Look, I don't want you ever to lie to me, not even to save my feelings."

The moon shone brightly above us. Whatever clouds had blocked it earlier were now gone. Gabe's eyes held a look I hadn't seen before—annoyance, affection, and something more that made me lean closer, press my head against his chest, and wrap my arms around him.

"I won't," I promised sincerely.

It was weird. He was shaking a little. He held me tightly. One hand went up and gently stroked my hair.

"What's wrong?" I whispered into his chest.

He sort of laughed, but not really.

"That thing told me something."

He paused. I heard his heartbeat pick up pace.

"What did it say?"

"It told me that there's no use fighting. It basically told me that we'll all die. But, honestly, that's not what upsets me."

I pulled back and looked at him with what I knew was an expression of surprise.

"Clara, I know I can kill these things. I can feel it. It was like instinct to fight them tonight, but I couldn't do it. I held it back because I didn't know how to do it without hurting—"

There was a hard look of pain on his face, just like I saw earlier tonight. He cupped my face in both his hands, stroking my cheek with one thumb. He seemed unable to speak at all for a long minute.

"I can't lose you," he said.

There was desperation in his voice so unlike him. From the moment I met Gabe, he was all control. Well, except for that one time on my porch when we both lost control. Yikes, fluttering in my stomach again. But, this was different. His brown eyes combed over my face as if memorizing it. I couldn't stand that strange look of agony. I tip-toed, pulling him down to me, and kissed him. His lips were unyielding, at first, then he softened, scooping one hand behind my back. I wanted the kiss to last longer than it did, but he pulled away. He let his eyes drop to the ground.

"Better?" I asked with a little too much perkiness.

He smiled then finally looked back into my eyes. That hard edge was gone now. Mission accomplished.

"Yes," he said quietly. "Much better."

He tucked one side of my hair back behind my ear. I felt the trail of heat his finger left behind. I wanted to kiss him again, but he'd already leaned away from me. His aura hovered in fuzzy shades of blue, purple, and red around his head, like a sad crown.

"I'll pick you up in the morning," he said, kissing me lightly on the forehead, leaving me depressed and wanting him more.

⁕11⁕

GABE

Canebrake Island wasn't really an island. There was an artificial land bridge about a mile long through swampy water to a piece of fertile soil about three miles long and wide. Local sugar farmers owned pieces of the land, which was all it was used for. Well, and apparently it was the home of the care-taker who lived on the island, the man Mrs. Fairfax called 'crazy old Homer.' During harvest and planting time, the land was dominated by bulky tractors hooked to massive tills and hulking trailer hauls bumbling from field to mill. For the rest of the year, it remained isolated and still. I wondered how this reclusive man spent his time out here all alone.

As we crossed the land-bridge, I looked out at the wispy fog blanketing the marshy water. A white heron was picking its way through the shallows near the bank. Gray moss clung to the branches of the many cypress trees thickening the swamp. I noticed that the spiky leaves were already tipped a russet brown, which seemed too early for that autumn change. Cypress knees jutted up out of the mist looking like the tops of little gnome's heads peeking out to look around. It was eerie how completely still everything was here, yet so alive at the same time. It was like being watched.

"My dad said that the riot last night was on the front page of the paper," yelled Jeremy from the backseat. "The headline was 'Family Football Turns into Frenzy.' He wanted to know if I'd had any part in starting the riot."

"Your dad has a strange impression of you," said Clara next to me.

"Yeah, well, I guess I can't blame him too much. Ever since I got caught for vandalism in the 8th grade, he thinks I'm a delinquent."

"You're not?" asked Ben.

I'd made Ben come along even though he really didn't want to. He's been paying me back by pouting and making mean-spirited comments the whole ride over.

"Not really," said Jeremy, apparently not offended by Ben at all.

"He should take the time to get to know who you are now, not who you were," said Clara.

"Yeah. Well, sometimes parents are more interested in their own lives than in their kids."

Clara opened her mouth to say something else, but closed it shut tightly. I took her hand, knowing what I sensed from her was that same anxiety she felt whenever someone mentioned inattentive parents. I knew that she was extremely close to her dad, so this bitter emotion must be for her mother. Clara seemed a little distant since last night. I couldn't blame her. I don't think I comforted her much after what happened with the shadow people. Actually, I still felt myself wanting to pull away from her, but it was only because I was afraid—of what I could do, what I couldn't do, of hurting her, of hurting others. I was afraid of myself.

Before long, the cane fields ended and the dirt road led us into a brackish wood thick with water oaks and leafy elms. The cover of trees opened to a flat piece of land dipping toward the swamp which wrapped itself around Canebrake Island. Squatting at the water's edge was a rudimentary house made of cypress, covered with a tin roof rusted along the rim. A cluster of cypress trees framed the backside of the house along the swamp's edge; thin fingers of Spanish moss dangled from its craggy arms.

"This must be the place," sighed Ben. "Looks about what I expected."

"Stop being so cranky," I said.

Ben just rolled his eyes at me. As the four of us neared the house, the sound of music grew louder and louder—a violin. The melody was a little sad. It sounded familiar, but the instrument seemed wrong. My mom always played classical music for her plants in the greenhouse. When I helped her in repotting or adding fertilizer, I would ask her sometimes why she only played classical. Her prompt reply was always, 'Nature is nurtured best with the best kind of music.' I wondered what Jeremy would think of my mom's little parable, then he shocked me by knowing the song.

"Humph, Moonlight Sonata."

"What was that?" asked Clara.

"It's Beethoven," said Jeremy confidently.

"Excuse me," said Clara with a smile on her face. "You know classical music?"

"Yes," he said harshly, "I know classical music. I took piano when I was little. So what?"

"Oh, nothing at all," she added, still grinning.

Right when we made it to the top of the rickety porch that wrapped all the way around the house, the music stopped. We glanced at each other for a few seconds then I knocked lightly on the door, whose white paint was chipped and falling away. No sound. No answer. I tapped again, louder. No answer still. A soft brush against my legs made me jump suddenly. An orange tabby cat gazed up at me from round green eyes. He meowed hoarsely.

"Come here, Newton," came a raspy voice beside us.

We jerked around to find a stout man somewhere in his forties staring back at us. He'd come from the backside of the porch with his violin and bow hanging in his hands. He looked like a cross between a hippie and a cowboy. He wore pale blue Levi's, a brown checkered shirt, and Roper boots with steel tips. His long black hair had a few streaks of gray and was pulled back in a ponytail. He also had a speckled gray beard. Although his tawny skin was leathery and lined with deep furrows along the brow, he had youthful blue eyes the color of the Caribbean. I'd never seen it for myself, but I saw a picture once in my mom's travel magazine. I was hoping to see it for my senior trip, but that looked doubtful now.

"Excuse me, sir. Are you Homer Rivers?"

"Hmm," he said with a thoughtful expression, "I was expecting five of you, not four."

We all glanced at each other, obviously confused.

"You were expecting us?" I asked.

"Yeah," he replied, "for a while now."

His accent was more country than Cajun. He set the violin and bow on a weather-beaten table next to a wicker chair then picked up Newton who was weaving between his ankles.

"Excuse me, but how could you be expecting us?" I asked. "We just heard your name for the first time yesterday."

"Well, Gabriel, I heard about you a long, long time ago."

"How?" asked Clara. "Where from?"

The grizzled man gave us a sheepish grin and his blue eyes sparkled as he tapped an index finger to his forehead.

"Do you know all of us?" she asked.

"Yes, Clara Dunaway, I do."

"This is so frickin' weird, I don't even know where to start," said Ben, taking a step backward.

"Benjamin LeBlanc, I suggest you stay right where you are because without you, without all of the Setti, many more will die than needs to."

His voice was firm, but his blue eyes still shone brightly. His words pinned Ben to the spot.

"Setti?" I heard myself mumble. "You said there should be five of us, so all of us together would be—"

"Yes, Gabriel. Setti refers to the number in the clan—six."

"But, I thought it referred to our sixth sense that we have."

"Sense?" then the man chuckled heartily.

Newton nuzzled under his bearded chin in response to his laughter, then Homer suddenly became serious.

"This sense that you've felt all your life is merely a side effect for what you can really do. What you've thought is some supernatural gift is actually just a shadow of the true power that you have within you."

When he said this, he looked at all of us, not just me.

"You said five. Who's missing?" asked Jeremy.

"The Creole girl, the Healer," he replied frankly.

"Melanie?" exclaimed Ben.

"Why don't we go inside? I think we should sit down for this conversation."

His screen door creaked open and slammed shut behind him. We all stood there for a second, glancing at each other for guidance. I shrugged then went in. The others followed. Ben was the last one in. I was expecting a dark interior and a musty odor to match the outside of Homer's hovel. I was surprised to find a warm, well-lit room that was much larger than I'd imagined. There was a wall of windows facing the marsh and double doors that went out to the back porch. The water glittered under a partly cloudy sky. There were kerosene lanterns, like the ones my Pop used when we went camping, propped up all over the room—on a wooden mantel above a recently used fireplace; on a roughened oak dining table; on bookshelves that were nearly completely full lining the far wall. There was a cushy-looking green couch with a blue and white quilt lining against its back and a matching chair facing out to the water, beside the book shelves. Homer sat in the chair and motioned for us to have a seat.

I noticed several photo albums spread out on the coffee table. One was open to a newspaper clipping entitled "Miracle Boy Survives Lightening Strike" with a large photo. I recognized the girlish-faced blonde slumped in the hospital bed right away.

"Hey! That's me," said Ben, picking up the album.

"Yes, that's you," agreed Homer, letting Newton curl up on his lap.

"Dude, you seem like a nice guy and all, but come on. Why are you saving clippings of me?"

"Not just you, Benjamin," he said. "I've been collecting evidence for years on who my clan members are. That was the only time I felt your power so strong, when that lightening struck you. I've had my doubts over the years, but the way you were drawn in to Gabriel and Melanie made me certain that you are one of us."

"Mr. Homer," said Clara, "can you please start from the beginning? What is this, this power you say we have? What is it for? What can we do? What—"

"Slow down there, Clara. You're right. I should tell you what we are. I suppose it's best if I start with me."

Ben had finally set down the album and grabbed a chair from the kitchen table for himself. Clara sat in between Jeremy and I on the couch. It was interesting how she was radiating a subtle joy. I glanced at her and saw that excitement in her hazel eyes, focused intently on Homer.

"I am a Tracer," said Homer. "My power is to unite us with other Setti. I can find Setti wherever they are, not just our clan but others. I also pass on the knowledge I have gained from others as I can see Setti not just in the present, but those also in the past."

"Others?" asked Jeremy.

"Yes, there are many more like us. Each clan has six members. We work as a whole. I can also sense the approach of the reapers. The ancient clans called them 'myrkr jötnar' or 'dark giants.' My job is to help us connect with other clans and to strategize when the reapers come."

"So, you're like our Obi-One," said Jeremy.

"Yes, I suppose so," replied Homer with a smile. "I've heard that other clans farther north are calling the dark giants 'reapers' now."

"Like the Grim Reaper. That makes sense," said Jeremy. "They are here to deliver death then?"

I would've thought Jeremy was making a joke with the hint of sarcasm in his voice, but there was a hard, cold expression on his face.

"Yes, Jeremy," said Homer, knowing his name just like he knew ours without any introduction. "Their power is very different from ours. They wield it to take energy from humans with frightening precision. I'm afraid we're behind in our training."

I felt a shot of fury rise up within me.

"If you knew all this, why didn't you contact us sooner? Don't you think it would've been wise to be preparing for this months ago, even years ago?"

"I understand your anger, Gabriel, but how exactly should I have done that? What would've been your reaction if I showed up on your doorstep even a week ago and told you that you were part of an ancient clan with the power to kill monstrous demons from another world. What would've been your parents' reaction?"

This silenced me pretty quickly. I know that I would've thought he was a lunatic. And, I'm pretty sure all of our parents would've put a restraining order on the man known as "crazy old Homer." It was Clara's gentle voice that finally broke the tension.

"And, what about me, Mr. Homer?" she asked. "I mean, I know that I can see auras, but you said that it's just a side effect of what I can do."

"You, Clara, are our Guardian. I know that you used your power last night. I sensed it and saw what happened, in my mind's eye of course."

"Of course. The ole mind's eye trick," mumbled Jeremy.

"You have the ability to protect others from the shadow scouts and the reapers," said Homer.

"Shadow scouts?" I asked.

"Yes, I've been in contact with a friend of mine, another Tracer in

Arkansas. They call them shadow scouts, because that's essentially what they are. They're here to scout the territory, to find the best time and place for the reapers to strike first."

"But, when we researched these things, there have been sightings going on for decades," I said. "Why have they been here so long?"

"Yes, I started seeing visions of them a long time ago. They have a trace of their masters' power on them, which made me see them in nightmares and even in waking dreams. They've been here for many years, watching and waiting to see when the climate was right for the reapers' return."

"What kind of climate is that?" asked Jeremy.

"A climate of fear, of course," answered Homer soberly, stroking the purring Newton. "The shadow scouts are drawn to it. They spread it."

"Yes," I said, "that's what they were doing at the football game."

"But, why?" asked Ben, listening very closely.

"Because humans are their weakest when they are filled with fear, and it makes easy prey for the reapers. They don't want a strong, confident force against them; they want to feed without a fight."

"I don't get it," said Ben. He seemed lost in all this.

"Benjamin, this may be a terrible analogy, but it's the best I can think of. Would you want your food on your plate to jump up, grab a knife, and start fighting you? Or, do you want that food just to sit still and wait to be eaten?"

Ben's face went pale. I'm pretty sure mine did, too. When he put it that way, it was scarily clear what we were up against and what was at stake.

"Fear," Homer continued, "is what you must push away from your hearts and minds most of all. Being able to master your own fears may be the difference between life and death."

I had a sudden flashback to Mrs. Jaden's class and our group discussion about *Lord of the Flies*. I remembered Clara's burning anger at Derek's suggestion that what is good or moral does not matter; it is only a question of the strong dominating the weak. That weakness which doomed those fictional characters was fear. I felt Clara squirm beside me.

"The constant terrorist attacks, rioting nations, the dirty politics, the economy, all of it," said Clara, "fear has become so much a part of our society that we don't even notice it anymore. It's almost normal."

"I knew you were bright, Clara, but you still surprise me," said Homer. "Yeah, we've brought the reapers here ourselves. They're intelligent creatures as much as they are hideous and deadly. They want little opposition, so they descend when we are our weakest."

"So, what is my role?" asked Ben, now very interested in what was going on.

"Benjamin, you are our Light-bearer. You have the ability to take in electrical, and even solar, energy from all around you. This means that you can weaken the shadow scouts and the reapers by taking it from them. That is what they feed on—energy."

"Why haven't I known about my power, or even had a hint of it, like Gabe and Clara?"

"Sometimes, Benjamin, the power is there all the time, we're just unable to recognize it. Tell me Benjamin, have you never felt any sensation before a thunderstorm? That's when you might've noticed it most, when electricity is thick in the air."

"Well, I get that tingly feeling all over my skin before it storms. You know what I mean?"

He glanced at us, but none of us responded.

"Y'all get that, too, right? Where it feels like tiny ants crawling up and down your arms and legs," he said, getting a funny frown on his face. "Y'all don't have that feeling?"

I shook my head, so did Clara and Jeremy. It didn't surprise me at all that Ben had been sensing his power his whole life, but was just too goofy to ever notice it.

"But how is that tingly feeling gonna somehow help me weaken these monsters?"

"I'm afraid that you'll be the one to make it happen, but we'll work on that in a bit, Benjamin. Of course, Jeremy must do his job before you can do yours."

"Dude," said Jeremy, "all I can do is break glass and plastic. Unless these reapers are made of plastic, we're in trouble."

"No, Jeremy," said Homer, chuckling lightly, which made his eyes sparkle again. "Your ability is to shatter the energy fields that the shadow scouts and reapers build around them. There is power in the sound waves you can create that can break these fields. The shadow scouts conceal themselves, like camouflage, with their protective shield. Guardians are the only ones who can see them when they're hidden. It's part of her gift of protection."

Clara nodded, more to herself it seemed, then Homer continued.

"You must be aware, Jeremy, that the reapers' energy fields are much harder to break than those of the shadow scouts. You must prepare yourself for an exhausting fight ahead."

"Awesome," said Jeremy, grinning with what I can only say was boyish delight.

"Tell me something, Jeremy. How many instruments do you play?" asked Homer.

What a strange question. Jeremy seemed to think so, too.

"What?"

"How many musical instruments can you play?" he repeated politely.

"Um, three. How did you know I liked music?"

"All Sounders have an affinity for music. It's in your blood."

"What instruments do you play besides the piano?" asked Clara, smirking at him.

"I played the trumpet through middle school then dropped the school band to learn guitar. I'm good, too," he added haughtily.

"I'm sure you are, *Sounder*," said Ben with a laugh.

"Hey, Sounder sounds pretty cool," said Jeremy, "It's better than Lightbulb."

"Light-*bearer*," said Ben.

"Whatever, Lightbulb."

"But, Mr. Homer," interrupted Clara, "why are the shadow scouts afraid of me?"

"I don't know for certain, Clara, but it seems that your protective aura is the complete opposite of theirs. Your shield of light burns them with fire, while their shield cloaks them in the darkness. They hate to be seen. They want to hide and do their dirty work for their masters in the shadows."

"What exactly do they do for their masters?" she asked, her vibe tensing next to me.

"Essentially, they freeze their victims with fear so that the reapers can consume their life energy and kill them."

I remembered last night how I fell into a trance of complete terror in the clutches of the shadow scouts. There were no reapers near me, yet it seemed they wanted me to react somehow to their torture.

"Why would they attack me last night without the reapers nearby?"

Homer turned his blue eyes on me, now closer to the color of brittle ice.

"They will do everything in their power to destroy you, Gabriel. You most of all. Perhaps, last night, they were testing you to see what you could do."

"I guess I failed that test," I said quietly.

Clara's hand went to the hand on my knee where she intertwined her fingers with mine. I gave her a small smile. It was all I could manage. Then, I noticed that Homer's brow had bunched up into a frown, while watching our hands together.

"Humph. Interesting," he mumbled to himself.

What did that mean? He was obviously concerned about this connection between Clara and me. Homer dropped the frown and stared unblinking at me.

"Gabriel, you are our Vanquisher."

"Now, *that* sounds cool," said Jeremy.

"You, Gabriel, can use your power to destroy reapers, shadow scouts, and ash-eaters."

"Yeah, we didn't get to talk about the ash-eaters. What's their deal?" asked Jeremy.

"From what I've seen of visions from the past, they're like parasites. They follow the reapers and eat what's left behind."

"Hey, kind of like those little minnows that swim alongside sharks and eat the algae and left-over fish parts," said Jeremy.

It was amazing. Death could be knocking at the door with giant dragon wings and fangs bared and Jeremy would be saying, 'Awesome, dude.' He was like a gamer geek plunked right down in the middle of his own fantasy quest. Only, this wasn't a game. I turned my attention back to Homer. There was something important I needed to ask him.

"In your visions," I stammered, "have you ever seen a warrior woman, kind of like a Viking?"

Homer's expression softened and his eyes twinkled again.

"Of course, I have. The Viking, or Nordic, and Celtic clans were the last to expel the reapers from our world. From what I've seen, the reapers have been here twice before. The first time was many thousands of years ago when mostly primitive people lived on the earth."

I thought of the pictographs made by the ancient people in Cuba. Clara squeezed my hand. I'd forgotten she was holding it.

"And, the second time was during the Dark Ages, which I think now was appropriately named for more than one reason. We have few records of what happened in that time period."

"Yeah, but that was because the Black Plague was killing so many people," I protested, realizing I was repeating one of Mr. Hamilton's history lessons.

"I think now that the Black Plague was more than a rampant virus. I think there were also the black giants that were killing just as mercilessly at the same time."

"Wouldn't there be some kind of records? Some sign that they existed?" I asked.

"Not necessarily," said Homer thoughtfully. "With the shadow scouts, they have the ability to watch people and even make them believe and say things that may not even be true. Think about the hysteria that the shadow scouts spread at the football game last night. Once fear takes hold, people will believe many things. Perhaps, the shadow scouts ensured that the fear of the plague was spreading, while their masters fed without detection. Another thing is that they didn't have the means of communication that we do now. The reapers could wipe out a whole village then let the ash-eaters suck up the evidence and no one would ever know they were even there. Of course, I think there is evidence in other ways that no one but a Setti would catch onto."

"What's that?" asked Clara eagerly.

"There are myths about creatures that stalk vulnerable humans by night and feed on their life force. Do you know what they are?"

"Vampires," snapped Jeremy.

"Yes. Of course, that life energy was changed to blood over time. The reapers have been twisted into mythical monsters, vampires and werewolves, all kinds of boogie-men. I think it's also interesting that so many cultures over the centuries have their version of the Grim Reaper. The Romans had a similar creature in their myths called Charon, the ferryman of the River Styx in the underworld. All gave it different names, but it always looks very similar to what the ancient clans called myrkr jötnar. And, its purpose was always linked to death."

Something he said bothered me about the 'mythical creatures.'

"Why did you say that people believed they were creatures who stalked by night?"

Homer looked puzzled for a minute.

"Oh, I suppose I forgot to mention that. The reapers feed only at night."

"Why?" asked Jeremy. "Do they get burned by the sun or something, like vampires?"

"No," said Homer, chuckling again. He apparently thought Jeremy was pretty funny, even when he didn't mean to be. "Actually, during the daytime, they rest by soaking up solar energy, taking away the light of our world. Have you not noticed the quickly changing seasons and the cloud cover spreading more each day?"

Of course, we had. Everyone thought it merely some freakish climate change. Scientists spouted their inane theories on a daily basis, speculating and hypothesizing on the atmosphere's odd behavior. Most of it was due to humanity's abuse of natural resources that seemed to be dooming us. But, that's all they had—theories. The truth was, no one knew why temperatures were dropping more quickly or dark clouds churned everywhere or a hurricane spawned out of nothing with no solid and logical scientific explanation. Perhaps, the scientists were half right. It was the fault of the human race. But it wasn't the overabundance of cars and pollution or the abuse of the earth that caused it. It was our ever-increasing spread of fear in this world, our faithless abuse of one brother to another that lured these dark beasts here to feed on the hopeless. The mere thought of what we'd brought on ourselves made me angry at our own ignorance. Homer had paused in his reverie, while we stewed in this new reality.

"You know," continued Homer, "there's another thing that made me wonder about the Dark Ages. Have you all heard of that old nursery rhyme: 'Ring around the rosy, a pocket full of posies—"

"Yeah, but that's about the Black Plague. My history teacher told me about that. It's a child's song about filling your pocket with flowers to keep away the smell of death everywhere, or something like that," I said.

"Yes, yes, I know. That's what's in the history books. But, think about it again. 'Ring around the rosie' could be symbolic of the circular formation the shadow scouts and reapers form around their victims before they kill them."

My mind suddenly wandered to the vision of the warrior woman, surrounded and impaled by four reapers. I snapped back, while Homer went on.

"The reapers are black, but the Europeans they devour who made up this little rhyme are generally fleshy pink, or 'rosie.' Then, there's 'a pocket full of posies,' which could be a reference to the fact that people in the medieval era carried posies, flowers, to ward off the black death, meaning the plague. But, the black death could also mean the black reapers."

"That's just weird," said Clara. "How can flowers keep away these killing machines?"

"You have to remember," said Homer, his blue eyes shiny and brilliant, "that this was a superstitious age. They surely thought these creatures came from some dark fairy world, which they believed was very real. I know that the Celtic people put floral wreaths on their doors during pagan holidays to keep fairies and mystical beings from stealing young maids during the night."

"How horrible it must've been when they came," said Clara softly, her voice lilting sadly.

"Yes," agreed Homer. "Just like the end of the nursery rhyme says, the flowers do nothing to stop the black death, being the plague or the reapers. Thus, it ends, 'ashes, ashes, we all fall down.'"

Homer didn't need to explain the final line. I think we all got it. Clara pulled her hand away from mine and tucked her hair behind her ears nervously.

"Homer," I said, "you mentioned that you have visions of these past clans. Well, I've had one, too, but only one."

I pulled the brown velvet pouch from my pocket that I'd carried ever since Theresa gave it to me.

"A woman gave this to me who found it in some ruins in Cuba," I explained. Homer had a look of deep understanding on his face. "The stone in here has been in my dreams. I know now that it is the remains of, well, she was a Vanquisher long ago. When I held it in my bare hands,

I saw her last moments, but she spoke in a language I couldn't understand."

"Old Norse," said Homer.

"Yes, I just realized that recently. But I don't remember the words enough to try and translate what she said."

"I know Old Norse," he said matter-of-factly.

"Really?"

"I've had quite a bit of free time in the past years out here."

"Yeah, I bet, without a TV or anything," said Ben sympathetically. "It must be awful."

Homer just smiled.

"I don't want all those things distracting me from what I need to do. I receive visions best when in solitude. Well, then, Gabriel, shall we step into your vision and see what the Viking Vanquisher has to say?"

"You can do that?" I asked hopefully.

"Of course, I can."

"Of course," repeated Jeremy, "he's got that whole mind's eye thing goin' on."

Homer stood up then sat on the coffee table directly in front of me. I'd never seen eyes so clear and blue as his.

"Clara, take the stone out for him," he said. "If you don't mind, Gabriel, I'll just need to hold onto your arms. I'll see the exact vision you see with physical contact."

"Sure. That's fine."

It was better than holding my hands, I guess, which would've been way too weird. His rough hands grasped my lower forearms. I glanced at Clara as she held the stone over my open palm. Her hazel eyes were warm and gentle as if she were comforting me before she let me go to this other place.

"Are you ready?" she asked softly.

Homer had closed his eyes and bowed his head. I nodded, feeling the weight and cold sting of the stone in my hands and hearing my last words sound muffled and distant.

"Here we go."

✷12✷

GABE

Here I was again, watching the fierce woman warrior defying the beasts to come closer. Something was different this time. I must've been propelled several minutes earlier than before. I was seeing more of the memory laced into the stone. The tall monoliths stood strong behind her with its swirling wormhole; electricity crackling in between. There was a bright light casting a circular glow and another warrior standing behind her. I don't know how I missed him. His long, dark hair was whipped by a fierce wind. He held his muscled arms up to the sky. There were intricate tattoos with interlacing knots weaving from his wrists all the way up his forearms and curling slightly to the tops of his biceps. He was a Guardian, holding his halo of protection in place.

"Heimta, Freya!" he bellowed.

His voice was deep and desperate. The warrior woman he called was edging closer to the rim of her Guardian's shield. Something had gone wrong, because their other clansmen lay dead outside the circle, close to the monoliths. There were nearly a dozen reapers circling the perimeter of the light shield, all hooded in strange, black garments with an unnatural sheen. I couldn't see any shadow scouts, but I could feel their menacing presence. Ash-eaters lingered in the distance, rustling in the dark.

"*Þeir ar próttigr, Blyn!*" she shouted over her shoulder.

She watched the circling reapers, edging closer and closer to the border of the halo of light. She crouched like a cat, waiting for the first attack. One of the giant reapers to her left swung his sword-like arm in the air then thrust it down upon the light shield just above her. Sparks spattered into the air, flinty and bright, but the arm never penetrated her Guardian's shield.

"*Heimta!*" he yelled again.

She glanced fleetingly in his direction, but it was the mistake they were waiting for. Invisible arms and hands seized upon her from the rim of the light shield, bursting into flame as they crossed the border and grabbed her. The invisible creatures, shadow scouts, shrieked as the Guardian's aura burned their flesh.

"*Neinn!*" he yelled, his bright eyes blazing. "*Freya!*"

The Guardian's shield vanished when he called out to her. I realized what he was hiding under a layer of furious anguish—love. In that blinking second that she was seized and his shield faltered, a blindingly fast reaper leapt through the air. In two swift bounds, the creature was face to face with the Guardian, thrusting his killing arm directly into his chest above his heart. The Guardian lifted one hand out toward Freya, but the beast's arm singed and petrified him within seconds into a statue of blackened ash. The echo of Freya's blood-curdling scream drowned out the ravenous sounds of ash-eaters rustling forward. That was the same scream I heard the last time I was here. Now I knew what had caused her so much pain.

With a vengeful slash through the air, the triumphant reaper scattered the Guardian's remains into a cloud of dust. The rest of the scene was sadly familiar. Four of the largest reapers stepped forward. Freya maneuvered herself near her companions in front of the monoliths. Her arms went out in a sacrificial stance. I saw in her eyes something I missed last time, a burning mixture of grief and fury that brought shining tears to her bright, green eyes. All at once, the four beasts impaled her with their killing arms. She grabbed the arms of the two fiercest in front of her, while looking back to her companions and saying those strange words I didn't understand.

"Setti, valr, svá váru þeir allir hraustir at engi talaði æðruorð."

When she turned her glowering gaze on her killers, I felt the humming vibration begin to tremble in the air as she spoke in a venomous tone.

"Myrkr jötnar, tekinn minn lífdagar. Vér nálægr þessi dyrr. Vér vili neinn andask. Minn kyn vili nálgask endr. Vér ávalt hafa."

As the power pooled inside of her, waiting to be released, I saw her head dip once toward the ground. I hadn't noticed it so much before that she had whispered something quietly. I heard the words this time.

"Blyn, minn astir."

Her head popped up and she unleashed her power in a fearsome yell. The reapers shattered as before into a black cloud of bone and dust. She continued that horrifying scream. The portal between the monoliths sputtered then snapped into nothingness. Squeals of pain escaped from the surrounding ash-eaters as Freya killed them all before finally sacrificing herself and exploding into glittering fragments of light.

My eyes shot open. Clara had her hand on my shoulder. Homer was already up and at the kitchen table, scribbling furiously on a sketch pad. Jeremy and Ben stared at me with wide eyes.

"Are you okay? Do you have a headache like last time?" asked Clara.

"A little," I admitted, feeling a dull throb against my temples.

"What did you see?" asked Jeremy. "The same thing as before?"

"I saw more. I saw two of them."

Homer rushed back over to his bookshelf and pulled out a brown leather-bound book then flipped anxiously through the pages. His fingers traced down one side then he scribbled something hastily onto the pad.

He finally returned to his chair, where Newton had curled up into a tight ball. Newton complained with a hoarse meow in being moved aside, but Homer was eager to tell us what he knew.

"Do you know what they said?" I asked. "Do you know why I have some link to them?"

He nodded.

"I've had visions of them before, but never this one, never their end," said Homer somberly. "They are our ancestors."

"What do ya mean?" asked Ben. "We're like, related? To Vikings?"

"Sweet," said Jeremy with that stupid grin.

"Our powers are passed down directly by blood," said Homer. "Not every generation knows they have it. It may lay dormant without being used or even discovered," he said, glancing at Ben. "Another thing I've noticed is that there are never any siblings of the one carrying the power."

I thought about that for a minute. It was true. Clara was an only child. Ben and I had always thought it was cool the way we were only children and also best friends, being completely spoiled by our parents. I guess that meant Jeremy was, too. I knew that Melanie was, because her mother had died in a car accident when she was little, leaving her to be raised by her grandmother.

"Do you have any children?" Clara asked Homer quietly.

"I do. A daughter, Penelope. She lives in Arkansas. It was on a visit to see her many years ago that I met the Tracer, Herrald."

"Does she have your power?" asked Ben.

"I'm sure that she holds it somewhere inside, but it is only awakened in one person at a time. I figured this out by comparing notes with other Tracers who noticed it, too."

"Can you tell me what they said, in the vision?" I asked, thinking of Freya and her Guardian.

He nodded again, his brow crinkling into a frown. He glanced down at the sketch pad in his hand.

"Can you share the vision with us first?" asked Clara. "We don't know what you saw."

"It was a stand-off," I said. "A Guardian and a Vanquisher were blocking a portal of some kind."

"Where was the rest of the clan?" asked Jeremy curiously.

I glanced at Homer, now realizing I was talking about our own kin. It became difficult to relate what happened, even though I didn't know these people any more than a character in a book.

"They were already dead," said Homer, rescuing me. "We didn't see how it happened, but they were overpowered by at least a dozen reapers who circled the Guardian's protective shield. The Guardian was Blyn, and he was your ancestor, Clara."

I felt a jolt of something from Clara, but it was not one emotion. It was many, too indistinct to name.

"What was he saying to her?" I asked. "He kept saying 'heimta.' What does that mean?"

"That was the one word I wasn't sure about that I had to look up," he said, glancing back to his pad. "It basically translates as 'get back.' He must've been able to see the shadow scouts, but she couldn't. She was carelessly close to the edge of his shield."

"What happened to her?" asked Clara.

"Shadow scouts grabbed her," I said.

"But how?" protested Clara. "I thought you said they couldn't come inside the shield."

"They can't. Not without being injured, that is. They risked being burned to get to her," said Homer.

"And that's when Blyn dropped his shield," I said.

"Yes. It was an emotional response. He lost concentration. That's how the reaper was able to get to him."

I felt Clara shudder next to me.

"What did she say to the other clansmen after she was stabbed?" I asked.

Jeremy and Clara had already heard this part of the vision that first time in Theresa's hotel room. Ben wasn't asking anymore questions. He was just listening. Homer looked down at the pad where he had quickly scribbled the words when he came out of the vision.

"She said to them, 'Setti, slain warriors, so brave were they all, that no one spoke words of fear.' It sounded like a battle poem of some kind. They were words of farewell."

"But, then she spoke to the reapers in a really harsh voice. What did she tell them?" I asked impatiently.

"Oh, yes, that was quite something. What spirit that Freya had," said Homer, musing to himself with a smile.

"Freya?" asked Clara. "That's a pretty name."

"She was a remarkable woman, and Vanquisher. I'll share other visions I've had of her some other time. But, to your question Gabriel, her last words were, 'Dark giants, take my life. We close this gate. We will not die. My kind will come again. We always have.' Then, using all of her power, she killed every reaper, shadow scout, and ash-eater left. Unfortunately, she killed herself as well."

There was a solemn silence after Homer repeated Freya's dying words. The weight of it hung in the air, pressing down on us. We were their legacy, a group of young teenagers without any experience in battle against murderous demons. Well, other than the occasional game of 'Halo 3' or 'Gears of War.' Those powerful words were daunting beyond my imagining. It seemed that Homer knew it, too.

"Don't fret now. Your powers are just awakening. You will soon feel like the warriors that you truly are."

My mind wandered to last night, how I couldn't even defend myself against the shadow scouts for fear of hurting someone else. How would I ever defend my whole clan against the reapers?

"How do I control it?" I asked, trying to keep the shakiness out of my voice.

"You'll have to practice," he said. "Shall we?"

Homer stood up and walked toward the door.

"Alright! This is what I'm talkin' 'bout," said Jeremy, popping up and heading outside in a skipping run.

Ben and Clara followed a bit slower. I stopped Homer before we were out the door.

"What did Freya say right before she died, when she bowed her head?"

Homer's eyes glazed a little.

"She said, 'Blyn, my love.'"

"That's what I thought," I said, ducking out the door to join the others.

Clara was watching me with her arms crossed. I avoided her eyes. Ben was staring off into the distance with his hands stuffed into his jeans pockets, while Jeremy paced anxiously.

"Okay, who's first?" asked Jeremy, practically hopping in place.

Homer eyed each of us carefully after he stepped off the porch.

"I think we should start with Ben first, since I think he needs the most help."

"You can say that again," mumbled Jeremy.

"Shut up, sound-system," said Ben.

"Is that supposed to be an insult?" asked Jeremy, "Because it's not."

"Okay, boys. Enough," said Homer calmly. "Tell me, Benjamin. You said before that you get a tingly sensation just before storms. Is there ever another time when you feel this way?"

Ben had that funny puzzled look on his face he got whenever I asked him things like whether he'd finished an essay paper for Mrs. Jaden or if he realized he had to bring up his ACT score for college. His eyes brightened suddenly.

"Well, sometimes, when I'm playing soccer and I'm running downfield, I do get a sort of rush and feel that way. But, I always just ignore it, because it reminds me of thunderstorms. I hate storms."

"I think that's where you've gone wrong, Benjamin. Instead of ignoring that feeling, you need to open yourself up and embrace it. You say it's when you're running that this happens?"

"Mm-hmm," he nodded, his blonde hair flopping forward.

Homer turned around and stared back toward the road where we'd come. He stroked his grizzled beard.

"I wish I had a soccer ball, but I'm afraid I don't keep those around," he mused with a smile.

"I've got one," I said. "My gym bag's in the back of the Jeep."

I jogged over and found my red and white Nike ball then started back, but they were coming to meet me.

"Okay, then," said Homer, turning to Ben. "I want you to just kick the ball down the path as fast as you can and when you feel that sensation that you get, focus in on it."

"You want Ben to focus?" asked Jeremy sarcastically.

Ben reached out to punch Jeremy, but he dodged around Clara chuckling to himself.

"Geez, boys, cut it out," said Clara.

"Fine," grumbled Ben.

Jeremy stayed defensively behind Clara, out of Ben's reach, grinning.

"Listen to me," said Homer more earnestly, "when you start to sense it, keep running. Let that feeling go. Don't block it out."

"But, how will we know if he's using the power?" asked Clara. "I mean, I've seen Jeremy, and I know Gabe can use his, but how will we know if he's pulling energy from around him? We can't exactly see energy."

"You'll know," was all Homer said. "Go, Benjamin. Run."

Ben shook his head then started dribbling the soccer ball along the dirt path, mumbling something under his breath. He was slow at first, zigzagging along the road, but then he picked up speed. We followed him to the mouth of the woods that circled the clearing. He disappeared around a bend. We waited.

Clara stepped close to me and put her hand in mine.

"Are you okay?" she asked.

"Yeah. Why?"

"Your aura. It's been sort of, well, sad-looking since you came out of the vision."

Her hazel eyes held me still. I wanted to wrap my arms around her and lose myself. I wanted to tell her that nothing was wrong, that nothing had changed, but I couldn't. My mind went back to Blyn and Freya. They had caused their own deaths, possibly even the deaths of their clansmen, because of their feelings for each other. It was a weakness we couldn't afford, that I couldn't allow.

There was a yelp of excitement and laughter in the distance. It was Ben. This gave me a reason to pull my hand away and walk closer to Jeremy and Homer who had stepped a few feet ahead.

"Well, well, well. Look at Firefly go," said Jeremy.

Ben was cruising back toward us, but he looked different. He was glowing, actually glowing. It wasn't like Clara was last night with a golden halo cast all around her. As he came closer, knocking the hell out of the soccer ball, I could see that there was an electric light shimmering on his face and arms, beaming through his white t-shirt, then dimming under his jeans and shoes. The ball skidded past us and bounced off the porch steps in the distance. Ben jogged to a stop, his chest heaving from the run. A goofy, but uncharacteristically arrogant, smile spread across his face that was shining with white light.

"What do ya think of this?" he asked, holding out his arms for us to see.

It's not like we could miss it.

"Very good, Benjamin. What was it like?" asked Homer.

"Well, first, when I started running, I was still thinking you were kinda crazy. No offense," he said, still panting.

"None taken."

"Then it started; that sort of itchy, tingly feeling. I did like you said. I started thinking about how it was running up my legs, my body, then down my arms into my fingers, so I started running faster. It was like the air around me was pushing me to go faster and faster. Then I could see it all over my skin. It was totally awesome, man," he said, clapping Homer a little too aggressively on the back.

Homer wasn't exactly a small man, but the force of Ben's pat nearly knocked him over.

"Oh, sorry," Ben said, laughing in an almost giddy way. "Man, I feel good! I always associated that feeling with the time I was struck by lightning, so I blocked it out. If I'd known it felt this good, I'd have been doing this a long time ago."

"Yeah," said Jeremy, "and you'd be locked up in a cage in some scientist's lab somewhere."

"Huh?" asked Ben, confused.

"You can harness all electrical energy, solar energy, even energy from plants around us, Benjamin. What you need to practice is pulling energy from specific elements, because the foremost purpose of your power is to weaken the shadow scouts and reapers when they come. Tonight, when you get home, I want you to practice with some kind of electrical source."

"Like a light bulb," suggested Jeremy.

"But, what is it that triggers it?" I asked.

"It seems that for Benjamin, it's any physical activity where he releases large amounts of energy, which actually makes perfect sense. When his body is losing energy that internal power takes over, trying to take in energy from the environment around him. But, just as it is for all Setti, your will has much to do with the strength of your power and your ability to control it."

"How do you mean?" I asked.

"Well, I'll tell you this. I didn't move out here in the middle of nowhere without cable TV or even a telephone just for the fun of it. I realized that my power was mostly internal, requiring great concentration on my part to wield it. I needed a place of solace so that I could meditate and receive connections from other Tracers. It wasn't until I moved out here on Canebrake that I started having full visions of past Setti. Before that time, it was like broken pieces of dreams."

"I still don't see what you mean about us. Our powers are different," said Clara.

"Yes," he said, smiling so that his cobalt eyes sparkled. "You are different. You, Gabriel, and Jeremy experience your power as an emotional response to what is going on around you."

"Yeah, I guess that's true," admitted Jeremy, "because it's always my music that brings it out, and well, you all know how I feel about my music."

"Yeah, we know," said Clara. "I guess that's true about us, too."

She glanced at me, and I knew she was thinking about last night. I remembered how furious anger lit up her face as she charged toward me and the shadow scouts. I wasn't about to add my own views on this subject.

"But, why emotions?" asked Clara.

Homer thought reflectively, pursing his brow into wrinkly lines.

"Emotions are reflections of our internal energy. Whenever we have emotions, our mind filters it out through our physical body, then our body reacts to these feelings in some form of energy."

"Whoa, isn't this getting a little too personal here?" said Jeremy, cocking one eyebrow up.

"What kind of emotions are *you* thinking about?" asked Clara sharply.

Homer ignored them and continued.

"Just think of it this way, any feeling that you have, whether it's joy, anger, sadness, desire, hate, whatever it might be, they all have a physical reaction. Think of the physical maladies, like heart attacks and ulcers, caused by emotional stress. It is this energy that awakens your power. Have you ever heard the physics theory that for every action, there is an equal and opposite reaction?"

"Yes," Clara and I said in unison.

Homer seemed surprised by such a quick response, then he went on.

"Your body's reaction to any heavy emotion on the inside is for your power to push outward forcefully. You'll find that some emotions will have a stronger impact than others. But, the ultimate goal is clear. For Sounders, it is breaking the energy fields of our enemies with a voice. For Guardians, it is an instant shield of protection. For Vanquishers, it is the ability to crush evil entities into dust. This is why it is imperative that you learn to control your own emotions."

This was unreal. I'd managed to block other people from seeing my true feelings my entire life, but I had never had any control over them. This was like telling a cop to avoid crime.

"Well, whatever, guys," said Ben, frowning down at his arms that were losing their golden luster, "but I'm gonna take another run."

"Remember, Benjamin, you must wield your power carefully. Do not take too much energy from any one living thing, until of course we meet with our great enemy. This will be your task, to focus on where you draw that energy from."

Ben's brows furrowed together for a minute then lifted in understanding. He turned abruptly and headed back up the path, without the soccer ball this time.

"Yeah, you go recharge, Sunshine!" yelled Jeremy after him. "So, who's next?"

Homer didn't say a word, but led us around the side of the house near a metal work-shed where his blue pick-up was attached to a trailer. In the bed of the trailer were thick pine logs with branches still poking out along the trunks. Next to the shed were three huge logs as tall as me with their limbs cut away. Homer marched over, heaved them upright and stood all three on end. For a man his age, he was strong.

"You have been expecting us," I said.

"Yeah," he said, walking toward us. "I've had these waiting for you, Gabriel. It's time to see what you can do."

I kept any fear away from my eyes. I didn't feel ready for this test. I was actually a little jealous of how easily Jeremy could turn his on and off. Homer must've seen my hesitation.

"Just stand right here and face the logs. I want you to focus just on one of them, then think of any time where you felt some intense emotion. That should draw it out."

My memory snapped back to when Clara and I were on her porch and I nearly killed her. I tried not to look at her, but my eyes slid to her anyway. A splotch of scarlet colored her cheeks while she stared at her feet. I suppose we were thinking about the same thing.

"Okay," I said "everybody just step back."

The three of them took one giant step behind me. I tried to block them out and just zone in on the center log. Seconds ticked by. I closed my eyes and thought of last night when those shadow scouts grabbed me. My first reaction was terror, but then it became a sort of caged anger. I thought about how Clara was coming toward me and how I had felt helpless to do anything. No reaction. I didn't feel a thing, not even the slightest sensation inside my gut. Jeremy shifted his feet, distracting me. Not opening my eyes, I took a deep breath.

Okay, let's try something else. I let my mind go back to that night on Clara's porch. I liked the way she looked in that long coat, her wide eyes gazing up at me in the dark. I couldn't pinpoint exactly what it was that had seized me, making me kiss her without even thinking. I had just wanted to be close to her, very close. When we were together like that, her intense emotions melded with mine, amplifying my own. I couldn't even express exactly what she made me feel. It was a jumble of things, good things—admiration, hopefulness, awe, and something more.

I sensed it rising abruptly, flaring up inside my chest. I opened my eyes, zeroing in on the target. I urged it on, willing it to break away from my body. My right arm shot out instinctively, reaching in front of me. I closed my eyes briefly, glimpsing Clara in the dark—hazel eyes, arms around me, pulling me closer. Without even thinking, an orb of pressure tore through my body, flowing out of my hand, careening toward the target then blasting all three logs. They splintered backward; one jagged log of wood tore straight into the side of the tin shed; the other chunky pieces and sawdust flew several yards into swampy water.

The strange part was that I felt completely calm. In fact, I felt great. It was like purging all of my emotions at once. I turned with a smile. They weren't exactly smiling. Well, except for Jeremy.

"Which one were you aiming for?" he asked.

"The middle one," I said. "Uh, sorry about your shed."

"Don't worry about it, Gabriel. I'd say there's no doubt that you can use it. You'll just have to try and harness it now."

Reflecting on what just happened, I realized that fear stifled my power. Only in that state of joy was I able to summon it.

Ben jogged up beside us, shimmering white again. It was so weird how he acted all casual about it. He was putting his phone in his pocket.

"I've been trying to call Melanie, but I just can't get a signal out here," he complained.

"No. Sorry, you can't get cell service out here," said Homer.

Ben turned to me.

"I think we need to go see Melanie. She needs to know everything we do. She needs to know she's a part of this."

Homer glanced at his old Timex on his left wrist.

"You might want to do that," he agreed. "It's about time for me to check in with Herrald, anyway."

"I thought you didn't have a phone," said Ben before it dawned on him. "Ohhh, I get it."

Jeremy snorted a laugh.

"We can continue tomorrow, and you should bring Melanie."

"Sure thing," said Ben, jogging back to the Jeep.

"You might want to turn your lights off, Sunshine, before we get back into town," said Jeremy, following behind him.

"How do I do that?"

"I don't know, but Melanie might freak out if you show up on her doorstep like a knight in shining armor, minus the armor."

As we drifted back to the Jeep, Clara stopped and turned abruptly.

"But, Mr. Homer, where did this power come from? I mean, why us?

How did this all start?"

Homer smiled and gazed across the water for a moment. He seemed to be recalling some distant memory. We circled back toward him.

"In my time on this island, I have spent many, many hours in deep meditation. I have tried to travel beyond those primitive people and their first encounter with the dark giants to seek the source of our power. But, it is beyond me, beyond my reach. When I travel as far back to the beginning as I can go, everything turns white."

"Whoa," said Jeremy, "so even Obi-One has his limits."

"Yes," agreed Homer with a smile, "we all have our limits. But, I can tell you this, we were given these powers for a specific purpose. It is not only our privilege to have them, but our obligation to use them well. Only then will we fulfill our destinies."

"Dude, I love the way you talk," said Jeremy, clapping him on the back and heading to the Jeep.

"Later, Obi-One."

"Clara," called Homer before she walked away. "I've been wanting to know something for a very long time."

"What's that?" she asked.

"What color is my aura?"

Her face lit up with a wide smile. Something flipped in my stomach.

"It's completely white. And," she sort of laughed, "it's got glittery sparkles all in it, kind of like Cinderella's dress. It's very, um, comforting."

Homer chuckled softly.

"Thank you, Clara. I've been curious for some time now. I'll see you tomorrow."

I lingered, waiting for Clara to move out of earshot. Homer waited patiently for whatever was coming.

"Homer, earlier today, you seemed a little disturbed by noticing that Clara and I are, well, that we're together. I was wondering why."

His face was completely expressionless, no hint of his thoughts.

"I suppose it's natural for you two to be drawn to each other—the sword and the shield. It doesn't surprise me, actually. However, there is the risk that your feelings for each other could endanger the clan and others that we must protect. I'm certainly a little more worried after sharing that vision with you today. But, Gabriel, you are your own person. You must decide what is best. I will not interfere in this."

He clapped me on the shoulder in a fatherly way. My eyes were on the ground.

"Put that out of your mind. For now, you must focus on wielding your power and making it obey your will."

I nodded, trudging back to the Jeep. 'Put it out of your mind.' Put her out of my mind? Easier said than done. How do you stop thinking? How do you stop breathing? I glanced ahead. Her head tilted back as she laughed loudly at something Jeremy was saying. She tucked her auburn hair behind one ear. Freya flashed to mind. My heart sank. If it kept her safe, I could do it. I would have to.

Part 2:

The Descent

"Do not go gentle into that good night,

Rage, rage against the dying of the light."

--Dylan Thomas

✷ ✷ ✷

A world of gray swirled in the heavens. The massive storm moved like a giant worm, inching slowly to earth where it would burrow a great, black hole. It was the perfect guise for the myrkr jötnar. The ghostly mass, shrouded in a veil of tempest, eked its way toward unsuspecting prey. Humans below were not aware that this oncoming storm was a harbinger of hell.

Hovering among his lesser brethren within the eye of the storm was a frightful beast; immense beyond the standards for any myrkr jötunn. His gleaming eyes were shadowed by the brow of his massive skull. His horns, the only dark giant crowned with them, twisted and pointed backward. An enormous cloak whipped wildly around him, and dragon-like wings beat against a rogue wind. To the slaves, he was Great Master; to his race, and even the Setti he battled in this world before, he was Bölverk. His body trembled with pleasure, sensing the oncoming descent and the awaiting feast.

A torrent of wind squeezed into the eye, but it did not move the creature from its fixed, mid-air position in the least. Miles below, a tip of brown earth emerged into sight. He bellowed a long, loud unearthly sound that echoed out across the eye and into the violent winds encapsulating the beasts. Hundreds of ash-eaters responded with anxious shrieks, flapping ghastly, tattered wings in the hurricane's circling gales. Tendrils of blue lightning streaked across the gray sky. En masse, the beasts descended as one.

The city was not nearly empty. The slaves had done their jobs well, instilling the fear that leaving would be as dangerous as staying. Half the population still cowered somewhere in the dark. Bölverk touched its clawed feet to the cobblestone pavement, sensing the humans' electromagnetic energy everywhere around him. He eyed the many tall buildings in this city, very unlike his last visit to this world. The humans of this era were more advanced. He smiled, pleased to see the human species had reproduced so well over the millennium. His race would feed in abundance and replenish its slave population before returning home. The screaming had already begun.

His chief slave appeared in front of him with bowed head and on bended knee as required.

"What words do you bring, slave?"

The blackened figure, a former human from their last feeding in this realm, was a larger creature of their specimen. He had once been a fierce warrior. This one had been the most loyal of the slaves to Bölverk, reporting more often than most, as if it felt true allegiance to its master rather than fear. The others reported when they were weak and needed to feed. This one came of its own will, drawn to the dark comfort of its master's presence. Even so, it would never rise above its station as servile pet.

"Great Master, there is only one clan of Setti within this territory. They are young and weak. I encountered their Vanquisher who is hardly even aware of his power."

"Power? They have no power. None that will hinder the myrkr jötnar."

The slave had not raised its head, waiting for its master's bidding.

"Have the outer bands begun their work?"

"Yes, Great Master," came the prompt reply. "They are feeding already. The city below awaits your mighty hand."

The colossal creature slit the air with its sword-like arm above the slave's head. The slave did not tremble, but waited in eager anticipation for its reward. The sharpened black arm split into seven bony fingers that wrapped entirely around the slave's head, even trailing slightly down the neck. With a small guttural sound from the giant's throat, its internal energy obeyed his will, sliding along its arm through its fingers and into the head and body of the slave. The slave shivered delightfully in response, feeling the beasts' power flow into him and his own strength multiply.

"Rise," said Bölverk. "Do your work."

He waited for his first meal. His dutiful slave along with another dragged a large human from one of the tall buildings. It was a male, well-built and strong, but trembling with fear shining in its bright eyes. Bölverk did not hesitate, having waited too long for his first feeding. His razor-sharp arm impaled flesh and bone, sucking out the human's life energy within seconds and transforming its body into a charred shell. Three ash-eaters slithered forward, inhaling the repast of leftovers. Bölverk closed his eyes, sensing the pleasure of fresh energy pulsing through his body, relishing the new life strengthening every part of him. This morsel merely whetted his appetite. His glowing yellow eyes popped open, slit like a serpent's glare. He gave the command his dutiful slave was awaiting.

"Next."

✻13✻

CLARA

I was used to Jeremy taking over the radio in Gabe's Jeep. He was leaning over the stick shift to change the playlist on his iPod plugged into the radio adaptor. We were halfway across the land-bridge, and Gabe was cruising like a bat out of hell.

"Dude, I've got to switch gears," Gabe said in a very annoyed tone.

"Got it. No problem, man. Just thought Guns 'n Roses might be more appropriate for our current situation."

A guitar solo and Axel Rose's screeching yell blared out the opening of "Welcome to the Jungle." I suppose Jeremy was alluding to the fact that our lives had taken a sudden turn into a dark and dangerous place.

"Do you have a playlist for everything in life?" I called back to him.

"Absolutely. There's a song for everything and everyone."

"Really?" I asked, quite curious. "What would be my theme song?" There was no hesitation which was a little weird.

" 'Firewoman' by The Cult."

I twisted around, sitting sideways in my seat. Jeremy had that crazy grin on his face. His eyes were hidden by streaks of black wind-blown hair.

"Well, thanks. I think. That's not a bad theme song," I finally said. "What about Ben?"

He had to think about this one. Gabe was brooding about something next to me. I don't know if he was irritated with Jeremy's flirty mood or just ignoring us altogether. It was hard to tell these days. He seemed farther and farther away.

"I'd have to say," said Jeremy, " 'Singin' in the Rain' by Gene Kelley."

I couldn't help myself. I burst out laughing. I'd seen that old Hollywood musical with my dad once where the tap-dancing Gene Kelley just sings merrily away while the rain pours down on him. That was definitely Ben—happily clueless.

"Who's Gene Kelley?" asked Ben, still staring at his arms where the light was fading.

Need I say more.

"Okay," I said. "What about you?"

"That's easy. 'Master of Puppets' by the almighty Metallica. Oh, yeah."

"You wish," said Ben.

I rolled my eyes. He was so full of himself.

"How about Gabe?" I asked.

"Ooo, that's a tough one. Let's see," he said, glancing around. We had just turned back onto the highway leading into Beau Chêne.

"Man, I'm starving," interrupted Ben. "Let's stop at Wendy's."

Gabe nodded, but was still silent. I was distracted from Jeremy's light entertainment by the way Gabe's aura was transforming from its mostly purple hue to its usual rainbow of color.

"You know," I said to him, "your aura changes when you use your power."

"Really?" he said, sounding completely disinterested.

"Yeah. It turns a dark purplish-blue, and it seems to wind around you like intertwining ropes."

He didn't even respond. Not even a grunt.

"Okay, then," I mumbled to myself.

We were coming up to the overpass when we saw the traffic. The outgoing lane heading north through Lafayette was bumper to bumper.

"What's that all about?" Gabe asked to no one in particular.

"Maybe there's a wreck," I suggested, but then I noticed that too many of the cars and SUV's had suitcases strapped to the roof. "Oh, no. That doesn't look good."

Gabe abruptly turned off the iPod and unplugged the adaptor to flip on the radio. Jeremy didn't protest. Something had happened while we were in no man's land all day. I pulled out my iPhone now that we were in range of towers.

"I've missed three calls from home," I said.

"Two for me," said Ben.

Gabe flipped the radio to a station out of Lafayette. Sure enough, there was no music playing, only the news. The normally perky DJ was droning on in a not-so-cheery voice.

"Officials say that Contra-flow will be in effect within the hour so that all lanes of Highway 90 will move more easily along the hurricane evacuation routes. The newest tracking has Hurricane Lucy still heading northwest. I'm afraid it hasn't veered from its earlier course this morning, which puts the eye traveling directly over New Orleans. Experts are baffled at the sudden and remarkable speed at which it has increased, now moving at 33 miles per hour, faster than any hurricane in recorded history. . . ."

My pulse was pounding in my chest. My throat had suddenly gone dry. It was really happening.

"Pull in to Wendy's, Gabe," Ben called from the backseat.

"Are you kidding me! Are you really hungry at a time like this?"

I was having trouble getting a hold of myself.

"Yeah," said Ben, completely unflustered, "I need food. Besides, I can find out a little more of what's going on if we stop."

Gabe careened into the parking lot. I nearly fell into his lap, even with my seatbelt on.

"Sorry," he mumbled.

Ben climbed out of the back and jogged inside with Jeremy right behind him.

"Do you want anything?" Gabe asked me.

"Are you kidding?"

"Yeah, I feel the same way."

Gabe didn't go in with the other two. I snapped open my cell and dialed home. Mom picked up on the second ring.

"Hey, Mom."

"Where are you, Clara? I've been trying you all morning. Do you know that the hurricane is heading this way?"

"Yeah. I just found out."

"Just found out? Where have you been?"

"No where. Just tell me what's going on."

Mom was used to my vague and evasive answers by now. Our conversations always ran somewhere along these lines, but her voice had a high-pitched hysterical tone to it that was beyond the norm.

"It's expected to make landfall this afternoon. Your dad's been outside, putting everything from the yard in the garage, and I had to face Walmart to get water, batteries, and everything by *myself*."

Geez, she could make me feel guilty.

"Well, are we evacuating?" I asked.

"To where?" she screeched another octave higher. "Everybody the south of us is blocking up the interstates, trying to get away from the coast. Besides, your father says we'll be safe here since the bad winds are on the east side and we'll be getting the west side of it, but it will still knock out the electricity. We'll be out of power for who knows how long. I want you home right away."

My mom was always a little melodramatic, but this time there was actually reason to be. I started to tremble, because I knew there was much more to fear than rough winds and a power outage, but I couldn't explain that to my mom. Was this all really happening?

"I'll be home soon," I promised and hung up before she could fuss at me anymore.

There was a buzz of cars moving around the parking lot. People were making quick pit-stops for food and bathroom breaks, then jetting back onto the interstate. Gabe was stewing in silence, watching a couple in his rearview mirror scurry into Wendy's with two toddlers waddling between them.

"So, what's going on with you?" I asked.

He jerked his head sideways to look at me.

"What do you mean?"

"You know what I mean. You're blocking me out. I want to know why."

He got that dumbfounded look on his face like the first time he'd given me a ride home. I think he was always shocked whenever I said whatever I was thinking. I was born without a filter. What could I say?

"I'm not blocking you out. I've just been thinking about things," he said, staring at his hands gripping the steering wheel.

"What *things*?" I said, unable to keep the ice out of my voice.

"I'm just worried, Clara. That vision I saw today. They died because they were *too* close to each other. I think they may have been responsible for the death of the whole clan."

"What are you saying?" I asked, feeling fire in my cheeks. Maybe Jeremy was right about my song. "That I would let anything happen to you or our friends or anyone I cared about?"

"Of course not, Clara. I don't think you would mean to. It's just complicated—"

"No! No, it's not complicated! You're just making it complicated. It's quite simple. We both care about each other, so we should be together. How the hell is that complicated?"

There was a sick burning in the pit of my stomach. I could feel the acid churn, making me nauseous. I couldn't believe this. He wouldn't talk, and I couldn't shut myself up.

"I can't believe you're even thinking about having this conversation with me when you know what's heading in our direction right now. If ever I needed you, it's now. But, you've got to pull that stupid dumb boy 'it's complicated' crap on me. Maybe you're afraid, but I'm not. I know how I feel. And there's no way in hell that I'd let anything happen to you, or my friends, or my family, or even complete strangers for that matter, just because of how I feel about you. If you're so scared, then maybe you should just—"

"Man, my mom's pissed!" yelled Ben, climbing over the back and hopping into the backseat, while digging for fries in his bag. "She's been worried about me all morning, trying to get me to go home."

"That's funny, because neither of my parents even bothered to call me," said Jeremy, climbing in next to him, slurping on a drink.

I was seething. I stared out the window, refusing to talk to anyone. Especially Gabriel! Idiot.

"What did you find out?" asked Gabe quietly, starting up the Jeep.

"Just that the whole town has gone totally insane," said Jeremy, "everybody's trying to get what they need before we lose power. They can't put us on mandatory evacuation because the hurricane is moving too fast and the entire city of New Orleans and surrounding parishes have to get out since it's headed right at them."

I was still staring out the window, trying to calm myself down. I couldn't help but think of my old friends in New Orleans, desperately packing their entire lives into one car before leaving their home behind. This kind of goodbye was more heartbreaking than most, because you didn't know what would be there when you got back, *if* you got back.

My eyes lifted to the clouds. They hovered low and moved in wispy gusts. What was coming? I had only seen the reapers in one or two dreams. They were always elusive and faded beyond the more distinct shadow scouts that haunted me. It didn't seem real. A prickling fear crawled up my spine. My eyes finally focused on what we were passing. It was the only Lowe's in a 30-mile radius. There was a huge

18-wheeler near the garden center, handing large boxes out to a swarm of people. A hazy blur of gray, black, and a dull crimson aura hung over the entire mass like a sludgy pool of grime.

"Oh, no," I mumbled.

"What?" asked Gabe quickly.

"That's not good," I said. "Their auras are horrible looking. All of them."

"What are they getting off that truck?" asked Jeremy.

"Generators," said Gabe.

Gabe suddenly banked hard right onto one of the many solitary roads without a sign trailing off the highway that cut through Beau Chêne.

"Where are we going?" asked Ben.

"Melanie's. We need a plan, and she needs to be in on it before I take you home. We also need to figure out how we're going to explain to our parents that we have to stay together when the storm hits."

"Stay together?" asked Ben.

"Yes," said Jeremy with a heavy sigh, "the reapers will be here soon, and we've got to stay together."

Ben was silent for a few seconds.

"I guess you're right. Man, my mom's gonna be pissed that I'm late."

"I thought you said she already was," said Jeremy.

"Yeah, but she's not used to me not doing what I'm told. I'm not like you, Jeremy. I actually listen to my parents."

"Well, Goldie Locks, nothing like the present to engage in a little teenage rebellion, eh?"

✳ ✳ ✳

I was sitting in one of the rocking chairs on Melanie's porch staring at her opposite me in the other one. The boys stood back, watching. I guess we were waiting for her head to pop off or something. She was just sitting there in her khaki shorts and "save the whales" t-shirt, studying all of us from those dark, almond-shaped eyes with her long curly hair waving loosely around her shoulders. We had obviously caught her off-guard, because she didn't look quite as prim as usual. She was prettier this way.

"So, what you're saying is that I'm one of these Setti, and that one of my ancestors was a Viking?"

We all nodded dumbly.

"Have any of you noticed the color of my skin? I doubt seriously that I have a giant, blonde-haired, blue-eyed great, great, whatever."

"No offense," said Jeremy, "but you look a little café au lait to me."

"I'm Creole," snapped Melanie. "We've got Spanish blood mixed in our family."

"Well, somewhere along that family line, a Spaniard took a detour and got busy with a Norse woman."

"Melanie," interrupted Gabe softly, "haven't you ever noticed your own abilities in healing? I know you said your grandmother is a *traiteur*, but you should've sensed something of your own power at some point."

Melanie's thin black eyebrows dipped down into a broken V. Her hands were clasped calmly in her lap. She opened her mouth to say something then the screen door creaked open.

"Mel? Your friends want some lemonade or something?" asked a white-haired woman with smooth, tawny skin peeking out the door.

"No, Gram. We're fine."

"You kids better get home soon before the winds pick up."

"Yes, ma'am," said Ben.

She nodded, gave us a closed-mouth smile then returned to the television that was blaring the latest on Hurricane Lucy. We all turned back to Melanie who was staring out across the yard. I followed her gaze. A line of maple trees along the drive shook their leaves in a flurry of wind. The clouds felt even lower than before. The outer bands of the hurricane were already sweeping over Beau Chêne. Melanie let out a soft giggle like someone who'd just heard a shameful joke. I turned back to her.

"It *was* me then," she murmured to herself.

"What was you?" I asked.

"One time, when I was very young, we had a dog named Moonshine. He was an old beagle that my grandpa used for hunting. My grandpa used to love to hunt. That was his favorite thing to do, and the only thing he loved more than me and Gram was that old dog Moonshine. Well, one late afternoon when he'd come back from the woods, he was carrying Moonshine in his arms."

"What happened to him?" asked Ben.

"He had gotten bitten by a water moccasin back in the swamp. There wasn't much hope for him. His whole leg and abdomen was swelling really bad with the poison by the time Gram started to work on him."

"What did she do?" I asked.

"I'm not supposed to reveal *traiteur* secrets, but mostly all she did was cut the wound and draw out what poison she could with a small suction, sort of like a mini-plunger. She stitched him up, put her herbal salve on it, then left him with me. My grandpa couldn't even be in the room with him, he was so upset. I remember curling myself up next to the old dog. I loved Moonshine because my grandpa loved him. This was after my grandpa had been diagnosed with cancer, and we knew my Gram couldn't do much to stop the inevitable. I didn't want that dog to die. It would've broken my grandpa's heart. So, I laid there on the floor, stroking Moonshine's head. His little eyes blinked at me, while I whispered to him. And, I remember wishing with all my heart that I could cure him, that I could make him better like my Gram made other people better. After about an hour, I fell asleep on the floor. I woke up to Moonshine licking my cheek and wagging his tail, completely cured."

"Wow. What did your Gram say?" I asked.

"She said it was a sign that I had the gift of a *traiteur*. So, I started seeing patients with her. And, every time she prayed over patients when they left, I wished strongly, just like I had with Moonshine, that they would get well. Gram even let me lay my hands on them in the parting prayers. It's funny how when we prayed together, not one patient ever returned with the same illness."

I was thinking that it was not a coincidence at all that the patients she put her hands on were all miraculously healed. It seemed to dawn on Melanie, too. She sucked in her breath sharply.

"Oh," was all she said.

"I don't think it's your grandmother with the true gift of healing," said Gabe. "It's you."

Melanie didn't say anything at first. Her mouth lilted into a small pout.

"That would break Gram's heart if she found out," she said softly.

"Mel, we have much more serious things to worry about than that," said Gabe sternly. "We've got very little time to figure out what we're going to do."

"How are we going to convince our parents that there are like these monster death-dealers coming?" asked Ben. "My mom's gonna freak."

My phone started buzzing in my pocket. I had turned it on vibrate when we got to Homer's, not wanting my mom to interrupt. It wouldn't have mattered since there was no cell service out there anyway. I saw Jessie's pic on the front when I pulled it out.

"It's Jessie," I told everyone, now staring at me. "Hello."

There seemed to be no one on the other end at first then I heard a hushed whisper. It was Jessie's voice sounding more shaky and panicked than I had ever heard in my life.

"Clara, Clara? Are you there?"

She was panting heavily.

"Yes, Jessie, it's me! What's going on?"

Gabe hopped off the porch railing, staring intently down at me.

"I think those things are here," she whispered, "the ones from last night at the game. Wait a minute . . . ."

"Jessie? Jessie! Tell me what's going on!"

"Shhh. I'm looking out the window. Wait. What in the world *is* that? Our neighbor, Miss Cindy, something's dragging her—"

There was a distant scream and Jessie's voice got louder.

"Mom? Mom, what is it?"

"Jessie, for God's sake," I was yelling, "what is happening?"

For a split second, she talked directly to me.

"I don't know, Clara, but I need you," her voice choked into a sob. I had never heard Jessie cry in my entire life, not even when she broke her arm falling off my trampoline when she was ten. "Hunter, stay here," I heard her say to her little brother, suddenly quiet again. "Get in the closet, and don't come out until I come back."

There was utter silence, but I could still hear her breathing very low on the other end.

"Jessie, we're coming right now," I said, practically leaping off the porch. "Just hang on. We're coming."

There was no sound at all on the other end, and I thought for a second that I'd lost the connection. Then, I heard a soft, desperate whisper. It didn't even sound like her at all.

"Hurry, Clara. They're in the house."

Before I could say another word, the call ended.

✺ ✺ ✺

I had vaguely heard Gabe give instructions to Melanie that she had to persuade her Gram to go out to his Pop's cabin on the bayou where we would all meet back up. Melanie hadn't protested at all, but seemed convinced that she could get her Gram to go. If Gabe was driving like a bat out of hell leaving Homer's, he was now flying down the road like a bee on crack.

"Did she say anything else?" he was practically yelling at me.

"No, no, nothing else. Something had dragged her neighbor outside, but she wouldn't say what."

I was biting my lip so badly, it had started to bleed. A bitter salty taste filled my mouth. Jessie only lived a few minutes away, but every second felt painfully too long.

"Ben," said Gabe, "call Zack and Mark and tell them to get their families out to my Pop's camp. They know where it is. And tell them that their lives depend on it."

"On it," said Ben, thumbing through his phone contacts.

We rounded the corner of Evergreen Lane. Only one more block. The wind had picked up speed, rocking the Jeep at every turn. As we passed a yellow house on the corner of Azalea Street, something caught my eye in the back yard beyond a white picket fence.

"Oh, God, stop the car! Stop the car!"

Gabe screeched to a jolting halt. Three shadow scouts were dragging a man across the yard to a tree. No. It wasn't a tree. The tree started to move. Its limbs were long, almost majestic, in their purposeful movements. It was a reaper—tall, slender, and shrouded in a dark cloak. The man was cursing and kicking out violently around him. The reaper stabbed him through in a quick, unyielding motion. Gabe jammed the Jeep into first and tore down the road toward Jessie's.

"What are you doing!" I screamed. "We have to go help him!"

"It's too late for him, Clara. We've got to save Jessie if we can."

My mind was spinning from the brutality of what I'd just seen. A man was pulled from his house and murdered in his backyard. What about Jessie? My aunt and uncle? What about my little cousin Hunter who was only five?

"Hurry," I said gravely to Gabe.

There was no need. Gabe jumped the curb, knocking a trashcan into the street, then tore across the front lawn directly up to the house. The four of us leapt out, launching ourselves up the steps through the gaping front door. It was too quiet. Then there was a scream coming from outside.

"The back door is through there!" I yelled, pointing to the kitchen.

Jeremy was closest, speeding like a demon through the house. We were right behind him. As we poured out the back door, we saw them on the lawn, near a pile of what looked like a broken statue, but I knew it wasn't. My Aunt Vanessa didn't own garden statues. Four shadow scouts turned their gleaming yellow eyes on us and hissed in unison, having their hands on Jessie to keep her still. She wasn't making it easy, struggling with captors she couldn't see. I wondered what this must look like from the others' eyes.

"Shadow scouts! Jeremy, now!"

Without a moment's hesitation, Jeremy yelled in one long drawn-out scream, sounding eerily similar to Axel Rose's jungle yell. That familiar humming sensation rapidly increased into waves of vibration, stirring my own power to life. It was like mine was responding positively to his. It was instinctual. I closed my eyes for just an instant to focus my thoughts. I needed to protect Jessie and my friends. My rage subsided into righteous anger, wanting only to shield us from this evil. When I opened my eyes, I wasn't surprised to see my golden halo shimmering like a fiery dome over the four of us. Jeremy's sound waves lapped in the air, shaking me where I stood. Then, I heard a sputtering crackle and the four shadow scouts seemed more vivid than before.

Jessie's face had gone pale, but she still struggled against the arms clamping around her. Her eyes went wide seeing the grotesque black figures holding her. That's when I saw the two reapers emerge from the shadow of an old, fat oak tree near the driveway. My heart nearly stopped. My light shield dimmed. Seeing them so close in the flesh was surreal, like watching a waking nightmare walk right up to you. They were ten to twelve feet tall, seemingly too big to be agile. But, their bodies were lithe, moving in a strangely fluid way, like they held some secret of our environment that helped them move without any obstruction from gravity or the earth's pull. While their bodies had the appearance of a man's, their skin was black with a dark green sheen, similar to how some dinosaurs are depicted in science books. The skin didn't look soft like a human's. It appeared to be a thick, tough layer overlapping a lean muscular frame. The most frightening part was that there was movement underneath it, like an invisible force rolling under the surface of the skin. The only clothing these beasts wore were tunics around the waist and long cloaks made of a black, rustic leather that shined with an unnatural luster. I shivered, wondering what animals on their home world had been the victim for their pelts. Their appearance was terrible, but their eyes were horrifying. If I ever cringed at the sight of the shadow scouts, I wanted to cower like a small child away from the sight of those eyes on me. They were glowing yellow with black slits for pupils like a serpent's, set in deep-set hollows of their massive skulls. They had no hair at all on their bodies, only that putrid greenish-black skin, rolling with the energy underneath it.

The tallest of the two stepped aggressively forward. It flared out a pair of massive dragon-like wings—bony frames webbed with taut, leathery skin between. It shocked me, because I'd never seen this in my nightmares of the creatures. After an instant, the beast folded the wings close to its back. It was trying to intimidate us. It was working. I tried with all my might to keep my shield up, but it wasn't as strong as before. We were all frozen, taking in the reality of what stood before us. Then, the creature spoke to us, and in our own language.

"Little Setti. You are no match for us. Go hide while you can. Your turn will come soon enough."

Its voice was deep, throaty, and fierce. There were tendrils of something black and wet between its lipless mouth when it spoke. I felt my shield dim to almost nothing, then Gabe snapped me out of that trance.

"Clara! Your shield!"

My eyes met his, giving me the strength I needed. Pulling the power from deep inside, I pushed it farther out in a shower of light. I hadn't even realized it, but while I was gaping at the reapers, Ben was to my right, moving closer to the shadow scouts. I glanced in his direction. He was beaming white, having drawn energy from them. One of them had even let go of Jessie's arm and had crumpled to its knees. Ben was draining them dry.

"Jeremy," said Gabe grimly, "again."

I knew he wanted Jeremy to break the energy fields of the reapers, having successfully done it with the shadow scouts. Jeremy's voice came out in a deeper tenor this time, low and steady. There was a hollow echo in his voice. It was like his power intuitively knew just what to do. I couldn't help but notice how his aura leapt around him in vibrations of fuchsia and orange. Had it not been for our current situation, I would've remarked at how beautiful it was.

The tallest reaper stepped toward Jessie, seeming no more worried about us than bugs buzzing around his head. Oh, God. My cousin's pale face went entirely white. All I could see were her bright blue eyes shimmering with tears as she looked up at the horrifying creature above her. A jarring pressure to my left made me stumble sideways as Gabe sent out his power. It didn't penetrate the creature's shield, but exploded the top half of a shadow scout holding Jessie's right arm. The lower half of the scout slumped to the ground in a pile of crumbling embers. I forced myself to remain calm and focused, knowing they needed my protection. The other reaper stepped forward to stand in front of me, glaring into my eyes. I was transfixed. Up close, I could see its face was nothing close to human. There were two tiny slits where a nose should be on a flattened face. It lifted its long arm that looked more like black steel sharpening to a point and slammed it directly over me. Green electric sparks spit up into the air. Then, it grinned. It had no teeth, but a row of slick, black slime where teeth should have been. It opened its mouth very wide. Tendrils of black ooze threaded across the gaping hole; bright green streaks of electricity licked inside the orifice. I knew my face showed my disgust. It gurgled and grinned at me again. It was like a lion who yawns to show its row of canine teeth just for the shock effect on its prey.

This must have gotten Gabe's attention, because I felt wave after wave of his power from the left, pummeling the reaper that was glowering at me. It let out a frightening growl, stumbling backward and turning its attention on him. Jeremy and Gabe had both moved in front of me, working on the reaper at the same time. The sound waves were slowly shattering the creature's shield. Gabe relentlessly pounded it with his own force. It lifted its sword-like arm as if to attack them, though they were still inside my shield. Gabe had his arms in front of him, making a huge pushing motion then the reaper exploded into fragments of black bone, dust, and its own echoing shriek.

Jessie screamed. The other reaper reached one arm out toward her. Its sharpened tip splintered into seven, bony fingers that encapsulated Jessie's tiny head. Ben was glowing brightly next to me. The shadow scouts had let her go and had fallen to the side, but it didn't matter. The great reaper held its protective shield in place, while Jeremy and Gabe continued to pound against its hulking back. Its other sharpened arm went up. I saw the sheer terror in Jessie's round blue eyes as it penetrated through her green t-shirt, singing the fabric then the skin. The reaper moved slowly, as if on purpose to torture us all even more. This wasn't happening. This couldn't be happening.

"NO!" I screamed, my heart sinking with the slow movement of the reaper's arm.

With violent finality, it plunged the arm swiftly into her chest, sucking the life from my cousin. Jeremy and Gabe did not relent. I could hear a splintering crack—the sound of the beast's shield faltering. There was a greenish glow flowing up the reaper's arm and rippling through his body. That crawling current crept under its skin. Jessie's pale skin slowly darkened to tan then brown then black. Her hair fell away. Her clothes singed to almost nothing.

"No," I heard myself whisper hoarsely.

My poor cousin. She couldn't be gone. I was waiting to see her freeze into a statue of ash. My heart had gone numb. I could feel my head shaking back and forth in disbelief. The reaper made a strange, gurgling sound before it withdrew its arm from her chest and its spiny fingers from around her skull. Jessie's eyes were closed. Her skin was not ash, but a shiny, sleek black, like scales. I was waiting to see her crumble into nothing. Instead, her arms twitched, her head tilted up and her eyes opened. They were a gleaming, ominous yellow. Horror made me tremble, sending a tremor through my shield and a pain in my heart. Jessie was a shadow scout.

·14·

CLARA

My power drained away with each passing second that I stared at my cousin Jessie. No, the shadow scout who once was Jessie. There was nothing left of her, but a smallish frame slouched in a posture that looked familiar. In a daze, I didn't notice at first the quick movement to my left. Jeremy had grabbed a metal trash can against the garage and was launching it at the reaper. He released a deafening yell that carried with the metal, reverberating outward like a giant tuning fork as it struck through the reaper's energy field then spiraled sideways. The reaper spun around, but instead of going for Jeremy, it turned on Ben who was doing his best to steal its life energy. Ben was glowing brighter than ever before, and had edged too close to the creature, which would've been fine if my shield had still been in place. I couldn't do anything but stand there stupidly, overwhelmed by my own grief.

"Clara!" yelled Gabe.

I snapped out of my misery and tried to focus on rebuilding the shield. My mind spun erratically into many thoughts jumbled together—light, hope, protection, safety—but it kept wavering back to Jessie. I was breathless, and I hadn't moved from this spot since we had come out the back door. Gabe sent out an onslaught of his power which missed the reaper but shattered the remaining shadow scouts, except for the small one, into a cloud of sooty smoke. That last scout crouched on the ground, seemingly confused and lost. The fearsome reaper lunged out at Ben, who was too fast for the beast. Ben twisted away, running for the small circle of light I had been able to rebuild. Before he could cross the halo's threshold, the reaper spat out a ball of black ooze which webbed out, wrapping over Ben's shoulder. He stumbled, but Gabe was there, jerking him fiercely into my light shield. When Gabe tried to use his power against the reaper a second time, its own energy shield was back up. The creature glanced at all four of us with a glimmer of something flashing in its serpentine eyes. Was it anger? Frustration? In a matter of seconds, it glided back across the yard, yanked the small shadow scout to her feet, and with two beats of its massive wings, it was airborne and gone. Jeremy tore off after them, stopping at the spot where they lifted off, staring into the sky as they vanished into distant clouds.

"Ben!"

I ran over to where Gabe was examining the gelatinous ooze snaking around Ben's shoulder. It had eaten through his thin t-shirt to the skin. The fabric had fallen away completely. Ben kept wincing in pain. Red whelps were rising at the edge of the black thing's grip. Gabe reached out to try and pull it off with his bare hands then flinched back abruptly as soon as his fingers touched the oozing slime. Ben cried out again.

"Damn it!" yelled Gabe.

"What is it?" I asked.

"I don't know. It sent an electric shock through me."

"A shock?"

The ooze had tendrils wrapped entirely around Ben's left shoulder, snaking around the bottom of the arm and up his neck. It moved of its own will, like an octopus wrapping tentacles around its prey.

"Yeah, it feels like the sting of a catfish, times a thousand," Gabe said gravely.

Even after saying so, he grabbed at the center mass again. The jolt rocked him backwards on his heels. Ben screamed, rolling his eyes in pain.

"Can't you try to kill it?" I asked. "I mean, with your power?"

Gabe gave me a grave look, then shook his head.

"I don't have enough control, Clara. I could kill Ben in the process."

One of the tendrils slithered across Ben's neck as if it were seeking to strangle him. Ben's bright eyes widened.

"No. You. Don't."

He reached up with his right hand and latched onto the black mass, screaming as he tried to tear it away from his body. Then, something bizarre happened. The spidery tendrils flailed crazily, shrinking back into the blob while smoke hissed and rose from the mass. Ben's glowing white light faded in a snap. Within a minute, the viscous ooze smoldered into a hard glob like charcoal, crumbling away from Ben's bare shoulder. He pulled away a chunk of it in his hand then fell backward, passing out.

"Ben!" shouted Gabe, shaking him, then looked at me. "What just happened?"

Before I could answer, Jeremy reappeared above us.

"Did anyone check on the boy?" he asked.

"Oh, no! Hunter!"

I jumped up and ran back through the house to Jessie's room. The door was cracked. Her bed was left unmade. There was a stack of graphic novels on her bedside table and a Blondie bobble-head next to her alarm clock. Above her bed hung, in all its glory, a giant British flag that she begged her mom to get her when we all went to the D-Day Museum in New Orleans two summers ago. Aunt Vanessa had asked her why she needed a British flag so badly, instead of an American one. Jessie's prompt reply was, "it's more symmetrical." Secretly, I knew she had longed to run away to England and join one of their underground punk culture groups. Nausea stirred in my stomach as I stood there among all her things. I leaned forward to look at the pictures taped to her vanity mirror. One was taken at their lunch table at school—Gabe was peering over a book making that half-smile expression; Ben was stuffing a po-boy into his mouth; and Melanie was smiling sweetly between them. Another was a picture someone snapped of her, probably Aunt Vanessa, the second she took off the towel when she dyed half her head purple. That was last summer. I hadn't known there was a hair dye that bright. The third was taken this past Christmas in front of their fireplace. It was me, Jessie, and our moms—the sisters who looked so much alike but had nothing in common. Aunt Vanessa was sort of the wild child, while my mom was the prim and prettier one. Jessie and I were wearing identical looks of take-the-dang-picture. I hadn't realized I was crying until I felt something wet fall on my hand that was propped on the vanity.

"Clara," said Jeremy gently behind me, "the closet."

I wiped my face with the back of my hand and plucked that last picture from the mirror, stuffing it in my pocket. When I turned around, I saw the tiny pale face of Hunter peering from the crack of Jessie's closet door. I opened it slowly, pulling the frightened boy into my arms.

"It's okay, Hunter. I've got you."

He wouldn't speak, which wasn't normal. Hunter was typically loud and obnoxious. I pushed passed Jeremy and carried him into the living room. Gabe entered through the kitchen, sliding his cell phone back in his jeans pocket.

"There's no cell service. I think all the towers are knocked out from the storm."

I glanced around and noticed how little light was left in the house. Although it was overcast outside, it was still darker than it should be. It was late afternoon and dusk had settled in.

"Looks like all the power is out," said Jeremy.

"Ben's still unconscious, and that thing left burn marks on him.

We've got to get him to Melanie at my Pop's cabin. Let's pray they've made it there already," said Gabe anxiously and looked at Hunter in my arms. "Is he okay?"

"Physically, yes," I said.

"Y'all go get in the Jeep while Jeremy and I get Ben. His breathing doesn't sound good. I'm worried that that thing did more damage than burns."

"But, Gabe, what about our parents?" I asked anxiously.

"As soon as we get Ben taken care of, we'll go pick all of them up."

"We can't wait, Gabe. My parents don't live far from here. The reapers could already be there. Let me go on my own, and y'all get Ben to Melanie."

"No! You won't," he yelled.

I flinched. He'd never talked to me like that. Actually, no one had ever talked to me like that.

"Clara, we *need* to stay together," he said more calmly, and I could see the look of concern in his eyes. "It's the only way to keep us all safe. I can drive fast. It won't take long."

I was stung by his harshness. I wasn't about to admit that he was right, even if he was. I walked away toward the front door to the Jeep, still parked practically on the front steps. I belted Hunter in the backseat.

"I'll be right back," I told him. "You don't move."

He nodded once, his blue eyes mirroring his sister's so much that it hurt. As I moved away from the Jeep, I stepped on something. Looking down, there was my iPhone, shattered beyond repair. A shattered reminder of our shattered lives. My breath came quickly as I reeled from everything that had just happened.

I left it where it lay and started up the driveway to see if they needed my help, then something else caught my eye behind Aunt Vanessa's Durango, glinting in the half-light. Next to a black spot of soot on the concrete was a set of car keys. My hands trembled as I picked them up, knowing that the black spot was all that were left of my Aunt Vanessa. Who knows what she was doing or where she was going, probably to get help, when the reapers surprised her, killing her on this spot. How horrible to vanish into air, like you'd never even been here. This would break my mom's heart, even more than mine. My mom. Dad. The keys jingled temptingly in my hands. My house was only a few blocks away. Before I could think twice about it, I jumped in the Durango's driver seat and screeched out of the driveway.

Gabe would be pissed, but he'd get over it. I had to get to my parents before those creatures did. I could protect them long enough to meet back up with the others at the cabin. I didn't know if I could keep my shield up while driving, but I had faith enough to make it happen.

The wind was really picking up. Tops of trees were bending unnaturally. Leaves and branches rolled in the street. A stop sign waved and wobbled on the street corner back and forth. I didn't stop at the stop sign. My tires squealed as I made a left turn, and I felt the truck try to lift. I had to admit that I wasn't an experienced driver. I hadn't been 16 long, and my mom had promised to get me a car only if I made straight A's all year. That seemed like an insanely long-lost goal, when it was only last week that I was sitting in class, thinking my life was normal.

I screamed as something suddenly flew through the air on my right, crashing into the passenger side window. It was a mailbox, torn loose from its post. It cracked the glass, but didn't come through. I hadn't meant to stop, but my impulse was to slam on the brakes. Looking around, it was spooky quiet. Only the wind was blowing things around. A little red tricycle rolled down a driveway like a ghost-child was taking it for a spin. I didn't see anyone running hysterically from their homes or driving frantically for help. Where would they go for help anyway?

I had to get home. Darkness fell heavier and faster. Two more streets then Gardenia Drive; come on, come on! Adrenaline was shooting through my body so fast I could hardly think straight. I had no idea what I was going to tell my parents to convince them we were being invaded by monsters. That is, if they didn't already know. My foot pressed the pedal even faster, turning onto my street. There didn't seem to be anybody anywhere.

Screeching to a halt in the driveway, I sprinted up the porch steps and through the front door. Everything was quiet. This was frighteningly familiar to Jessie's house. Maybe they were in the greenhouse. I crossed through the kitchen, seeing the stacks of bottled water, batteries, and canned soup on the table. My mom's purse was turned over on the tiled floor, lipstick and cell phone toppling out. There was a heavy sinking sensation in my stomach. Slamming through the back door, I sped across the stepping stones to the greenhouse when my mom's voice stopped me.

"Clara! Run away! Hurry!"

She was pinned against the huge live oak tree whose branches were so thick and heavy they dipped close to the ground. She was held tightly by two shadow scouts. Her eyes darted from me to something else. She was watching the ghastly, black figure stepping toward the crumpled shape of my father near the shed. One shadow scout had his hand on my father's back to keep him still, but he wasn't struggling. He was unconscious, or worse.

"Dad!"

I ran as fast as I could, trying to cut the reaper off before he reached my father. A flaming anger shot through my body surrounding me in golden light. I didn't even have to think about it. My power was up and ready. The reaper hadn't taken notice of me yet. When I leapt over my dad, the shadow scout hissed then cowered backward quickly out of reach of my burning aura. This shadow scout had a strange face. Although it was taut and shiny black like the others, it had a deep, greenish gash cut across the forehead. Glancing down at my dad to see if he was breathing, I noticed the pruning shears he used for overgrown bushes clutched in his hand. I saw the slow rise and fall of his chest then wondered what had made him fall unconscious. That's when I noticed the dark shadow looming largely over me.

My shield was strong, but small, which allowed the reaper to walk right up to me. It was strange how similar it looked like the others we encountered at Jessie's, but it also had a subtle difference in its angular face. I thought they would all be carbon copies of each other, like some kind of lizard or snake, but they weren't. Like any race on earth, there were subtle differences. While its glowing eyes looked at me more like an animal than a man, there was a frightening sense of intelligence hiding behind that glare.

"What is this?" it bellowed in perfect English, though its voice sounded like the rumble of thunder. "A little Guardian, is it?"

The shock of this beast speaking my language wore off quickly. I realized it was toying with me. There was no need to answer. I heard a stifled cry. My eyes flashed toward my mom where the third shadow scout had found its way to keep her still, pressing her throat against the bark of the tree. Then I realized that she was staring at it, as if she could actually see it. I studied the shadow scouts, noticing that they were clearly visible to the human eye, not just my own. I suppose they didn't bother wasting energy in camouflaging themselves once the prey was caught.

"Ready, master," said the scout with the scar.

The reaper's gargantuan head tilted toward my mom. I must've made a noise, because it snapped its eyes back on me with splintering speed. It could see my terror, building, threatening to overwhelm me. I sensed my power beginning to weaken. It seemed the reaper sensed it, too. It lifted its long, black arm, snaking it along my protective shell in an S-pattern as if showing me how it could sever my body in half were it able to get through my shield. Tiny electric sparks showered down on the outside. Only a thin, transparent layer of light held him back, but it was enough to keep it from crossing over all the same.

"Ah," I heard a gasp and cry from my mom again.

The scarred one yanked her head back by the hair.

"Get away from her!" I screamed taking two long steps toward them before realizing my shield followed me, leaving my dad's arm exposed. I leapt back with maddening speed.

The reaper grinned, showing me a slick line of black ooze. I shivered, remembering Ben. There was a creepy, knowing look in the reaper's snake-like eyes.

"Humans are strange creatures," it said in that bellowing voice, "Let us experiment."

With those weird words, it stalked toward my mom less gracefully than the others. Oh, God. No, this wasn't happening again. I grabbed my father's leg and tried to drag him, barely moving him an inch. He was dead weight. There was no way to move him with me and get him across the yard in time. I turned abruptly, watching the reaper step slowly toward my mom whose eyes were on me. Her beautiful red hair was damp with sweat and tears, sticking to her pale face. I closed my eyes, frantically focusing on my power, trying to pull it from deep inside so I could push it outward and reach her. I opened my eyes, seeing the golden halo extend a few more feet.

The reaper didn't block my mom's body, as if he wanted me to see this. Uncontrollable tears were spilling down my face.

"No! Please! Please don't!"

I couldn't believe I was begging, but I didn't know what to do. The more I panicked, the less control I had on my power, and the closer he stepped toward her, the more my fear grew. Finally, it was in front of her. It flipped its cloak back over its shoulders and flared its wings upward and outward like the one before, revealing all the power in its massive, grotesque body. Even the hood fell away, revealing an impenetrable, knotty skull. Its head seemed to be made of hard bone, as if it bore a dense, exoskeleton from the neck up. I briefly wondered what kind of world created this monster. It glanced toward me as one pointed arm severed into seven fingers, grasping my mother's skull. The scarred shadow scout stepped away, since the others held her wrists.

I started to run toward them, turning to see that I could only move one yard before my dad was out of the shield of protection. The scarred scout dashed to the periphery above my dad, just waiting for me to move too far. I turned back to the beast. I knew that its huge size was no hindrance on its speed. As soon as I left my dad, the thing would have him in its grip. I realized that it was staring at me with interest.

"Choices," it said with no feeling at all, "which will it be?"

I shook my head in disbelief.

"Choose?" I heard myself ask.

How do I choose? Was it even possible? What an evil, perverse thing to ask of anyone. Then, I remembered this thing wasn't from my world. Whatever dark hole it had crawled from, there was no touch of humanity or mercy in that place. It was then that I realized what a dreadfully, menacing force we were up against.

The wretched creature twisted my mom's delicate head toward me, so that she was forced to look at me. I could see the raw fear filling her eyes. In that moment, I'd forgotten every fight we ever had. All I could see was my sweet mother. The one who helped me make that pretty lemonade stand with blue gingham curtains to sell on the street corner. The one who brought me mint chocolate chip ice cream whenever I had a sore throat. The one who made the most perfect cupcakes for my birthdays, always letting me lick the bowl. The one who used to sneak in at night and check on me in bed when she thought I was already asleep. The one who read Dr. Seuss to me every night because she knew it made me laugh. My mom, the one who I'd pushed away for the past few years, even when I knew she loved me as much as I loved her.

This foul creature held her in its grasp and there was nothing I could do. I shook my head violently, feeling my shield ebb away.

"It's okay, Clara," she said in a shaky voice, a willowy arm reaching toward me, "it's okay, it's o—"

The reaper's rapier arm had slid under her ribs in a swift, silent movement, cutting off her breath.

"Mom!"

I heard myself screaming, but it sounded so distant, like it was happening far away. I wailed over and over, watching the unimaginable in front of me. My beautiful mother blackened to cinder as the reaper sucked the life out of her, her mouth agape and her eyes hollow. I fell to my knees, unable to absorb what I'd just seen. I knew that my shield was no more. I knew it because the shaking flames of fear were licking up my spine; the scarred scout had his hands on my shoulders, sending his energy of terror through me. Strangely, the fear had no place inside of me. It kept twisting into despair, the longer I looked on the ashen statue of my dead mother. Hot tears spilled down my cheeks.

A high-pitched shriek echoed around me. As the reaper stepped away from what was left of my mother, an ash-eater slinked up toward her. It had been waiting in the shadows. Morbid fascination made me watch how it didn't seem to have any limbs under its pasty gray, crackled cloak. Wait, it wasn't a cloak. It was frayed wings, thin and tattered, lagging heavily on that skeletal body. Its bare head had no features at all, only a yawning, hungry mouth. As it drew nearer, I looked away. I couldn't watch what it was about to do. There was nothing I could do to stop it. Everything seemed to slip away from me in a feeling of overwhelming hopelessness. I didn't even care that the reaper was standing above me with no shield between us. My head was bowed in defeat.

"Strange creatures you humans are. While humans think of others before themselves, we serve ourselves first. This is why we are dominant, and you—"

I felt a sharp sting under my chin, lifting it upward. It was one of the creature's sharpened finger tips, making me look into its demon eyes.

"—are food."

"Go ahead," I said, choking back a sob, "just get it over with."

"No," it said, dropping its voice even deeper, "I will kill you slowly. I may even keep you as a slave. Setti make such faithful slaves."

In that instant, I felt a flare of power in my gut. Without even trying, a burning light instinctively lurched out in a small burst. The beast felt it too, growling fiercely, then slashed at my face with its clawed finger. A stinging burn sliced across my left cheek, sending a searing pain and an electric shock through my entire body. It radiated from my face, down my neck and spine, rippling farther downward in agonizing torture. My mind took over, carrying me away from this place of pain. As my body began to tip sideways and slip from consciousness, I became faintly aware of a building pressure rushing through the air above me. In the muffled distance, I heard Gabe calling my name.

15

GABE

"She did what!" I yelled.

"She took Mommy's car," repeated Hunter, shrinking back into the seat cushion.

"Get in, Jeremy! Now!"

I knew I sounded like an ass, but I didn't care. He jumped in the back next to Hunter without saying a word. That's what I liked about Jeremy. He had good sense. I made sure Ben was strapped in securely, because I couldn't promise we would make it to Clara's house safe and sound. I tore a hole in the lawn, spinning out of the yard.

What was she *thinking*? Had she completely lost her mind? No. Maybe not. Maybe I *was* being an ass. I didn't even consider how seeing her own cousin transformed into a shadow scout might affect her. I wasn't even taking a second to think about how it affected me. After all, Jessie had been my friend for most of high school, but I couldn't focus on that right now. There was too much at stake.

Clara was just too damn impulsive. She didn't even consider that separating from us put us all in danger. I was worried about my own mom and grandfather, too, but we had to act rationally. Going rogue wasn't the smartest plan in the world, especially after seeing what these creatures could do. Above all that, my heart pounded at a maddening speed because she was endangering herself and risked encountering these things on her own. I needed to be there, to be with her.

"Watch that—"

Jeremy was warning me about a mailbox in the middle of the street, but I'd seen it already, swerving like a maniac without dropping speed. I understood now what Homer meant about needing to control your emotions. Clara was thinking with her heart, not her head. At the moment, so was I. I felt physically nauseous not knowing what was happening to her.

"Watch that—"

Jeremy pointed at a red tricycle that had rolled into the road, but I crashed right into it, sending it spiraling across a yard. Gusting wind spun around us and night had nearly come. There was no electricity anywhere. Without street lights and the yellow glow from windows, it felt like we were painfully alone. Finally, I turned onto Gardenia Drive, shifting quickly up into fifth gear speeding to the end of the street.

Before I'd even turned off the engine, I felt them. An overwhelming sense of negative energy permeated the air.

"They're here," I said to Jeremy.

"Stay put," I heard him tell Hunter.

I ran straight around to the back of the house where I sensed that gloomy presence. The first thing I saw when I rounded the corner was a ghastly ash-eater sucking up the bottom half of a burnt female figure. My heart lurched, thinking it was Clara, but then I saw her, kneeling before a hulking reaper that had its sharp fingers dangerously close to her face. An overpowering surge of anger welled in my chest then poured out in violent bursts. I was running toward them, not giving a damn whether Jeremy was close behind me to shatter the reaper's energy field. Shield or not, I was going to break this beast in half. The reaper slashed at Clara's face, sending her sprawling to the ground.

"Clara!"

I was within ten feet of it by the time it turned in my direction. This creature had no idea what it had just done. My power surged out of me in a fountain of furious energy, showering forward onto the massive reaper. While its protective shield was transparent, I could see web-like cracks appearing, like a capsule of broken glass wrapped entirely around its body. I wasn't thinking anymore, only reacting to this drive inside of me. I sprinted headlong, twisting sideways and leaping into the air to do a scissor kick as I'd done a thousand times before to shoot the ball into the goal. My leg landed dead center of the reaper's chest, knocking it away from Clara. I heard an electric crackle then shattering sound. Its protective shield disintegrated. Glancing sideways, Jeremy had found a pair of huge pruning shears and was swinging it in wide arcs above his head. He channeled his resonating voice through the metal, screaming like a madman and lunging out at the three shadow scouts that circled around him. I heard one hiss and shriek as he sliced through its shield and arm. My eyes were back on the reaper whose demon glare scoured me with intense hatred. I had no fear at all. Somehow, I knew my power was greater than his. No matter how fierce it looked swinging out its sword-like arms in the air above me, I was going to kill this vile creature that dared to even touch Clara. It sliced its blade toward my head, but I ducked and dodged in a semi-circle motion. It came again, swifter and lower. I dodged again, but its sharpened tip nicked the back of my neck. It just barely pierced through my shirt to the skin, but it sent a stinging shock through my body, like liquid pain streaming into my blood. The jolt knocked me to the ground. I crouched on all fours, needing to refocus. I felt the reaper's nauseating presence, like an acrid stench, bounding toward me. Jerking swiftly to my feet, I pooled a raging ball of energy then launched it at the beast. Its demon eyes went wide, sensing my fatal power the instant before it obliterated it into dust from shoulders to skull. I aimed just a little too high. Its lower half slid into a lifeless clump on the ground.

I turned just in time to see Jeremy, still using his sound-embedded scissors, slashing out at the last remaining shadow scout. It had a gash across its scaly, black forehead. As I sprinted toward them, it spun and fled, disappearing into the twilight. Jeremy dropped the shears and leaned over, panting. I noticed what was left of the other two scouts. Their bodies lay sprawled on the ground. One was nearly severed in half; the other had a deep slice across the chest. Their bodies were fractured from top to bottom, like the skin had literally cracked into pieces, leaking out that black ooze that one of the reapers had spat at Ben. It seemed harmless now, soaking into the ground, dying along with its hosts.

I knelt next to Clara and felt for a pulse in her neck. Yes. She was alive. I knew that even a small nick from that reaper's blade carried intense pain from the sting I felt coursing from my neck. I couldn't imagine the level of pain a full claw across the face could carry.

"Clara," I whispered, turning her head gently toward me, sweeping her hair back.

No response. The angry whelp across her cheek burned brightly against her pallid skin. We had to get to Melanie. I lifted her in my arms and carried her to the Jeep. Jeremy waited and guarded Mr. Dunaway. When I returned for Mr. Dunaway, I found Jeremy studying the dead scouts.

"What exactly did you do?" I asked him.

"I'm not sure," he said thoughtfully, "I remembered that my power carried in that garbage can back at Jessie's when I threw it at the reaper, so I thought I could do the same with those."

He pointed at the garden shears that had become his killing weapon.

"I didn't know you could kill them with your power," I said, excited at this new revelation.

"I don't think I can with just my power," he said. "Not like you. I had to go at them over and over, pushing my power through the shears. Once I'd broken their shields, it seemed like I was literally breaking them each time I cut through their skin. It just took a lot out of me."

He appeared aggravated and somewhat confused, gazing down at the lifeless creatures.

"Don't worry. This is a good thing," I assured him. "Homer will be glad to hear about it and I'm sure he'll have some sort of advice. For now, we need to get the hell out of here. Let's get Mr. Dunaway in the Durango and see if we can find the keys then you take the Durango and follow me."

Luckily, Clara had left the keys in the ignition. We did a quick sweep for supplies, since I knew Pop's cabin had next to nothing in the cupboards. I found Clara's terrified cat cowering under the kitchen table. It didn't take much coaxing to get her to come to me. Within ten minutes, we were on the road again. Night had finally wrapped itself around us, a smothering cloak to hide us from our enemies and our enemies from us.

❋ ❋ ❋

The headlights beamed into the darkness. The woods surrounding Pop's camp had never felt so ominous, pressing in on us as we drove deeper into them. I was half expecting an ambush of reapers to attack from all sides. Jeremy followed only a few feet from my bumper, which was actually comforting rather than annoying. Ben had woken up on the ride over, but still seemed groggy. I had explained briefly what had happened.

"So, Clara's Mom? She got—"

"Not now, Ben," I said, pointing to Hunter in the backseat who was stroking Misty curled up in his lap.

Ben nodded. Only the sound of crickets greeted us as we rolled to a stop. There were two cars parked close to the brush. I recognized the Ford Taurus as the one that was parked in Melanie's driveway. The other was Zack's dad's Chevy pick-up.

"I guess you'd gotten through to Zack earlier?" I asked Ben, having long forgotten that I told him to call earlier today. That seemed like ages ago.

"Yeah," said Ben. "I wasn't sure if he'd come the way he sounded on the phone."

"I'm glad he did," I said, stepping out of the Jeep and walking to the other side.

"Here, Hunter. Take this flashlight and shine it ahead of us right along that trail," said Jeremy, pulling a flashlight from a backpack we'd found at the Dunaway's.

The little boy stayed close, lighting our way with one hand, carrying Misty with the other. I lifted Clara from the Jeep to follow. Jeremy and Ben were pulling Mr. Dunaway from the Durango, and not very gently.

"You sure you can handle this?" Jeremy was asking Ben.

"Yeah, man, I'm fine. Stop looking at me like that."

"Like what?"

"Like that," whined Ben, "like I might faint or something."

"You did faint, Sunflower. Fell just like a stone."

"Shut up."

"Hey," I interrupted, "why don't you both shut it up and get moving."

"Well, you get the feet then," said Jeremy, "just in case."

I didn't have to look back to know Ben had a nasty look on his face. Melanie was waiting on the small deck of the cabin, looking out and holding up a kerosene lamp as if she knew exactly when we were coming.

"Finally," she said anxiously, "I was expecting you almost an hour ago."

"We got a little side-tracked," said Jeremy, moving backwards up the steps, carrying the upper end of Mr. Dunaway.

"Yes, I know," said Melanie, "but you still took a long time in getting here."

"We needed supplies," said Jeremy, "wait, how did you know—"

"Homer told me," she said frankly.

"What? He's here?" I asked eagerly.

"No," she said, holding the door open for us, "he told me another way."

Gram was at the door, ushering young Hunter near the fire. While it wasn't exactly cold outside, there was certainly a chill in the air. The glow of firelight flickered warmly, a stark contrast to the bleakness surrounding us. I quickly noticed Zack staring wide-eyed into the fire, not bothering to see who was coming in. He was holding his little brother, Noah, in his lap, who was doing the same. While Zack's gaze never left the fire, Noah watched Hunter curl up on the rug with Misty.

"In here, sweetheart. Don't knock his head."

Gram led Jeremy and Ben with Mr. Dunaway to the first bedroom off the main area that was the living room, dining room, and kitchen altogether. I followed Melanie with Clara to the other.

"What did he tell you?" I asked Melanie who had already prepared a bed for her.

Melanie set her kerosene lantern on the bedside table then folded back a clean quilt that I didn't recognize as being one of my grandfather's from the old cedar chest. She must've brought this from home. I placed Clara gently in the bed. Melanie already had a basin of water and some kind of pungent herbal ointment at the bedside.

"How did you know? Did Homer tell you everything? Did he see everything that happened?"

"I don't know if he saw everything. He only told me that Ben, Clara, and her father had been hurt, and that Clara had the worst injury."

She dipped a soft cloth in the water and gently cleaned the wound on Clara's face. After patting it dry, Melanie ran her index finger along the length of the cut. I watched her, motionless and filled with anxiety.

"The cut didn't bleed. Why is that?" I asked.

"I'm assuming one of those reapers did this to her?"

"Yes," I replied.

"It's like the blade was hot when it cut her, almost cauterizing the wound."

I heard a soft grunting noise and at first thought it was Clara, finally waking, but it was Melanie.

"What is it?"

She sighed.

"There is something dark poured into this wound. It's not just a cut, or burn, actually."

"Can you heal her? Do you know how to use your power yet?"

Melanie darted her eyes at me as if I'd lost my mind.

"Of course, I know how to use it. I've been using it for a long time, just not like this," she said, turning back to Clara. "Healing arthritis and chronic bladder infections is a lot different than this."

"Still, can't you—"

"Shh."

Yes, Melanie actually shushed me. I realized that my own anxiety was affecting her ability to concentrate. I stood back and waited. She placed one palm on Clara's forehead, the other softly across the wound. She mumbled words under her breath that I couldn't make out. I thought perhaps that there was no outward sign of her power, since it was an internal gift. Then I heard a gradually building sound. It was like a high-pitched note building to a crescendo, yet it was very quiet, not piercing. It made me think of my dad and how he used to drink a glass of wine every night at the dinner table. Sometimes, he would dip his finger in the water glass then rub the top rim of the crystal wine glass, making a high-pitched humming that sounded like music. That was what Mel's power sounded like, only it was softer and really swift. Within a few seconds of the sound mounting, a shock of blue light radiated out of her hands onto Clara's face. The light illuminated her closed eyes and scarred skin, then just as suddenly the sound and light were gone. When Mel pulled away from Clara, the reddened cut didn't seem quite as bright. Other than that, there was no change in Clara at all.

"Does this happen all the time when you've used your power in the past? Is that the norm for *traiteurs*?"

"No," said Mel nonchalantly, "this is definitely new. It's only the third time I've actually seen my power working. I mean, like this. I've been practicing ever since we got here."

"On what?" I asked.

"Gram's bad knees. I was on my third healing when I heard Homer's voice in my head," she said, turning to me with an arched eyebrow, "does he really look like a hippie-cowboy?"

"Yeah," I said, smiling and wondering what a telepathic message from Homer felt like. "What did your Gram think? Did she freak?"

"Not at all. She actually confessed something she'd been waiting to tell me. Her grandfather had the same power, the one who passed his traiteur secrets onto her. Usually, traiteurs pass on their gift to a relative of the opposite sex, but she said she knew all along that I was special, that I had a gift. Of course," said Mel with a stifled laugh, "I thought she was just exaggerating, being the doting grandmother, you know?"

"Yeah," I agreed. "I've been wondering which one of my own relatives passed my gift onto me, too. This all feels so surreal, doesn't it?"

Melanie nodded then looked at me with more tenderness than I'd ever seen in her eyes.

"Yes, Gabe, but it also feels like fate," she said, turning back to Clara. "We need to help each other through this attack on Beau Chêne and our loved ones, because I think our greater purpose is well beyond this first assault. We're going to have to push past a lot of pain to survive."

It was such a great thing to ask of someone, to ignore the loss of life, to delay grieving, so that you could continue to fight.

"Will she be okay?" I asked.

Melanie sighed and turned back to her.

"I think so. To be honest, I think it's her own mind that's keeping her unconscious, not the injury. I removed all of the pain from the reaper, but she may be dealing with another kind of pain which she's not ready to face. It's up to Clara now."

Mel dimmed the lantern, but left it at her bedside. I followed her out, turning for just one more glance at Clara who seemed to be sleeping peacefully on the pillow. Ben and Jeremy were talking in low voices to Zack near the fire who had finally snapped out of his daze. Mel disappeared into the other room to see Mr. Dunaway.

"I know," Zack was saying. "I even went by there to pick him up when he wouldn't answer his phone, but when I got to his house I couldn't even get out of the car. They were everywhere. If I'd stopped, they would've gotten Noah."

"Who do you mean?" I asked.

"Mark," answered Ben, so that Zack wouldn't have to repeat it. "But you said you didn't see Mark. Maybe he still got out."

"Maybe," said Zack doubtfully.

"So, your dad, too?" I asked. "He didn't make it?"

Zack shook his head, looking down at Noah who was playing quietly with Misty next to Hunter. Noah was dangling a fishing lure with no hook above the tabby cat who appeared completely content to swat at it as many times as Noah swung it above her head. Zack went on.

"I knew something was wrong before I even got that call from you, Ben. I was watching the news in case I needed to do something, since my dad was drinking himself into a coma in the garage and didn't seem to care what happened. Then there was this freaky broadcast. They aired a cell phone call from the middle of the French Quarter in New Orleans. Their power had already gone out, and the news anchors were trying to find anything to put on the air. I think they regretted it as soon as the call started rolling. All you could hear were these horrifying screams in the background and these awful noises; they were inhuman. The caller just kept pleading for help before the line died. Right then, I got Ben's call. While I was packing, our power went out. Dad wouldn't come, so I, I just left him."

Zack leaned over in his chair, cupping his face in his hands.

"You can't blame yourself," I assured him, "if you hadn't left when you did, chances are you and Noah would be gone, too."

Zack turned up to me with a bewildered look on his face.

"What is going on? Is this the end of the world or something?"

I glanced at Ben and Jeremy who were both staring at me, wondering what to say.

"There's something we should tell you—" I started to say when Melanie came back into the room.

"He had a cut on the back of the head, similar to Clara's, but he'll be alright now."

"Is he awake?" I asked.

"Yes, sort of."

"Shouldn't I go tell him about Mrs. Dunaway? Or, should we wait?" I asked, not really wanting to give that news to him.

"Gram is with him. She's explaining everything that happened. Gram has a way of calming people and making them feel better just by talking to them after something tragic."

"But, how does she know what happened?" Jeremy asked.

"Homer told me everything he saw. I, of course, explained it all to my Gram, who had worried about me when I went into, well, sort of a trance for half an hour."

"Wicked," Jeremy mumbled.

"What else did Homer say?" I asked.

Melanie had made her way to the dining table with her salves and ointments. She pulled Ben over and made him sit in a chair. He obeyed quickly. Ben still had only half a t-shirt on. Melanie took a pair of scissors and cut the rest off, examining the wound on his shoulder.

"Mel? Are you going to tell us?"

"He said that you were smart, Gabe, in making us all gather in a secluded area like this one. He tried to reach you first, but immediately saw that you were 'indisposed' as he said when he tried to communicate with you. He was concerned that I might not be receptive, since we'd never formally met," she said, dabbing at the raised whelps on Ben's shoulder.

"Ow," he complained.

She didn't stop her prodding and thorough examination.

"He also said that we should get all our families here and that we should be safe through the night. The reapers shouldn't sense us out here."

"What do you mean?" asked Jeremy. "They can track us?"

"Not exactly," said Melanie, "they can track energy. They go wherever the strongest amount is first, which will of course be in town. Geez, Ben, what did this?"

"Reaper spit," he replied casually.

Melanie gave him that raised eyebrow look.

"It's true. Right, Gabe?"

"Yeah," I agreed, "it gives off an electric shock."

"It hurt like hell," said Ben, "it felt like needles sending shockwaves through me."

"I guess that explains these little pock marks," said Melanie, "did it go up your neck?"

"A little," said Ben. "But then I got really ticked off. It felt like it was going to strangle me."

"Yeah, Ben. What did you do to it? How did you kill it?" I asked.

He gave me that typical, blank-Ben expression then something dawned on him.

"I was just thinking about how I wanted to shock this thing like it was shocking me, so I grabbed it. I think I must've like zapped it with my own energy."

"No way," said Jeremy with that mischievous grin. "So Light Bulb becomes Lightning Bolt. That's pretty frickin' cool."

"Did Homer say anything else?" I asked Melanie.

"Yes, he said that he'll be in touch in the morning, unless he senses anything else we need to know."

"What about the reapers?" asked Ben, wincing at something Melanie was doing to his shoulder.

"I asked him that, too. Actually, I *thought* it, and he must've heard my thought then he told me that they don't attack during the day, because they essentially sleep while soaking up solar energy."

"Man, that was some telepathic phone call," said Jeremy.

This whole time, Zack had listened in silence. Until now.

"Excuse me," he interrupted, "but can anyone explain what you're all talking about? I feel like I just walked into the Twilight Zone."

"We'll have to explain later. There's not enough time now. Come on," I said to Jeremy, "we've got to go."

"Wait, I'm comin'," said Ben, trying to get up but Melanie shoved him back down.

"I'm not finished, Ben. Now, everybody just settle down for a minute."

Melanie's tone was snappy, but commanding. A hush fell over the room as we watched her work her power. She took three deep breaths, placing her hands on Ben's shoulder. Again, she whispered something under her breath, repeating some phrase I couldn't make out. Just as before, I saw a pale blue light burn brightly from her hands then dim as suddenly as it had come, that singing sound coming and going. When she opened her eyes, Ben had that goofy smile spread across his face. He rotated his arm back three times to test out his shoulder.

"Awesome," was all he said.

"What the—?"

Zack jumped up with wide eyes, knocking over his chair, scaring Hunter and Noah who had been wrapped up in their own little world on the hearth rug.

"Mel, we don't have time," I said, gesturing toward Zack.

She nodded. It was her turn to do the explaining.

"Give me just a minute, Gabe," said Jeremy, rummaging through drawers in the kitchen.

"I need one, too," I said, quickly leaving the room.

Clara hadn't moved. The low lamplight cast a soft glow on her pale face. Her hair was still pushed back, revealing the raised mark of the reaper's claw that had killed her mother. I sat next to her on the bed, wondering if that was why she wouldn't wake up. Perhaps, she knew that she would have to face the cold reality that she hadn't been able to save her. This brought on my own sense of urgency to get home, to get my mother and grandfather to safety. All the same, it felt almost painful to leave her like this. I tucked a lock of hair behind her ear and leaned close to her.

"Wake up, soon, Clara. We need you," I whispered, brushing a swift kiss on her forehead, "I need you."

When I passed back through the living area, Melanie was sitting in a chair watching the two boys on the rug. Before I made for the door, I stepped close so that only she could hear me.

"Mel. Keep your mind open. If they come here, your only warning may be from Homer. If I know him, he's doing his best to watch over us."

"Don't worry about us. You be careful."

I found Ben, Jeremy, and Zack on the back deck, waiting for me. Ben was shaking his head at Jeremy, while pulling on a blue Aéropostale shirt that Zack had just handed him.

"What is it?" I asked.

"He's raided your Pop's entire collection of knives from the kitchen," said Ben. "Can you believe that?"

Jeremy looked at me and shrugged.

"I was able to channel my power through objects today. I thought these might come in handy," he said, looping the strap of a canvas tackle bag over his shoulder.

"Good idea," I said.

"What? Are you kidding me?" Ben asked in disbelief. "What if he accidentally kills us instead?"

"You didn't see him in the last fight," I said in Jeremy's defense.

I could feel Jeremy grin, more than see it in the dark. When we stepped off the porch, Zack started to follow us.

"Wait, wait a minute," I said, putting my hand up to stop him. "Where are you going?"

"With you guys, of course."

"Zack, I need you to stay here and protect the others."

I could see the look of pain in his eyes, but there was no way he was coming.

"Well, what do I do if they come? Jeremy's taken all the weapons."

Jeremy rolled his eyes, putting a protective hand on his bag of arms.

"Don't try to fight them. Get everybody in the car and get as far away as you can. As a matter of fact, if you have to go, drive out to Canebrake Island. Homer lives there and he'll know what to do."

Zack nodded, but seemed more unsettled now that we were leaving without him.

"Don't worry," I said, stepping off the deck with Ben and Jeremy behind me, "Homer said it would be safe here."

We walked toward the path and Jeremy tossed the Durango's keys to me. Guess he knew I was a bit of a control freak about driving. I'd thought Zack had already gone back inside, but then I heard him ask a question that we had no time to answer.

"Who's Homer?"

✷16✷

GABE

There was no moon to light up the darkness. There was no light at all, except for the beams of the Durango straight ahead of us. Cruising down Main Street felt like driving through a ghost town—no lights, no people, no sound, nothing. There wouldn't be anyone here during a hurricane anyway, but this felt more desolate than when other storms had hit. We were headed to Ben's house first, since it was on the way to mine, and this was the quickest route.

"Weird," said Jeremy.

"Yeah, it feels like the whole town is deserted," said Ben.

"No, I was thinking it felt like déjà vu, like I've seen this before. Wait!" I slowed the SUV, but didn't stop.

"What? What is it?"

"Over there, Gabe. Pull in."

Jeremy was pointing to the gazebo at the center of the plaza.

"Look, I know it sounds crazy, but I saw this in one of my dreams. I saw a family killed here, and look, there's someone hiding there."

"Where?"

"In the gazebo!"

I'd never heard Jeremy so agitated. I was almost past the plaza then turned sharply into the long empty parking lot. He was right. As my headlights swiveled across the gazebo, I saw someone's head duck quickly below the railing. It definitely wasn't a reaper or shadow scout; it was a person who was terrified. I parked right up next to the gazebo.

"Hello," said Jeremy, hopping out before I'd turned off the engine. "You can come out. It's okay."

Ben and I were right behind him. Someone slid up cautiously from a corner. I couldn't believe who it was.

"Mrs. Jaden?" said Ben.

"Mrs. Jaden, are you okay?" I asked, stepping speedily up the gazebo steps.

She looked nearly hysterical. There was a wildness in her eyes that made my heart pick up speed.

"Get down, boys. Get down," she urged us in a hushed voice.

Instinctively, we did so, half-kneeling inside the enclosure. We'd always done what Mrs. Jaden told us. She'd been our English teacher for years. But this wasn't our friendly, whimsical English teacher. This was a frantic, frightened woman. As soon as I knelt down, I saw a little girl crouched in the corner. I knew that Mrs. Jaden had a daughter from the pictures on her desk at school and the stories she told in class.

"What happened?" I asked.

"It's my husband," she said breathlessly, "he left the house an hour ago to get some things at the store."

She glanced over the railing across the street. I remembered that Mr. Jaden owned and managed Beau Chêne's only book store, Books on Bayou Rouge.

"Our electricity had gone out, so I was lighting candles around the house when I heard my neighbor screaming. I ran to the back door, which looks out over her yard, thinking a tree fell on her house or something, but what I saw, what I saw was so horrible."

Mrs. Jaden broke off, shaking her head and remembering what I knew must have been a reaper killing her neighbor. She wiped her eyes with her sleeve, obviously trying not to break down entirely.

"We know, Mrs. Jaden. We've seen them, too. Why are you waiting out here for your husband?"

She shook her head again, glancing across the street.

"After I saw my neighbor with that thing, I grabbed Michelle and rushed over here to get Joseph. While I was walking across the plaza, I saw two shadows that looked like tall men just vanish right through the door to our store. They didn't open it. They just walked through it."

She said it as if she was trying to convince us she wasn't lying or delusional. Sadly, she didn't realize how well we knew what she was talking about.

"They're not even bothering to camouflage," said Ben beside me.

"Yeah, we know what they are," Jeremy said to Mrs. Jaden, "they're scouts that help the other ones, the bigger ones."

It was interesting to hear Jeremy dance around the harsh truth with Mrs. Jaden. He didn't use terms like dark giants, reapers, or killing monsters, which might've thrown her over the edge.

"We'll go get him," I said. "You and Michelle wait here."

"No, boys. It's too dangerous," she said, grabbing my arm to stop me, "I should go. If you'll watch Michelle, I'll—"

"Look, Mrs. Jaden," interrupted Jeremy, "there's no way in hell we're gonna let you stroll in there just cause you're our teacher and you're an authority figure. Those rules don't apply to this. Just trust us. We'll take care of it."

Michelle stared out from behind her mother with round, brown eyes.

"How long ago was it that you saw them?" I asked.

"Just before you pulled up."

"Let's go," I said.

We stepped out of the gazebo, walking speedily across the parking lot. I heard her faint whisper behind us as we moved farther away.

"Be careful."

It sounded less like a human and more like the wind, which had died down from what it was earlier. Now, the wind blew softly, making a hollow whistle along the empty street. When we made it to the entryway of the bookstore, Jeremy was on the verge of yanking the door open when I grabbed his arm. I'd been to this bookstore a thousand times and knew what noise would warn the shadow scouts that we were here. I pointed upward where a bell dangled above the entrance. Jeremy gave a quick nod—then retrieved a sharpened knife from his canvas bag. With a swift cut, the bell came down, and he tucked it in his pocket.

I eased the door open then the three of us slid inside. All was dark, and there was no sound of anyone or anything. I gestured for them to follow me along the wall of Fiction that trailed up to the register. We pressed ourselves against the bookcase, moving slowly and quietly. Then I felt the shadow scouts; their eerie presence prickled the hairs on the back of my neck. Looking in every direction across the aisles of books, I didn't see them. I turned to Jeremy and Ben, mouthing the words, 'do you see them?'

All three of us swiveled our heads in opposite directions, trying to find any sign of them. My eyes were starting to adjust to the lack of light in this enclosed space, but I still had to feel my way along the wall of books behind me. Jeremy stepped one row over through a cross aisle, moving alone parallel to us. We were almost to the front where the rows stopped and wire racks of bookmarks and decorative journals stood. Then I heard a noise, a shuffling sound. Somewhere behind the register, I saw the thin beam of a flashlight cross the ceiling then return to a desktop. Peering closer, I saw it was Mr. Jaden, juggling the flashlight while pulling papers from a cabinet and stuffing them in a briefcase. He was completely unaware of our presence or the shadow scouts. Just as I stepped forward to call out his name, two black figures leapt onto him from both sides.

Mr. Jaden gasped.

"It's them!" I yelled.

In a split second, the pressure built in my chest then flowed out of my body through my outstretched hand toward the shadow scout on the right. Two pairs of yellow eyes turned on me, gleaming in the dark. One pair went out. I heard a sharp hiss and then shriek of pain from Mr. Jaden. I couldn't tell what damage I'd done, but I knew the other shadow scout had instantly cloaked himself.

"Jeremy," I called.

"I know."

He was right beside me, beginning to sing an old song I knew all too well—*Enter Sandman* by Metallica. If I didn't know him better and what he was doing, I would've thought he'd lost his mind. I stopped trying to figure Jeremy out a long time ago. The familiar melody and lyrics grew louder and louder as did a steady, building vibration coming from him.

"Tuck you in, warm within, keep you free from sin, till the sandman he comes. Sleep with one eye open, gripping your pillow tight—exit light, enter night, take my hand, off to never-never land."

I jumped suddenly when a light appeared on my left, but it was Ben. His skin was beginning to glow white as he absorbed the energy from the hidden shadow scout. Jeremy continued to sing as we all moved closer to the counter.

"Ben, get Mr. Jaden."

"What do you want! Get back!" Mr. Jaden yelled from behind a cabinet, holding one hand to his bleeding forehead and lifting the flashlight over his head as if he was ready to strike.

"No, wait, Mr. Jaden," said Ben, "We came to help you. Your wife and daughter are outside."

"No, Ben! It can hear you," I said.

There was a whooshing sound passing me and running for the door.

"Come on, Jeremy. Now!"

"Off to never-never land!" he screamed.

An electric splintering sound vibrated near the door, revealing the scout who was silhouetted by the grayish light outside. I pushed out forcefully, blowing the shadow scout the last few feet to the exit, sending him crashing into and shattering the glass door.

"Come on, Mr. Jaden," I heard Ben trying to coax him to go with us. "We'll explain."

Someone outside screamed. It was Mrs. Jaden.

"Sarah!" yelled Mr. Jaden, dashing past us and out the door.

We ran after him, leaping over what was left of the shadow scout. Mr. Jaden was fast, but Ben was faster.

"Get him out of the way!" I yelled.

I didn't even need to. Ben was already thinking like me. Mrs. Jaden was running toward us, crossing the parking lot with her daughter in her arms. Behind her stalked a fearsome reaper. He moved in long determined strides, but seemed in no hurry at all. It was like a snake with a mouse in a hole. He knew he would get his prey eventually. The creature hadn't even taken notice of us as it came steadily on. Or, if it did, it was completely unmoved, thinking us more food for him.

"Jeremy, break his shield. Now!"

There was no time for his serenade. He knew it. Ben tackled Mr. Jaden down to the ground in the middle of the street.

"Get down, Mrs. Jaden . . . on the ground!"

I passed Ben, who was struggling to keep Mr. Jaden on the ground. He was fighting like mad to get to his wife. I couldn't blame him, but there was no time to explain that he would only get in the way. Jeremy was running alongside me.

"Now, Mrs. Jaden! On the ground!"

She dropped to the pavement, cradling Michelle underneath her. Jeremy let out a short, staccato yell at the same time he released a sharp object from his hand. It glinted in the air on the way to its target. A meat cleaver embedded into the invisible shield a few inches from the reaper. Green sparks of electricity spattered outward where the cleaver hit, then it fell to the concrete. The reaper stopped instantly, finally realizing what we were—Setti.

I immediately threw out a sphere of energy, shooting it across the parking lot. With a wave of its sword-like arms, the reaper rebuilt its shield. My energy crackled around its massive frame into nothing, not even touching the beast.

Jeremy and I both stopped, sizing up our opponent. It gave us a wide grin, showing us that viscous black fluid lining its mouth that glittered with electricity. I felt a jolt of anxiety from Ben behind us. The thing whipped its cloak back over its shoulder, exposing its muscular body in an attempt to prove it was mightier. Even in the dark, I could see the electric current rolling under its greenish-black skin, giving it morbid vitality. Its gleaming eyes shifted from Ben to Jeremy to me. I knew what it was trying to determine, whether one of us was a Guardian.

"This time," I said in a low voice, "we're going to do this simultaneously and you're going to have to give it all you've got."

"No problem."

Without warning, the creature jolted into a sprint closing the distance between us. Jeremy let out a long, barbaric yell, while I pushed out an unending stream of power. I could feel his sound waves vibrating through me. As the creature bounded toward us, a shower of green sparks flew into the air, bouncing off of its shield. It was stronger than the other ones. My thoughts went back to Clara and the last reaper I'd seen. Fueled by a new rage, both my arms went up, pushing out my power with brutal force. The reaper was a few yards from us, a wicked glint in its glowing eyes. Its shield finally gave way, splintering then cracking under the pressure. I continued my attack, pushing even harder than before. The creature wielded its sharpened black arms perpendicular to its body, preparing to stab us both through at the same time. Unyielding, Jeremy and I refused to back down. The reaper was nearly within arm's reach, growling as it came. I took one quick breath, yelling as I loosed a final blow out through my chest. Upon impact, the reaper's skin crackled then exploded into black fragments and dust. A cloud of odorous ash swept over and past us with the momentum of the creature's stride.

It took a second to realize we'd done it. The adrenaline finally slowed. Jeremy and I were both panting from the exertion. I looked at Jeremy whose face was covered in sooty ash. He was smiling at me, all white teeth in a gray-powdered face.

"Well, Gabe. It's a dirty job, but someone's gotta do it."

He chuckled at his own joke.

"Jeremy. That's a bit lame, even for you, man."

I laughed anyway. I could always count on Jeremy to lighten the mood, no matter how utterly dark it was. I brushed some of the ash out of my hair, turning to see Mr. and Mrs. Jaden hugging one another with their daughter in between them. Ben was beaming more brightly than I had ever seen him.

"Hey, look at this," said Jeremy, "we've got our own lighthouse to lead the way."

"Mr. Jaden," I called back to the others. "The three of you need to go to my Pop's camp. Right now, I think it's the only out-of-the-way place that's safe. There are others hiding there. It's three miles south of Badger Bridge on Old Spanish Trail Road. The turn is kind of hidden. It's a gravel road on the right-hand side."

"I just can't believe what I just saw. What were those things?" he asked.

I didn't know how to answer that question.

"I guess you could think of them as the new terrorists," said Jeremy.

"What did you do to it? *How* did you do it?" asked Mrs. Jaden.

My teacher had the most peculiar look on her face, a mix of confusion and amazement.

"I don't know how to explain it, Mrs. Jaden. But, I think it's safe to say that maybe some of those ancient tales you used to teach us about magic might have been true. I wish I could tell you more, but we truly have to get going."

"Mr. Jaden," interrupted Jeremy as we started back to our cars, "what did you come out here for anyway? What did you need from the store at this time of night?"

He lifted Michelle into his arms, who laid her head on his shoulder.

"I was coming to get our insurance policies, thinking we'd certainly get storm damage. I know that it's first come, first serve, so I wanted to be ready to call them if I needed to."

There was an awkward silence. Leave it to Jeremy to break it.

"Well, Mr. Jaden, I don't think you'll need that policy or that number anymore," he said lightly.

It was slowly dawning on all of us that the world would be irrevocably changed from what we had always known. As the reapers spread across the state, the country, the world, our entire way of life would change. Insurance companies becoming obsolete would be the least of it.

"Look on the bright side," said Jeremy, grinning.

"What's that?" asked Mr. Jaden.

"You won't have to wait on hold for an hour listening to crappy elevator music."

"We've got to get moving," I said to Ben and Jeremy more urgently. "Like I said, Mr. Jaden, it's about three miles past Badger Bridge. Look for the gravel road on the bayou side."

"We'll find it," he said, shifting Michelle to his other side, and extending his hand for me to shake. "Thank you for, for helping us."

"Just get to my Pop's camp quickly and safely."

We all shook his hand, which seemed strangely out of place but I suppose the most appropriate thing at the time, then marched back to the Durango and headed away from town.

※ ※ ※

Ben still held the note in his hand telling him that his parents had gone to his grandmother's since she had the generator.

"Don't worry. Your grandmother lives right down the street from my house. As soon as we grab my parents, we'll get yours."

He remained silent, still emitting that white glow from his skin. The streets were deserted, but that was to be expected. Wind bands were coming and going, like the storm was breaking apart and spreading in different directions. My house was only one of three on the street. It was old land, passed down through generations. Pop had built this house set on a plot of ten acres when he was first married. It was always nice living out here in peace and quiet, but now it only made me feel more anxious, more isolated. The trees seemed to close in on us. As we pulled up my long drive, I heard a noise, a loud motor.

"What's that?" asked Jeremy.

I looked at Ben and we said it at the same time.

"A generator."

"That should be good news, right?"

"We'll see. Ben, you hang back just a little on the porch."

"Why?"

"If everything is okay, then I'll need a minute to prepare them for your, uh, condition."

"Oh, right," he said, looking at his glowing arms.

Jerking the car into park, I ran up the steps with Jeremy behind me, busting through the door. I had prepared myself for all kinds of horrors, but I'd never imagined what was actually waiting there.

Pop was sipping iced tea and cutting into a steak at the dining room table. There was a Scrabble board, half-finished, spread out on one end with two lamps and a fan blowing. All the wires were plugged into an extension cord that disappeared into the kitchen. I knew Mom had it trailing to the generator on the back porch. Pop looked up, unsurprised, stuffing a piece of steak into his mouth.

"Hey, boys. Come pull up a chair and get some dinner."

Then my mom shuffled into the room, holding a second fan on a long stand.

"There you are, Gabriel. I've been worried sick about you. Where have you been all day? And, what in God's name have you got all over you?"

"Mom," I said calmly, not stopping to explain that I was covered in reaper ash, "we've got to leave."

"No we don't, baby. The evacuation isn't mandatory. That's what they said on the radio before the power went out, and that's what I'm going by. Get that worried look off your face. We'll be just fine. I've got a couple of fans. We'll have to make beds in here so we won't sweat to death, but I—"

"No, Mom, you don't understand," I said gravely, crossing the room, "we all have to leave. Now."

"Why, Gabriel? I've got all that meat from the freezer, so we've got plenty of food. That is if the ice holds out in the ice chest. Of course, your Pop had to have the steak tonight and—"

I grabbed hold of my Mom's shoulders, gently but firmly, and looked at her directly in the eyes. Her brow pinched in the middle the way it did when she was worried about something.

"Mom. Listen to me very carefully. We are leaving right now. I know it sounds crazy, but this storm has brought something terrible to Beau Chêne. People are dying. We're going to Pop's cabin where it's safe. Others are there waiting for us."

"I don't understand," she said, shaking her hand. "People are dying? From what?"

"They're, they're," I stammered, knowing full well how absurd it would sound coming out of my mouth, "monsters. They're killing people."

"It's true," said Ben, coming in behind me, glowing like a damn candle.

"Oh, my word, Benjamin," she exclaimed, "what in the world has happened to you? Did you fall into some sort of chemical spill?"

He had dimmed somewhat on the way over, but he still had a bizarre, ghostly look to him.

"No, Ms. Nancy. That's another story that we can tell you along the way. But, Gabe's telling the truth. We need to leave."

My mom stared skeptically at all three of us. She hadn't even bothered to ask who the new kid was beside me. Jeremy just waited silently. I hadn't noticed that Pop had disappeared and was now reentering the room, holding a 12-gauge shotgun.

"Alright then. Let's go."

"Daddy, what do you think you are you doing with that thing?"

"Nancy, I've known this boy all my life. He doesn't lie and he doesn't make up stories. If he says we're safer out there, then we're safer out there. Get your purse and let's go. I've got all I need."

She looked back into my eyes, considering what to do, weighing everything as she always did.

"Trust me, Mom."

Finally, she sighed heavily.

"Fine. But one of you boys needs to get the ice chest in the kitchen. I've got a month's worth of frozen meat in there and I'm not going to let it spoil."

It took close to ten minutes, but we eventually got Mom and Pop in the Durango along with an ice chest, a gas grill, two fold-out cots, and a pile of sleeping bags and blankets.

"And, whose Durango is this, Gabriel?" she asked in an accusing, motherly way.

"We had to borrow it from Jessie," interjected Ben, thankfully.

"Why?"

"Mom, we just did. It's too much to explain right now."

"Well, you've got a whole lot of explaining to do when we get there."

In three minutes, we were pulling up to Ben's grandmother's house. The white shell driveway crunched under the tires. Pop was already dozing in the backseat. Jeremy and I followed Ben up to the front door.

"Well, this should be interesting," said Ben.

Their generator rumbled loudly on the backside of the house. Faint lights came from the two windows in the front room. It seemed like all was well. No reapers.

"Sounds like everything is okay here, too," I told Ben whose anxiety was pouring over me like a tidal wave.

"Yeah, except my parents don't believe me as easily as your family believes you," he said. "You know what? Why don't y'all wait right here. They hate surprises, and they're only expecting me. It'll be easier if I do this alone."

"Okay, we'll wait here," I said, gesturing to a garden bench on the side of the walkway up to the front door. "But, we need to hurry. We've got to go to Jeremy's house, too."

He nodded and went in to face the firing squad. I glanced at Jeremy when we sat down, wondering why he hadn't seemed in any kind of a hurry to get home to his parents. He had plugged his earphones in and was tapping his knee to the rhythm of whatever was playing. I pulled out his right earphone.

"Did you ever get a call from your parents before the cell towers went out?"

"Nope."

"Do you think it's going to be hard to get them to come with us?"

He pulled the other earphone out and stretched out his legs, crossing his ankles.

"I don't know what they'll do."

"What do you mean? What are they like?"

Jeremy had always spoken so cynically about his parents, but I wondered how he really felt about them. Was he just playing the bad boy or did he truly not care about them?

"What are they like? Well, my mom's a heavy smoker, snuffing out at least two packs a day. She plays bingo down at Veteran's Hall three nights a week. She hates cooking, so I pretty much live off of Ramen noodles and Easy Mac. And, I've heard her say more than once that she was glad she only had one kid. My dad works at Bayou Pipe from 6 a.m. to 6 p.m. When he gets home, he falls into his recliner with whatever fast food he picked up on the way home and basically ignores the world around him while he watches Spike TV. And, as far as they're concerned, I'm pretty much invisible."

That was way more than I was prepared for. I knew my expression must've shown a bit of shock. Jeremy sort of laughed.

"Don't worry, man. It really doesn't bother me. Not anymore. I practically raised myself, and if I do say so, I did a damn fine job."

I tried to smile back.

"Do you think they'll come with us?"

"Quite frankly, I'd be surprised if they're even there. They left for that hurricane last year to my aunt's in Baton Rouge without telling me. I came home kind of late and found a note with bottles of water, cans of tuna fish, and a variety pack of chips."

There was a building anger rippling out from him. I had no idea that his home life was that bad. It made me feel a little guilty for having people who cared about me so much, when he really had no one. Well, now he had us—his clan.

"Do you even want to go by there?"

Jeremy cut his eyes at me. There was deep sadness there.

"Yeah," he said, almost reluctantly, "I need to go, just in case they stayed."

He knew as well as I did that it would be a death sentence to leave them unprotected. After all their neglect of him, Jeremy still had a heart to protect them. He always seemed to be surprising me.

Ben came out the front door with his tiny, white-haired Grandma on his arm and two bickering people behind him. All four of them were talking at once.

"This is just ridiculous, Ben. I don't know what you're talking about," said his blonde-haired mother.

"Son, this is all uncalled for. You can't take Grandma to a cabin in the woods," said his sandy-haired father.

"Wow," said Jeremy next to me, "a whole family of Light Bulbs."

"I believe you, Benjamin," said his Grandma, looking up adoringly at her grandson and patting his arm.

"Dad, you're just going to have to trust me. Now, Gabe's mom and grandfather are waiting on us."

"Gabriel," said Ben's mom, "would you please tell him he's being ridiculous? You're just being ridiculous, Ben."

They followed Ben all the way down the walkway, griping the entire time, but still following him as he hobbled slowly so Grandma could keep up. I have to say, it did look a bit ridiculous, just like his mom said. What was surprising was that Ben's parents were still trailing behind their son without a full explanation why they had to leave. Actually, knowing Ben's easy nature to follow others, it shouldn't have surprised me at all. Apparently, the apple didn't fall far from the tree.

"Hey, Mr. LeBlanc?" I called behind them.

"Yes, Gabriel?"

"Would you mind if I borrowed a car? I'd like y'all to caravan straight to the cabin, but Jeremy and I need to get to his parent's house."

"Well, we'll go swing by there with you," he said, nodding hello to Jeremy.

"No, sir. I think it's best that all of you get off the road as soon as possible. We won't be long."

"Okay, then," said Mr. LeBlanc, pulling a pair of keys from his pocket. "We'll take Grandma's car. Angela! We're taking your mother's car."

She was still complaining to Ben and Grandma who shuffled toward the Chrysler instead of the Honda minivan. I gave instructions to my mother to drive straight to the camp without stopping and that we'd be there shortly. I also warned her to expect quite a few house guests. Her only response was that she'd at least have someone to feed all the meat that was going to spoil.

"Ben," I said, as he put his Grandma in the front seat of the Chrysler, "I think you need to drive them there."

"They can find it on their own, Gabe. I'll go with you two."

"No," I said. "They may encounter some of the scouts or reapers. If they do, they'll probably panic, not having seen them or know what they are. And, you'll be able to weaken them enough that you can all get away."

"You think so?"

"Of course," I said confidently, knowing that Ben needed it. "Besides, I think I've figured out that the reapers are going for easy prey. I think they know there's enough people out there for easy taking that they won't fight that hard to get people in fleeing vehicles. Still, I'd feel better knowing you were with them and will get them all to the cabin in one piece."

"Don't worry, Gabe. I'll take care of them," he said with his big Ben smile.

"Let's go," I told Jeremy.

We jumped in the minivan and backed out of the drive. I waited until the other two vehicles were safely ahead of us, then I turned back toward Beau Chêne, back to where the shadow scouts lurked and the reapers searched.

"Well, Gabe," said Jeremy, "this is different."

I glanced at him in the passenger seat of the minivan, wondering how in the hell we'd ended up in this situation. Just the two of us, heading back into a den of demons in the most laughable ride imaginable, without our Guardian—Clara. I was suddenly in a great hurry to get this over with and get back to the camp, gunning that little minivan straight toward town.

✶17✶

GABE

Jeremy's neighborhood was spooky quiet. No noisy generators broke the silent night. Creeping into the back door with a flashlight, Jeremy found a note on the counter, just as he'd predicted. He scanned it, then balled up the paper and tossed it on the kitchen floor.

"Yep. Gone to Aunt Lydia's in Baton Rouge."

I could feel that same bitterness as I did earlier coming from him.

"Sorry, man," I said, standing halfway in the doorway, "but we better go."

"Yeah, just give me a minute to get some things."

He disappeared with his flashlight to the back of the house. I couldn't help but glance toward his father's worn recliner in the den after what Jeremy had told me about him earlier. Even in the dark, I could tell this was a depressing environment to grow up in. Jeremy tromped back up the hall with a backpack over one shoulder.

"Let's hit it."

"I was thinking it might be better if we go straight out to Sugar Mill Road from here then skirt around town to Old Spanish Trail," I said, jumping back into the driver's seat of the minivan.

"Yeah, it's probably faster," he agreed.

There were so many houses packed tightly in this neighborhood, but there wasn't a soul in sight. Jeremy didn't have any jokes to tell anymore. We were both too busy watching every shadow, and I think his thoughts were troubled by his missing family. Whether it was because they'd abandoned him again or because he knew there was a likely chance that he'd never see them again, I wasn't sure. I pulled out onto Sugar Mill Road without bothering to stop at the sign. There was no need. When we neared the intersection where the sugar mill was, I actually started to feel the first moment of relief that I'd had all night knowing we were getting close to Pop's camp.

As we rolled up to the intersection, a heavy dark energy hit me like I'd been punched in the gut. Then I heard the noises, the screams.

"Holy hell," said Jeremy, staring past me at the sugar mill.

It took me a second to register what I was looking at. It's like my brain was trying to explain it to me in slow motion. I knew that the tractors stopped hauling cane during hurricane warnings, but I'd forgotten that the mill didn't stop running. Not for anything. They had massive power generators. Just like the local hospitals, they powered themselves up and kept right on working. Apparently, the shadow scouts and reapers figured this out.

I couldn't even count how many shadow scouts were swarming in and out of view from the warehouse-style building to about a dozen reapers outside, waiting. I watched in horror, the same way you would watch a car wreck, completely unable to remove your eyes from the scene. Though it was hard to see them in the dark, I could make out the outline of shadow scouts hauling workers from the building one by one, taking them to whatever reaper wasn't already draining the life from a man. As each reaper plunged its arm into the chest of someone, I could actually see the greenish glow of the stolen energy light up the reaper's skin, just for an instant. The dreadful screams of the men echoed into the night. All the while, ghostly ash-eaters shrieked in agony, skirting the perimeter and waiting their turn.

"Go, man. Go!" yelled Jeremy.

Then I saw what he saw, a shadow scout watching us. He was far away, but I could swear he had a long greenish gash along his head. Right before I pressed the accelerator, I saw him get the attention of a reaper and point in our direction.

I slammed on the pedal, spinning out onto Old Spanish Trail. Power was welling up in my chest, but there was no way Jeremy and I could take on that many reapers alone. I was confident, but I wasn't stupid. We'd gone about a mile. Jeremy was staring out behind us, while I kept checking the rearview mirror.

"You think they'll come after us?" he asked, pulling his canvas bag of Pop's kitchen knives up into his lap.

"No. Why would they? They've got plenty to feed on without chasing us—"

Then, boom. An impact like a freight train hit the driver's side, rolling the minivan off the road. All I could hear was the crunch of metal and breaking glass, watching the world spin in front of me. The minivan flipped all the way over twice, showering glass down on us then rested on the passenger side. I was suddenly thankful that I'd always worn my seatbelt and that Honda built sturdy cars. Knowing I wasn't exactly a safe driver, it was bound to happen eventually. Of course, I realized this wasn't just a traffic accident. I unbelted and kicked out the front windshield which was only partially intact. Scrambling out and facing the direction of where I felt the reapers coming near the road, I pushed out my power. It rolled over the shields of two reapers and the shadow scout, glistening an electric green as it was deflected. Jeremy was quickly beside me, pulling knives from his canvas bag and throwing them one after the other as the reapers advanced, yelling out his sound vibrations at the same time. The smaller reaper was only 8 feet tall, as opposed to his partner who was quite a few feet more, and had taken flight, advancing on us much faster. It swooped down toward Jeremy, who spun around and sent a butcher knife and two skinning knives flying overhead. All three hit directly into the reapers' invisible shield before it cracked. I was a little erratic, sending out my power in bursts, some overhead, some behind us as we kept running. I felt the air above me move and automatically rolled to the ground. The airborne reaper descended, his killing arms thrust toward me, hissing as he came. Instantly, my power reacted, shooting from my chest and out through my fingertips. A second later, the beast screeched in agony as its left arm and shoulder exploded into dust. The creature fell bodily to my side.

"Come on!" yelled Jeremy.

No need for encouragement, I was off, sprinting as before, while the creature writhed on the ground. We were several paces ahead, but not slowing down when Jeremy pulled something from his sack of metal toys.

"Use this!"

I glanced down at the ax in my hand, recognizing it briefly as my Pop's for wood kindling, then did what I thought Jeremy was suggesting. I turned around to see the wounded reaper sprinting at us with a fierce gleam of hatred in its serpentine eyes. Pulling all of my energy up into my chest, I hauled back the ax then channeled the power straight down my right arm as I released it. The ax did four revolutions then hit dead center of the reaper's abdomen, exploding the beast into powdery soot in a blink. The other reaper and shadow scout were moving leisurely toward us as if deciding whether we were worth the effort.

"Come on," I told Jeremy, pulling his sleeve and running.

We were on Old Spanish Trail which paralleled Bayou Rouge, snaking its way farther south toward Pop's cabin. I knew that nearly every house on the bayou had a boat. That was sort of the status quo. Of course, Pop just had a little pirogue that had probably rotted from lack of use. I was hoping that one of these more expensive houses which lined this part of

Bayou Rouge would have something a little bigger, and faster. I could see a plantation-style mansion looming up out of the gloom ahead of us. I glanced back over my shoulder, but couldn't see them following.

"Where are we going? We could've taken them," Jeremy was arguing.

"I'm not so sure," I said, using the adrenaline to keep my legs moving.

It was strange. I hadn't been afraid the first and definitely not the second time I fought these creatures, but there was something gnawing at my gut this time. I didn't know if it was the scene of the swarming shadow scouts and reapers at the mill or if it was the way that shadow scout had pointed us out and followed us.

"Keep running," I said.

We passed the open garage where a Lincoln Navigator and Mercedes Benz still sat. I didn't even think about the possibility of anyone being alive inside. There was no sound of a generator motor, and this house would definitely have one running if anyone was home. We jumped the wicker furniture on the stone patio, jogging down the sloped lawn toward a short pier. There was a long flat barge and a small speed boat tied to the dock.

"Should we take the party barge?" asked Jeremy sarcastically.

"Not even remotely funny. Come on."

We jumped into the speed boat, then I started untying the ropes.

"See if you can find a key," I called back.

"What would make you think these people would leave a key in their boat?" asked Jeremy as he ducked under the steering wheel.

He was right. I was acting irrationally now, just hoping we might catch a break and get lucky. Then I heard the motor sputter on, gurgling up water from the rudder.

"You found them?"

I was completely shocked.

"No. I had to go with a *keyless* ignition," said Jeremy, steering us carefully away from the dock.

Apparently, Jeremy had a few hidden talents, some of them borderline criminal, but helpful nonetheless. Now was no time to question where he had gotten such skills. I was just glad he had them.

"Nice job. Now just head down with the current and we'll be there soon enough."

"Aye, aye, captain."

He shoved us up another gear and picked up speed now that we were in the clear. There was still no moon, but a dim grayish light penetrated through the cloud cover above. The bayou water ahead looked like a flat sheet of black glass. I was almost in a state of calm after this last episode when a trigger set off my emotional sense. I turned in time to see a giant cloaked figure taking three long bounds on the embankment then flying through the air onto the boat in front of me. The reaper's hand severed instantaneously into seven fingers as he grappled for my throat. He had his electric hand splayed across my collar bone, pressing me down against the side of the boat for leverage. It all happened so quickly that only three seconds passed from the instant I saw him to now where he had me pinned with deadly force. The sting of electric shocks shooting from his hand threatened to paralyze me. A sudden anger spilled out of me and I pushed up against him, grasping his throat though my hand only spanned one fourth of it. His slits of yellow eyes peered down into mine as I pushed outward with my power. It wasn't working. His shield was up, preventing any of my energy from breaking through.

"What is this?" the reaper asked through a mouth slicked with black ooze. "A Vanquisher with no power? Perhaps, you're not even worth draining."

It lifted its other sword-like arm, readying to strike. I pushed out again, but it still had no effect. Then I heard Jeremy yell, sending out violent waves of sound. I saw him leap onto the creature's back, stabbing viciously into its neck area, cracking the shield with each jab. In the split second that the reaper released me to turn on Jeremy, I pooled all that was in me and threw the hardest undercut that I could. The moment my fist landed under his chin, I felt a crack as his head jerked back, then his body crackled and shattered as my power splintered through his body. It fell apart in chunks onto the floor of the boat. Its massive arms that had me pinned moments ago broke from the body like weak branches from a towering tree. I was panting, completely exhausted. Jeremy looked no better.

I searched the boat and the embankment thinking that the shadow scout might be nearby; then realized we were veering onto shore. I moved as quickly as possible which felt entirely too slow, grabbing and righting the wheel before we went aground. I winced in pain, trying to get a good look at my hand. I knew I'd broken several bones. Jeremy was still laying on his back, propped up on his elbows, looking at the pile of charred black pieces that was the reaper who almost killed us both a minute before. He stood up slowly, picked up what was once its head, then drop-kicked it overboard. We heard a hollow splash. Jeremy sat back down on the floor, still winded then looked over at me. I just nodded.

"My sentiments exactly."

✳ ✳ ✳

CLARA

I was staring at the ceiling, watching the way the lamp-light flickered in pretty patterns on the cypress wood. Misty was curled up beside me, purring softly as I stroked her. I had woken up earlier when Mrs. Jaden had come in and tucked her sleeping daughter in beside me. How strange. My English teacher and family had joined us out in our hide-away in the woods. She recounted what had happened with Gabe, Ben, and Jeremy. I was elated, thinking they'd all come back safely. Then she told me 'no,' they were still out there. Again, my heart fluttered when I heard several voices and footsteps enter about an hour later. Mel came in to check on me, examining me carefully, while giving me the news that Gabe and Jeremy were still gone.

Dad had come in once since then. He didn't say a word about Mom. He just held me close, saying, "Thank God, you're alright." I'd noticed how his eyes followed the length of the scar spanning the left side of my face from the top of the cheekbone to an inch above my mouth. He didn't say a word about that either, but there was a pained expression on his face. I had made Mel give me a mirror earlier so that I could see what was still stinging after two of her healing sessions. I knew how awful it looked.

It was past midnight now, and I could tell by the low voices through the closed door that only a few people were still awake. I glanced at the two cots beside my bed that had been set up for Zack's brother Noah and Jessie's brother Hunter. They slept soundly as if there was nothing at all wrong with the world. Their yellowish auras shined dimly in the room. I started to wonder why most children had yellow auras. Misty's purring had finally stopped, and she settled into sleep, making a low wheezing sound. The warm glow of the lantern played on the ceiling, giving me a distraction as I waited. I was thinking about how I used to lay outside on my back with my mom in the summertime, making shapes out of the puffy clouds above us. I remembered how she would agree that she saw whatever animal or object I imagined in the sky. That aching emptiness was sinking into me when I heard someone entering the cabin in the next room.

"She's awake," I heard Mel say.

It had to be Gabe. Adrenaline pumped quickly through my veins. My stomach lurched in a panic, but I didn't know why. Then I heard Mel's muffled voice again.

"What happened to your hand? Wait a minute."

There was silence then a funny, high-pitched noise then silence again. A minute later, the door to the room creaked open. It was Gabe. Oh, crap. That's a little scary. He had such a serious expression on his face, while his aura spun around him in intertwining ribbons of deep purple and blue. He walked to the edge of the bed, still not saying a word. I watched quietly as he paced just a little, enough to make me more nervous. His right hand was swollen all along the knuckles.

"What happened to your hand?"

He didn't answer me, just shook his head. Was he still ticked that I'd left Jessie's without them? He finally came and sat on the edge of the bed, not touching me at all.

"What possessed you to take off by yourself?" he asked, obviously trying to maintain his cool.

Yeah, he was still ticked, to put it mildly. I pulled myself up into a sitting position, not caring that I was wearing just my pink cami pajamas. Rules of indecency and proper etiquette for a southern lady were kind of irrelevant right now.

"I wanted to save my parents," I said.

"Clara. You could've killed yourself as well."

His voice had softened.

"So," I said bitterly, feeling a lump in my throat.

"So?" he said much louder. "Are you kidding me?"

I couldn't respond. My cheeks were flushed, and I could feel a burning in my eyes. The stormy look in Gabe's dark eyes made me tremble. He looked so angry. He stood up and paced again. Misty lifted her head, apparently annoyed.

"Is that helping?" I asked, knowing full well that being a smart-ass wasn't exactly a wise decision.

He turned on me then, sitting very close on the bed and grabbing me roughly by the shoulders. I was kind of scared all of a sudden. Misty had had enough and jumped off the bed.

"Damn it, Clara," he said gravely, "don't you understand what that did to me?"

"No," I said, trying to keep the fear from my eyes. He really was scaring me a little with his stern looks and hostility.

"Don't you even care?" he asked lower, gripping me tighter.

"I didn't do it to hurt you. I did it to save my parents, Gabe. But, I couldn't save them both anyway, could I? I watched my mom die right in front of me," I said in one breath.

All sarcasm had leaked away. Hot tears poured down my face. I was a sobbing mess. I was ashamed of what I'd done, of leaving them when I shouldn't, of being too weak to save my mother, of crying shamelessly about it now when it couldn't change a thing. It was the deepest, darkest grief I'd ever felt. I just wanted it to go away. Gabe loosened his grip and pulled me into his arms.

"I'm sorry, Clara. I should've listened to you, but I just was trying to do what was best for everyone."

There was a moment of silence where only my muffled sobs could be heard.

"He made me choose, Gabe," I said through the tears. "How could he have done that?"

He pulled away and gazed at me tenderly.

"The reaper made you choose between . . ."

"Yes. My parents," I finished for him.

That stern look crept back across his brow.

"They're cunning, Clara. The reaper knew exactly what to do to weaken you."

He was definitely right.

"I just can't believe she's gone," I said.

Gabe cradled my face with his hands, wiping the tears away.

"I'm sorry, Clara. I wish, I wish I would've listened and gone there with you, then it might've turned out differently."

I hadn't intended to make him feel guilty for something I failed to do. It wasn't fair. I was wrong, and I knew it.

"We can't live our lives with regret, Gabe," I said.

How ironic, since I'd been regretting being unable to save my mother ever since. Even now, that sickening feeling deep inside continued to weigh me down. I felt so hollow.

"You're right," he agreed.

My mind wandered back to that moment I watched my mother evaporate into ash. The pain of it was too much to bear. Then I thought of Jessie—my willful, vibrant cousin now a slave for these abominable creatures. That pain was even greater. At least I could imagine my mother free of this place, of this world where nightmares stalk the living. This was no longer a world she would've been able to endure. I could at least be thankful she was at peace.

"I'm glad your mom and Pop made it," I finally managed to squeak out; trying my best to find some way to escape the well of grief I was in.

"Thanks," he said, holding my hand and tracing the lines on my palm distractedly.

"I can hardly believe that last week, we were just sitting in class, thinking that everything was normal, just trying to figure out if these creatures were real or part of our crazy, overactive imaginations."

"That feels like ages ago," he agreed, looking up at me with sad brown eyes.

I don't think Gabe knew what else to say to comfort me. There was nothing he could say. The pain was too sharp, too new, like a fresh cut that continues to bleed no matter how many times you dab it clean. I had to close my mind off to it, to the loss of her, or else my heart would never recover.

"When he struck me," I said, noticing Gabe flinch, "I heard you saying my name before I fell unconscious. I didn't imagine that, did I?"

"No. That's exactly when I ran up."

A flash of anger passed over his eyes, but I didn't want him to be angry anymore. The dark feelings threatened to dig wounds too deeply that would leave us both scarred. I wanted everything to be normal, just for a little while. I wanted to forget the heartache that wouldn't go away and the agony of the unknown that lay ahead of us.

"So," I said, scooting closer, needing the comfort of being near him, "should the maiden reward her knight in shining armor with a kiss?"

I asked the question as playfully as I could, though tears were still damp on my face. To Gabe's credit, he played along.

"Well, Jeremy helped."

"Oh, should I give him a kiss, too?"

"The hell you will," he said, leaning into me.

I sank back onto the pillow, smiling, but he wiped that stupid look off my face pretty dang quick. This was the Gabe I'd been missing. The warmth of his lips on mine made me forget what had happened, where we were, and what was still left to do. I savored every second, knowing that an aching hole waited to swallow me up with despair if I let it. Gabe pulled apart and looked at me, tucking my hair away from my face. Defensively, I pulled my hair over my left cheek, trying to hide that hideous scar. Gabe grabbed my wrist gently and pulled my hand away. He tucked the hair back behind my ear.

"Don't even think for a second that this makes you any less beautiful," he said, trailing a finger along the outside of the scar.

Did he just call me 'beautiful'? Wow. That was a first from any boy, except my dad, but he doesn't count. Gabe was obviously happy with my reaction. I felt a flush of pink fill my cheeks, and I couldn't help but smile timidly.

"Good. Now I know another way to render you speechless—with compliments. Push over."

"Why?" I asked.

"Because I'm exhausted and I want to get some sleep. There's plenty of room. Michelle there barely takes up any space at all."

"Oh, no, Gabriel Goddard. You're not sleeping with me. My dad's in the next room, and he wouldn't allow this at all."

"Clara. That's not what I meant. First of all, I'm sleeping next to you, not sleeping with you, with you. I really don't think your dad is worried about any of that going on. I mean, come on," he said, gesturing to the three children lying asleep around us, "we've got chaperones."

Gabe was a gentleman. I knew that, but I eyed him carefully all the same, inching over very slowly into the middle of the bed. Michelle was all the way on the left.

"Hands will stay above the covers. I promise," he said, showing me both of his hands.

He shoved off his filthy shoes and pulled a blanket draped over the foot of the bed up over him. I lay back down, facing him, and smiling. He looked at me for what seemed like a really long time like he was trying to memorize my face. Then, he pecked me quickly on the lips and flipped over.

"Goodnight, Clara."

I couldn't help but stare at the back of him. His purplish aura was so distracting. It had started to slow down and stop spinning so crazily. Then I noticed what a mess he was. There was some kind of dirt all over him and, wait a second, right at the base of his neck above his t-shirt there was a reddened, raised mark.

"Gabe? You've got some kind of cut or burn right here," I said, touching the small whelp.

I felt him shiver as my fingers lingered and brushed his neck. He reached over and doused the light of the kerosene lamp.

"Stop that, Clara," he warned, "or I won't be able to keep my promise."

I didn't know what he meant for a second and then it dawned on me. Note to self, his neck is a sensitive spot. A small laugh escaped me as I tucked my hands under my pillow.

"Yeah," he whispered groggily, "very funny."

✷ ✷ ✷

I woke up to the smell of bacon frying. My stomach rumbled expectantly. I couldn't even remember the last time I ate, and I was starving. I was alone in the bedroom, but I could hear the romping laughter of kids in the next room. As I shuffled the covers off, I noticed my gym bag on the side of the bed with a few pairs of jeans and some of my other clothes stuffed inside. I slipped on a pair of jeans and changed into a soft cotton t-shirt that had swirling patterns of green vines all around it.

The back door was open, leading out toward the bayou. I could see my dad, Mr. and Mrs. Jaden, and Ben's dad all talking quite seriously, while drinking coffee at the picnic table. There were sleeping bags piled all over the floor, which made me realize how lucky I was to have one of the few beds in the cabin last night. Gabe's mom and Melanie's grandmother were shuffling around the kitchen making breakfast. Gabe, his Pop, and Ben were at the table eating heartily. Gabe looked cleaned up since last night.

"Good morning," he said, taking a bite of a buttered biscuit.

There was a basket of biscuits, a plate of fried bacon and fried ham spread out on the counter.

"You hungry, Sweetheart?" asked Ms. Goddard. "We've got plenty. Of course, we didn't bring any eggs, and all we've got is water to drink. I didn't have time to empty all of the fridge, because someone was in such a hurry to get going," she said, swatting Gabe on the shoulder as she set a bottle of syrup on the table.

"It's good enough for me," said Pop, pouring syrup all over two biscuits stuffed with slices of ham.

"Wow," was all I could say, then something dawned on me. "Wait a second. How did you cook all this without electricity? I don't hear a generator."

"No, we didn't have time to bring that either," said Ms. Goddard. "Come to find out, we've got our own."

I knew I looked puzzled.

"It's Ben," said Gabe, pointing to the blonde-haired mess next to him.

"What do you mean?" I asked, completely confused.

"Well, we were talking this morning about how he burned that black slime that the reaper spat on him yesterday and killed it. Ben said he shocked it to death. Then, I wondered if he could shoot electricity into something else, so we tried it."

"Yeah," said Ben, still chewing, "so I held the plug to the toaster and zapped it and it worked just like it was plugged in the wall. Cool, huh?"

"That's when Ben suggested trying it on the oven so that my mom could get some breakfast going. Of course, he had to zap it five separate times to keep it hot enough to bake biscuits."

"But wasn't it worth it, son," said Pop, biting into a soppy biscuit.

"Mm-hmm," agreed Ben, chewing happily.

"Well, that will definitely come in handy," I said, "It seems a bit coincidental that you all wanted to test it on food appliances," I said.

"I don't mind. It gave me something normal to do," said Ms. Goddard. "This whole thing is so weird to me that I've stopped trying to understand it."

"I know it's difficult to believe," said Mel, walking in the room and looking as if she hadn't lost a wink of sleep with her long hair pulled neatly into a ponytail, "but I'm just glad that you trusted Gabe and came with him, not even having seen the creatures for yourselves."

"I heard enough from Sarah Jaden to know that you're all telling the truth. Besides," she said, glancing at Gabe, "I've always known that my son had a special intuition. I just didn't think it was supernatural-special."

Gabe glanced at her, but didn't comment.

"Everything happens for a reason," said Gram, "these kids have been friends for a long time. Something has kept them together."

"Well, except for Jeremy," said Ben.

"Has anyone seen a knife around here?" asked Ms. Goddard, opening and slamming drawers shut. "I can't find one sharp knife in the whole dang place."

"Humph," was Ben's comment with a roll of the eyes.

"Speaking of Jeremy, where is he?" I asked.

"He wanted to go back into town for something," said Gabe.

"By himself?"

"He'll be fine during the daytime," assured Mel. "That's what Homer said."

Knock, knock, knock. We all looked at the door, but no one moved.

"I don't think a reaper would knock," said Mel, crossing the room and opening the door.

It was Homer with his orange tabby cat Newton in his hands. He had on the same kind of plaid shirt, but a green and brown one today, and his Roper, steel-tipped boots. His hair was pulled back in a ponytail like yesterday, too. Was it really only yesterday that we'd met?

"Good morning, everyone," he said, stepping inside. "I'm happy that everyone appears to be safe and sound. You must be Melanie. It's nice to meet you face to face."

"Same here," she said, shaking his hand.

"I'm Melanie's grandmother," said Gram, shaking his hand, too.

"This is my mother, Nancy Goddard," said Gabe.

Ms. Goddard wiped her hands on a towel then shook his hand lightly.

"We've heard quite a bit about you this morning, Mr. Homer," she said.

"Oh, just Homer please."

Geez, how long did I sleep? It seemed like everyone knew about everything, but then I realized I hadn't left the bedroom since we got here. I imagine they were all talking well into the night about everything that had happened.

"Would you like some coffee, Mr.—, I mean Homer?" asked Ms. Goddard.

"That would be wonderful. Thank you."

Misty swept my ankles, staring intently up at Newton in Homer's arms. Newton made a hoarse, grumbled meow, so Homer put him down. The two cats ran up and touched noses then Misty flitted away with Newton close behind. It made me smile. Then Homer walked up to me and put a hand on my shoulder, asking gently, "Are you feeling okay, Clara?"

There was such genuine sympathy in his voice and in his eyes that I felt the sting of tears welling up suddenly. I swallowed hard.

"Yes, Homer, as well as can be expected."

"Good," he said, "because we all have a great trial ahead of us."

Hearing that, Gabe and Ben left the table to join us. We gathered on the beat-up sofa and mix-matched chairs. Mel pulled a chair from the table to sit next to me. Gram joined us, too. Ms. Goddard brought Homer a cup of coffee then milled around the kitchen but she seemed to be keeping an attentive ear on us. Pop brought his coffee with him and stood behind Gabe.

"First, I think we should talk about what happened with you and Jeremy last night, Gabe."

"What happened?" I asked hastily.

"We had a run-in with some reapers when we passed the mill," he said, not completely holding my gaze.

I realized he was leaving something out about the mill, but I wasn't going to press the issue. Obviously, it was something pretty unpleasant.

"Yes. It was a close call," said Homer. "I was concerned when I was tracing you, because everything became hazy after the car accident."

"Car accident!" I exclaimed. "Why didn't you tell me about an accident?"

I was staring straight at Gabe, probably making him uncomfortable, but I didn't care.

"There was no need. We made it just fine," said Gabe calmly before turning back to Homer. "Why would they come after just two of us in a car when they didn't need to?"

"They knew you were Setti, and they knew you were separated from your clan. That's of course when it would be easiest to pick you off, pardon the expression. You have to understand that the reapers are an arrogant race of creatures. Because they dominate humans so easily, they have a sick pride about killing Setti, who have a power equal to their own. They would never agree that we're equal, but when we work together, we are actually greater than them. They saw the opportunity and took it."

The back door opened and Jeremy stepped through with his backpack over his shoulder. He had pep in his step for some reason, bobbing his head to his iPod.

"Hey," he said too loudly and unplugged his earphones, "what's up, Homer? Come to join the party?"

"Hello, Jeremy. We were just discussing yours and Gabriel's escapades last night."

"Yeah, that was something else," he said, spinning a chair around that was facing the fireplace and sitting. "Thought we were wasted when that reaper jumped in the boat."

"In the boat!" I exclaimed.

"It's okay," said Gabe, trying to calm me, "we all made it just fine."

I realized then that they wouldn't have been in danger if I'd been there. Gabe was right about needing to stick together. I couldn't act on my own selfish whims anymore, not if I planned to keep everyone safe.

"You know, Homer," said Jeremy, "I was wondering if you knew why we had all those nightmares. I mean, Clara had one that didn't exactly come true, but then it sort of did. Then last night, I remembered my dream about Main Street and seeing people killed there in the plaza. That's what made me look and stop where Mrs. Jaden was. Are these dreams we're having like visions? Like what you have?"

Homer pressed his lips together and scratched his bearded chin.

"Not exactly. They're not visions of the certain future. I don't even have those kinds of visions. What I see is always connected to the power of the Setti and also the myrkr jötnar, or the reapers as we call them. Your dreams are connected to the power of the Setti in the same way. I've talked to my friend Herrald in Arkansas and he claims that his clan members have all had nightmares, too. I think it's like an innate warning system that comes with the power that binds us, that shows us and prepares us for what is coming."

"Well, I'm glad to hear that," said Mel. "I mean, that it's not a vision of the future."

"Why?" I asked. "You told us you hadn't had any nightmares."

"Well, I didn't. Not recently anyway. But, I did have one really frightening nightmare over a month ago. I asked Gram to help me do the traiteur ward against nightmares, which worked. I didn't realize I'd basically blocked them myself."

"Well, what was the one dream?" asked Gabe.

Mel's eyes flicked to Ben then away again to Homer.

"It wasn't about monsters. At least, I didn't see any. I guess that's why I didn't make any connection to the reapers."

"What was it then?" asked Jeremy.

"I dreamed that Ben exploded."

"So Firefly becomes Firecracker," said Jeremy.

"Drop it," said Gabe a bit too sternly.

Jeremy was always joking about Ben, but something hit Gabe wrong this time.

"I wouldn't worry about that dream," said Homer reassuringly, "these nightmares aren't predictions of the future. They're only warnings to prepare us for what we must face."

"Humph," grumbled Jeremy, "then I wonder why Melanie was dreaming about Ben."

Mel's eyes darted fiercely to Jeremy. Ben was oblivious to the comment, but I wasn't to Mel's reaction. Her aura was always golden, just a slightly deeper shade than those around children, but it flared deep orange when Jeremy made his not-so-polite comments about her dreaming of Ben.

"What we need to be concerned about are the reapers still left in Beau Chêne," said Homer.

"Left?" I asked, "then some have gone?"

"Oh, yes. I've been tracing them all night. This is only a small band that is attacking this region. The reapers' leader, Bölverk—"

"Wait. The reapers have a leader?" asked Ben.

"Yes. Unfortunately, they do. They are organized and efficient. But, Bölverk doesn't even care about our little clan of Setti. He's certain that his soldiers behind him will take care of us. He's moving north to Baton Rouge then hitting every large city as he goes up the country."

"How can you be sure if you can't see the future?" asked Jeremy.

"Because I've witnessed enough visions of the past to know how they operate. They go where there is the most food first, which are the cities thriving with energy."

"So, how far out have they gone?" asked Melanie.

"There are bands already spreading into Mississippi, Arkansas and east Texas."

"Man, I wonder what the rest of the world is thinking," said Ben absently.

It was an interesting thought. For a moment, none of us dared to comment, then Homer continued.

"Herrald has told me that the president has declared our state a disaster area, sending multiple troops of the National Guard into the state. The newscasters are baffled, he said, because no one can get down here then get word out as to what is happening."

"They are brilliant, aren't they," I said.

"Who?" asked Ben.

"The reapers," Gabe answered.

"Yeah," agreed Jeremy, "they knock out the electricity and cell towers, so we can't communicate to show the world what's really going on, so we send more people straight into harm's way who are just expecting fallen trees, floods, and maybe a few looters, not death-dealing demons. Yeah, they're pretty smart."

"Is that why the shadow scouts have been here for so many years?" I asked Homer. "So they can see what our civilization is like in order for the reapers to make the best attack."

"I think you've summed it up rather well."

"Wait a minute," Gabe interrupted, "you said that there are still reapers in Beau Chêne and that their leader, this Bölverk, left some of his soldiers as you said to get rid of us. That means they'll come here."

Mel gasped, turning and looking at Gram.

"They also detect the energy of humans," I said, "we've gathered quite a group here now. Won't they sense all of us?"

"Don't worry. I've got a shotgun, and she don't miss," said Pop.

"Everyone just calm down. That's why I've come."

"You've got a plan," said Gabe, not as a question.

"I've got a plan," assured Homer. "The reapers will go to wherever they detect the greatest amount of energy, both electric and electro-magnetic energy. Well, we've got our own supply to lure them to us."

He turned and looked at Ben who glanced quickly between all of us.

"What?" he asked absent-mindedly.

"I get it," said Jeremy, "You're gonna be bait, Light Bulb."

"What do you mean bait?"

"But we can't stay here," I said, "there are children. They could all get hurt."

"I know, Clara. We will go where there's no one nearby that can get hurt. We can lure them all to us and finish it so the rest of Beau Chêne will be safe."

"Canebrake Island," said Gabe.

Homer's eyes sparkled bright blue as he took a long sip of coffee then nodded. "Canebrake Island."

18

CLARA

"You've been really quiet since we left. Are you okay?"

Gabe gave me a stiff nod and a smile that faded too quickly. It was meant to be reassuring, but it wasn't. His aura flickered a pale blue with flecks of gold and orange haloing his head. It was the strangest color I'd ever seen around Gabe. His eyes kept darting to the woods lining this long road to Canebrake Island. At least I was in a familiar place, sitting next to him in his Jeep. Jeremy was lounging across the backseat in his own musical world with his hoodie pulled up and his earphones on. Gabe drove much slower than usual since we were following Homer, Mel, and Ben in his old pick-up truck.

I wondered if his mood had something to do with the scene we left back at the cabin. At first, all of our parents and grandparents were arguing back and forth because Homer suggested that we had to leave to confront the reapers. I thought Ben's parents were going to shoot off into orbit with their ranting. It was complete mayhem until Homer finally told every single one of us to demonstrate what we could do so that our parents could understand. So, we put on a little show. I created a bright dome of light; Melanie healed the red whelp on the back of Gabe's neck which nearly disappeared; Ben did his thing and started glowing like, well, a light bulb; Jeremy shattered a jar of fishing lures with one shout; and then, Gabe shattered a log into splinters with a wave of his hand. After that, everybody shut up. Homer gave a nice long speech, explaining our special abilities and our purpose as a clan. He even mentioned the fact that this ability is passed down through our ancestors, some of them knowing and using the power, others never knowing it at all. This sparked another whole conversation about who gave us this ability, like it was a disease, not a gift. My dad tried to be reassuring, but he had no idea where it came from in our family. There was no history at all on his side, not that he knew of. Homer finally concluded by reassuring everyone that we would all be safe traveling during the day and that he had a plan that would protect us all, including those people still left in Beau Chêne. After another hour of loud protesting then quieter bickering then finally relenting and hugging, we left.

Gabe scanned both sides of the road again with that determined expression on his face.

"What are you looking for?" I finally asked. "Homer said the reapers don't attack during the day."

"Yeah, I know. I'm just wondering where they are. I can sort of sense them, but it feels strangely distant."

The day was gray and still with wispy clouds passing smoothly overhead. We were just about to cross the land-bridge when Homer's truck veered off to the shoulder. Gabe pulled up behind him and stopped.

"What's up?" said Jeremy, sitting up quickly.

"I don't know," I said, hopping out to join the others beside Homer's truck.

"Is something wrong?" asked Gabe.

We all congregated on the blacktop. There was no need to worry about cars passing out here, if anyone was even venturing out of their house.

"I wanted to show all of you something," said Homer.

We gathered around him in a huddle, staring intently like he was about to do a magic trick.

"Do you remember how I told you that the reapers soak up solar energy during the day?"

We all nodded dumbly but kept our mouths shut. Homer got that stern glint in his eye.

"Everybody look up."

Six heads bobbed backward as we stared up into the sky. There was nothing to see but gray clouds and more gray clouds.

"I don't get it," said Ben, "are they invisible?"

"Look closely," said Homer.

Melanie gasped.

"You've got to be kidding me," said Gabe.

Then I saw what they saw. There was a brief moment where the thin clouds became thinner, revealing what appeared to be a black sheet above them. As if fate wanted us to get a good look, a hollow space separated two banks of cloud cover. This void moved across the sky, allowing hazy sunlight to come through. Silhouetted against the light were orderly rows of reapers floating on their backs. Their shiny black cloaks whipped around them. It was a menacing army at rest hovering between heaven and earth.

"So, monsters that actually like the sun?" asked Jeremy lightly. "That's a new one."

"They don't just like sunlight," said Homer, "they're soaking up its energy and keeping it from coming down here where it's needed and gaining strength in the process."

"Won't that kill the plants?" asked Mel.

"It would if they stayed indefinitely. I'm not sure what will happen, because we don't know how long they'll be here."

There was a moment of silence as we watched the hollow space move beyond us, revealing the end of the rows.

"How many do you think there are?" asked Ben.

"Forty-four," snapped Gabe.

He'd actually had the presence of mind to count them.

"You said that their leader was leaving a small group behind?" I asked Homer. "Is forty-four a small group?"

"By their standards, yes," he replied.

"Where are the ash-eaters?" asked Jeremy. "Why aren't they with them?"

"The ash-eaters don't feed on energy," said Homer.

"Yeah, I know," said Jeremy, "but aren't they some kind of watchdogs or something?"

"I don't think so," said Homer. "In my tracings of the past, the ash-eaters only follow the reapers when they feed, sort of like scavengers."

"Why would the reapers allow them to do that?" I asked, feeling a punch in my stomach when I remembered the ash-eater at my house. "I mean, the reapers don't seem like the kind to want pests following all the time."

"I'm sorry I can't answer that either. My visions only ever show them doing what we know they can do. But I can tell you this. The reapers are self-serving. If they're allowing the presence of the ash-eaters, it's because they're getting something in return."

We were all staring up. I felt a familiar chill creep up my spine. Instantly, I looked around us in the woods. Three pairs of luminescent eyes flashed then disappeared into a thicket of tall oak trees.

"We're being watched," I said as calmly as I could.

All eyes followed mine. Gabe took two steps toward the woods with his hands outstretched, then there was a strange burst of pressure waving out through the trees. The tall weeds flattened as Gabe's power passed, but there was no sound of pain from any creature hiding there.

"It's good that they're watching. They'll lead the reapers straight to us when night comes," said Homer, studying the sky as if it might turn dark any minute. "Still, we'd better get going."

No need to tell us twice. We hopped in our vehicles and tore across the land-bridge. The first thing I noticed when we pulled up to Homer's house was a funny kind of bulls-eye spray-painted in the middle of the clearing. Gabe veered around it, like Homer, parking back by the shed. I jumped out and walked toward the formation. At the center was a bright yellow solid circle about three feet in diameter. Five feet out from it was a red circle, then a neon blue circle ten feet from that. The final circle was about ten feet from the blue, a fluorescent green.

"Okay," said Jeremy, "you've got my attention. What's this, Homer?"

"Glad you asked, Jeremy, my boy," he said, clapping him on the shoulder. "This, my friends, is our battle zone."

"Sweet," said Jeremy.

"How do you mean?" asked Gabe.

"Clara. Come here, dear," he said, taking my hand and guiding me to the center of the bright yellow circle.

Once there, I glanced around at everybody staring at me, waiting for me to do something. I shrugged.

"I don't know what's going on any more than you do."

"Let me explain," said Homer. "I thought it best that we have a strategy to work together. Setti are most effective and the safest, mind you, when they fight as one. Clara, here, is our anchor. If anyone strays from her shield they become vulnerable, and I don't think I have to explain that tonight we'll be fighting a great force that will take advantage of any weaknesses."

Uh, no you don't, Homer, now that we know we're outnumbered by like seven to one. Thanks for the terrifying reality check.

"What are the painted circles for?" asked Ben, standing on the red line.

"Well, I'm not sure if you are aware of this or not, Clara," he said with his twinkling eyes on me, "but you have the ability to enlarge your shield at will."

"Yes," I said, "I was able to do it at Jessie's house, but then later, something happened at my house. I couldn't keep it up."

That nauseating emptiness filled me up, remembering how I couldn't push the shield out to protect my mother. Then my eyes started to sting.

"Your personal grief caused you to lose focus," said Homer sympathetically. "And, I am terribly sorry for your loss."

He paused a minute, giving me the most tender smile I think I'd ever seen. I looked at the ground as a tear slid down my cheek. Mel reached out and touched my shoulder to comfort me.

"Try it now, Melanie," said Homer.

I looked up confused. Mel's hands shimmered a vibrant blue on my shoulder. That high-pitched sound I'd heard before at the cabin outside my door came and went, and so did that sickening feeling in the pit of my stomach. I felt perfectly calm and steady though the sadness was lingering far away.

"What just happened?" I asked Mel.

She smiled.

"Homer explained on the way over that my healing ability can extend beyond the physical. Of course, just like I can't take away the scars from physical injuries, I can't completely erase emotional wounds either. I can only soothe the pain, temporarily," said Mel, glancing at Homer. "He told me that my purpose during the fight would be to help you maintain control and stay calm, because the reapers would find ways to weaken you."

"I'm sorry, Clara. I didn't intend to upset you right now. I know that the reapers will try," said Homer. "You will need Mel close by your side tonight, because they gain a sick pleasure from taunting their enemies. They will seek out the weakness in all of you in order to defeat us."

"Thanks for the pep talk, Homer," said Jeremy, "don't try to lift our spirits too high now. I mean, Gabe and I were almost killed by just two of them last night. Hell, forty-four oughta be a piece of cake, right?"

Jeremy's solid orange aura was waving crazily around him. Homer smiled in his nice, but dismissive way.

"I know that it sounds bleak, but the truth is that we can defeat forty-four just as easily as we can defeat four. That is, as long as we keep together. I know that you're just discovering your power, but it's as old as time, unending through the lines of your families and far beyond. Don't fear their numbers. Just be wary of their cleverness."

I glanced at Gabe whose eyes were fixed on me. His aura had faded entirely blue. I couldn't tell if he was worried about me because of my constant despair about my mom or if he was worried about all of us tonight. His steady gaze made me shiver. I finally looked away. Homer walked to stand next to Ben on the red line.

"Now, back to the plan. Clara will stay in the center yellow circle. Mel will stay next to her in the red circle in case Clara needs her healing assistance. If any of you are hurt somehow during the fight, Mel will come to you or you to her, whichever is easiest."

"But, why would we get hurt if we stay close to Clara under the shield?" asked Ben.

"You shouldn't, but what my visions of past battles and even the one Gabe showed me about Freya is to expect the unexpected with these creatures. I will watch all sides from the blue circle and give you guidance. Ben, you should stay in the blue as well."

"What do I do?" asked Ben.

"It will come to you naturally. As soon as Jeremy breaks their shields, you'll be able to feel their energy in the air. Take away as much as you can from them."

"And me?" asked Jeremy.

"You and Gabe will fight from the green circle. It's best that you're the closest to them and that we stay out of the way behind you, but watch the line. Don't stray too close. The shadow scouts are known to cross into a shield to get to a Setti."

Homer glanced at Gabe who seemed unmoved by the comment, yet his aura was rippling like sloshing water.

"I suppose, Homer, that you want me to keep my shield pushed out to the green line," I said.

"Oh, yes. Sorry, I forgot to explain that. Now, this is important. We have to be prepared that we're up against a great force."

"I don't think you have to explain that," said Jeremy.

"There is a possibility that Clara's shield may fall back. It's not that I don't trust your abilities, thinking that your shield may shrink," Homer said to me, "I just know that they'll be crafty and may find a way to try and weaken us. If that happens, I'll tell you all to move back to a certain line, whichever the shield shrinks to. Of course, you'll probably see it yourselves, but you might be a little distracted to notice, so I'll keep watch. Any questions?"

"Yeah," said Ben, "have you got any food? I'm starving."

Mel laughed.

"Actually, I do. Why don't we go inside," he replied.

"I'm gonna do a little target practice," said Jeremy, hiking his backpack up on his shoulder and heading to the back by the shed.

The rest of us followed Homer into his little house. It was so nice and cozy that for a little while, I actually felt at ease. I curled up on the couch with a quilt. Mel and Ben disappeared into the kitchen. Gabe wandered over to the coffee table where the newspaper clipping of Ben still sat. Gabe picked it up, scanned over it, put it down, then came over and sat on the couch really close to me. He folded my hand into his, but still didn't say anything.

"Would y'all like some cake and coffee? The cake is store bought from a few days ago, but Homer says it's still good," asked Mel from the doorway to the kitchen.

"Sure," I said, "lots of cream and sugar, please."

Gabe shook his head then Mel disappeared back into the kitchen.

"So, what's on your mind?" I asked as casually as possible.

He shrugged.

"Gabe. Please talk to me."

He looked at me then. His dark brown eyes were so intense staring into mine then his eyes wandered to the scar. Self-consciously, I turned away.

"I'm afraid, Clara. Not of the reapers, but of anything happening to us," he said in a low voice, pulling my hand into his lap and studying my palm, "especially to you."

"Don't worry so much," I said, using my best acting skills possible, "we'll be fine. Homer has faith in us."

"Yes, but Homer has his doubts, too. I can sense it even if he's not letting on to us. And after this then what? We know what these creatures are doing, spreading around the country and killing people. Do we just sit back here and let it happen? I don't think so."

Then Mel walked in carrying a plate with a slice of carrot cake and a rich-smelling cup of coffee in an over-sized green mug. Ben took a seat with two slices on his plate and started shoveling it in before his butt hit the cushion. Homer walked up with a plate and cup, handing it to Gabe.

"I know you didn't want any, but I think some caffeine and sugar will do you good."

As Gabe took the refreshments, I saw him staring intently at Homer's arm, whose sleeve was riding up.

"What's that, Homer?"

Homer sat into his cushy chair, smiling with a twinkle in his eye. He flipped over his arm and pulled his sleeve up to his bicep. There was a black tattoo, a swirling pattern of interlacing knots weaving up his forearm and around a sword crossing a shield. From behind the shield a dragon roared whose face was turned upward with its mouth agape as if it were in pain. The interlacing knots closed around the dragon's head then swirled farther up and disappeared beyond Homer's shirt sleeve.

"That's the tattoo I saw on Freya and Blyn in my vision," said Gabe.

"Yes," said Homer, "I've had several visions of their clan in the past. I suppose it's because we are descended from them and they were the last to battle the reapers before us. When they came together, they branded themselves as a show of unity. I'd seen it so often that I finally sketched it then got the tattoo. I think I needed to feel that it was all real, not just in my head. For a while, I was a little crazy, I think, wondering if what I saw was real or not. The tattoo helped me ground myself."

"Yeah," said Ben through a mouthful, "the librarian at our school thinks you're totally nuts."

Mel shushed Ben. He gave her the 'what' look then kept on eating.

"It's okay," said Homer, "I understand what others think of me. It doesn't matter, especially not now."

"Homer," I said quietly after a sip of coffee, which was really good and warm. I wanted to know something that I knew no one else would bring up. "What can you tell us about the shadow scouts, about how they're made?"

Tension filled the small space of the room. Homer's features went dark.

"I know why you're asking, Clara, and again I am sorry for your cousin, Jessie."

The mere mention of her name made the whole tragedy more real. I shifted anxiously in my seat, feeling Gabe's eyes on me again.

"Apparently, the shadow scouts are all former humans. I don't know anything about how the reapers do it. I've seen that in the past some humans don't even survive the process."

"How can they have shadow scouts who have been here for so many years now, watching us, when the reapers just came into our world?" asked Mel.

"The shadow scouts who've been here and who are serving them are those they captured and changed the last time they were here on earth."

"Over a thousand years ago?" I asked. "But how can they live that long? Humans aren't immortal."

"They no longer need food or water or anything that humans need," said Homer soberly, "they survive on the dark energy that the reapers give them. The shadow scouts depend on the reapers for it, and so they do whatever is required of them."

"So, the reapers are immortal?" asked Ben, licking his fingers clean, completely un-phased by all this. He was a strange anomaly.

"No, Ben," said Gabe, "they can die easily enough."

It took a second for Gabe's comment to sink in. It felt good that he had so much confidence. We needed it. That made me think about that time I saw those creepy shadow scouts in my living room, how they flinched away from me when I made like I was moving toward them.

"Why do the reapers hate us so much?" I asked. "I can feel it when they look at me."

"Perhaps they envy what they have lost," suggested Homer, "they've lost their humanity. I once saw a shadow scout being made in a vision I had when Freya's clan was attacked in a Celtic village. A large man was transformed by a reaper, and when he was, he seemed disoriented and confused. One of the reapers grabbed him by the arm and quickly took him away. I still don't know exactly why."

"Can you guess? I know that you've given it some thought," said Gabe.

Homer nodded.

"As a matter of fact, I have. I think that the longer the shadow scouts live, feeding on the dark energy of the reapers, they lose more and more of their human souls. The reapers are evil through and through, living off the murders of others. Anything that comes from these creatures is full of their malevolence. I believe that when they're first made, they're confused by the transformation and need some kind of assimilation into their new existence. Now, how this is done, I don't know."

I noticed then that Gabe was staring at me. What I hadn't noticed was that I was crying quietly. I couldn't help but think of Jessie, and how wrong it was that she was doomed to live on forever, becoming more like these wicked beasts. I wondered where they'd taken her, what they'd done to her, and if she would be there tonight when we fought to kill them all. It was so unfair. I wanted it all to go away, this empty sadness from the loss of two loved ones—my mother now dead and my cousin a slave to these foul demons.

"What if," I said in a half-whisper, "what if Jessie is with them tonight?"

I couldn't even meet Homer's gaze, but I felt the empathy in his voice.

"She is no longer your cousin Jessie. Not anymore."

Mel sat next to me on the end of the sofa and touched my arm. I knew what she was going to do. I almost wanted to shrug her off, feeling like I deserved to feel the grief and pain, knowing it was my failure that caused my mother's death, wondering why I was the one who lived and not Jessie. But, I didn't shrug her away. Just as she began soothing me with her healing art, Jeremy walked through the door. By the time he made it to our circle near the window, I could feel that despair floating away somewhere. It was a temporary fix, but I was glad to feel that grief drifting away.

"What are you doing out there?" Ben asked Jeremy as he plopped down in a chair next to him.

"I've been getting ready, Sunshine."

"What's all this?" asked Ben, pointing to a small canvas bag attached to Jeremy's belt that looked weighted down.

"My ammunition," said Jeremy, grinning. "I have one for you, too, Gabe."

Jeremy tossed Gabe another small canvas bag that had a loop to belt it on. Gabe opened the flap of the pouch and pulled out a shiny metal Chinese throwing dart.

"What the—?" started Ben.

"Nice thinking," said Homer. "I was pleasantly surprised when I saw how you managed to wield weapons with your power, Jeremy."

"Thanks, Homer. I like how much easier it is to channel my sound vibrations through metal."

"Hey, let me see one," said Ben, holding his hand out to Jeremy.

Jeremy took one out of his little bag, apparently impressed at his stash of different shapes of pointed stars. I saw the sly grin on Ben's face just as Jeremy passed the star to him. A tiny thread of electricity passed from Ben to Jeremy through the metal star with a little popping noise.

"Ow! Damn it! Why'd you do that?"

Ben laughed.

"Sorry, man. Just seeing if I could."

Jeremy scowled nastily, rubbing his hand.

"Hey, Homer, does this mean I can shock the reapers and kill them?"

"No, I don't think so," he replied, which made Ben slump into a pout. "They feed on electricity. You'd only be giving them power. The shadow scouts, too. However, you might be able to destroy the ash-eaters. It would be worth a try to get rid of as many of those as we can anyway. They're such cold, menacing spirits to have floating about."

"Yeah, that sounds way cool," said Ben, happy again.

"Whatever," said Jeremy a little bitterly. "Anyway, Gabe, I thought you might try it out for size, since I saw how well you channeled your power with that ax last night."

"What ax?" I asked, but was completely ignored.

"It's true," said Gabe, "I was able to aim and hit the reaper using a physical object to guide my power through. That reminds me. Homer, you said that you traced and saw us fighting on the boat last night. It was a difficult fight that we almost lost with just that one reaper. Why was that?"

"Well, I think it was difficult for two reasons. One reason is because you seemed to start to doubt yourself. Instead of facing the creature, you backed away. It's always more difficult to defeat this enemy when you are the one being hunted and they have the element of surprise. The second reason is simply because you were nearly exhausted, both physically and mentally. Just because we have these powers doesn't mean we're invincible. And, while the power Melanie and I hold is an internal ability, we will still grow fatigued after using it continuously over a length of time or using it intensely."

"You know, there's something that's been bothering me," said Jeremy, "how did they travel in that hurricane? Did they create it?"

"Not exactly. Somehow, they are able to use their energy to control winds and storms. How did they get it? I'm not sure. But, I do know that their mere presence on earth alters the atmosphere."

"I wish we could sit one down and ask them some questions," said Jeremy.

"That would be an interesting interview," said Gabe.

"Yeah, like that would ever happen, Sound Garden," Ben said snidely to Jeremy.

"Okay. Sound Garden is a band. And just for the record, that's still not an insult. But, keep trying, Flash. You might actually come up with an offensive name for me one of these days."

Geez. Those two never stopped, and while it was usually quite entertaining, I could feel that my nerves were on edge. I sipped my coffee. Homer pulled out his violin and bow that were propped up in a case against the wall of books behind him. He always knew just what to do. Not even asking if we cared to hear music or not, or whether we wanted to further discuss this fearful enemy we had to face in a few hours, he started playing. It was just what we needed. I suppose that was part of his gift, too.

He didn't play a piece of classical music this time. It was an old Acadian song that I'd heard at festivals, like at the Gumbo Cook-off and the Crawfish Festival. It started out as a slow melody. His bow moved up and down the strings of the violin in a steady rhythm. While it was slow, it wasn't sad. The song gradually began to increase in rhythm, moving into merrier notes that made me think of happy times of my childhood. I drained the last of my coffee and set the mug down then shifted my body into a curled up position, laying my head in Gabe's lap. Like Homer, I didn't bother to ask permission, even though I knew Gabe wasn't really big on public displays of affection. He didn't seem to mind though. We were all mesmerized by Homer's melody, the notes lifting and lilting across the room, taking us away from our present reality. It was the perfect medicine, putting us all in a peaceful state of mind and body. I felt Gabe's hand combing through my hair. He pulled it away from my face, exposing my scar. I didn't care right now. I closed my eyes, completely lost in Homer's lovely music and the gentle touch of Gabe's hand in my hair.

19

GABE

    Clara had fallen asleep. I didn't want to wake her. Not yet. Jeremy had gone back outside for more target practice. Ben and Mel lounged in the corner, speaking in hushed tones. Homer was playing his violin listlessly. He had wandered into some classical music. This one was familiar; something my mom used to play for her plants in the greenhouse. Vivaldi, maybe? I looked down at Clara, wishing she could be this peaceful all the time. Since yesterday, I could only feel waves of anxiety pouring out of her. Sometimes it felt like grief, sometimes a slight sadness, then other times complete despair. I marveled at Mel's ability to calm her, soothe her, when I couldn't. There was no amount of wishing that I could do to bring back her mother and cousin. I only hoped that we would all make it through the night alive and keep the rest of our family safe on the other side of Beau Chêne. This made me wonder about something.

    "Homer," I interrupted. He stopped and turned to me. "Why did you leave Newton at Pop's camp?"

It was obvious to me that Homer's cat was important to him, and I hadn't even thought about why he left him there until now. He gave me a sort of wistful smile that faded while he packed away his bow and violin.

"Newton is a passive fellow," said Homer. "He'll do better away from all the noise and ruckus here."

"Is that the only reason?" I asked pointedly.

Homer chuckled.

"I know what you're thinking, Gabriel. That Newton would be abandoned if we all die here, that I brought him to the cabin knowing he'd be taken care of if we didn't make it," he said, raising his dark eyebrows, his only facial hair that had no spots of gray in them. "Rest at ease, Gabriel. That wasn't my intention. And while I am not ignorant to the fact that this is a serious trial ahead of us, I am certain that we will succeed. I have slight misgivings on us all making it through unscathed, but we will win. I have no doubts."

At that moment, Jeremy burst in the door, a bit out of breath with a wide-eyed look.

"It's getting dark," he said "and a storm is coming."

"Yes," said Homer, "come, Benjamin, it's time for you to get started."

I roused Clara, which didn't take much effort. She was not in that deep of a sleep. I glanced out the wall of windows. Yes, the sky had darkened since we'd come inside. The swamp extended far into the distance; the water's flat surface reflecting the dark gray of the sky. A wind was moving from the south, sending short ripples in our direction. The cypress trees dappling the marshy water waved their fingers of moss, like ghosts saying farewell.

"It's time?" asked Clara, clearly awake now.

"Yes," I said, taking her hand and following the others outside.

Before she walked out of the door, I pulled her back to me instinctually. I couldn't explain why. I just had a sudden urgency to kiss her. So I did. I may have been a bit too aggressive, but I couldn't help myself. I wanted her to know what I felt about her, in case we didn't get the chance again. I pulled her close to me and lowered that wall that held my emotions inside. I wrapped all that she meant to me into a tight ball in my chest, letting it slide directly out to her in a slow hum of pressure. She shivered. I remembered what I did the last time that I'd lost control and knocked her unconscious. This time, I was able to keep it in check and give her a brief show of what I felt. It was probably the only time I'd ever knowingly and willingly shown anyone how much they meant to me, especially in this bizarre supernatural way. It was definitely the only time I'd been able to control my power enough to use it in this manner, tenderly and gently. Before this, it had always been sheer force and violence. When I finally pulled away from her lips, she had a complete look of shock on her face. For a second, I thought maybe I had done something wrong.

"Are you okay? Did I hurt you?"

"Are you kidding me?" she asked, smiling sheepishly. "Can we do that again?"

I certainly wasn't the blushing type, but I felt a flush of heat crawl up my neck anyway.

"Stay focused, Clara, during the fight," I said.

"You should've thought of that before you kissed me and did that whatever it was you just did."

I swept a swift kiss on her forehead, tucking her hair back behind one ear.

"Seriously," I said, looking intently at her, "stay focused."

"I will," she assured me, and I sensed that her emotions were strong and steady.

We walked out hand-in-hand to the others. Homer was talking to Ben who was obviously on edge.

"Whatever feels natural to you," Homer was saying when we approached.

"Yeah, I feel better when I run," said Ben, starting to jog along the interior of the blue line in our multicolored bulls-eye.

"Are you sure they'll all come?" asked Jeremy.

"Oh, yes," said Homer, "quite certain. The reapers always seek out the greatest energy in a region, wanting it for their own. Once Benjamin works up his power, they'll flock here together, thinking they've hit the jackpot, so to speak."

"Won't some of them leave then when they realize it's only the six of us?" asked Mel.

"I doubt it," said Homer, "they'll see that we are Setti and will want to try and defeat us."

"By defeat," said Jeremy, "you do mean kill us."

Homer nodded.

"Don't think of our possible defeat," he said, "it will only weaken you. Remember that this would be to their advantage. Instead, remember those who we are fighting for, the ones we've lost and the ones still counting on us for survival."

Ben had lapped around us three times, picking up speed, and was starting to beam brightly through his t-shirt, even slightly through his jeans. There was a rumble of thunder in the distance.

"Clara, come to the center now," said Homer, his voice becoming more commanding.

She did so, planting her feet right in the middle of the yellow circle. Homer was saying something so that only she could hear—words of encouragement, I'm sure. Mel walked a little past me, looking out at the swamp not so far away from the clearing. I turned and stared out in the direction of the thunder as well. There was a slight ripple of worry coming from Mel.

"What's wrong?" I asked. "I mean, besides the obvious."

She gave me a half smile then turned back to the sound of the oncoming storm.

"Ben," she replied. "I can't help but think about that dream I had so long ago."

"Forget about that," I said, "Homer said that those dreams didn't mean anything. They aren't predictions of the future."

"Really?" she said in her dry, sarcastic way, "then why did I dream that he exploded in this exact setting in the darkness of a storm with circles of color all around him? It all came back to me just now when I heard the thunder."

I glanced behind us at the spray-painted circles on the ground, our target for battle. Ben was still running, working up a sweat and glowing like crazy.

"Forget it, Mel. Clara will keep us protected, because you will keep her calm and steady. Have faith."

She looked at me, raising that one eyebrow into a peak.

"It's pretty pathetic that you're giving me the 'stay calm' advice, isn't it?"

I didn't respond, but laughed, just a little. I wouldn't let on that her dream now had me slightly worried.

"I'm fine," she finally said. "Let's get ready."

She walked back to Clara and Jeremy joined me. He folded the flap back of the small bag looped through his belt.

"I need easy access," he explained. "Hey, where's your pack?"

I'd forgotten it inside.

"Here it is," said Homer, coming up behind us. "That was a very good idea, Jeremy. You have quite a large collection of Chinese throwing darts. A hobby of yours?"

"Yeah, sort of. I picked up the rest this morning at a shop in town," he said, looking a little guilty. "I mean, I don't think the guy's gonna be open for business any time soon."

"I'm sure you're right," said Homer.

Jeremy seemed relieved that he wasn't going to get a lecture about stealing, then he started thumbing through his iPod. I think Homer agreed that now wasn't the time to worry about such things, when we now knew that the store may or may not ever open again.

"Gabriel, do you still have that pouch with the stone, the relic of Freya?" Homer asked.

I'd almost forgotten about it. I felt around in my jeans pocket and pulled it out.

"Here," said Homer, taking the pouch and threading a leather strap through the short draw strings, tightening the ends into a knot. "I thought it might do you some good, keeping it close to you this way."

He looped the leather strap over my head. The pouch with the black stone that was literally a piece of my ancestor, a great Vanquisher, fell at the center of my chest, close to my heart. Homer patted the pouch.

"Remember what you are and whose blood runs in your veins," Homer said, giving me a fixed, sincere gaze.

"I will," I assured him.

"Good," he said, stepping back, "then we're all ready."

"Let's rock and roll," said Jeremy, almost bouncing with excitement a few yards away.

Homer ambled back to the blue circle. Ben had slowed to a jog, but he didn't appear out of breath at all from his rounds. He seemed the opposite, completely invigorated with a brilliant white light shining off of every part of him, even his hair. Clara and Mel were talking together. Clara nodded to something she said. Another rumble of thunder pulled my gaze toward the swamp.

"What's on the music agenda for tonight?" I shouted to Jeremy.

Jeremy grinned in that mischievous way he had about him.

"Iron Maiden, my friend. It's time for Eddie to do some damage."

"Eddie?" I asked, completely confused.

Jeremy looked at me like I was an idiot, as if it were common knowledge to know whoever Eddie was.

"You know, dude. Eddie, their skeleton mascot," he said, like I was a fool for not knowing. I guess in Jeremy's world, I was. Then I remembered an art project he did last semester. Mrs. Fowler asked us to recreate a masterwork. Jeremy's idea of a master didn't include Monet or

Munch. It was an Iron Maiden album cover entitled "Piece of Mind" where a chained skeleton man, Eddie, fought to get free from his padded cell. Now that I saw where Jeremy came from, it all made sense. He was mumbling to himself as he apparently scrolled through songs.

"Yeah, 'Revelations,' that's the one. Perfect. Bring it, man."

His bizarre enthusiasm made me smile, despite the fact that anyone else would've thought he was a mental patient. Hell, maybe his odd music was his own way of self-medicating. Who was I to judge what was weird or normal?

Turning my attention back to the water, I watched as a bank of heavy, dark gray clouds drew closer. I took a deep breath. It wasn't six o'clock yet, but the sky rolled in the smoky darkness, plunging us into an artificial night. There was a rustling sound growing louder and louder, the only sound other than the wind. I knew this sound. I'd heard it in my dream where my skin broke into thousands of pieces and the ash-eater inhaled what was left of me. This was the very spot in that nightmare where I'd carried the black stone to the edge of a swamp, watching the storm carry the reapers and other creatures toward me. I grabbed the pouch at my chest, holding the remnant of my ancestor long gone. As if Freya knew what approached, even after a millennium of death, I felt a pulsing sensation quiver out of the stone, moving through my body. The rustling grew closer. A streak of purple lightning splintered across the sky, revealing the army of reapers stealthily moving toward us, riding on the wind. My power awakened instantly, building steadily, waiting to be released. It trembled through my veins.

"It worked, Flash!" shouted Jeremy gleefully back to Ben, jumping up and down. "All our friends have come to play!"

An orb of golden light suddenly surrounded me, pushing several feet past the green line, which was the border Homer wanted us to stay within. I glanced back at Clara. Her hands were raised as if she literally held up the dome of light. There was such a peculiar combination of serenity and strength in her face. We could do this. I was sure of it now. In addition to Clara's sphere of protection, there was Ben, who beamed out well beyond our circle. The reapers were coming into view. Jeremy started to sing his strange tune, which somehow seemed exactly right for tonight.

"Bind all of us together, ablaze of hope and free, no storm or heavy weather, will rock the boat, you'll see . . . The time has come to close your eyes, and still the wind and rain."

His voice rose loudly, sending sound vibrations out around us. There was an electric crackle and five or six shadow scouts popped into view, standing directly on the other side of the shield opposite me. Clara had created her shield of protection just in time. Their yellow eyes glowed with an unnatural luster. They hissed at Jeremy for removing their camouflage. He kept belting out his song. More crackling, more shadow scouts appeared, bursting into view around Clara's shield. I counted as the reapers spread out, encircling us slowly. All forty-four had come, and was it ever a sight. Their massive black cloaks whipped wildly and their wings beat slowly as the wind carried them over the water onto solid ground. It was like a band of demons had come straight from Hell, wandering out of the murky gloom. Night was truly taking over. Ben's glow reflected off of cypress trees which seemed more alive with the wind stirring their branches and gray moss. Where I thought they should look more like guardians to protect their own, they took on the appearance of additional fiends, waiting to finish us off if the reapers failed. Another shaft of lightning split the sky, silhouetting the cloaked creatures rapidly descending on us.

One very large reaper approached me, fully twice my size. He rubbed his two sword-like arms against one another, making an eerie noise, a sharp clanging of metal on metal. Greenish sparks sputtered around his arms. I wondered how these organic blades of bone could sound so much like metal, when Jeremy snapped me out of my reverie.

"You ready, captain?"

"Ready."

Not needing any more prodding, Jeremy stopped singing and started a series of short yells, each flinging out with silvery darts into the darkness. I could see the metal stars glinting as they flew through the air, hitting their targets, shattering the shields of five reapers in front of us. The stars spun to the ground not making a mark on the reapers, but having done their job well. I threw the first dart, but the gargantuan reaper looming in front of me deflected it with his rapier arm. He wielded that massive arm above us, smashing down onto Clara's shield. A vibration of golden light rippled around the dome. Clara made a startled sound behind me. I glanced back. She still stood fiercely, but there was a quizzical look on her face as if she didn't know what had just happened.

"Stay focused!" shouted Homer from the blue circle.

Ben stood still now, breathing heavily with his arms at his sides and his head tilted upward. He was glowing brighter and brighter. I faced the reaper in front of me. He glared into my eyes with a look of deep hatred.

"Come now, Vanquisher," he said, "Did you think we'd just stand here and let you kill us without a plan of our own? You have much to learn. Too bad you won't have the time."

He took two steps backward and spoke in a low guttural voice in a language I did not know that all of the reapers were able to hear around the circle. I only knew they could hear, because they obeyed him instantly and in unison. The language, if it could be called that, was harsh and bestial. Yet, its' rhythmic cadence denoted intelligence, rather than animalistic calls. Then the creature spoke in our language, as if allowing us to know their thoughts would instill more fear in their prey.

"Enclose," he said, then half the reapers filed in a perfectly spaced circle around the entire radius. The other half stayed in the back with him, then he spoke again.

"Deteriorate."

All sharpened arms pointed upward into the sky and came down in one loud clang against Clara's shield. I heard her shriek. The reapers' arms went up again, pounding down with a hellish yell. Their rhythmic chant increased the fierceness of each blow.

"What the hell are you waiting for!" yelled Jeremy.

I realized then that my power had built to a boiling point. I raised my arms and pushed outward with a fierce wave of energy, incinerating four reapers in front of me. The leader of this demon band made a throaty growl at me.

"Again!" he shouted, while the ring of reapers pounded down again.

The shield of protection shrank slightly. I had expected them to be clever as Homer forewarned, but I hadn't expected their military-like maneuvers, operating as one cohesive mass.

"To the blue circle!" shouted Homer from somewhere behind me.

Jeremy had thrown four darts in a row carrying his sound, all sticking the reaper in front of him. It refused to back down to him.

"Slaves," I heard the creature growl, making a forward motion with one sharpened arm.

Before I could react, two scouts that were invisible appeared suddenly within the golden dome, only because their flesh caught on fire. They squealed in pain while laying their hands on Jeremy.

"Down, Jeremy!" I yelled.

He jerked away and hit the dirt, the sleeves of his shirt smoking. I flung a sphere of energy out, catching them as they tried to escape. They burst into leafy ash.

"Come on, Jeremy," I called to him. He jumped up over to me. "We've got to move around the circle. You go ahead of me. As soon as you break the shields I'll be right behind you."

"Let's do it," said Jeremy.

The reapers pounded again, but this time Clara hadn't weakened. I glanced in her direction and saw Mel standing next to her with a hand on Clara's shoulder. Ben was even brighter than before if that were even possible. Jeremy started running, letting out a long, loud unending scream. I followed, pushing my power through my arm as I shot out the throwing darts he'd given me. This time, I didn't miss. Every time they landed, whether in the reaper's chest, shoulder, or gut, the reaction was the same—instantaneous explosion into black shards of charred bone and sooty dust. Gradually, I saw Clara's dome of light eking back out to the green line. We were gaining ground.

Then, the unexpected happened. Even though Homer warned us to beware of their cleverness, I still didn't see this coming. Perhaps, that was because I hadn't realized that while this protective shield kept the reapers and their dark power outside, that wasn't true for the natural elements.

We had made a full circle, and I'd run out of Chinese throwing darts, killing at least a dozen reapers in the process. Of course, a dozen more stepped up from the ranks in the background to fill their spaces. I saw the leader, his gleaming eyes no longer on me. He'd severed his arms into two giant seven-fingered hands then made a sweeping motion with them. Obeying his will, a gust of wind scooped up two tons of water. I watched it closely, wondering what the hell he was doing then it shot like an arrow straight at Ben. The effect was horrifying. Ben's body was full to the point of bursting with electricity from the shadow scouts and reapers around him. As soon as the water touched his body, a powerful shock wave ruptured out of him sending a shower of white sparks into the air. Ben screamed and crumbled lifelessly to the ground. His light went out, plunging us into darkness.

"Ben!" I yelled, starting to run to him.

"No, Gabe. Focus, son. Focus! Don't let your emotions rule you!" shouted Homer.

Mel ran away from Clara, falling to Ben's side. The shield of light was shrinking again back behind the blue line, almost to where Ben had fallen. Several dark shapes loomed just on the periphery of the shield where Ben lay. I looked back at Clara who stared intently at a shadow scout across the dome of light opposite her. I followed her gaze, recognizing the tall scout with the greenish gash on its head as the one who'd attacked her parents. It was also the one who'd led the reapers on us last night from the mill. The scout appeared to be taunting her.

I was distracted, and so was Clara. I hadn't noticed that their leader had wielded the wind and lifted a fallen cypress tree.

"Gabriel!" yelled Homer.

He was pointing up. All I saw was an oblong object flying swiftly through the air straight for Clara. Seeing it coming, she dropped to her knees, still holding up her shield. Without even thinking, I flung a bolt of power through my arm directly at the tree soaring for Clara. It cracked and split, falling in two large pieces on either side of Clara, nearly crushing Homer in the process.

"Are you okay?" I yelled over to him.

He crawled up from behind the trunk, making his way closer to Clara. I looked at her, trying to gauge her emotions to see if she was still holding strong. She seemed to know.

"Don't worry," she said confidently, "I'm not letting this shield go."

She pulled up from her knees, holding the protective dome now half its original size in place. There was no fear coming from her. I clutched at the pouch hanging around my neck. This remnant linked me to this Vanquisher from the past. There was power left in this stone, undaunted by centuries of time or death. The power seeped outward. I quivered as it pulsed through me. The power beat from it stronger than ever before. I could visibly see my chest shaking, but I was no longer filled with bitterness or hatred for these creatures who had stormed into our world, taking innocent lives in a ruthless rampage. I was filled with an unwavering emotion that felt something like anger, but less hostile, something more steady and true—it was a deep desire for justice. There was no way that I'd let it end like this, these beasts killing us all. Clara's shield shrank further, then I saw that shadow scout pacing just behind the ring of reapers in her view. The leader of this demon band leapt on top of the split trunk that protruded from the shield so he could get a good view of us. He flung his black cloak wide over his shoulders puffing out his massive chest and urging his sinister fiends on.

"Okay, Jeremy and Clara; listen up," I said in a low voice, still staring ahead at the leader who ordered another barrage of beatings against

Clara's shield, longer and louder this time. The clanging noise drowned out my words which was only to our advantage. "We're going to gather everything we've got and push it out all at the same time. Clara, your shield can burn them and look how close they've come. Their confidence is their weakness. Let them come in just a bit closer, then I'll say when."

"Keep your friends close and your enemies closer, eh," said Jeremy, though his flippant remark had a nervous edge to it.

Clara's eyes kept darting around us as she continued to focus on holding up her shield.

"Jeremy, you need to pool all of your power into one fierce yell that shatters as many shields as you can at the same time. This may be our only way—for Ben, and for everyone else. Are you ready?"

Both Jeremy and Clara nodded with heavy, steady looks in their eyes. I turned back to the rhythmic beating of the reapers. Their persistent pounding against the shield spit up green sparks chaotically into the air. With each hammering blow, their demon chant continued. As Clara's shield shrank and they drew closer, I could finally make out the ghostly figures of the ash-eaters behind them, slinking further forward like hyenas to the lions' prey. The leader gloated at me from high on his cypress platform as the relentless hammering brought them closer and closer. I was trembling with the power filling every inch of my frame. Clang, clang, clang. They stalked even nearer. The sight of those serpentine eyes glaring at us in the dark would have frozen me with fear if I hadn't known deep down that my clan could, and would prevail.

"Now!" I yelled.

Clara's shield spilled outward, Jeremy's sound wave blasted, and my power detonated into the darkness lighting every shadow scout and every reaper on fire. In that split second of victory, I watched that ghoulish shadow scout that taunted Clara burst into flame, screeching into the night as it died. The malevolent leader's monstrous face showed a milli-second of fear as it was blown from atop his dais then exploded into shards of bone and splintered flesh. In one deafening blow, the last of the reapers, shadow scouts, and ash-eaters incinerated into a massive cloud of black dust that coated all of us. I looked to Clara and Jeremy near me, who gagged under the weight of the ash. Then, a kind of miracle happened. A gusting wind carried the dark ash into a mushroom cloud that curled upward. A clap of thunder echoed into the night, seeming to split and open up the sky. Our heads tilted upward as a torrent of rain began to fall, washing away all evidence of the demons who'd come to slaughter us. I watched as Clara's face was washed clean of the dark powder, hardly believing what we had all just done.

Mel's singing sound from her healing power shook me from my daze. I ran toward her where she bent over Ben, shaking with sobbing cries. No. I couldn't bear the thought that we'd done it at the cost of my best friend. He laid flat on his back, motionless, the rain pouring down on top of him, cleansing him from the caked black powder. Mel was blocking his face from view. I almost didn't want to see his face, to see the lifeless, vacant look of death on such a dear friend. Ben was the kind of person that brought life into the room the moment he stepped into it. I'd never thought I'd have to face the day when he wouldn't be there. Mel's shoulders still shook with sobs. I bent down to gently pull her away, but when I did I realized she was only half crying—and half *laughing*. She leaned back and looked up at me. Ben was staring stupidly up at all five of us standing over him.

"What's up?" he asked. "Did we do it?"

"Damn, Light Bulb," said Jeremy, "I thought you'd blinked out for good."

Unbelievably, Jeremy actually looked relieved to see that Ben hadn't died after all. Homer started laughing. Ben sat up, and then Melanie very uncharacteristically threw her arms around him. I turned to Clara, who stood there smiling sweetly. She was looking at me. The rain had plastered her long hair to her face. I wrapped myself around her and looked up into the night that dropped sheets of wonderful rain down on us. Gazing back into Clara's hazel eyes, I couldn't think of much to say.

How could you sum up what we had gone through, what we had managed to overcome and survive? So, I just stated the obvious.

"It's raining," I said.

"Yeah. It's raining," she said with a giggle. "Kind of a silly observation if—"

I stopped her mouth with a long kiss. She didn't seem to mind. The others helped Ben limp back into the house. The rain poured down, drenching the air, the earth, and us. That feeling of triumph leapt through me, racing through my blood. I'd won many championship soccer games with my teammates, but fighting for victory was a very different emotion than fighting for the life of friends, of family and her. Clara pulled back and gazed up at me with that bizarre smile on her face that she wore when she observed my aura.

"What?"

"I wish you could see it," she said, "The ropes of light are braided now, weaving steadily around you. It's so amazing."

I smiled, tucking a wet lock of hair behind her ear and pulling her to me. The rain continued to fall, but it didn't bother me. Clara was close and I was warm. The cypress trees were finally still, their moss falling in motionless tendrils. Their menacing appearance had faded, now seeming like sentinels protecting us from further harm. I didn't know what lay ahead, but for now I wasn't worried. I couldn't think of anything at all but the one in my arms, and just for that brief moment, all was utterly and completely right with the world.

✷20✷

CLARA

The newborn kittens had just opened their eyes. Noah was cuddling a tiny calico to his chest. She mewed softly, wobbling her head shakily. We'd tried to move Misty and her kittens to a blanketed box on Homer's back porch, but the next morning we found them all transported back out here to the shed. Noah and Hunter had been visiting them every day.

"What's that one's name?" I asked, pointing to the one in Noah's lap.

"This one is Princess Leia."

"Really? That's a pretty name."

I had remembered suddenly that Jeremy had given Noah and Hunter his entire collection of Star Wars action figures from his house two weeks ago.

"And this one?" I asked, picking up an orange tabby that looked identical to its father, Newton.

"That's Obi-One," said Hunter, stroking a fuzzy orange ball in his arms.

"What about those two?" I asked, pointing to the smoky gray and the runt who were nursing on Misty.

"Luke Skywalker and Yoda."

I giggled, seeing the roly-poly runt named Yoda nuzzling up to Misty, unable to move its fat little self.

"And yours, Hunter?"

"Oh, this is Chewbacca."

"So, no Darth Vader?" I asked.

"No," said Noah, "we need Jedi Knights. We need good guys."

These little boys had been through hell on earth. We all had. It shouldn't surprise me that they wouldn't think of naming any of their precious pets after a dark cloaked figure who wielded evil power.

"I couldn't agree with you more," I said, scratching behind Obi-One's ears.

"Clara," called Mel from the porch, "we need you inside."

"Okay."

I gave the kitten to Noah, who was more than happy to take him off my hands.

Walking across the yard, I glanced over at my dad who was examining the exterior of the framed-up house on the edge of the woods, one of several that would be built on Canebrake Island. Zack was standing next to him, listening attentively. Ms. Goddard and Gram had brought another truckload of vegetable plants from Gabe's house and were carrying them one by one into the greenhouse. Ms. Goddard had all of us transport her greenhouse here, piece by piece and pot by pot. I heard her telling Gram something about tomato plants and making it through the winter.

"Oh, they'll last Esther, you mark my words," said Ms. Goddard. "I've got the best fertilizer in the world."

"I believe you, Nancy. I think we'll do just fine."

I walked on, observing how much we'd done since that night we'd fought the reapers here on the island. The first two weeks after we destroyed them were the hardest. My dad, being the most logical of us all, wrote down a systematic plan to comb the town for survivors. By splitting up into teams, we were able to find everyone left, which included the owner of the café in town, Martha Mirabelle; seven terrified children under the age of ten from three different homes, and a sugarcane farmer named Ed Dugas who lived on the outskirts of town. Ms. Mirabelle had moved in with Ben's grandmother for the time being, helping to feed and raise the seven orphans there until their new house could be built on the island. My dad suggested to all of the survivors that we live in close proximity; thus, the new construction taking place on Canebrake Island. Dad's logic was that it was probably better if we live away from town since any stray reapers would pass through looking for surviving humans. Homer agreed, saying this secluded area would probably be safest for all. What I hadn't thought of, which I overheard my dad telling Gabe, was that he was also worried about the surviving humans from other areas who might have ill intent. Basically, he was concerned about the breakdown of society now that there was no one policing the area against criminals. It made me think of Mrs. Jaden and her lessons on *Lord of the Flies* about how man often reverts to its primitive behavior when civilization is lost. I was really beginning to wonder what was waiting for us out there.

    It was Mrs. Jaden's idea to have some kind of memorial for those who passed away. We knew that the reapers understood our language and would recognize signs of survivors still living here, so it had to be something small and inconspicuous. Mrs. Jaden suggested a simple sign on the gazebo in the center of the town's plaza with a memorable quote to signify our farewell to them. So, one sunny morning at the end of September, we all gathered around the gazebo, while Mrs. Jaden led the ceremony. With the help of her husband who made the marker with carved words and a whittled leafy border, they held it up for all to see.

    "This plaque will mark this place in remembrance of those we loved and lost. It reminds us that they are not fully gone, that their memories live on in us forever. These words by the poet William Shakespeare will serve as a memoriam to the Beau Chêne that was and to all of the wonderful people who lived and perished here," she said solemnly before reading the sign:

> "That time of year thou mayst in me behold
> When yellow leaves, or none, or few, do hang
> Upon those boughs which shake against the cold,
> Bare ruin'd choirs, where late the sweet birds sang.
> In me thou seest the twilight of such day
> As after sunset fadeth in the west,
> Which by and by black night doth take away,
> Death's second self, that seals up the rest.
> In me thou seest glowing of such fire,
> That on the ashes of his youth doth lie,
> As the death-bed whereon it must expire,
> Consum'd with that which it was nourish'd by.
> This thou perceiv'st which makes thy love more strong,
> To love that well which thou must leave ere long."

With those words, Mrs. Jaden's daughter Michelle, Zack's brother Noah, my little cousin Hunter, and the seven orphans all laid one white flower each at the foot of the wooden sign. Again, we didn't want bouquets of flowers that would draw attention from unwanted people traveling through town. I thought the men were all being paranoid, but Homer agreed with them, and I trusted his judgment. I suppose they knew better. I wanted to think the best of mankind, but they just wanted to be sure we were all safe with such small numbers to defend ourselves. It didn't seem like much to mark the life of my mother and all the others who'd died here, but it would have to be enough.

As I stepped up to Homer's porch, I heard Pop and the sugarcane farmer Ed Dugas laughing about God knows what on the far side of the clearing. Out of everyone, these two seemed the most unaffected by the sudden change in our lives. They looked at the construction of new houses as just another job to be done. They did more resting than work, which hadn't seemed to bother my dad too much. As always, he was so patient with everyone, even while I know he was still grieving inside. So was I.

I pulled the photograph from my pocket, the one I'd taken from Jessie's vanity mirror. I touched the faces of my Aunt Vanessa, my mom, and Jessie. This was my remembrance of them; this happy moment snapped in a blink that I kept with me wherever I went now. Sometimes, when I would feel my strength faltering and my heart sink as I thought of that day I couldn't save my mother and Jessie, I pulled out this photograph and remembered this day—one of doting mothers and loving daughters. We all have suffered so much and suffer still when we realize what has been lost. But I must focus on the goodness that we had and is still to come. As if to mark this moment with that thought, Hunter's sweet laughter echoed in the air. I looked back to see him and Noah chasing a waddling duck near the water's edge. The pudgy kitten Chewbacca bounced gently in Hunter's arms.

When I walked into Homer's house, I saw the other five standing around the dining table where a map of the eastern United States spread wide. Homer was pointing his finger along a line that trailed through Mississippi toward the north.

"Clara," said Mel as I joined them, "Homer's had contact with Herrald in Arkansas again."

Of course, by contact, she meant a telepathic conversation of sorts.

"What's up?" I asked curiously.

"We'll have to leave soon. There's no time to help finish the building," she said.

"Why?"

Homer looked up and saw me standing there.

"Clara, the clans are gathering about 60 miles outside of New York City. They're using a former summer camp for training and living quarters. Herrald and others agree that Bölverk's strategy seems to be to go straight north to all of the large cities along the way to Chicago, then he'll head east to New York. We need to leave soon and beat him there."

"How long will it take him to get there?" asked Gabe, still focused on the map.

"There's no need for him to hurry. He still doesn't see any of us as a threat. Again, their overconfidence is their weakness. We'll need to beat the snow that will begin to fall soon in the north, which will slow our progress. I still think we have plenty of time as long as we leave within the next two days."

"Two days?" I heard myself exclaim. "I haven't even told Dad we're leaving yet. He'll freak out."

I could feel myself starting to unravel. That was when Gabe came around the table close to me.

"Clara, I know this feels sudden, especially since we're just starting to feel normal again, but the reapers won't wait for us to be ready for them. We need to make it north to the other clans before they destroy a city full of millions of people."

"What about the millions they've already killed in all the small towns already?" I asked, knowing I sounded like a spoiled brat. As usual, I couldn't stop my mouth. "What about them?"

"We can't strategically block every town in America, Clara, and you know this," he said calmly, making me even angrier because he was so freakin' patient. And right. "We do know that a huge majority of them, including their leader, will be drawn to the energy of New York. Along with the other clans, we can stand against them."

I knew I was biting on my lower lip. Gabe's stern expression slipped into a half-smile.

"Come on," he said, taking my hand and leading me toward the door.

When we stepped outside, I heard Zack's hammer echoing through the woods. I could see Noah and Hunter right by the shed where they'd brought their feline friends out to play. Misty circled them nervously, but didn't interfere. It was so pleasant and peaceful here now. The thought of leaving opened an aching hole in my chest.

A gust of chilly air passed over me, promising that winter was near. Autumn had come and gone more quickly than usual around here. Now at the end of October, we were already wearing layers to keep warm. In a normal season, we would've been in shorts and t-shirts even into part of November. I had wondered if it had something to do with the presence of the reapers sucking all the life out of our atmosphere, but decided not to ask Dad. I didn't want to remind him at all about them. We still hadn't even talked much about Mom's death. I don't think either one of us knew what to say without dredging up horribly painful emotions.

I zipped up my green hoodie, tucking my hands into the pockets and waited for Gabe's lecture. I was watching my dad and Zack work from the edge of the porch. Gabe stood behind me, wrapping his arms around me.

"They need our help to finish in time before it gets too cold," I said sulkily.

"They'll have Homer's house now with all of us gone. And maybe with our absence, my Pop and Mr. Dugas will put in a little more effort. Besides, Mr. Jaden comes every day to help even though they won't build his house till last."

I sighed heavily, trying to find something else negative to say about leaving.

"I know you don't want to go, Clara," said Gabe.

He sensed my emotions without saying a word. Geez, that was annoying sometimes.

"It is nice here, now," he continued. "But we've got to think about others who still have a chance for survival. Mel is fully recovered, so there's no reason to delay."

Homer had been right about the repercussions to our bodies when we overextended our powers. We hadn't realized it at the time, but

Ben had actually stopped breathing that night we fought the reapers. Mel was able to bring him back, but she had to lie in bed for a week, and then she was only able to move around very little for weeks after. Ben was like a doting puppy dog, fetching everything she needed. They still hadn't admitted anything, but I was sure there was more than just friendship there.

Right then, Ben came swiftly out the back door with Jeremy in pursuit.

"No way, dude. I'm not doing it," said Ben, passing us by.

"Come on, man. You owe me," insisted Jeremy.

"I don't owe you nothin'."

"Yeah. Remember when you zapped me. That hurt like hell. Come on."

Jeremy was actually begging, holding his iPod in his hand. Ben stared at Jeremy for a minute, then rolled his eyes and sighed.

"I will on one condition," said Ben.

"Anything."

"That you stop calling me names."

Jeremy stood there stupidly for a minute.

"Come on, man. That's all play. Besides, I really don't have any control over that. It just sort of spills out of my mouth."

"Okay. One month, no mean names, and I'll charge it up for you."

"One month. No mean names. Deal," said Jeremy without even blinking.

Jeremy handed the iPod to Ben. Within a few seconds, there was a short electrical snapping sound then he handed the iPod back to Jeremy.

"Sweet!" he exclaimed, scrolling through songs. "You're the man, Light—, I mean, Benjamin."

His voice went from normal, crazy Jeremy to a pathetic, fake British accent when he said Ben's name. It still put a smile on Ben's face that he had something over on Jeremy. Ben walked over to help my dad and Zack. Jeremy disappeared back around the porch plugging his ears giddily with earphones.

"That was interesting," said Gabe, laughing against me.

My mood had lightened, and I knew he was right.

"Fine," I finally said. "But, it's going to break my dad's heart."

"We'll tell him together tonight. He'll understand. Come on," he said, stepping off the porch and holding out his hand. "Let's go help while we can. We'll be packing tomorrow."

Gabe had that tilted half-smile spread across his handsome face. Even now, after everything, he could soften my resolve with just one look. I laughed and shook my head, then finally gave in. I took Gabe's hand and walked with him side by side, content that at least we would be together for the long journey ahead of us.

Excerpt from *Saga of the Setti: Book Two* . . .

CLARA

"Whoa. Look at this," said Jeremy, pointing up ahead.

An eighteen-wheeler had jack-knifed and was overturned sideways across the road. There was a pile-up of cars. Gabe eased the Yukon onto the shoulder, swerving around the mass of metal and wreckage then back onto the interstate where there were no cars at all far into the hills.

Gabe's aura flickered brightly. When I'd first met him, he had a rainbow of colors around him. Then as our powers became stronger, his aura slowly changed to a deep midnight, almost indigo blue with weaving ropes of brilliant blue light. It was a sign of something though I knew not what. We were all so new to these powers and what we knew of them was very little. Well, except for Jeremy. According to him, he was an expert at being a Sounder. And he just might be right.

"It's a shame we just got the open road," said Homer, "because we're getting off at the next exit. It's time we ventured off this main interstate. Let's put your father's plan into action, shall we, Clara?"

"When do you think we'll be at Lake Catherine?" I asked.

"Oh, it'll be a few hours yet. Why don't you get some sleep?"

I nodded then wedged myself into the corner. I'd balled up Gabe's sweatshirt for a pillow, but the cold still seeped through the window pane. I wondered how cold it would be in New York. Closing my eyes, I focused on the soft hum of rubber on cement beneath us. The steady vibration lulled me into a dreamy place. Gabe filled my head as I snuggled closer to the sweatshirt that smelled of him. Before long, I was somewhere else entirely. It might as well have been a different world. Actually, it was. A vision of high school that was far into the past, never to come again. I was standing on a dance floor in an emerald green halter-dress under a canopy of twinkling lights. It was the dress my mother had bought me for the Homecoming Dance; the dance I never had the chance to attend. Gabe held out his hand, looking at me with that crooked grin as if he had not a care in the world except to know whether I would take his hand, and his heart along with it. He looked amazing in a coffee-colored suit and a thin black tie. I couldn't resist those eyes and that smile. Taking his hand, he pulled me in close, swaying to some tune that was vaguely familiar. What was that song? It was an older one. "Far From Home," that was it. When had I heard it last? My dream Gabe leaned down to me, whispering softly in my ear. "You're so beautiful, Clara." I smiled and looked up at him. His aura was pale blue, a turquoise sea, not those writhing, tangled ropes of light that surrounded him of late. His brown eyes were warm, sweet. Gentle. A disco ball spun silver sparkles around the room on him, me, the many dancers in the room that were nothing more than background to this wonderful dream. I glanced at our reflection in the mirror covering the right wall. The image was perfection. Gabe's handsome, dark features complimented my fair ones. There was no reddened scar marring my face. There were no worries at all. I liked this dream. I loved this dream. The chorus of the song surrounded us in a haze. "*And it's almost like--,*" crooned the singer. I leaned my head against Gabe's chest and sighed heavily. "Why can't we be like this forever?" His answer was no surprise. "It's always like this when I'm with you." So perfect. The singer crooned on, "*Your heaven's trying everything to keep me out. . . .*" I let the moment surround me in its splendor. His warmth seeped into me. Then the music began to slur and blur and slow to a disturbing murmur. A cold tremor prickled up my spine then a voice bellowed down from above. "So kind of you to save a dance for me." It wasn't Gabe. The smell of smoke and ash and fear slammed into me. I felt the bony grip of something powerful on my shoulder and wrapping entirely around my arm. Trembling, I looked up. Way up. The yellow serpentine eyes of a ghastly reaper glared down at me. Eyes that penetrated deeper than the surface of my skin. The creature smiled, bearing a black slick of slime coating its mouth. I shook my head. This isn't real. This isn't real. I tried to pull back, but was paralyzed. How? By what? His dark, otherworldly skin began to ripple and glow green. Something rolled out of him and into me. "No," I heard my paltry plea. My skin began to transform, darken, wither. I jerked my head to look at our reflection, knowing I would see my dream-self becoming a lifeless statue. But, no. It was worse, horrifying. My hair had fallen away and my skin darkened further. I knew what I was becoming, but my mind wouldn't register. I gazed at myself changing into something unnatural, all the while the song played on and dancers moved silently around us under glittery light. He still held me in a locked embrace. I gaped in frozen shock at our reflection, this macabre dance with a devil. The worst part of all was the feeling of it. It wasn't painful. No, the very opposite. He fed me pure energy. It rolled under my skin like a balm to a wound I never knew I had. The raw power surged inside my veins, no longer needing blood or a heart to function. All I needed was this; this feeling of sheer supremacy and strength. So what if the package was ugly; my whole being changed to something that no longer cared about appearances. But, wait, the inside would become as ugly as the outside. I turned my face back up to my ghastly captor, rejecting this so-called gift he was using to enslave me. "No," I repeated more confidently, summoning my power buried deep within. He felt the burning sensation rising out of my body. Those snake eyes narrowed to slits. He drew back a seven-fingered hand and slashed down toward my face.

About the Author

Stephanie Judice calls lush, moss-laden New Iberia, Louisiana, home where the landscape curls into her imagination creating mystical settings for her stories. She shares her small, southern lifestyle with her husband and four children. As a high school teacher of English and Fine Arts, she is immersed in mythology, legends, and art that serve as constant inspiration for her writings. Some of her favorite things are autumn leaves, southern accents, Gothic architecture, Renaissance festivals, family movie nights, and, of course, William Shakespeare. Writing is her haven for self-expression where imagination rules and dreams do come true.

Friend us on FaceBook to chat about characters you like, events with the author, and exciting news on book two. Follow us on Twitter and learn more about the author on LinkedIn.

Made in the USA
Charleston, SC
20 October 2011